R.J. KAISER

D0042565

Black Sheep

He was risking everything he had
to win everything he'd ever wanted

He thought the past was dead and buried
but it just walked back into his life.

GLAMOURPUSS

R.J. KAISER

"With the surefooted ease of
one who's walked the walk,
Kaiser...pens [a]...delightful
romantic mystery."
—*Publishers Weekly*
on *Fruitcake*

R.J. KAISER

Squeeze Play

A double murder sets off the
biggest squeeze play San
Francisco has ever seen.

"...Kaiser authors know how to
have fun. R.J. Kaiser is one
of them."

Also by R.J. KAISER

SQUEEZE PLAY
HOODWINKED
GLAMOUR PUSS
FRUITCAKE
JANE DOE
PAYBACK

R.J. KAISER

Black Sheep

MIRA®

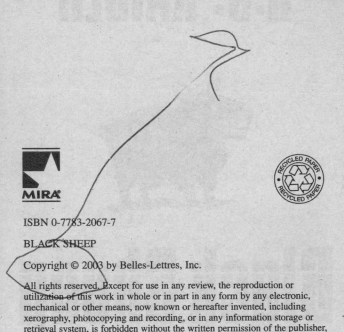

MIRA

ISBN 0-7783-2067-7

BLACK SHEEP

MIRA and the Star Colophon are trademarks used under license and registered in Australia, New Zealand, Philippines, United States Patent and Trademark Office and in other countries.

www.MIRABooks.com

Printed in U.S.A.

For John Green and Marti Kramer

Part ONE

Black Sheep

Tuesday
December 11

Hong Kong

Jonas Lamb hadn't played the ponies in thirty years, but the images, if not the fever, were still in his head. Maybe that was because his life was a lot like a horse race. He was coming around the clubhouse turn, still at the rear of the pack, but through the flying mud, the thunder of the hooves, he could see the finish line ahead. Jonas knew this was it, his last chance. If he was to go out a winner, it was now or never.

"Jonas," she said, "come back to bed."

Ignoring her, he continued to stare out the window of their twenty-third floor hotel room at the lights of Kowloon twinkling in the darkness of predawn. He was naked. He was depressed. He was limp.

"Jonas…"

Still he did not respond.

"Honey, it's all right. It's not important. Honest."

"Easy for you to say," he muttered.

"Baby, you're exhausted. Look at the day you've had."

There were times when a woman's understanding could be annoying to the point of aggravation. He did not want sympathy. He wanted an erection...or, more accurately, he didn't want to *not* have one. Plus, it was embarrassing.

"Jonas, please come back to bed."

"That's never happened to me before," he mumbled, half to himself, half to her. "Have you ever known me not to be able to get it up, Crystal?"

"No," she replied, "you're a fantastic lover. Always...well...always able."

"Until now." He didn't say it out loud, but he thought, *Today, of all days!*

The thing was, Jimmy Yee was a stud, and Jonas admired that because...well, he was a stud himself. Sexual prowess had been a part of their friendship, going clear back to Seattle when they'd talk business, negotiate, then cruise the topless bars and strip joints, getting drunk and competing with each other to see who could stuff more twenties into G-strings. And then there were Jimmy's mistresses. Damn if he didn't always have the prettiest Chinese girl on the planet hanging on his arm.

Of course, that was the better part of twenty years ago when they were both younger and, in Jimmy's case, several billion dollars poorer. God, how times had changed. Jonas was now on his sixth wife with one bankruptcy under his belt, while his old pal seemingly owned half of Hong Kong, as well as some pretty big chunks of the rest of the planet.

But despite the passage of time, women, Jonas had

discovered, were still a matter of considerable interest to Jimmy Yee. No sooner had Jonas asked if he could come to Hong Kong to talk a little business than Jimmy had said, "I'd love to see you, old boy! Will you be bringing a lady friend, or shall I arrange something for you?" Same old Jimmy. It had been heartwarming to know some things hadn't changed.

Of course, Jonas was going to supply his own companion. He'd had a first-rate mistress for more than six months, which was remarkable considering he could offer little other than a reduction in the rent and fantastic sex. (Now, it seemed, she was down to a break in the rent.) But he was lucky. Crystal was a knockout, if not the most sophisticated woman he'd ever bedded, plus she was a real sweet girl. She deserved a little something extra. What better treat than to bring her to Hong Kong, all expenses paid? No small thing for a girl who'd never previously ventured farther from California than Nevada.

"Maybe if you lie down and try to relax," she said.

He turned and looked back at her in the darkness. "Crystal, will you give it a rest, please? You're not helping matters by trying to make me feel good about it."

"I'm not trying to make you feel good about it. I'm telling you it's not your fault."

"Well, it sure as hell isn't *your* fault!"

"Look," she said, "it's what, five in the morning? You've hardly had any sleep. You flew clear across the Pacific Ocean yesterday. That's enough to incarcerate anybody."

Jonas couldn't help but smile. Crystal's malapropisms were among her more endearing qualities.

"Seriously," she said, "it could happen to a man half…"

"Half my age?"

"No, I was going to say half as stressed. You said today could be the biggest day of your life. You tossed and turned all night. If that doesn't put a guy under pressure, I don't know what would."

She had a point. How could he expect to focus on getting laid when the world was literally at his feet and he had but to grasp it? He'd been waiting for an opportunity like this his whole life. "You could be right, babe. I have been preoccupied."

"Come here," she said, her tone commanding, but not too commanding. "Come hold me."

Jonas felt the vinegar draining out of him. What was it about women? Sometimes they knew just what to say. The fact was, Crystal was a gem. The perfect mistress—not demanding, not spoiled, though she did have a bitchy streak that surfaced now and then. But he could hardly complain. She'd been a godsend, coming along at just the right time.

Too damn bad American culture didn't understand the social value of the kept woman like they did in, say, China or France, Japan or Italy. No, American men were at a severe disadvantage, having only three choices: fidelity, infamy or serial marriage (the latter nothing more than infamy dressed up in propriety, a truth he knew all too well).

Aware he'd been worked, but liking it, Jonas returned to the bed and plopped down next to Crystal. He put his hand on her bare thigh, giving it a perfunctory squeeze.

"You're first rate," he said. "I hope you know that."

"And you're the sweetest guy I know."

He looked at her in the darkness, only barely making out her pretty features. "You really mean that?"

"Of course."

"No, I'm serious."

"So am I."

"I'm a randy old fart who gives you a break in the rent, that's all."

She gave a little laugh. "Jonas, the world is full of randy old farts. That's not what attracts me to you."

He wasn't going to fish for a compliment, so he didn't ask the obvious. Besides, he knew. They had lots of laughs and great sex (normally). And neither of them made excessive demands on the other. It was an equal relationship with well-defined limits—limits drawn by Crystal as much as by him.

He stared up at the ceiling, his mind half on his upcoming meeting with Jimmy and half on Crystal. But when she scooted against him, pressing one of her one-hundred-percent-natural, perfect breasts against his arm, Jonas's mind let go of Jimmy. She lay her hand on his furry chest and gave a little sigh as though merely touching him was enough for fulfillment.

Crystal's fingers migrated south, bringing good old General Sherman to life. (His third wife, Gloria, loved national parks and was especially fond of the giant sequoias in Yosemite—the General Sherman tree being the most prodigious.)

"It seems you *do* love me," Crystal cooed, kissing his neck.

Why it was working now when it hadn't earlier, he didn't know. But he was sure as hell relieved. Considering he was still on the sunny side of sixty, Jonas figured he was much too young for his equipment to fail. Sure he'd had a few nips and tucks, some of the hair follicles on his head rearranged, but he could legitimately claim to be in his prime. Besides, if a guy couldn't get it up with a girl like Crystal Clear, there was something wrong with him.

"You've definitely got a talent," he said, knowing she'd been just as talented thirty minutes ago.

The difference was that earlier she'd made the mistake of bringing up his meeting with Jimmy. "Sure you don't need to get more rest?" she'd said. "If my whole life was depending on what happens tomorrow, I'd want all the sleep I could get."

That was when things sexual had begun going south. This time it was different. And Jonas knew if it was going to turn out better he'd have to push everything out of his mind but Crystal's tush and her bazooms.

He caressed her nipple and she moved still closer, running her tongue around the shell of his ear, her hand, meanwhile, gripping his cock.

"This Chinese enough for you, Mr. Lamb?"

Jonas had to smile. On the flight over he'd given her a primer on the social role Chinese women played in the business world. Maybe he'd been a little too frank in explaining things, but he didn't want her caught flat-footed. Jimmy Yee had a wife, a concubine and a mistress or two, he'd told her, the wife being in the number one position, the mother of his grown children. The concubine, a somewhat younger woman, was sort of an unofficial wife. Jimmy provided her with a home and had children with her, as well. The mistresses had only temporary status, serving at his pleasure.

Crystal considered that. "So, in other words, you brought me along for my tits and my smile."

"Well, I wouldn't—"

"That's okay, Jonas, I don't care. How else am I going to see Hong Kong? Just don't get any kinky ideas involving your friend."

At the moment all of Jonas's kinky ideas began and ended with Crystal's talented fingers. "Sweetheart, there are a billion Chinese girls, and not a one of them can hold a candle to you."

"You're so full of shit," she replied. "But that's okay. Keep saying it. It turns me on."

She rolled onto her back then and pulled him on top of her. The gods be praised, he'd gotten his rhythm back. Just in time, too. The last thing Jonas Lamb had wanted was to face Jimmy Yee feeling only half a man.

A few hours later he felt like a million bucks as he walked out of the hotel with Crystal on his arm, ushering her into Jimmy Yee's black Mercedes limousine. She was wearing the black mink she'd borrowed from one of her customers for whom she did weekly tarot card readings. The fortune-telling was a sideline, something she did when she wasn't tied up at her shop in Sausalito or looking after her five-year-old, Tamara.

Under the coat Crystal wore the little gold cocktail dress Jonas had bought her at Nordstrom in Corte Madera before the trip. It was inappropriate, considering the time of day, but this was Crystal's only chance to show off her attributes for Jimmy. Though perhaps a bit long in the tooth for a trophy mistress, Crystal "cleaned up pretty good," as his first wife, Rae Lynn, a Texan, used to say, and Jonas was proud to put her on display.

Crystal was getting her first look at Hong Kong by daylight, practically sitting with her nose pressed to the window of the limo. "Will you look at that!" she'd mutter. Or, "Wow, I've never seen so many Chinese. God, this is neat."

Jonas, who hadn't been to Hong Kong since an R and R visit during the Vietnam War, occasionally peered out the window, though he was preoccupied with his upcoming meeting. Hell, his stomach was in a knot. The dream of a lifetime was hanging in the balance.

Within a few minutes they reached the vehicular ferry that would take them from the island to Kowloon for their meeting at the Peninsula Hotel, where they'd have an early brunch, after which Jimmy's girl would take Crystal shopping while he and Jimmy repaired to the headquarters of Yee Industries. Jonas did his best to effect a cool demeanor, but the truth was he was dying.

Sure, Jimmy was a friend, but how could Jonas ignore the fact that, while he was barely clinging to financial respectability (thanks mostly to the largess of his current wife, Elise), Jimmy had used the years since their last meeting to move several billion dollars closer to immortality. The fact that their financial fortunes had taken off in opposite directions had made it tough for Jonas to pick up the phone for a "Hi, Jimmy, howzit going?" chat. What guy entering ten-digit net worth territory wanted to consort with some schmuck listing assets under two hundred thousand and liabilities of half a million?

On the other hand, how often could you call up a billionaire investor and say, "Hey, Jimmy, I got a deal that will make you king of the world. Interested?" Jonas had a fantastic proposition in his pocket. That was the golden goose he'd ridden to Hong Kong. And it was the golden goose that could turn his fortunes around and put him on top of the heap with Jimmy.

As soon as the ferry pulled away from the dock, Crystal said, "I've got to get out, Jonas." She threw open the limo door. "I want to see everything! Come on!" She hurried to the railing and stood there, taking it all in as the wind blew her ruddy curls across her face. "This is so exciting!" she effused, all but jumping up and down as Jonas slipped his arm around her waist. "I'm really glad you brought me." As she said it, she gave him a big kiss on the cheek.

It was then that Jonas spotted the guy on the half deck above them taking rapid-fire pictures. He wasn't taking shots of the skyline or the harbor. The camera was aimed right at them.

"Hey!" Jonas shouted, "what are you doing?"

Crystal turned to see who Jonas was yelling at. The guy snapped a couple more shots before retreating.

"Who was that?"

"Some guy was taking pictures of us. Come on, let's get back in the limo." Taking her hand, he led her back to the vehicle.

"What's the big deal?" Crystal said, slipping into the seat. "It's happened to me before."

"I hope that's all it was, babe," he said. But he wasn't at all sure. In fact, it unnerved him, considering the millions of people who potentially would be affected by his deal—and therefore interested in his every move. He'd been relying on secrecy, but considering how high the stakes were, nothing could be taken for granted.

"What else?" she said.

Jonas saw no point in explaining. Crystal had been content in her ignorance about what had brought them to Hong Kong and he wasn't about to burden her now. "I don't know."

"Well, what did he look like?"

"I didn't get a good look because he mostly had the camera in his face," Jonas replied. "But he was white and big. Crew cut. Fortyish, I'd say."

"Doesn't sound like anybody I know."

"Let's not worry about it," he said. "It was probably nothing." Until he knew differently, that was what he would assume. The last thing he needed was to allow himself to be distracted. He settled back in the seat and tried to relax, clear his mind and think positive thoughts.

A day didn't pass that Jonas didn't marvel at how well everything had fallen into place. In a very significant way, he had Elise to thank for it. Their four-year-old marriage had started out as his most pragmatic. Usually his wives had used *him,* but this had been one occasion where he'd gone into wedlock as the one seeking pecuniary advantage. Under the terms of their prenuptial agreement, his rights to Elise's estate were limited to a million dollars, which he was to receive upon her death, the bulk of her considerable wealth going to her adult children. (Elise appreciated the value of leverage and had made his fidelity a condition of inheriting under her will.) It was a generous arrangement nonetheless, which Elise had supplemented with a number of expensive gifts over the years.

Jonas had no complaints, though the fact that he'd entered the marriage with mercenary intentions had resulted in a certain amount of guilt, especially after Elise had been diagnosed with cancer and was told she had less than a year to live. It was a terrible blow to them both. Theirs was a marriage of convenience in many respects, but he liked Elise. He truly did.

After the onset of her cancer, Jonas had redoubled his efforts to behave honorably, keeping his end of the marital bargain, which called for companionship, respect and a certain amount of forbearance or, as Elise put it, "not rocking the boat." The woman was no fool. She knew sacrifices were called for from them both, especially after she became ill.

To gain financial security he'd given up a lot. His previous four wives had been fifteen years his junior on average, whereas Elise had been a year his senior. From the start, life in her boudoir was antiquated compared to the frothy zestfulness of his younger wives. And, needless to say, considerable adjustment was required on his part. Even so, the way Jonas saw it, the match had compensations apart from money. He no longer had to compete with phantom lovers half his age. For a man of fifty-eight, this was no small thing.

But there was more to Jonas's sixth marriage than financial security and sex (or the lack thereof). Elise had proved herself to be a quality human being, a person he'd grown to respect and admire immensely. It was nearly a year ago, after she became ill but before her condition was grave, that she'd had her finest hour. "You've promised to be faithful, Jonas," she'd said, "and to the best of my knowledge you have been. I expected fidelity so long as we could have a normal relationship. I realize my health affects things and that conjugal relations are no longer possible. I don't want you to suffer. If you feel the occasional need for some…companionship…of the sort I can't provide…I won't object—under the condition that you're discreet, that it's not someone in my circle of friends and that I don't hear about it. I'm turning a blind eye in other words, but respect me."

He'd been moved to tears by his wife's generosity, which he considered enlightened and definitely above and beyond the call of duty—not that he intended to run out instantly and get laid. (The gentle advance of years had dampened his ardor a wee bit, thus affording a civilized measure of self-control.) But, after a couple of months passed without sexual congress, Jonas had felt the pillars of rectitude shaking like a palm tree in a California earthquake. He succumbed, as it turned out, on a Sunday (why always on a Sunday?), and not without shame.

The angel who'd rescued him was, of course, Crystal Clear, his dream companion. How fortunate he'd been. How many men could claim to enjoy both the tolerance and beneficence of a wealthy wife and the cheery devotion of a comely mistress? He was doubly blessed and doubly grateful, all of which meant it was probably too good to be true. So far, though, the other shoe hadn't dropped.

If there'd been a downside, it was the impact of the arrangement on his pride. The million-bucks bequest from Elise was a godsend, considering he'd gone into the marriage flat broke with retirement (and the prospect of spending his golden years as a grade school crossing guard) awaiting just over the horizon. But even a million was no elixir for a proud man who'd wanted little more than "to make it," preferably through his own cunning and guile.

The thing was, life in America wasn't about money so much as it was about proving yourself. Unfortunately Jonas had reached this point in the game with a lot to prove and even more to live down. The worst thing he could imagine was to die a failure, and inheriting a little money was not his idea of success. No, the only way to be a man was to go for it, then live or die.

From his present perspective in a chauffeur-driven limo, on his way to make the sales pitch of his life, his mink-clad sweetie gleeful with excitement at his side, he himself sporting a new suit and gold Rolex (thanks to Elise's generosity and the financial success of her first husband, the late Jean de Givry), Jonas had reached the defining moment of his life, and he had the sweaty pits to prove it. This, he knew all too well, could be his last hurrah.

Like most Chinese, Jimmy Yee was superstitious, he believed in joss, he regularly consulted fortune-tellers and he liked women with large breasts—the latter an unfortunate predilection for an Asian male. On the other hand, money solved many problems—Jimmy's girls all got boob jobs, on the house, performed by the best plastic surgeons in the world.

Jonas hadn't exactly planned it that way, but Jimmy really took a shine to Crystal. The one-hundred-per-cent-natural tits were the starting point. And he probably found her outspoken fearlessness a refreshing change. But the kicker, doubtlessly, was the fact that she read tarot cards and carried a small set in her purse "for emergencies." Brunch had barely been cleared from the table in the ornate private dining room where they'd been served before Jimmy insisted on a reading.

"You don't mind, do you, old bean?" Jimmy asked Jonas, in the half Chinese, half British accent that had been with him since his public school days in England.

"I never make a move without consulting her myself," Jonas replied airily. "Be my guest."

Crystal gave him a look, but didn't remark on the mendacity of his comment. Lily, Jimmy's girl of the hour, a stunning beauty in her late twenties and a minor force in Hong Kong cinema (doing great love scenes reputedly being her principal, perhaps only, forte) appeared less than pleased. Crystal had been a touch too vocal during the meal, which did not please Lily and concerned Jonas until he saw that Jimmy was enchanted by her.

As Crystal got out her tarot deck and Lily crossed her arms under her nicely enhanced bust, Jonas leaned back in his chair, cigar in hand (he did not smoke, but Jimmy loved his cigars and this was, after all, Rome), and took in the scene with cautious optimism.

"I don't like to do readings for people I don't know," Crystal said with a tone approximating a surgeon general's warning.

"Why is that?" Jimmy asked, setting his cigar in the ashtray at his elbow.

She loosely shuffled the cards. "It's important to know how what I say might affect people. Interpreting signs is a big responsibility, you know."

"I'm very brave, my dear," Jimmy said, grinning. He gave Jonas a wink.

Jimmy Yee had changed considerably in the last twenty years. His black hair was now silver. He'd put on weight and wore glasses. Remarkably his billions had mellowed him, but his perfectly tailored suits and shirts were still perfectly tailored and his bearing reflected the stately grandeur of the numerous glass-and-steel edifices in his global portfolio. Scarcely a score of people in the world were his peers, and yet, to his credit (and Jonas's relief), he still had quite a bit of the nice guy in him. Jonas had been received as an old and dear friend. His foot was in the door and he was hopeful.

After shuffling the cards slowly and deliberately for a very long time, Crystal set them down in front of Jimmy. She put them in three stacks, and when she asked Jimmy to pick one, he touched the middle stack. Crystal picked up the cards and then laid them down in a complicated pattern. When she'd finished, she contemplated them like a chess player studying the board. Jonas was uncomfortable. She did not like what she was seeing, he could tell.

"Is it *that* bad?" Jimmy asked after a while.

Crystal took a moment, then said, "My advice to you is to be very, very careful, Mr. Yee."

Jimmy glanced at Jonas. "Are you saying my financial prospects are a concern?"

"No, I'm talking about your health, your life," Crystal replied. "I see danger."

"Can't you elaborate?"

She shook her head. "I'd rather not, if you don't mind."

A brief frown creased his brow. "What about money?"

"Favorable," she replied.

"And love?"

"Solid."

"Well, two out of three's not bad," Jimmy said, chuckling. He picked up his cigar and took a drag, ceremoniously blowing smoke toward the ceiling. "And what are the indications for Jonas, if it's not a breach of etiquette for me to ask?"

Crystal glanced at Jonas and he shrugged, knowing there was no way to tell her that billions of dollars were at play, and the less said, the better. Subtlety not being her forte, she plunged ahead. "His financial prospects are very favorable," she said, "though I see problems in his personal life. I also see physical danger in his future. Actually, the two readings are very similar."

"Jonas," Jimmy said, "I guess we can't take the same airplane."

Relieved, but still wary, Jonas smiled. "I'll make a note of that, Jimmy."

Jimmy Yee chuckled again, but Jonas could see that despite the quip he was a bit disturbed. There was no reason to believe Crystal knew what she was talking about, but Jimmy was not one to take omens lightly. Jonas remembered the *feng shui* master Jimmy had brought with him to that development project in Seattle. Before he signed a contract he'd wanted an analysis.

"Well, this has been delightful," Jimmy said, formally bringing the reading to a close, "but if I'm not mistaken you ladies have shopping to do. Perhaps the four of us can reconvene for a drink this afternoon. Lily, I'm putting Crystal in your capable hands."

Lily smiled so sweetly her pretty mouth looked as if it might shatter like the glaze on a doughnut. "My pleasure." She excused herself and headed off to the ladies' room, the men rising to their feet.

Meanwhile Crystal gathered her tarot cards and put them in her purse.

"Thank you for the reading, Crystal," Jimmy said. "I appreciate your candor."

"I couldn't very well lie," she said. "The cards say what they say. Besides, I've got nothing at stake, Mr. Yee. Except brunch. And I've already eaten that."

Jimmy seemed to appreciate the honesty. "Surely, though, you care how things go between Jonas and me." He gave Jonas a knowing look.

"I don't even know what the two of you are discussing," she said, rising, "so I can't really comment. But if he wants you to climb Mount Everest with him, I'd advise against it."

Jimmy chortled. "Excellent! Very good!" He turned to Jonas, who sensed things were going well. "You've got a clever lady here, old bean."

"Yes," Jonas said, "brains and beauty."

Jimmy Yee clasped him on the shoulder. "If you'll excuse me for a moment, I've got a phone call to make. Once the ladies are off, we can go to my office. I'll be back shortly."

Jimmy left the room and Jonas stepped over to Crystal. "That was clever," he said. "You handled him perfectly."

"Thanks, but I don't know what I did that's so special."

"The good news, bad news thing. It was brilliant. If you'd have been all rosy, Jimmy wouldn't have believed a word. I liked the way you finessed the financial forecast, by the way."

"Jonas, I didn't finesse anything. I told him the truth. The man's in danger. I didn't say this, but you could be part of the problem. Jimmy was exactly right when he said the two of you had better not get on the same plane."

Lily returned, followed moments later by Jimmy Yee. The four of them chatted while a waiter went for the women's furs—Crystal's borrowed mink and Lily's silver fox—and the men's topcoats. After kisses for their fellas, the miniskirted pair went off, affecting cheerful giggles.

"Your young lady's a pistol," Jimmy said, as they put on their coats. "How'd you find her, if you don't mind me asking?"

Jonas recounted the tale, sanitizing the details that cast a less-than-favorable light on him. "Our initial meeting, as fate would have it, was sadly ironic," he said.

"How so?"

Jonas explained how he'd met Crystal while doing Elise a kindness. He'd gone with his wife to her doctor's appointment on a sunny morning the previous March, but had some personal business to take care of, as well. The houseboat he owned in Sausalito had been vacated by tenants the week before and he needed to ready it for market. "Why not take care of your rental, then have a nice lunch in Sausalito, dear?" Elise had said when they got home. "It's silly to stay cooped up in this house with me when you have things to do." Jonas had stayed with her, anyway, until she had fallen asleep.

This was a couple of months after Elise had cut him loose from his vow of fidelity and he was getting that old, familiar itch. He'd been having sexy dreams (an early warning signal) and found himself thinking more and more about what he *wasn't* getting.

Jonas went on to explain to Jimmy how the houseboat had been his bachelor pad prior to his marriage to Elise. It represented madcap sex, his habitual means of coping during those difficult hiatuses between marriages.

His heart tripping, he contemplated the dispensation his wife had so magnanimously granted. Afternoon trysts were the sort of bacchanal she'd had in mind, weren't they? And yet, he'd continued to resist running off in pursuit of pussy, hopeful some more noble impulse would arise. Surely, he reasoned, Elise had hoped his love for her would trump his baser needs. His wife's true wishes aside, Jonas wanted to vindicate himself, to be a better man than she could hope for him to be.

Alas, he was inadequate to the task. Women were his weakness, his addiction, and they would doubtless prove to be his undoing. Hell, they already had. The sad truth was, he was powerless to resist temptation.

Having tidied up the houseboat enough to be

shown to prospective tenants, he left, telling himself he should go home. But it was too late, lust was in his heart. Nominally, he was on his way to lunch, but actually he was on the make.

Fate, it turned out, was a sorry co-conspirator. As he strolled along the bayside promenade, it seemed the town was a veritable riot of gams and boobs and firm, round asses. If he was to survive this chaste, he was badly in need of distraction.

Spying a shop with the curious name, Crystal Clear, Jonas peeked in the window. It was one of those New Age places that sold merchandise related to the holistic arts and various forms of unconventional spirituality. There were books, tapes, crystals, amulets, tarot cards, equipment for yogic pursuits, aromatherapy, massage. It was all there. Elise had talked about Eastern healing arts. Jonas decided to see if he could find a book or tape on the subject to take home with him as a gift.

No sooner was he inside the door when he realized he'd walked into a trap. The proprietress, a pretty redhead in a green sweater who he judged to be a D cup, between thirty-three and thirty-seven years of age, was seated on a stool behind the counter, looking perky and available. She smiled. He melted.

Crystal, who wore no rings and was presumably divorced, helped him find a book and a tape for Elise. But Jonas, so freshly off his love boat, was flush with carnal desire. He lingered, he chatted, he leered, he discovered that the condo the poor dear girl had been renting was sold out from under her, leaving her in dire need of lodging. (Finding an affordable rental in Marin was no walk in the park.)

Jonas saw his opening and rushed right in, not bothering to wrestle with his dark side. The question flowed off his tongue as if he knew the answer, which in his gut he did. "Ever have an urge to live on a houseboat?"

On the following Sunday, April 1, he helped Crystal Clear and her five-year-old daughter, Tamara, move into his one-time *barque d'amour.* They labored all afternoon, getting the place set up with a combination of her things and his. At dusk Jonas went to pick up a six-pack and some Chinese takeout while Crystal bathed Tamara and put her to bed. Upon his return he found Crystal had changed into a little T-shirt dress and piled her rusty tresses up on her head in that careless way that suggested the hair could come tumbling down with the least coaxing.

They dined by the light of a candle stub. Crystal's fortune cookie said, "An older, wiser person will change your life." Naturally, she had to find out if Jonas was to be that person. She did a reading for him. The cards were allegedly favorable, though he had to take her word for it. They screwed in his four-poster bed until she cried uncle, professing herself fulfilled and him amazing. (In matters of sex, like most everything else, first impressions were usually the ball game.) Her bubbly giggle still ringing in his ears, Jonas didn't stagger home until midnight. The next cycle had begun.

"Ah, lovely story, that," Jimmy Yee said, beaming

when Jonas ended with a shrug. Jimmy clasped his shoulder and they went out of the dining room where Jimmy's two bodyguards waited to escort them out of the hotel.

"After Crystal's reading," Jimmy said as they walked through the lobby, "maybe I should double my security detail."

"Once I'm out of town you'll probably be perfectly safe," Jonas replied with a wink. He was being glib, but an image of the guy on the ferry, the one taking pictures of him and Crystal, did cross his mind. He wasn't going to bring that up, though.

After they'd settled into the back seat of the limo, Jimmy said, "So, tell me frankly, Jonas, why the 'king of the world' hoopla? You could have rung me up and gotten a meeting without the hyperbole."

Jonas peered out at the streets of Kowloon. "What I meant to say was that I have something that can make you richer than the Saudi royal family, the prince of Brunei and Her Majesty, the Queen, all rolled into one. I guess king of the world is stretching things a bit. My apologies if I overbilled it."

Jimmy laughed. "I almost think you're serious."

"I am."

"Okay, king of the world, but at what price?"

"I don't know. A few hundred million, a billion, something like that."

"Sounds like a bargain."

"I should warn you, Jimmy, guts and vision are required. And a little luck, too. This one isn't for the faint of heart."

The headquarters of Yee Industries was located in Kowloon in a cylindrical architectural marvel sixty stories above Victoria Harbour. Jimmy's suite was on the penthouse floor. They accessed it via a private elevator. As he stepped out, the sight took Jonas's breath away, though he did his best not to gape.

He'd seen some nice office suites in his time, but Jimmy's digs were magnificent. The walls were constructed almost entirely of glass, a crystal doughnut encircling the building's central core. It was like being in a giant, glass-enclosed eagle's nest, a twenty-first-century version of Mount Olympus, complete with a silver-haired god of finance and industry in a hand-crafted gray suit and vermilion tie.

Opposite them, standing next to a reception desk about the size of a motel swimming pool, was a tall slender woman of forty. Neither the words *pretty,* nor *beautiful,* nor *handsome* described her, though she was a touch of each. She had the obsequious grace of a courtesan. She wore a simple gray wool skirt, white silk blouse, dark stockings and a string of fine white pearls. Her ebony hair was twisted loosely, but carefully, on her head. Her manner screamed discretion, integrity, intelligence, loyalty. She moved toward them, bowing slightly as Jimmy lay his coat in her arms.

"Jonas, this is my long-time assistant, Joy Wu. Joy, Mr. Lamb."

"Welcome, Mr. Lamb," she said, her eyes sparkling with a sincerity that made him want to throw an arm around her shoulders. Then the woman leaned close to her employer and whispered a few words in Chinese.

"Ah," Jimmy said, "an urgent matter has come up, Jonas. There's a chap in Tokyo I must ring up. It shouldn't take but five or ten minutes. Will you indulge me?"

"Of course, Jimmy. Take as much time as you need."

"Thank you. Joy will show you to my office and I'll join you shortly."

Jimmy headed off, and after Joy Wu took Jonas's coat, she led the way into Jimmy's private office, which had to be the better part of three thousand square feet, occupying a large chunk of the doughnut. The office was more landscaped than furnished. There was a running stream, plants in abundance, a virtual ecosystem. To the north were the New Territories and the mountainous face of the most populous nation on earth, stretching to infinity. To the south, the sparkling skyline of Hong Kong Island and the South China Sea beyond.

The furniture was oversize. Jimmy's desk, itself a hardwood sculpture the size of a small dance floor, was the focal point. *Zeusian* was the word that kept entering Jonas's mind as he glanced around.

Joy Wu showed him to a grotto of ferns containing two overstuffed couches, located some distance from the massive desk. She gestured for him to sit.

"Please make yourself comfortable, sir. I will bring tea." She bowed and left.

Alone, Jonas glanced around, wondering if something like this could be in his future. His heart raced at the prospect. And though he remained nervous over what lay ahead, he was hopeful, feeling like a guy on a first date with a woman who seemed to be sending all the right signals.

For a man with a checkered past, Jonas was as humbled by his good fortune as he was elated. There'd been others who'd bloomed late, realizing their destiny on the eve of their first social security check, but they were few and far between. His good fortune had begun when Patrick, the son he hadn't seen in years, phoned out of the blue the previous August. Jonas had planned to take Elise to a concert in the summer series that night, but she hadn't felt up to it, so he'd given the tickets to a neighbor. He'd just walked in the door when the phone rang.

"It's your son, Patrick," the strange voice had said. "Have any plans for dinner?"

Jonas was shocked.

"I'm not a kid anymore," the boy said. "I've got a Ph.D. There's no reason I can't take the first step."

Jonas was flattered and pleased by the overture. They had dinner (on Patrick), then talked until three in the morning in Elise's front room, catching up, expressing regrets and getting hurt feelings off their chests. Jonas, having lived with so much guilt about his paternal shortcomings, felt better afterward and told Patrick so. "That makes two of us," the boy replied. "I move we wipe the slate clean."

As far as Jonas was concerned, their reconciliation couldn't have come at a more propitious moment.

He'd never felt the need for family, but with Elise failing and dreary times looming, Patrick was a godsend. Over the course of the previous twenty-eight years, he'd seen the boy a grand total of perhaps a dozen times. Not that he'd planned it that way, but with the matrimonial landscape changing year to year, how could a boy of eight or ten or twelve be expected to understand his father's capricious approach to conjugal relations?

Which is not to say the two of them had no relationship. Jonas liked to think of their encounters as "quality time" in the purest sense. Patrick, who used his mother's surname, Mayne, wasn't quite as sunny in his recollections of those years. During their heart-to-heart conversation that first night, he'd confessed that while he had some fond memories of time they'd spent together, there were periods when he would have had trouble picking Jonas out of a lineup.

It was during a subsequent backpacking trip in the Sierras—undertaken for bonding purposes—that Patrick first revealed his other, more pragmatic reason for the reconciliation. A microbiologist by training, he had made a scientific discovery of earthshaking import, but didn't know what to do with it. Maybe Patrick, who was an idealist, more into realizing scientific and philosophical objectives than making money (a notion that was as alien to Jonas as debt service), simply needed his old warhorse of a father to help him realize his destiny.

Jonas had listened, incredulous, his eyes glistening in the light of the campfire as his son told him about the genetically modified organism (GMO) he'd created that converted the sugar in corn into a substance that changed the character of ethanol, thus affecting the oxygenation process of petroleum fuels. Incredibly Patrick's GMO enhanced the energy yield of a tank of gas, for example, tenfold.

Jonas didn't understand the science, but he was no fool. He saw the opportunity of a lifetime rising out of the ashes of a misspent life. A chance at redemption in the hands of his very own son!

"Do you have any idea of the import of what you're saying?" Jonas asked. "You could single-handedly turn the world economy on its head."

This was not hyperbole. Jonas knew a thing or two about economics and quite a bit about business. He'd seen the sunny side of a seven-figure net worth more than once in his financial life, though the dark side of seven figures—the *very* dark side—was more familiar territory.

"It has to be proved outside the laboratory," his son replied. "There are a few hurdles to get over and to do that I need money."

Jonas hadn't spawned a dolt. The timing of their reconciliation did correspond with Patrick's need for a cash infusion, but what the hell, human beings had kept their love and their money in the same purse since Cro-Magnon subtlety had supplanted Neanderthal implacability. So how could a man who changed wives as frequently as he changed his long-distance company complain about the symbiosis of devotion and gold?

"Odds?" he asked, hearing the tinkle of cash register bells more clearly than the gurgling of the nearby stream.

"Seventy-five percent probability I can pull it off," Patrick replied.

"Fifty-fifty and a man would be a fool not to put his life savings into it," Jonas had said, meaning it. (Hell, maybe even borrow the money and put up his soul as collateral.)

"Then perhaps the world economy *is* going to get turned on its head."

They decided to form a company to market the technology. Jonas would own and operate it as a front man with Patrick a silent partner. The boy wanted to be insulated from public scrutiny with his participation a secret. "It's the best way to protect the technology," he'd argued. After giving it some thought, the name they'd settled on was Global Energy Technologies.

There was a minor problem, however. While Jonas lived well and appeared rich, in fact his lifestyle was a product of his wife's largess. He told Patrick he didn't have much in the way of investment capital, but he thought he could get the money from Elise, as a sort of advance on his "inheritance." Her cancer was terminal by then, and she was in a settling-of-one's-affairs state of mind. It gave her pause, though, when he told her he wanted to form an investment firm but that the undertaking was so sensitive that even the broad outlines of the enterprise could not be revealed. He did, however, suggest that she might serve as an officer of the corporation, since the law required at least two officers. (Out of respect to his son's wishes, he didn't tell Elise about Patrick's involvement.)

Her skepticism notwithstanding, Elise was inclined to accommodate him, provided Jonas would look her in the eye and tell her it was the right thing to do. "There are never any guarantees," he'd replied, "but if the money was coming from my life savings, I wouldn't hesitate to write the check." Bravado, he learned that day, was like toilet paper during a shortage—something best used sparingly and only when absolutely necessary.

"In a sense it *is* coming from your life savings, dear," she'd replied, the flick of her brow reminding him once again there were no free lunches. "I'll give you the money, but I'm sure my attorney will be particular about how it's done."

He'd patted his wife's hand. "I understand fully."

The attorney, not surprisingly, wanted Jonas tied up every conceivable way. He proposed that ninety percent of GET's stock would be issued in Elise's name. Jonas had the option of purchasing the stock from her at any point during her lifetime for a hundred thousand dollars plus interest. Upon her death, Jonas would inherit the stock under the terms of her will, provided the million-dollar bequest in his favor was reduced by one hundred thousand dollars. If for any reason Elise changed her will, Jonas had the option of purchasing the stock for a hundred thousand dollars plus interest.

Microeconomically speaking, Elise hadn't lost a

thing by doing the deal. But in a world ruled by the twin gods of capitalism and plunder, money wasn't the issue, at least for Jonas—the issue was the opportunity money bought. What he hadn't shared with his dear wife was that he was convinced that Patrick's project would make him king of the world. (Why distress a dying woman with appearances of selfishness?)

In the months since Elise had written him that check, he had formed Global Energy Technologies, Inc., renting a small suite on Montgomery Street in the shadow of Telegraph Hill. Elise held the title of secretary of the corporation, though her signature on the incorporation documents was the extent of her involvement. With capital available, Patrick pressed ahead with his research, reporting that experiment after experiment had come up roses. Still, it would be a while before they had the results of what Patrick had termed "the definitive test, in the only laboratory that counted—Mother Earth."

Had it not been for Elise's cancer, Jonas would have been on cloud nine. (For all his pecuniary preoccupation, he did have a sense of decency.) Sadly, though, his dear wife was moving into the final phase of her illness. The doctors were giving her a couple of months at most. Again the terrible dichotomy of sorrow and joy.

Recently Jonas had been spending half his time with Elise and the other half at the office with occasional forays to the houseboat. Time moved with agonizing deliberateness. Everything seemed to be hanging in abeyance. So he worried, not just about his wife, but about his revolutionary venture with Patrick.

For all his bravado, Jonas was smart enough to realize he was probably in over his head, given the scale of their dream. At the beginning of the month he'd called for a powwow with Patrick.

Jonas had been direct. "Our capital will only last so long. I think we need a money partner, Patrick. And I don't just mean for seed capital. If we're going to knock the world on its collective ass, we'll need hundreds of millions, not hundreds of thousands."

"What are you getting at, Jonas? That we take it to an energy company?"

"No, that's only good for a nice fat annuity. We need somebody who'll put up the capital to create, then control, the world market for your little organism thingy."

Patrick had laughed at Jonas's rather unscientific description of the GMO. "I was going to make this a surprise for later," he'd told his father, "but maybe this is the time to tell you. I've given the organism a name. I'm calling it 'Black Sheep,' in honor of you."

Jonas had been touched. He'd told his son how his own mother had bestowed that epithet on him—the family "black sheep." It wasn't intended as a compliment. Barbara Lamb considered her son a clone of his old man, who, in her telling, was a reprobate and a scoundrel. Even so, Jonas wore the appellation proudly, if only because it harkened to his habit of doing things his own way.

"You've made my day, son," Jonas told him. "Maybe my life."

"You can do that yourself," Patrick replied, "if you know someplace to pick up a hundred million bucks or so."

Jonas had been ready for the comment, which had come right on cue. "As a matter of fact, I do."

"Oh? Is it a secret?"

"Hong Kong," Jonas told his son.

And now here he was in Jimmy Yee's eagle's nest on the rim of the Asian continent, the future tantalizingly within reach.

That was when Jimmy came in. "Sorry, old bean."

"No problem. I've been enjoying your view."

"Yes, it is nice, isn't it?"

Jimmy had no sooner sat down than Joyce arrived carrying a tray with a tea set, cups and saucers, which she placed on the highly polished teakwood coffee table. With a cant of the head she asked if Jimmy wished for her to serve the tea. His response was a subtle flick of the wrist, sending her away.

Jimmy unbuttoned his jacket and sank back into the cushions of the sofa. "Jonas, you have my full attention."

"I'll get right to the point," Jonas replied, affecting his patented "executive manner," a subtle mixture of testosterone and guile. "I have access to a biological organism that can increase the potency of ethanol by a factor of ten. It effectively reduces the cost of renewable biological energy sources by the same factor of ten. It makes ethanol a ready, economical substitute for petroleum fuels or can be used in hybrid fuels, lowering the demand for petroleum-based fuels by as much as ninety percent. My organism can be produced cheaply in many countries around the world, the supply virtually inexhaustible."

Jimmy gave him a long blank stare, his eyes seeming to glaze over. He did not smile; he did not frown; he seemed scarcely to breathe. After several moments he said, "What you're saying, Jonas, is you have a technology that can turn Saudi Arabia back into a playground for camels."

"That's about what it amounts to, yes."

There was another pause for reflection. "Is this theoretical?"

"No, it's been proved in a laboratory. The organism is a by-product of genetically engineered corn."

"You're saying it's proven? It exists?"

"Yes."

"And you have control of this technology?"

"Yes."

"Who knows about this, Jonas? Who's involved?"

"Three people on earth are aware of its existence," he replied. "You, me and the scientist who discovered it."

"You're certain?"

"Yes."

"What are you looking for, exactly? When you rang me up, you spoke of an investment opportunity."

"There are several ways to go. We can sell what we have to an energy company and let them develop it and take it to market, or we can develop and market it ourselves. If you're talking about replacing a substantial portion of the world's energy supply with a cheaper alternative, you're talking about much more than a few acres of row crops and a few service stations."

Jimmy said, "You're talking about a worldwide infrastructure."

Jonas nodded, taking a business card from his pocket and handing it to Jimmy. "And the scientific discoveries that make it possible are owned by Global Energy Technologies, Inc."

Jimmy Yee looked at the card. "Which is you."

"Which is me. Capital is what we need, Jimmy."

"As you said earlier, hundreds of millions, perhaps billions."

Jonas shrugged. Jimmy remained silent for a long moment before speaking.

"Naturally, I—or, for that matter, any serious investor—would need to see concrete evidence that you have what you say you have and that it works."

"Understandable."

"Can you do that?"

"A series of laboratory tests have already proven out. All that remains is a large-scale field test."

"Is it possible to see anything now?"

"Yes, but I wasn't going to carry anything around in my briefcase. I guess what I'm looking for, Jimmy, is an understanding in principle."

Jimmy Yee scooted to the edge of his seat and reached for the teapot. "Care for some green tea?"

"Thank you."

Jimmy poured Jonas a cup of tea and handed it to him. Then he filled another cup. Leaning back, cup and saucer in hand, he crossed his legs and stared at

Jonas. "I'm very interested, my friend. But I consider this conversation preliminary."

"I do, too."

"Once you give me scientific proof that your biological gizmo, the super ethanol, works, I'll have to bring in experts to evaluate it. I'd also want to talk to some experts on infrastructure and market issues. My expertise lies in real estate, as you know. And, though I have invested in technological ventures, I tend to avoid them."

"Ironically, this is both high tech and basic industry. We're talking energy."

"Yes," Jimmy said, "I appreciate that fact."

"Until you have need for your experts, please remember that secrecy—total secrecy—is paramount. Even rumors could be a problem. If you have preliminary conversations with anyone, please be discreet."

"Of course. Your name won't be mentioned."

Jimmy sipped his tea. Jonas did as well.

"Where do we go from here?" Jimmy asked.

"At some point, good-faith money might be required. That's when I'd bring my scientist in on it, perhaps with some technical data and so forth."

"Makes sense." Jimmy Yee drank more tea. "Listen, old man, as a token of my appreciation for thinking of me, and as proof of my interest in pursuing this, I'd like to pay for the expenses of your trip. Will you accept my check for twenty-thousand, U.S.?"

"That's not necessary, Jimmy."

"I insist. Absolutely insist."

Jonas, whose income for the year wasn't sufficient

to buy Jimmy's desk, relented, deciding not to fight merely for the sake of show. Besides, his old friend probably knew the details of his finances down to the date of his last bounced check.

For a while Jimmy Yee stared off at the distant mountains, seemingly lost in thought. "You know, Jonas," he finally said, "you were right."

"About what?"

"King of the world."

Jonas smiled the smile of a man who'd just been shown his crown. This day had been longer in coming than he'd hoped, but time had a way of sweetening long-awaited dreams. "I'll be honest, Jimmy. We still have a way to go. And I say again, secrecy is absolutely essential."

"Yee Industries, my friend, is more tightly sealed than Fort Knox."

3:13 p.m.

Joy Wu worked for an hour transcribing the conversation that had taken place that morning between her boss and the American. It was a time-consuming process, but that was the way Yee liked it. Fortunately, his habit also served Joy Wu's purposes.

After printing the transcript, she looked through it, removed four critical pages of text, took them to the copy room where she made a single copy, returned to her desk, reinserted the pages and filed the transcript. Then Joy wrote several words of explanation on the top of the first page of the excerpt, placed the copies in a plain manila envelope, sealed it, wrote the name and address on the front and called downstairs for a clerk to come for the envelope. She knew the courier would be arriving in less than twenty minutes.

Once the clerk had come, Joy went into the kitchen behind the elevators, where she made a pot of green tea, then placed it on the silver tray, along with a cup and saucer, a spoon, a linen napkin. She carried the tray into Jimmy Yee's office. He was at his desk, immersed in financial reports. He said nothing. He did not look up. She placed the tray on the corner of the desk. It was exactly 4:00 p.m. when Joy left the office, closing the door behind her.

5:06 p.m.
Wu Lo Noodle Shop, Hong Kong Island

After the courier left, Chi Chungwang took the envelope from the wire basket and set it aside. Then he filled a large foam container with noodles and called the boy from the back. Chi handed him the container of noodles and the envelope. The boy placed them in his delivery basket and left the shop, trotting up the street to the corner, where he turned and hurried down the alley thirty yards, stopping at the door next to the tailor shop. He rang the bell and was admitted when the door was unlocked by an electronic buzzer. The boy climbed the stairs and was met at the top by the old ah mah. He opened his basket, handed her the envelope and the container of noodles, then left.

The old woman took the envelope into the cluttered office where the director, Tang Gan, worked at his desk in the dim evening light that filtered through the half-closed *shutters. When the* ah mah *handed him the envelope, he glanced at it and motioned for her to leave. Tang turned on his desk lamp and opened the envelope. He read the pages. By the time he finished, beads of perspiration had formed on his brow. He realized that what he held in his hands was potentially of earthshaking importance. The implications for his country could be momentous. Tang carefully wrote a summary of the transcript pages that would be delivered to the communications center at Central Headquarters, to be encoded and dispatched before morning to the analysts in the Tenth Bureau of the Ministry of State Security in Beijing.*

WEDNESDAY
December 12

Hong Kong

Jonas Lamb awoke with a champagne hangover, but he didn't care. It was the best hangover he'd ever had, and that said a lot. Birthdays and anniversaries aside, there'd been his six honeymoons (though the first had been celebrated with a couple of six-packs), four divorces and one annulment. The latter, like his bankruptcy, hadn't been a champagne occasion, though he'd gotten drunk both times. Definitely the low points of his life.

But that was then and this was now. It was beginning to look like he'd finally hit a hot streak. Boy geniuses like Bill Gates probably took success for granted, thinking they were so smart victory was inevitable, but they didn't know that it was a lot sweeter when you had to pay your dues before your ship came in. On the other hand, if Lady Luck showed up a bit too late, a guy could have a coronary and miss the party. Maybe God did elect to get involved in these things, after all.

Jonas couldn't exactly claim he deserved his good fortune—and there was nothing to say things couldn't still go wrong—but he was determined to enjoy the good vibes as long as he could. (Hope had been the one singularly abundant commodity in Jonas Lamb's colorful life.)

A grin on his face, he listened to Crystal singing lustily in the shower. The last thing she'd said before they dropped off to sleep in a boozy, sex-satiated haze was, "Thanks for bringing me, Jonas. I'm having a hell of a time."

They had gotten a good start the previous evening. After they'd had a drink with Jimmy and Lily, Jonas told Crystal he'd take her anywhere she wanted for dinner—"The sky's the limit." Showing there was ample blue collar under the gold dress, she opted for one of Aberdeen's floating restaurants. Jimmy had warned them that the restaurants were about the tackiest things Hong Kong had to offer, tourist traps of the first order, but as Crystal told Jonas, "All due respect to Mr. Yee, I don't give a shit."

And so they'd taken a taxi to Aberdeen on the south side of the island where the ferries shuttled patrons out to the floating restaurants in the middle of the harbor. Jimmy had told them the pier where they could catch the ferry was located right next to the Marina Club, where he kept his yacht. He suggested they drop by for a drink and get a tour of the boat. Jimmy had a previous engagement, but arranged for his captain to do the honors.

When they'd arrived at the marina, Jimmy's man,

Captain Lam (he and Jonas joked that maybe they were distant cousins), clad in a crisp white uniform, escorted them to the yacht. The ship (it seemed unduly harsh to call it a boat, given its size and grandeur) was a gleaming white mini cruise ship, protected around the clock, the captain told them, by armed guards.

"Is security a problem?" Jonas asked.

"A man like Mr. Yee can never be too careful."

The comment brought the guy with the camera to mind, making Jonas wonder if the incident could have been connected with Jimmy, rather than him and Crystal.

At the end of their tour Captain Lam took them to the main cabin, where a sweet little miniskirt-clad hostess served them dim sum or, as Crystal called them, "Chinese snacks" and champagne. Then it was off to the floating restaurant. There were three to choose from, but Crystal wanted to eat on the Jumbo (her husband, Dennis, had eaten there once when he was in the service) and, since it was her night, that was what they did.

It was difficult to say what the floating restaurant most resembled, but Jonas finally settled on a combination of Las Vegas casino, Mississippi riverboat, Main Street at Disneyland and a carnival fun house, plus, as Crystal said, "one hell of a lot of Chinese takeout." It was also a bit like a floating lightbulb with enough juice going through it to illuminate a small town in the middle of the Christmas season. The inside was one enormous three-story banquet hall containing several huge million-dollar chandeliers. The structure was capped with those "Chinesy roofs" (Crystal's term) "that looked like paper hats with a happy face." The food was almost an afterthought, though the usual take-out fare at home was a poor imitation. But Crystal was happy, and as far as Jonas was concerned, that was all that mattered.

The real party began back at their hotel. Jonas had told her that his meeting with Jimmy had gone quite well, but he hadn't elaborated. When Crystal saw that *two* bottles of iced champagne (Cliquot, the queen's favorite) were waiting in their room, she said, "It looks like you plan to fuck my brains out. Apparently the meeting *did* go well."

"Yep. Fantabulous."

"Does this mean you're going to buy a love boat like Mr. Yee's?"

"Possibly."

"Dibs on first screw."

"Done."

With Crystal still in the shower doing a tune-up for her next big record deal, Jonas decided to touch base back home. He checked his watch, calculating that it was yesterday afternoon in California. His first call was to Patrick.

"My meeting was a success," he said cryptically. (They were always cautious in their communications.) "I would go so far as to say a big success. Of course, before he writes a big check, he wants proof your little Black Sheep organisms are for real."

"As expected."

"Yes, as expected. The point, though, is that it's there, if and when we want it."

"I guess that's reason to celebrate," Patrick said.

"I've been doing my share. But I shouldn't be the only one. Why don't you run out and pick up a bottle of champagne? There must be some sweet young thing willing to celebrate with you for unknown reasons."

Patrick's social life—or, more accurately, his love life—was the part of his existence that Jonas knew the least about. The boy never talked about girls or women. For that matter, he hardly spoke about his mother (Jonas's second wife, Tess, the spouse who'd gotten the annulment, leaving their child—in utero at the time—a nominal bastard), an indication that women generally may not have been a subject Patrick felt comfortable discussing with the old man. Jonas hadn't pressed the issue.

"Maybe I'll hold off until it's in the bag," his son said. "But I want you to know I appreciate your efforts. I couldn't have done it on my own."

Jonas was touched by the compliment, though he wasn't at all sure Patrick hadn't had other alternatives. The first surprise had been that he hadn't gone to his mother for the initial seed money. Jonas hadn't kept up with Tess, apart from having heard that her second husband had died. He knew nothing of her financial situation beyond the fact that she'd been in commercial real estate for years and had connections with a number of rich and influential people. But he couldn't bring himself to press Patrick for details about his mother's life.

Jonas's putative marriage to Tess had ended in a messy, unfortunate scandal for which he, and he alone, was responsible. She had been an innocent victim and she'd suffered terribly. Her one request was that he get out of her life, and so he had.

"Any news on your end?" Jonas asked his son.

"Nothing special, no."

"Well, just keep feeding those little Black Sheep so they grow up big and strong."

The quip brought more laughter from Patrick. "I'll do that. And congratulations on your coup," the boy said.

"Just trying to earn my keep." Jonas hung up, feeling a bit choked up. Funny how a guy didn't appreciate the value of family until he had one. His marriages had rarely given him that same warm feeling. Even Elise, who'd come equipped with a home and children, seemed more like a partner than a mate. Yet he owed her so much—including this trip. Which, naturally, made him feel more ashamed of himself than ever. He decided to make another quick call. Crystal's concert in the bathroom was over and the hair dryer was going full tilt. He figured he had a few more minutes. He telephoned Elise.

"How sweet of you to call," his wife said. "How's your business trip going?"

"It's going fine, thanks. How are you feeling?"

"About the same. I'm living from pill to pill, Jonas, same as before."

There was resignation in her voice. They both knew she was dying and it broke his heart. They probably never had truly loved each other, though there'd been genuine good intentions and mutual respect. Theirs was the bond of dear friends, very dear friends. Jonas wasn't sure that he'd given as much as he'd received. He felt badly about that, but Elise had never complained. "It would have been nice if you'd loved me," she'd once said in a moment of candor, "but it's not like I've never had that. You're a lot of fun, and I like you. Don't take this wrong, Jonas, but you're the perfect after-dinner drink."

As he talked to his wife from seven thousand miles away, those words, uttered months earlier, grabbed him in the gut and he felt himself starting to choke up. No, she wouldn't have resented him for being with Crystal. In her way, she'd encouraged it, but it still got him in the guilt complex. As much as anything, it was the fact that he survived while she faded away that ate at him. It was like Vietnam where he'd seen others die, not understanding why he'd lived.

He cleared his throat, trying to get the lump to go away. "So, what are you doing?" he asked, even knowing it was the last question he'd want her to ask of him.

"Oh, watching a little television, reading. Nothing special."

"You in bed?"

"Yes."

"Me, too."

"What time is it there?"

He checked his watch. "A little after eight."

"Tomorrow morning."

"Yeah, tomorrow morning."

"It never quite has sunk in how that works," Elise said. "I guess we have to accept it as a matter of faith."

"Sort of like the world being round. The people who say so are experts for a reason."

Elise laughed. "Silly goose."

The bathroom door opened and Crystal appeared, naked as a jaybird. Jonas clasped his hand over the mouthpiece, gesturing for her to be quiet. She was rubbing body lotion over skin that he'd been luxuriating in only hours ago.

"I should probably let you go," he said to Elise as his eyes marked the curves of Crystal's body, his conscience giving way to lust.

"Let's see, you have another day there, don't you?"

"Yes, we leave tomorrow morning."

First came the silence, then the terrible echo of his own words. "*We*," he'd said. God, where was a gun so he could shoot himself? But then, practiced as he was at the game of infidelity, he found the necessary words. "Patrick and I" flowed as if by magic from his mouth.

"Patrick is with you?"

"Yes, didn't I mention that?" He felt like a shit.

"No, I don't believe you did. I thought everything you did was hush-hush."

"Patrick's sightseeing while I tend to business. When I heard he'd never been to Asia, I thought, why not invite him along?" He glanced up at Crystal, who had the good grace not to laugh, though in a way she'd caused his gaff, her body being the distraction that had induced his foot to enter his mouth…not that he actually *blamed* her.

"Well, give him my best," Elise said.

"I will."

"I miss you, dear. And I look forward to seeing you."

"Me, too," he said. Then God and truth and all things holy notwithstanding he added those words that opened the universe or damned the soul (depending), "Love you."

Then he hung up.

It took a minute for his eyes to meet Crystal's. She still didn't smile, though it would have been easy to mock him. Like Elise, she was a decent human being. He was blessed with the women in his life.

She'd finished putting lotion on her long, shapely legs and moved around the bed, sitting next to him. Wrapping an arm around his neck, she said, "Know what, Jonas Lamb? You're a sweet man."

His shoulders slumped. "Now, doesn't that take the prize. My naked girlfriend listening to me talk to my wife on the phone and complimenting me for being nice."

"Goodness doesn't have to come in predictable ways."

"Maybe they'll put that on my tombstone."

There wasn't time for her to respond before there was an earsplitting crash and the door flew open, splintering down the middle and causing Crystal, whose back was to it, to shriek. Jonas, who had a full view of the action, saw a large white guy in a Gortex jacket fill the doorway. He took a few steps into the room and began to take pictures, the flashes going off as if they were on the red carpet Oscar night. It was the guy from the ferryboat.

Crystal screamed again and burrowed into the bed, her butt still hanging out and the camera still clicking away like a fifty-caliber machine gun before she thought to reach back and fling the covers over her derriere. Meanwhile, Jonas's aging synapses finally crackled into operation, enabling a response.

"What the fuck are you doing?" he cried, his fists clenched, but the fight-flight response was still a few seconds from kicking in.

The guy, who Jonas could only say had the look of an ex-marine (crew cut and bull-necked), seemed in no mood for discourse. He spun on his heel to depart, not having uttered a word, when a couple of Chinese guys appeared in the hallway. While not quite the size of the camera guy, they were close.

As Jonas sat on his bed, Crystal still screaming and hugging his legs like a middle linebacker nailing a running back, the Chinese guys jumped Mr. Paparazzi. A wordless battle of karate kicks ensued, complete with thumps and grunts and crunching bone. It ended with Mr. P. flat on his face in the hallway. Then the two men took the big guy by the arms and dragged him away. A couple of seconds passed before a third Chinese man appeared in the doorway. He had a stricken look on his face.

"Very sorry, Mr. Lamb," he said bowing. Then,

reaching in, he pulled the shattered door closed as best he could.

Jonas was in shock.

Crystal stuck her head out from under the covers and peered toward the door.

"What the fuck was that?"

"Sweetheart, you're asking the wrong guy."

The maintenance people had a new door on in twenty minutes. Nobody from the hotel had offered an explanation nor, for that matter, had they asked any questions. Jonas was flummoxed, Crystal annoyed to the point of pissed.

"If my ass ends up in the *National Enquirer*," she fumed, poking at her scrambled eggs, "I'll sue."

"Sue who?"

"The goddamn hotel! Or if all else fails, you, Jonas."

"If your ass does make the *Enquirer*, nobody will know it's yours. My celebrity may be marginal to nonexistent, but to tell you the truth, Crystal, I think my face is more recognizable than your derriere."

"How will I ever be able to look people in the eye?"

"Keep your pants on and you'll be fine."

"Ha, ha. Very funny."

Joking aside, Jonas was concerned, *very* concerned, considering his mission. On the other hand, he had no idea what to make of the incident. "It was the guy who took our picture on the car ferry yesterday, so he's obviously been stalking us."

"I can tell you right now," Crystal said, "Elise is behind it."

"No, it's not her style. Besides, we have our understanding."

"Jonas, you're so naive. That had the fingerprints of a woman all over it."

"How do you get that?"

"Someone wanted to know what you were doing here... Duh."

"Sorry, I don't buy it. Elise doesn't want to know what's going on. Besides, if she did, there have been plenty of opportunities back home to catch us in flagrante delicto."

"In what?"

"With our pants down." He gave her a wink.

She flipped him the bird. "If it wasn't Elise, who was it?"

"I don't know." He saw no point in bringing up his deal with Jimmy Yee, but it made more sense that the incident was somehow related to that than Elise.

"That's what I figured," Crystal said when he didn't have a ready answer. She slathered her toast with marmalade.

There was a knock at the door.

"Maybe we're about to find out," Jonas said, getting up from the table.

He expected the hotel assistant manager, but it was Jimmy Yee. Jonas was surprised as hell.

"Sorry to intrude, old boy," Jimmy said, "but we need to talk."

There were two security guys in the hall. They stayed outside. Jimmy, a small sports bag in hand, came into the room. As always he was impeccably dressed, this time in a double-breasted charcoal pin-stripe and purple tie.

"Good morning, Crystal," he said.

"Hi, Mr. Yee. Welcome to *Sex and the City.*"

"I beg your pardon?"

"TV joke," she said.

"Crystal's had a bad morning in the dignity department," Jonas said, motioning for Jimmy to take the only armchair in the room.

"Yes, I've heard," Jimmy said.

"Oh?"

Jimmy Yee put the sports bag on the chair, unzipped it, removed a camera, then carried it to the table, handing it to Crystal. "This may help assuage the embarrassment."

"What's this?"

"The camera used by the intruder. My people recovered it a short while ago."

"Digital camera, huh?"

"Yes. The disk is intact."

"Those guys who grabbed him," Jonas said, "the karate kids, they belong to you?"

Jimmy returned to his chair and sat, crossing his legs. "Let me explain."

"Please do."

"I tend to be cautious," Jimmy Yee began. "After your arrival, I had my security people keep an eye on you…as much for your protection as for mine."

"Then you knew the same guy tailed us yesterday, took pictures of us on the ferryboat."

"Yes, you'll find those shots in the camera, as well.

At any rate, I told my men to watch the guy closely and make sure no harm befell you. This morning they followed him here, but before they could prevent the intrusion he knocked in the door and...well, you know the rest."

"Who was he?" Jonas asked.

Crystal began looking at the camera's display, scrolling through the shots.

"We aren't sure yet," Jimmy replied. "American. Beyond that, we won't know for a while. I'm sure the authorities are looking into it."

"The police know about the incident?"

"No, I didn't want to bring it to their attention without first consulting you, Jonas. Let me explain. After my men subdued the intruder, they took him down a service elevator and out a back entrance. They had him in a car and...well, underestimated the severity of his injuries. Apparently he feigned unconsciousness, then at a traffic light jumped from the vehicle and ran right into an oncoming bus. He was killed instantly."

"Jesus," Crystal said, sounding distressed.

"I wouldn't expect *you,* of all people, to shed a tear over him," Jonas said.

"No," she replied, "not him. I'm looking at this picture of my fat ass. I've got to make a beeline to Jenny Craig, like now!"

"Some camera angles are not the most flattering," Jonas said, trying to keep a straight face. "Back to Mr. Paparazzi, Jimmy. Did he have any ID?"

"No. None at all. My people grabbed the camera and left before the police arrived. Nobody knows about the photos but us. Regardless, my connections are such that any investigation will not involve anyone in this room."

"Thank God," Crystal said, getting up. "Maybe I'll get dressed and duck down to the hotel gym for a quick workout. Excuse me, Mr. Yee."

Jimmy shook his head with amusement. Once the bathroom door was closed, he said, "Quite a bint you've got there, old bean."

But Jonas was more concerned about the unidentified intruder. "I don't suppose your people have any theories about what's going on?"

"No, I was hoping you would."

"No idea," Jonas replied.

Jimmy brushed a speck of lint from his pant leg. "One thing's bloody certain—somebody wants something awfully badly."

10:38 a.m.
CIA Headquarters, Langley, Virginia

Ted Myers, an economics analyst in the Office of Asian Pacific and Latin American Analysis of the Directorate of Intelligence, didn't like falling behind in reading the CRES log of message intercepts for China. And, unlike some of his colleagues, Myers was a stickler for scrutinizing the logs carefully. Rarely did anything of genuine importance show up, but like so many things in economic-intelligence gathering, the patterns, the gestalt, could be as revealing as any single piece of information. He was always on the alert for signs of sea changes, which was about the most one could expect to pick up from such low-level sources.

As he perused the log, an item under the "technology" category caught his eye. The summary line read: "Investment (U.S.)—energy technology, groundbreaking development." The intelligence source was described as "undercover agent, industry." The official who'd filed the report was the deputy station chief of the Guoanbu, the Ministry of State Security (MSS), Hong Kong. It was an unusual item, the U.S. connection being particularly intriguing. Myers decided to order a complete translation of the intercept.

Hong Kong

After the disastrous start to their day, Jonas decided to indulge Crystal, telling her she could have a thousand bucks to spend any way she wished. She opted to return to one of the shops she'd visited the previous afternoon with Lily. "Only this time, I'm buying." She'd seen some jade-and-diamond earrings that she said she'd have bought, except for the fact that she'd already tapped out the credit line on her Visa card, getting ready for Christmas.

After they'd picked up the earrings, they'd taken a helicopter tour of Hong Kong, checked out Victoria Peak, visited the Man Mo Temple and the Bird Market on Hong Lok Street in Kowloon. They ended up at the Night Market on Temple Street, where a fortune-teller told Crystal that she would "marry a rich craftsman and be very happy in a beautiful new home." Jonas dryly observed that one way or another, his days seemed numbered.

They had a light meal on Temple Street and took the Star Ferry back to the island, arriving late. Crystal was happy to see the door of their room still intact. Jimmy had left a message on their voice mail. "According to the police, the cameraman was an American private investigator from San Francisco named Chuck Haggerty. He arrived in Hong Kong Tuesday, a few hours after you."

"See," Crystal said, "told you."

"Just because he's from San Francisco doesn't mean he's working for Elise. His employer could just as likely be some rich craftsman."

"You make fun," she said, "but I think that fortune-teller could be on to something. A funny feeling went through me when she said that stuff about getting married."

"Crystal, why would you want to ruin a perfectly beautiful relationship?"

"Not to *you*, Jonas. You're already married. Duh. Besides, you're anything but a craftsman."

"This is bad?"

"You heard my fortune."

"Hmm," he said, rubbing his chin. He decided it was probably a good idea to change the subject. "So, moving on, how do you want to spend your last evening in Hong Kong?"

She laughed, knowing what he was doing.

"Seriously," he said, "this is your chance."

"Well, for starters, I want to take a hot bath, but first I might call my baby. I've been thinking about her ever since we went up in the helicopter."

"Whatever you like. How about if I order a bottle of champagne?"

Crystal sidled up close, pressing her fingers to his cheeks. "Know what? I don't mind fun and games, but I don't want to drink tonight. Would you mind?"

"No, of course not," he said. "Whatever turns you on. Or not."

She gave him a kiss. Then she got her address book from her purse so she could phone her ex-husband, Dennis, to talk to her daughter. Jonas decided to go down to the lobby and buy a newspaper to give Crystal some privacy.

In the hotel shop he bought a day-old copy of the *Los Angeles Times*. Figuring it was too early to go back upstairs, he opted for a short walk. The air was brisk and cool. Jonas hadn't gone a block before he realized he was being followed. The guy was Chinese. Jimmy's man playing guardian angel? he wondered.

A few more minutes of walking convinced him the guy either had nothing to do with Jimmy or Jimmy's motives had changed. This guy definitely was trying to avoid being noticed, and he wasn't nearly as well dressed as Jimmy's guys.

About then he noticed another suspicious character lingering in the shadows ahead. Both guys could be innocent, but Jonas found himself in the unhappy situation of not being sure. Meanwhile he was stuck between them. Adrenaline pumped in his veins. It was fight or flight. The problem with the flight alternative was he no longer had much spring in his legs. A spirited lope was about the best he could hope for. Maybe the thing to do was to face them down, preferably one at a time.

Turning on his heel abruptly, he headed back toward the hotel, prepared to duke it out with the tail, assuming the guy chose confrontation. But he'd only gotten a few steps when a black sedan came roaring up the street, stopping next to him.

Jonas was about to take off at a Senior Olympics clip when the rear car door swung open and Jimmy's security man, the one who'd apologized for the break-in, stepped onto the pavement.

"Please, Mr. Lamb," he said, "get in."

Jonas slid into the seat and Jimmy's guy followed. The car took off.

"I was being followed, wasn't I?" he said to his rescuer, glancing at the two other men in the car as he did.

"It seems yes," was the cryptic reply.

"Who were they?"

"Don't know, Mr. Lamb. Very sorry."

"Common criminals?"

"Hard to say, Mr. Lamb."

Jimmy's guy was better at rescues than communication, though there was no way of knowing if he was being circumspect or was merely ignorant of the facts. A couple of turns and they were back at the hotel.

"Please, Mr. Lamb," Jonas's knight-errant said, "better you not walk alone late at night."

"I take your point."

The door was opened for him and Jonas stepped out. The doorman greeted him with a welcoming smile. His newspaper under his arm, Jonas took a deep breath and walked inside. Back in the room, he found Crystal soaking in the tub.

"How's the kid?" he asked.

She looked up at him. He could see that she'd been crying. "Jonas, she cried when I said goodbye."

"We'll be home this time tomorrow."

"It was selfish of me to come, wasn't it?"

"No, of course it wasn't. You have a life, too."

Crystal bit her lip. Jonas knelt down next to the tub and gave her a tender kiss. He could see that if there were to be fun and games that evening it would be preceded by lots of hand-holding. Women, by definition, were high-maintenance creatures.

4:51 p.m.
CIA Headquarters, Langley, Virginia

Ted Myers attended a three-hour training seminar that afternoon and forgot completely about the full translation of the message intercept he'd ordered until, upon returning to his office, he found it in his in-box. As he read the text he was amazed. His heart was beating nicely, even as he told himself the translator may have taken liberties or the author of the original report could have been duped by his source. Then, too, the whole thing could be a hoax. Myers had never heard of this American entrepreneur, Jonas Lamb, but he knew a thing or two about Jimmy Yee, who was not a frivolous man and wouldn't waste his time on nonsense, yet this was…well, incredible.

Myers got on the phone and called ISS. He asked the reference specialist for all available information on Jimmy Yee, Yee Industries in Hong Kong and a California com-

pany called Global Energy Technologies, Inc., based in San Francisco. He also asked for anything available on Jonas Lamb, president of GET, Inc.

THURSDAY
December 13

Mid Pacific

"I could get used to this," Crystal said, putting her hand in his.

"Yeah, me, too."

He'd upgraded their tickets to first class and they'd been drinking mimosas halfway across the ocean.

"You're going to be rich, aren't you?" she said.

"That's a strange question coming from a fortune-teller," he said, giving her a wink.

She gave him a playful whack on the arm.

"Yeah," he said, "that's the plan. To make a bloody fortune."

"It's important to you to make it big, isn't it?" Crystal's tone was pointedly philosophical now. "You want to be somebody."

He gave her hand a squeeze. "I guess we all have something to prove, if only to ourselves."

"So, how did such an insightful guy manage to screw up so many marriages? I mean, what happened, anyway? They divorce you or you divorce them?"

"Some of both. And there were a couple of mutuals. Half the time I had to buy my way out."

"And you wanted out because…"

Jonas reflected. It was a subject he no longer thought much about. After his third divorce the subject lost its emotional sting. It was a bit like one's sex life. The first time meant something. And maybe the second. After that each partner was more like a new box of chocolates than the be-all and end-all. "I suppose disappointment," he said.

"You ever love any of them?" Crystal asked.

He pondered her comment, not having to think too long. "Tess."

"She was number…"

"Two."

"Your son's mother."

"Yeah."

"What happened with her? You never said."

"For starters, we probably didn't belong in the same town, much less the same bed. Tess had class and brains and I was a migrant cowboy…not even the real McCoy. But she knocked me on my butt and I decided I had to have her, come hell or high water. I guess I heard my mother's voice telling me I was unworthy, so naturally I wanted to prove Ma wrong. I wanted to believe I was good enough for anybody who made the bells ring."

"So what went wrong?"

"I made a bad mistake. My marriage to Rae Lynn had fallen apart. I'd left Texas, wanting a fresh start, expecting Rae Lynn to handle the divorce. I ended up in California and in love. Unfortunately Tess had a mother who saw right through me."

"Meaning?"

"Meaning she realized that I was a drugstore cowboy with a charming grin and not much else. Tess saw more...or she saw less, I've never quite figured out which. The long and the short of it is that I was afraid to mention Rae Lynn and my past for fear of blowing my big chance at the girl of my dreams. So I didn't."

"You married without telling her about your first wife?"

"Texas seemed so damned far away, I figured I was safe."

"And Tess found out."

"Not only that I'd been married but that my divorce hadn't gone through. She was about eight months pregnant at the time."

"Oh, shit."

"That pretty well summed it up. Needless to say her mom ran my ass out of Dodge. I tried to save the marriage both before and after the divorce from Rae Lynn finally went through, but no soap. It was too late."

"You broke her heart."

"This scarlet *A* on my forehead doesn't stand for *adulterer,* it stands for *asshole.*"

"Poor Jonas," Crystal said, touching his hand.

"Do you know how rare it is that I get sympathy from a woman when I tell that story?"

"Well, you *were* a stupid shit."

He grinned, though sadly. "Yeah, that I've heard."

"But there's something sweet about it, too. I mean,

you didn't intend to hurt anybody. And look at you now. You haven't done all that bad."

He was grateful, but unconvinced. "Six marriages, one bankruptcy and a couple of near bankruptcies later and where am I? Living on my wife's first husband's money."

She leaned toward him, pressing a luscious breast against his arm. He was surprised to see a tear brim her lid and start running down her cheek. Crystal Clear pressed his fingers to her wet cheek. "This may not be the best time to tell you, but I've been thinking that maybe it's time I find myself that rich craftsman."

He blinked, realizing she wasn't kidding.

She wiped her cheek with the back of her hand. "I've been playing games since my divorce, same as you," she said. "But I don't want to be playing them when I'm fifty-eight. No offense. Just being honest here."

Jonas had a feeling he'd just been dumped. He wondered if that's what all this philosophizing had been about. She'd been preparing him. A pain ran right through the bones and muscles of his chest to his heart. "Do what you need to do, sweetheart," he said. "And don't worry about me. I'm cool with that."

"Are you?"

He laughed. "How many times do you think this has happened to me? And how many times do you think I've been on the other end?"

She started to say something, then censored the thought. After a moment, she said, "If you don't mind, I think I'll take a nap. Can I borrow your shoulder?" Crystal wedged a pillow against him. "You're a nice man, Jonas Lamb," she murmured, sounding already half asleep. "A very nice man."

Ted Myers had requested an expedited response from ISS, which probably explained why the dossier on Lamb and GET was so thin. According to the report, Lamb was fifty-eight, a Vietnam veteran, a former army-enlisted man who received an honorable discharge in 1969. He was married to Elise de Givry and resided in Kentfield, California. GET was a closely held company, lightly capitalized, incorporated for just three months and was headquartered in San Francisco. The only other officer was Elise de Givry. The business purpose was listed as scientific research and investment. The report Myers had gotten from Research contained nothing new on Yee or his company, nothing that would indicate any interest in biotechnology.

Myers read the intercept again and wondered if it could be disinformation. If it was, he couldn't see the point of it. Could the Chinese be putting up some kind of smoke screen for Yee? The author of the report had certainly gotten worked up over his subject. Not many low-level intelligence documents contained terms like "global economic dislocations," "catastrophic market disruptions" and "revolutionary shifts in global wealth." Were it not for the involvement of Jimmy Yee, Myers would have discounted it. As it was, he saw no alternative but to investigate further.

He started by sending a query through secure channels to the station chief in Hong Kong, requesting available information on Lamb, GET and Yee. Then he went to talk to his section chief, Ken Kellerman. He told Kellerman he had an intercept of a Chinese field report claiming Jimmy Yee was working with a small American firm that had developed a biological substance, some sort of super ethanol made from a genetically engineered variety of corn that dramatically boosted the energy yield of petroleum fuels. Kellerman agreed the report was dubious at best and speculated that the Chinese were probably jerking somebody's chain. He agreed, however, they should follow up and approved Myers's suggestion that they put a request through to the FBI for all available information on Lamb and GET, Inc.

Honolulu

About an hour from Hawaii one of the jet's engines began to sputter. The captain announced that it was being shut down as a routine precaution and that they'd be stopping in the islands to change aircraft. Crystal was upset and began worrying about her daughter.

"Mr. Yee had the smarts not to get on a plane with you, Jonas, but look at me. What was I thinking?"

"Probably not that my company is well worth the danger."

"Joke about it if you want, but I bet you won't scoff at my tarot cards in the future."

Jonas tried to be supportive and Crystal distracted herself by comforting a pregnant woman across the aisle who was even more hysterical than she. Jonas, having nothing else to do, leaned back in his seat and retreated into his thoughts. The concern foremost in his own mind was that he might die before becoming king of the world. What an irony that would be.

The tarot gods notwithstanding, the captain made a perfect landing within sight of Pearl Harbor. Crystal and the soon-to-be mom hugged. Jonas, more relieved than he might have thought, pondered his next move in his battle to conquer the world. (A guy on the threshold of destiny couldn't afford to take his eye off the ball.)

Since it was going to take a while for the airline to get a replacement aircraft for the trip into SFO, Jonas decided to avail himself of the opportunity to get a little work done. In a final conversation that morning, Jimmy Yee told him that if he had any further news of interest, he'd leave a message on Jonas's machine at his office in San Francisco. With Crystal and her new friend ensconced comfortably in the waiting area at the gate, Jonas went off to find a pay phone.

Jimmy Yee had, indeed, left a message for him. "Your little adventure is turning into quite the affair, old bean. I took the liberty of having some friends in San Francisco check out your photographer-detective friend, Mr. Haggerty. You might wish to give me a jingle and I'll tell you what I've learned."

Jonas immediately put in a call to Yee Industries. Jimmy was unavailable, but his assistant, Joy Wu, gave Jonas a cell number where he could be reached. The second call did the trick.

"So glad you rung me up," Jimmy said. "Most intriguing development. It turns out that the gentleman flattened by the bus is very much alive and well in San Francisco. A trusted associate of mine spoke with Mr. Haggerty at his office last evening, California time. He is a private investigator, but claims to have no knowledge of anyone in Hong Kong who might be using his name, and he'd never heard of either you or me."

"Jimmy, you're shitting me."

"No, my friend, I am not. Haggerty did say there was a somewhat similar occurrence in San Diego last year where he was questioned by the police about an incident that took place there while he was up at Lake Tahoe, so it's nothing new."

"You mean we're talking about *two* Chuck Haggertys? One in the morgue in Hong Kong, the other alive and well in San Francisco?"

"Yes. It's apparently a case of stolen identity."

"The plot thickens," Jonas said, thoroughly befuddled.

"It does, indeed."

"Maybe I should make some inquiries of my own."

"Keep me informed," Jimmy said.

"And you the same."

They ended the call and Jonas bought a candy bar at a newsstand and then wandered back to see what Crystal was up to. Her pregnant friend was in the ladies' room. Jonas sat down in the vacant seat.

"I'm not sure how to tell you this, Crystal," he said, "but you know Haggerty, the guy so enamored with your posterior that he recorded it for posterity?"

"Yeah?"

"Well, it seems that was an assumed identity. The

real Haggerty is alive and well in San Francisco. I'm going to try to talk to him when we get back."

"Jonas, what have you been smoking?"

"A Butterfinger. But that's all right. I didn't inhale."

"I think you're having a nervous breakdown."

"No, Crystal, I just lead a very interesting life."

4:04 p.m.
CIA Headquarters, Langley, Virginia

Myers received a cable from Hong Kong indicating they had no information on Jonas Lamb or GET in their files and that Jimmy Yee had no known business interest in biotechnology ventures. They confirmed that an American by the name of Jonas Lamb had been in Hong Kong three days, having left that morning for San Francisco. They were checking to see if Lamb had met with Jimmy Yee.

Myers also received a memo from the FBI indicating that it had no information on file concerning GET and very little on Jonas Lamb. There was nothing intelligence-related in Lamb's background, though he had a criminal record consisting mostly of minor misdemeanor infractions dating back nearly forty years, the three most serious being an assault conviction in the State of Washington when he was nineteen and two DUIs, one in 1970 and the other in 1974, both in California. Lamb had also been a defendant in several business-related civil cases, one involving fraud. He went through bankruptcy in 1985.

Lamb's background, Myers decided, was not that of a Rhodes scholar, but neither was he Al Capone. What stood out most, as far as Ted Myers was concerned, was that Lamb did not seem like a man who would be engaged in earthshaking scientific research or espionage. Nor did he seem like someone who would move in the same circles with one of the wealthiest men on earth.

Myers took the information he'd gathered to Ken Kellerman, saying the involvement of Jimmy Yee and the interest of the Chinese made an otherwise innocuous piece of intelligence noteworthy. Kellerman instructed Myers to pass the file on to OPS for review by the President's Analytical Support Staff (PASS).

FRIDAY
December 14

Davis, California

Kenny Jarrett lay under the covers in his bed, fully clothed, staring at the dark ceiling of his dorm room, waiting for the clock to reach 2:00 a.m. K.J., as he was known by his friends on campus, hated being called Kenny—only his mother did that anymore. And he wasn't particularly proud of the name Jarrett, considering his old man was a capitalist pig, a big shot in agribusiness down in Bakersfield. Being related to Cal Jarrett was cause for shame in itself, yet another reason K.J. had to prove himself, which was what he planned to do.

The boy knew that corporate America, including his father, didn't give a shit about people, except to exploit them. He hadn't been on campus six months before deciding to dedicate his life to doing something about that. Thanks, of course, to Tina Richter.

Tina had changed his life. She was the smartest girl he'd ever known. And probably the most beautiful.

Best of all, they were comrades-in-arms, revolutionaries for the environment. They both wanted to teach corporate America a lesson.

Tina had recruited him into Save the Seed, a secret militia of eco-warriors dedicated to the fight against genetic engineering. They'd met in September when Tina was passing out flyers outside the Student Union. They struck up a conversation, which became spirited. Her attention was flattering as hell, first because she was a senior and second because she had the most totally fantastic body in the world. Maybe it was his passion for the environment that drew her to him, but there was no denying the fact that ten minutes after he'd met Tina Richter, he was in love.

The trouble was K.J. was a freshman. What hope did he have of winning her? After he'd attended his first few meetings of Save the Seed and saw that, as a group, they were mostly talk, he realized that to get anywhere with Tina, he had to win her respect. It was pretty clear that Tina, too, was frustrated with the group's inaction. "You know what the trouble is?" she'd said as they'd walked together after a meeting. "We've got lots of good ideas, but nobody's got balls."

K.J. had decided then and there that he would change that—single-handedly, if necessary. Tonight was the night it would all begin.

Determined as he was to become a hero in Tina's eyes, he was still nervous. Totally. Hell, he had to piss again. The second time in half an hour. It had to be nerves. He decided not to succumb. If a guy was going to be a man among men, he had to learn to hold his water.

He tried to distract himself by fantasizing about Tina. He wished they'd be meeting after the operation tonight, but that wasn't the plan. Once they'd made contact and he'd done his thing, he was supposed to sneak back into the dorm. God, he wished he could go to her apartment instead.

Nice as that thought was, K.J. was still having a problem with his bladder and all the sexual fantasies in the world wouldn't change that. Throwing back the covers, he left his room and headed down the hall to the communal toilets. Fortunately there was nobody around. He should probably have put on his pajamas, just in case he encountered somebody else on his floor with minimal bladder capacity. But he wanted to be ready when the time came, and he figured he wouldn't as likely fall asleep with his clothes on. He'd set his alarm as a precaution, but if somebody should hear and remember the time, they could put two and two together. Brad Kozik, his team leader, had told him not to let anybody see him. That was critical.

His escape from the dorm went without a hitch. Sucking in the cool night air as he walked across campus, he felt vital and alive. It was sort of like having sex, though maybe that was only because he'd be seeing Tina.

She wasn't at the rendezvous site when he got there, but she showed up on her bike within two minutes of his arrival. A navy stocking cap covered her beautiful dark hair and she was dressed in dark clothing—those tight jeans that showed off her ass to perfection, a pea coat and gloves. K.J. searched her face for signs of fear. He wanted to know he wasn't alone. She smiled, her lips tight, the crease in her forehead persisting.

"So, is the rookie secret agent ready for his first test of fire?" she asked. "No pun intended."

K.J. sucked up his courage and said, "I am, how about you?" His voice was deep and husky. He hoped she couldn't tell it was from nerves. "You got the stuff?"

"Of course, did you think I'd come without it?"

"Let's do it, then," he said, effecting a macho tone.

They began moving in the direction of the Ag Building, Tina riding her bike, K.J. walking.

"You remember the drill?" she asked, apparently playing her part as the senior operative.

"Yeah."

"Let's go over it again."

"When we get there, you give me the bottle. I wait in the bushes while you put the note on the door. I wait three minutes, then I walk up to the building, light the wick and toss the bottle through the corner window where Mayne's office is, then I walk away."

"But not the way I go."

"Yeah, not the way you go."

"And what if you get stopped?"

"I act dumb. Say I couldn't sleep because of my midterm, so I went for a walk."

Tina rode along in silence for a while, checking out

their surroundings. "You know this is our first major operation. Brad talks about all the stuff we've done, but it's nothing compared to this."

"Yeah, I know. I plan to make a difference, Tina. Hell, if you had my old man for a father you'd fly a kamikaze into a battleship, if that's what it took." K.J. was really feeling it now.

"Don't worry about your father, worry about the sonsovbitches fucking with nature. This is about saving the planet, K.J."

"I know, Tina. I'm a soldier for all living things." And he damn well meant it, too.

Thirty minutes later Kenny Jarrett lay in his bed in his shorts and T-shirt. He was sweating profusely, his heart racing. His window was open and every once in a while he'd catch a whiff of acrid smoke. He'd been listening to the sirens, feeling powerful and heroic, recalling with pride the sight of those flames shooting out of the building. He'd almost peed in his pants, but by God, he'd pulled it off. He'd struck a blow for nature, putting Patrick Mayne out of business, at least for now. K.J. was a champion for living things, a full-fledged soldier of Save the Seed.

He couldn't wait to see Tina's face. And all the others, for that matter. God, he'd never felt a rush like this!

There was only one bad thing. He couldn't tell his father. Maybe someday he would, though. It'd kill the sonovabitch. Totally. Man!

Gordy Roberts, a national security adviser to the vice president, and William Evans of the President's Analytical Support Staff (PASS) briefing team, arrived at the V.P.'s Texas ranch for the daily intelligence briefing. The vacationing vice president met them in his study. After the oral briefing Roberts brought an item from the supplemental report concerning Jimmy Yee and the PRC to the V.P.'s attention. He thought the V.P. might be interested because of his close connection with the oil industry. The V.P. read the report and his mouth sagged open. Roberts agreed that it was incredible. When the V.P. asked if any effort was being made to verify the information, Roberts told him that routine follow-up was under way. The V.P. said that if some Chinese billionaire was intent on shaking down the world energy markets, the U.S. ought to have more than a routine interest in the development. He instructed Roberts to talk to the president's national security adviser. If the report proved to have credibility, perhaps the matter should be on the agenda of the next meeting of the National Security Council.

Kentfield, Marin County, California

When Jonas awoke in the guest suite of the home he shared with his sixth wife, he did not feel like the king of the world. He didn't even feel completely at home, which was the way it had been from the day he'd first moved in with Elise. This was still Jean de Givry's house, and in many ways Elise was still Jean de Givry's wife, though she'd be aghast to hear he might feel that way.

Jonas had moved into the guest suite when Elise's illness became debilitating. In times past it had been occupied by Elise's elderly mother, who'd predeceased Jean, which was why it was known even now by the de Givrys as "Mom's" or "Gram's" room as well as the guest room. Only Elise would refer to it as Jonas's room. (During his absence she'd had her decorator add a few holiday touches, including a small flocked Christmas tree with twinkling white lights.)

The de Givry adult children, Melanie and Wilson, had never really accepted him. In fact, they'd bitterly resented Jonas's very existence, considering him an opportunist and an interloper. Of all the crosses he had to bear in connection with this marriage, "the children," as Elise called them, were the most onerous.

The irony was that "the children" understood Jonas's motives a little too well. They had his marriage to their mother pretty well pegged. The problem was they only saw the negative side of the equation. Elise was cognizant of the quid pro quos in the arrangement, whereas Melanie and Wilson were not.

What it boiled down to was that a fight over Elise's considerable wealth was brewing. The signs had been there even before the wedding. The way her children saw it, their mother's marriage had not so much produced a stepfather as it had placed an asp in the family coffer. Jonas, to his credit, had no intention of being mercenary, and he hoped that Melanie and Wilson de Givry would find it in their hearts to let him slip quietly away with his duly earned inheritance. He wasn't holding his breath, however.

Of the two de Givry progeny, Melanie was far and away the more dangerous. First, she was a lawyer, and that was never good. Second, she had a mean streak in her a mile wide. Wilson was simply greedy. He lacked balls and let Melanie do the talking for him.

The children had their own homes, of course, but with the holidays upon them and Elise failing, Jonas knew he'd be seeing a lot of his stepchildren. He could only hope they would make as much of an effort as he to keep things civil, for Elise's sake if for no other reason.

It was early, and though jet lag had completely messed up his sleeping rhythm, Jonas decided he might as well get cleaned up and dressed. There was a good chance he'd find Elise up. She still liked to go down for breakfast with the assistance of her nurse. It was often the only meal she didn't take in her bed, the poor thing. "I have a little strength in the morning," she'd say. "I might as well make use of it."

When he'd arrived home last night Elise was already asleep. He'd gone to her room and kissed her forehead, but hadn't awakened her. He still had to say hello and look into her eyes without guilt, a capacity he'd unerringly (but not happily) perfected.

He was shaving in the company of Gram's tiny bathroom TV when Paula Zahn informed him of the firebombing incident at U.C. Davis, perpetrated by a group of eco-terrorists called Save the Seed. Since that was Patrick's domain, the news got his rapt attention.

The TV screen was so damned small, though, that he had to put on his reading glasses to see the video clips, half of which he missed while trying to wipe shaving soap from the lenses. By the time he was ready for eye contact with Paula, the building fire was extinguished, but he did manage to see a university mug shot of his beloved son. There on national TV was Patrick, looking more like the Unabomber than the victim of a band of arsonists bent on endangering human life so that nothing could enter a human digestive tract that didn't bear Mother Nature's stamp of approval.

According to Paula, nobody had been hurt, which meant his son was safe, but Jonas's heart pounded against his sternum just the same. There had been considerable damage to the building and laboratory, which gave him pause. Could their precious little organisms have gone up in smoke?

Jonas rushed for the phone and dialed his son, getting the answering machine. He left a brief message. "I heard the news and assume you're okay. Hope the Black Sheep are, as well. I'm sure the authorities are keeping you busy, but give me a buzz."

His stomach doing contortions, Jonas paced. It could be a while before he heard from Patrick. Rather than wait, he decided to hop in the car and drive on up I-80 and get a reading on the situation. But first he'd have breakfast with Elise and give her the silk bed jacket and nightgown he'd bought for her while Crystal was busy picking out her jade-and-diamond earrings. He hated running off so soon after returning home, but Elise was a mother and she'd understand.

What he wouldn't tell her, though, was what he feared most—that if Patrick's research had been destroyed and the little Black Sheep were dead, there might not be a revolution after all. No crown. No coronation. No glory. No redemption.

1:21 p.m.
Smithwick, Texas

After a lunch of venison and roast turkey, the V.P. and his guest, Harmon Shelbourn, CEO of TexasAmerican Petroleum, went for a stroll to get out of the house and away from their wives and families. They were, of course, accompanied by the Secret Service. After chatting about developments in the industry, the V.P. asked Shelbourn if he knew anything about an experimental biological additive, some sort of super ethanol, being developed by GET, Inc., a small company in California that purportedly would boost the energy output of petroleum fuels by a factor of ten. Shelbourn asked if it was a joke. The V.P. assured him it wasn't. The government knew very little about it, but there had to be scuttlebutt floating around the industry. Shelbourn, visibly shaken, indicated he would ask around and see what he could learn.

Davis, California

Tess Vartel had been pushing eighty most of the way up the interstate from San Francisco. She should have known better. With the big silver university water tower just coming into view, she saw the red light in her rearview mirror. A highway patrol cruiser was right behind her, a couple of car lengths back.

"Damn," she said, glancing down at the speedometer. Eighty-one. She eased up on the accelerator. "I don't need this," she said aloud.

And she didn't. This would be her third speeding ticket this year. Traffic school again. She'd promised herself no more tickets, for her self-respect if nothing else.

She put on her right turn signal and moved over one lane at a time until she was able to pull off onto the shoulder and roll to a stop. The patrol car was right behind her.

Tess already had a headache. This wouldn't help. Plus, it wasn't getting her to her son's place any faster. She took her wallet out of her purse, her fingers trembling as she removed her driver's license.

Looking into the mirror again, she saw that the officer was still in the patrol car, probably on the radio. It was a woman. Tess wasn't sure whether to be glad or not. Tears wouldn't do any good. That was certain. Not that tears were her style. Anything but. On the other hand, she was in a very emotional state and had been ever since receiving Patrick's call. A child in trouble and tears did go together.

She'd been in the pool at the YMCA, working with the children afflicted with cerebral palsy as she did every Friday morning, when one of the boys in the office came to report that Patrick was on the line. She couldn't imagine why her son would be calling her there. She was surprised he'd even remembered her schedule, which, over the course of the week, had her all over town—her office some mornings and other afternoons, the women's shelter, the Y, Legal Aid, the law library. And then there were other responsibilities like board meetings. Half the time she herself had to struggle to figure out where she was supposed to be.

In ways, she enjoyed her two hours in the pool with the disabled children most. Perhaps because it was so different from everything else she did. Holding those little babies in her arms, seeing the joy on their faces as they flailed feebly at the water, living proof that goodness and virtue came in the most unlikely packages. But then there was the kid standing there at the edge of the pool in pants with a crotch starting at his knees, saying, "Somebody named Patrick is on the line and he wants to talk to you."

At least it wasn't somebody wanting to talk to her *about* her son. Every mother's nightmare.

Tess had hastily dried herself at poolside, slipped on her terry robe and padded off barefoot to the office, fighting the ominous feeling in her belly. There, on the cement floor, standing next to a well-worn wooden desk that was probably as old as she, Tess picked up the phone and punched the flashing button.

"Patrick?"

"Hi, Mom."

"Are you all right?"

He laughed. From the time he was thirteen Patrick had found her maternal affectations amusing.

"You've heard the news, I see."

"What news?"

"There was an incident early this morning in my building on campus."

"Incident? What do you mean, *incident?*"

"Some vandals tried to burn the place down. They got my wing. Several offices and the lab before the firefighters got it under control. Hell of a way to end the quarter, huh?"

Tess felt a chill in her blood. "You were the target, weren't you?"

"They're just misguided, ignorant kids, Mom. Nothing to worry about. That's why I'm calling...to ward off any possible attacks of hysteria."

Water from her suit running down her legs, Tess had begun to shiver, unamused by her son's flippant tone. "What happened, exactly?"

Tess Vartel had never practiced law—had never done litigation or worked in a law firm—but her legal training, her instinct to probe for facts, kicked in when confronted by situations like this. "You aren't calling because it was a nonevent," she said.

"No, I'm calling because, like I say, I didn't want you to be alarmed when you heard the news reports."

That was vintage Patrick, always protecting her, playing single child-father to her single parent-mom. Even when he'd have one of his asthma attacks he'd somehow fight off the panic while she'd be practically apoplectic, certain her child was going to expire before her eyes. Then, afterward, he'd make some smart remark like, "Thought for a while I was going to lose you, Mom."

Sometimes it seemed they'd grown up together, and in a sense, they had. She was only nineteen years his senior, though there were times when it seemed more like ten—to him as well as to her. "They threatened you, didn't they?"

"Not exactly."

"Patrick, you're being evasive. I'm over the shock. I'm not going to start crying, for God's sake. I want to know exactly what happened."

He recounted how the Molotov cocktail had been thrown through the window of his office, causing a fire that had destroyed everything. And he told her about the note taped to the front door of the building.

"What did it say?"

He read her the text. "Professor Mayne, keep your hands off Nature, stop the genetic mutilation or pay the price. This is your last warning."

"Was it unsigned?"

"No, it was signed 'STS.' The police think it's an underground group called Save the Seed. I've gotten some crank letters from them in the past."

"Then they're eco-terrorists."

"Yeah, crop-busters, eco-warriors. They see bio-engineering as an attack on nature. Talk about Frankenfood scares people and fuels the passion of the extremist. Essentially it's ignorance."

"Yes, but they're violent. Arson is a serious crime."

"To their credit, Mom, they did it in the middle of the night, not when the place was full of people."

"Maybe because it was easier to do then. I don't think you can dismiss this as nothing. That note was a clear threat."

"Mom, the point is it's nothing like what happened to Richard."

Maybe her son knew her too well. Naturally, the horror of what she'd been through with her husband had popped into her mind. The gruesome crime, her terrible embarrassment and guilt, the police, the investigation, the eventual arrest, the prosecutors, the trial. The worst, though, was her moral failing and the guilt, a burden she continued to carry. The fact that she'd come out of it whole, still believing in humanity, in herself, had been something of a miracle. But then, maybe this showed she wasn't quite as whole as she thought.

"I still want to see you," she'd told her son. "For my sake, if not for yours."

"I'll be spending most of the day with the authorities. How about if I come see you this weekend?"

Tess had agreed, but the more she thought about it the more she was convinced her son was far too cavalier about his personal safety (how she'd survived his surfing years, she had no idea) and that a heart-to-heart talk couldn't wait. It would be like Patrick to make some cheeky remark to the press and incite someone to throw a firebomb in his bedroom window without waiting to see if he'd abandoned his work on genetically engineered crops.

And so she'd decided to drive up to Davis to counsel him. After finishing with her swimming lesson, she'd phoned Walter to tell him what had happened. Not unexpectedly, he was as concerned as she.

"I don't know whether I'll be back in time for dinner or not," she told him.

"Well, don't worry about it, dear. You do what you have to do. I understand."

It was vintage Walter Bronstein, always considerate, always putting her interests first. He was so wonderful that way. "I'll call you," she said.

"You just look after Patrick. I'll be here."

And so she'd headed across the Bay Bridge on her way to the valley—a mother fighting her maternal instinct, even knowing that, if not infallible, it was the glue that had held the species together over the millennia.

There was a rap on the window beside her head. Tess pushed the button, lowering the window. The highway patrolwoman leaned down to check out the interior of the vehicle. "May I see your driver's license and registration, please?" she intoned.

Tess handed the woman her license, then reached over, removing the vehicle registration from the glove compartment, and handing it over, as well.

"Keep your hands on the steering wheel where I can see them, if you would, please."

Tess, her heart pounding, gnawed on her lip, waiting for the right moment to speak.

"Do you have any idea how fast you were going, Ms. Vartel?" the officer asked.

"Eighty, Officer."

"Uh-huh. You know that's in excess of the limit."

"Yes, I'm sorry."

"You've got a problem with speed, don't you, Ms. Vartel? My computer says you've had two citations in the past twelve months."

"I did have a problem, Officer, you're right. But I got control of it. I reformed. This is different. A sort of emergency."

"What kind of emergency?"

"I was in a hurry to see my son."

"Your son? He in the hospital or something?"

"No," Tess said, "his office at the university was firebombed this morning. I was very worried and anxious to see him. I was hurrying too much."

The officer leaned down for a closer look at her. "You're the mother of that professor?"

"Yes."

"You gotta tell me what face cream you use, honey. I think I'll get me some."

"I was a child bride, but thank you."

"Vartel," the woman said, studying the license. "That wasn't the professor's name, was it?"

"No, Patrick's name is Mayne. That's my maiden name. Vartel is my married name."

"And your kid's got your *maiden* name?"

"Vartel is from my second marriage. My first husband and I had our marriage annulled because—"

"That's all right. This is California, we could be here all night. I'm on my fourth last name myself. Let's move on."

Tess looked up at the woman, liking her. Human beings sometimes connected under the oddest circumstances. Like her first encounter with Jonas Lamb, for example. They'd met when she and some other college students picketed a construction site north of Santa Barbara that was endangering a frog habitat. Jonas, a construction foreman at the site, supposedly a blue-collar charmer (though she'd found out later it was all an act, Texas drawl and all), got out of his truck, walked up to her and said, "Frogs, ma'am? You mean we could be trampling on the little fellas and not even know it? Golly, if you've got a net with you, let's catch the rascals. Maybe together we can find them a safe home."

Tess's college girl sensibilities had been ruffled, and she was mightily offended by Jonas's arrogance and seeming unlimited supply of gall. But then, he did have a sense of humor and another side that was much more endearing. When he'd looked into her eyes and said so convincingly, "I really had no idea we were a danger to any living thing, ma'am. I'm not a conservationist by instinct, but I've got an open mind and I'm willing to learn. Would you care to save me from my ignorance?" it was all over. She was toast.

Tess doubted his sincerity, of course, knowing she'd be a fool to trust him, and for good reason, as it turned out. (He admitted later he'd approached her because she was the prettiest protestor in the group.) But she ignored her better judgment and accepted the challenge, figuring she could convert him to environmentalism. "Who knows," he'd said, his manner so disarming, "you might succeed where the Baptists failed." Jonas was a lot smarter than he'd let on. And though he'd spent some time in Texas, he'd later confessed he was Seattle born and bred, a phony cowboy—"all hat and no horse, as they say in the Lone Star state."

In a manner of speaking, that twist of fate had brought her to this moment on the shoulder of Interstate 80, under arrest, seated in her BMW next to a cornfield. Patrick was, after all, *their* child.

"Here's the problem," the officer said. "What happens if while rushing to your son's aid you kill some other mother's child? That doesn't make a lot of sense to me."

"You're right, Officer. I let my emotion and my fear get in the way of my judgment."

The patrolwoman thumped her pen on her citation pad. "Because you're a mother and I'm a mother, I'm letting you go with a warning, Ms. Vartel. But let's not forget the other lady's kid, okay?"

"Thank you, Officer."

The woman gave her a final look in the eye. "Vartel, Vartel. Why is that name familiar?"

"My husband was the victim in a notorious murder case in San Francisco a few years ago."

"That doctor who was brutally murdered in his own house. Stabbed, wasn't it?"

"Yes."

She stepped back, tossing her head. "Get out of here. Go see your son."

Jonas stood in the bay window of his son's Victorian in Davis, looking out at the street where, under a leaden sky, the Channel 13 News truck was pulling away from the curb, on its way to a murder, a rape, a robbery (or, if the community was having a good day, perhaps a broken water main). Next to him was Patrick's perfunctory four-foot, artificial Christmas tree, which the boy had propped up on a box covered with white tissue paper, a bachelor's nod toward the holiday spirit. A perky little brunette reporter from the *Sacramento Bee* was seated with Patrick on the chrome-and-leather sofa, doing an interview, tape recorder rolling, mike in hand.

They'd been talking for about five minutes, starting right after Patrick had finished with the TV guy, having taken enough of a break in the interim to go to the bathroom, then get himself a glass of juice. But not until he'd put Jonas's mind at ease with a thumbs-up, a smile and a quick "Don't worry, the Black Sheep are fine."

Jonas was relieved. They'd dodged a bullet. There probably wasn't a better feeling in the world than seeing yourself climb out of a casket and do a jig just when the Grim Reaper thought he had you by the balls.

The cute little reporter bore no resemblance to Crystal, but she brought his erstwhile lover to mind, perhaps for no other reason than the fact he was at loose ends, sexually speaking.

As it turned out, Crystal's philosophical musings on the plane weren't alcohol-induced delusions.

When he'd dropped her off at the houseboat, she'd chosen to say her goodbyes on the deck, under a string of unlit Christmas lights, her eyes glistening.

"I won't invite you in," she'd said. "We've had an intense few days. And anyway, you want to get home to Elise…or *should* want to get home to Elise." (The word *should* on the lips of a woman, when used in connection with a man's attitudes, was always a danger sign.) Actually, though, Elise wasn't so much the issue as Crystal's own needs. "I have enough respect for you, Jonas, to be frank. That fortune-teller in Hong Kong really made me think."

It was apparent to him that his bounteous sex life was about to go down the drain. Still, aplomb was called for. "I see," he said, his tone reasonable and gentle. "You've decided to go looking for a rich craftsman."

"I think we need to take a step back and reflect."

That, he knew perfectly well, was woman-speak for "It's over, unless I change my mind, which, being a very real possibility, is reason enough to keep the door open." Then, too, Crystal had the sexual appetite of a man, having less tolerance for dry spells than most women. Unless another guy entered the picture soon, a mercy fuck in, say, a couple of weeks (around New Year's Eve would be a good bet), remained a very real possibility, suitably disguised, of course, with patter about being unable to get him out of her mind. Jonas never understood what was so bad about the simple, direct admission that she wanted a good thumping and preferred the tried and true over the unknown.

Having seen and heard it all before, he chose the pragmatic course in formulating his response. "I want you to be happy, and I'd like to be part of your happiness. But you know what's best for you better than I." He'd kissed her lightly on the lips then and left.

Already in honeybee mode, Jonas was on automatic pilot, aware once again there was a world of womanhood out there. He was a master at rationalization, telling himself there was no need to invest his happiness in a solitary specimen. Hence, even in times of high stress like now—with the dominion of planet earth at stake—he could notice a pretty girl, the little reporter from the *Bee* being a case in point.

He'd arrived at the same time as she, following her up the flight of stairs to Patrick's front door. If called upon, he could testify that she had great legs. And, having listened to her, he could also vouch for the fact she was a bright, serious young woman, though, of course to her, he was just Patrick's old man, over by the window, hanging out until he could get a few words with his son.

"But never mind the radicals for a moment, Professor Mayne," Jennifer said earnestly. "What do you say to the thousands of ordinary citizens who are uncomfortable with the notion that their food is being engineered in a laboratory? Let me quote from a tract distributed by Save the Seed, the group that claims responsibility for this morning's attack. 'We can't allow three billion years of evolution to be destroyed by corporate greed. Mankind must step forward to save itself by saving all living things from the evil conspiracy of the corporations and their mad scientists.' What do you say to that?"

"I'm sure those folks are well meaning," Patrick replied in an impressively calm voice, "but with all due respect, they don't understand the facts. Look, most crops grown today are not the product of an evolutionary process controlled by nature. For centuries crops have been intentionally designed, altered—engineered, if you will—by man. The wheat and corn and peas we eat didn't come that way from nature. They're the product of crossbreeding controlled by human beings. Distinct strains of plant life have been artificially created by people using breeding techniques that result in unique gene structures."

"But that's different than what you do, isn't it?"

"What bioengineers do is the same thing, but on a more refined and targeted scale. It's changing gene structures on a limited basis. It's quicker and more economical than the shotgun approach of mixing separate strains of plants. The primary difference is technique. It's all the same DNA, don't forget. Nature provides the building blocks. We move them around to get a different end result. Is that any more reprehensible than the people who took the wolf and turned it into a Pekingese or a poodle?"

Jonas had to admire his son's deftness. Watching the couple on the sofa, he could see that Jennifer was fascinated. Patrick was smart enough to impress anyone. He was also charming and engaging. Jonas, a wily veteran of the seduction game, understood a woman's body language, and he imagined Jennifer's heart was doing the hootchy-kootchy.

When she crossed her lovely legs and gave the hem of her skirt a discreet tug, Jonas realized where her mind was—never mind his own. So he turned to the window to watch the street, knowing that the most effective antidote to the wayward impulse was simple distraction. It was certainly far more efficacious than principle or prayer.

Driving up the interstate that morning, he had flirted a bit with his paranoia. Was it possible the fire-bombing of Patrick's lab had something to do with his Black Sheep discovery? Was it really the work of a bunch of crazy kids who aspired to playing God in an adult world they didn't understand and therefore felt compelled to despise? Could it be that the same forces that had spawned a phony Chuck Haggerty were also responsible for this? Or, was it simply a matter of *everybody* being against good old Jonas Lamb and his son?

The little *Bee* reporter and Patrick started making coming-down-to-the-wire sounds, which she capped with, "Last question, Professor Mayne. Would you be willing to grant another interview in the event of significant future developments in the case?"

Smart girl. Had it been Jonas on the sofa, he probably would have suggested they discuss the matter over dinner. But this was a more jaded and cynical generation where girls didn't always get their way and boys often didn't care enough to make an issue of it. Patrick was cool, answering with a simple "Sure, give me a call."

Jonas had little doubt she would. Continuing in his role of voyeur, he watched Jennifer turn off her tape recorder, then sway her clamped knees to the side so she could bend over and pick up her briefcase from the floor. Patrick was already on his feet. Jennifer got everything packed away, then came to attention. She extended her hand and Patrick took it, his expression indicating distraction, Jennifer's little heart doing a double back flip, seemingly for naught.

She didn't glance Jonas's way until the last moment, smiling as an afterthought, her mind, understandably, onto other things. Patrick didn't see her to the door—that I-can't-be-bothered Gen X thing. Instead, he looked at the old man and gave a weary sigh.

When the front door clicked shut, Jonas said, "Cute girl."

Patrick—a tall, darkly handsome young man who favored his lovely mother in all respects save his blue eyes, which were carbon copies of his old man's—nodded. "Yeah, but my words will come out twisted, you watch."

"I think she liked you."

"It won't make any difference."

Jonas decided it was a fruitless line of conversation. Patrick was far too serious to let his priorities slip. On to business. "What was all that talk about genetically engineered food?" he asked his son.

"My cover," he replied. "My daytime job."

"You don't think this incident had anything to do with Operation Black Sheep?"

"Nope."

"You sure?"

"Jonas, nobody knows about it but you, me and now your friend in Hong Kong. This Frankenfood phobia has been around for a while. The firebombing was about the food supply, not the energy markets."

He was relieved, but also aware Patrick was continuing to be circumspect. Jonas wasn't offended, though. Patrick had said the less he knew, the less he had to worry about, which was good enough for him.

"How about I buy you lunch?" he said to the boy.

"That sounds good," Patrick said, "but would you mind if I had a quick shower first? Things have been hectic since before dawn."

"Take your time. I'm at the age where you either embrace hunger or surrender to fat. Vanity can be just as effective as exercise, you know."

Patrick, amused, headed off.

Jonas turned once again to the window. As he pondered the joys and sorrows of his life, a BMW pulled up, parking in a space across the street. The driver, a woman, got out. Jonas watched her slip on a trench coat. There was a certain grace in her movements. She wasn't a kid, like Jennifer. She was a mature woman. Attractive. And she was crossing the street, headed for the house. Another reporter?

About the time she reached the sidewalk out front, the synapses in Jonas's cerebral cortex fired in coherent fashion and a familiar picture filled his brain. The woman was someone he knew. A wife. Or more accurately, an ex-wife. His second ex-wife. It was

Patrick's mother, the woman who'd once been the girl bent on saving the frogs. Tess. *Shit.*

Why he felt panicky he could only guess. Maybe it was because Tess had exiled him, cast him into the darkness, made it perfectly clear she had no desire to see him ever again. His impulse was to slip out the back door—not out of fear so much as consideration. Tess and guilt went together like law and order, crime and punishment. Facing your victim was never easy, at least for anybody with a shred of decency in his soul.

"Patrick!" he called halfheartedly toward the back of the house, perhaps thinking the fruit of his union with Tess could save them from each other. Former spouses (a subject on which Jonas considered himself an eminent authority) were, after all, the quintessence of contradiction. They were beloved for what they'd once been and damned for what they'd become, familiar yet alien, living reminders of one's most egregious shortcomings. Former spouses were mistakes with attitude. Friendly or hostile, it almost didn't matter. The essence of an ex was failure.

There was a rap on the front door. Jonas could hear the faint sound of a shower running in back somewhere. Patrick would be no help. Jonas moved toward the door, preparing himself for good cheer.

Holding his breath, he opened the door, the plastic Christmas wreath appended to the outside flopping gently against it. Tess's eyes rose to meet his. The expected shock was there, then a long, frozen moment of comprehension, calculation and judgment. Perhaps the best way to describe what he saw was dismay.

"Hello, Tess. Long time no see."

Her jaw went slack. She had a pretty mouth and she was a pretty woman. Yes, he realized, it was Tess standing on the porch, but not *his* Tess. The Tess he knew existed in memory, in a place that was no more. This was another Tess, a metaphysical joke of sorts, an Einsteinian trick of time and space that defied understanding.

"Jonas, what are you doing here?"

"Well, how can I put it? Sometime after that business with the frogs, we had a son and…"

"I'm sorry, I didn't mean it that way. What I meant was I didn't expect to see you."

"I didn't expect to see you, either, but when you leave DNA behind, these things happen." He grinned thinly. "Patrick's in the shower, so on his behalf I'll invite you in."

"I've come uninvited. I wouldn't want to interfere."

It was then he noticed the huge diamond on her ring finger. It was emerald cut. It had to be ten carats. Patrick had told him Tess had been widowed. Was the ring from her marriage or something current, a new relationship? He cleared his throat. "I came uninvited myself, Tess," he said, moving on. "Think nothing of it. The little bastard deserves a surprise. I don't know about you, but I can't wait to see his face."

Tess smiled the smile he recalled surprisingly well. In his experience, lovers get imprinted on each other with an emotional stamp that time can repudiate, but not erase. Love may be gone, but it can't be forgotten.

Jonas held out his hand, inviting her to enter. Tess stepped across the threshold.

Her surprisingly familiar scent pleased him, as did her trim waist, closely cinched by the belt of her trench coat. Her dark hair had a sheen and a richness that contrasted so dramatically with the look of his other wives, who'd tended to be blondes of one stripe or another. He again caught a glimpse of the rock on her finger. Elise had some pretty impressive jewelry, but nothing like this. It made him wonder.

"Let me help you with your coat."

Tess put her purse down on a chair, unbuttoned her coat and let him slip it off her shoulders. He took it to the closet. When he returned, she'd walked across the hardwood floor and was standing next to the tree where he'd been moments ago. She wore heels and a dark brown business suit and cream silk blouse. Tess had always been stunning in her simplicity. The girl he'd disgraced was gone, but not her spirit, not the intelligent dark eyes that had once peered into his heart.

"This is strange," she said, summing up the situation perfectly.

He searched for something to say, but found himself simply staring, taking her in, remembering. She was what? Forty-six or seven and hadn't lost her figure. "Tragedy throws people together, I guess."

"Yes. Speaking of which, how's Patrick?"

They were standing on opposite sides of the room, the gulf between them somehow natural. But in the few minutes they'd been together, he already recalled why he'd once loved her. There had been something terribly solid about Tess Mayne, something that had cut to the heart and soul of him, bypassing all the intermediate steps that normally had to be negotiated in getting to know a person. It was a combination of seriousness and sensitivity, intelligence and insight. Oh, how he'd hated being unworthy of her.

"Patrick's fine. Too fine, maybe. Not as shook up as I was when I heard about it on the news."

"That sounds like him."

Jonas wanted to say something positive and reassuring, like "Our son's a gutsy young man," but it was too presumptuous, too familiar. He settled instead for "You okay?"

"Yes, considering. What do you make of the firebombing? Has he opened up to you at all?"

"We only spoke for a few minutes. There's been a stream of reporters here all morning."

"I hope he wasn't provocative. Patrick has a tendency to be combative, cheeky even."

"I don't know about the cheeky part, but I know where he got his idealism. It wasn't from me."

She stared at him as though she was remembering some incident or event from long ago. He hoped it wasn't one of those he'd regretted. After a moment she drifted to the sofa and sat down. "So, how have you been?"

"Busy," he replied.

She nodded.

"And you?"

"The same."

He went and sat in the chrome-and-leather armchair that matched the sofa. "This is my first time here."

"Oh, really?"

He detected in her a touch of pleasure at his comment. Then it occurred to him—they were, in a sense, competitors.

"Patrick and I tend to meet at restaurants or bars. It's a guy thing."

She nodded and, having trouble keeping eye contact, glanced around the room. It was Spartanly furnished, containing few other pieces of furniture besides the sofa and chair. Apart from that there was a sound system, a few unframed posters and lithographs on the walls, and the tree.

He wanted to say something funny, something to make her laugh, but it wasn't in him. Mostly he didn't want empty small talk. It was far worse than the truth, which was what was needed.

"I still feel guilty," he said.

"About?"

"Us."

She laughed. "Don't waste the energy. That's all ancient history. Anyway, we were just kids."

"I wasn't," he replied. "Maybe that's the problem."

"So, what are you doing these days? You still in construction?"

"No, you're several careers behind. I don't do a lot, actually. Look after my investments, such as they are."

"You're living in Marin, if I recall correctly."

"Yes, Elise and I are in Kentfield."

Tess smiled a cocktail party smile.

"Elise is seriously ill," he told her. "Terminal cancer."

"Oh, Jonas, I'm terribly sorry. I wasn't aware."

"No reason you should be."

"You either bear up or give up," she said. "That's what I discovered when Richard died."

"It appears you've adjusted. That isn't costume jewelry on your finger, is it?"

"No," she said, looking down at her finger. She fiddled with the diamond. "No, I was recently engaged."

"Oh, really?" A twinge of jealousy went through him. (There was a certain proprietary feeling associated with spouses that persisted even after they moved into the "former" category, and Jonas was feeling it now.) "Congratulations."

"Walter's a very old and dear friend who was widowed last year. We've always been close, but were very happily married to others. Then..."

Jonas nodded. "Funny the way things work out sometimes, isn't it? I mean, who would have thought you and I would be sitting here like this, twenty years after the fact, talking?"

"It's closer to thirty, Jonas."

They heard footsteps in the hall and turned to see Patrick in stocking feet, jeans and a sweatshirt appear in the doorway. "My God," he said, seeing his parents seated in his living room.

Tess went over to her son, taking his face in her hands. "I couldn't wait till the weekend, so I came barging in, not realizing your father was here."

"I wasn't expecting either of you," Patrick said, his expression teetering between amusement and horror. "How many times have the three of us been in the same room, anyway?"

"Half a dozen at most," Jonas replied. "When you were a kid, mainly."

He studied them. "Is this just awkward for me?"

Jonas said, "As you age you forget what pissed you off. Unless you want to be mad for no reason, you let go. Am I right, Tess?"

"Yes," she replied, giving Patrick's waist a squeeze.

"I've got an idea," Jonas said. "Let's take your mother with us to lunch."

"If you two have plans, I won't intrude," she said.

"No, no," Jonas insisted. "Nothing livens a party like the presence of a lady."

Mother and son exchanged small smiles.

"Let me put on my shoes," Patrick said. He left the room.

Jonas moved closer to her, close enough that he could see the smallest details of her pretty face. Subsequent encounters with his other wives hadn't been this poignant. Was it because of Patrick? The circumstances? Or his feelings for her?

"Apart from being happily engaged, how are you, really, Tess?"

"Fine," she replied. "I'm really fine. And I'm a grown-up now."

"I don't know I can say the same. And the jury's out as to whether that's good or bad."

She chuckled. "We are who we are, Jonas. That's one lesson I've learned."

He understood the words, but not necessarily the concept, maybe because he was never one hundred percent sure who he was. "So, who's Walter?"

"Walter Bronstein."

"The big real estate magnate?"

"Yes."

"You worked for him, didn't you?"

"Yes, still do. He brought me into the business, taught me everything I know. Walter was a mentor and...as I said, a friend. He's been very generous to me and also Patrick, who he's considered the son he never had. I didn't marry Richard until Patrick was already in college, so if there was a father figure in Patrick's life, it was Walter."

Jonas didn't say anything.

Tess only then realized what she'd said. "Sorry, Jonas. I didn't mean that as a knock on you, but it *is* true that you weren't around for Patrick during those years."

"You're right, but I am trying to make up for past sins and omissions."

Patrick returned, effectively ending the conversation. "If you two are up to this, let's go."

They went to the closet to get their coats. While Jonas was helping her on with her trench coat there was a crash accompanied by the sound of falling glass. Tess flinched. Jonas spun around. They heard the sound of screeching tires outside.

Patrick hurried to the front door and stepped onto the porch. Jonas followed. A vehicle disappeared around the corner.

"It was an old pickup truck," Patrick said calmly.

They went back in the house to assess the damage. There was a large rock in the middle of the front room floor with a note tied to it. "At least it didn't hit the Christmas tree," Jonas said as he started to pick it up.

"Don't touch anything," Patrick told him. "The cops said if I receive any suspicious mail or if notes are left not to touch them. Anyway, I can pretty well tell you what it says."

2:49 p.m.
Smithwick, Texas

Harmon Shelbourn was no sooner in his car than he grabbed his cell phone. Before he and his wife had driven out the gated entrance to the V.P.'s ranch, he had Phillip Persons, head of the research division at TexasAmerican Petroleum, on the line. Shelbourn asked if Persons had heard rumors about super-ethanol research being conducted out in California by GFT, Inc. Persons knew nothing about the research, this was the first he'd heard about it, or the company. Shelbourn gave him a rundown on what he'd learned, adding that the federal government wasn't involved, but that there was awareness of the project in the highest levels. Persons promised to check with colleagues and report back.

Davis, California

Tess had been sitting on Patrick's front steps for ten minutes, watching the traffic go by. The police had been there for half an hour and once the note had been examined ("You've had your warning. We'll be watching") she was too upset to stay inside. So she'd put on her trench coat and come out for some air.

The lead police detective, a ruddy-faced man with

the curious name Noel August, had put on surgical gloves to examine and read the note. It was all so reminiscent of the ordeal she'd gone through when Richard was murdered.

Why was it that when her life seemed set that something terrible or worrisome always happened? And why was it that Jonas Lamb was so often in the mix?

When he'd opened the door and she saw him standing there, it was more than a shock. It was a blow. Jonas, no longer the folksy charmer he was at thirty, yet still a good-looking guy. Tawny-headed with traces of gray at his temples. Manly. Fit. Still robust, but in a quieter way. Worldly and sophisticated without being urbane. He was a middle-aged Lothario, a salesman, basically. Always on the make.

Not that she couldn't handle seeing him. She was well beyond the emotion and the pain, but his unexpected appearance had added personal embarrassment to an already traumatic situation. But this wasn't about Jonas, it was about Patrick. And the parallels with Richard's murder were enough to chill her blood. She'd failed her husband with a moral lapse, and she couldn't allow the same thing to happen with Patrick.

She'd been an overly protective mother, perhaps trying to compensate for having raised Patrick in a broken home. But he made it clear early on that he was his own person. When he graduated from college he decided to use the money his grandmother had willed him to do some traveling before graduate school. But instead of the grand tour of Europe, Patrick had opted for an adventure in the Amazon. She was sure he'd never be seen again, unless it was on a string of shrunken heads adorning some aboriginal's hut.

The night before he left, they'd had a heart-to-heart talk over a bottle of wine. "Mom," he'd said, "I know this isn't what you'd have chosen for me, but at some point you'll have to accept the fact it's my life. Me being on my own is going to be as good for you as it is for me."

She'd laughed. "I hate to say this, Patrick, but I think there's a little role reversal going on here."

"Mom, you've got to loosen up. The only thing you've ever done that wasn't orchestrated was marry my father and get pregnant."

His bluntness had taken her aback. "Maybe I learned something from that."

And now Jonas, whom she'd all but forgotten, was suddenly back in the picture. She could deal with him, but the man spelled trouble. He'd failed her in the worst possible way, showing he was without honor. That would never change.

Jonas found what the police had to say much less interesting than did Patrick. Or maybe he was preoccupied with the woman outside. Once she'd stepped out the door, he'd mentally gone with her.

Deciding it wouldn't hurt if he talked to her—the better they understood each other, the less likely there'd be trouble between them down the road—he slipped away. Tess was sitting on the steps. She turned at the sound of the door.

"Are they finished yet?"

"Almost," he replied. "Mind some company?"

"Suit yourself."

He sat on the stoop next to her. "You okay?"

She looked into his eyes in a way that suggested the question was somehow offensive. "I'm upset about Patrick, obviously."

"He'll be fine, Tess."

"Jonas," she said, her tone shifting, her demeanor more engaging, "if you don't mind me asking, what *is* your relationship with him?"

"The best way to put it, I guess, is that we're trying to catch up."

She did not look pleased. "Better late than never, I suppose."

"If it's any consolation, Patrick and I are as much business partners as anything."

"Business partners? You mean that literally?"

Oh, shit! he thought. *Me and my big mouth!* Patrick had told him that the less his mother knew about their relationship, the better. Now he'd spilled the beans.

"Jonas, have you lured Patrick into one of your schemes?"

"No, Tess, I haven't," he said emphatically.

She seemed not to believe him, and he doubted there was anything he could say that she would fully trust. "I'd rather you tell me it's none of my business than lie."

"I'm not lying."

"Well, you're being evasive."

"Our deal has nothing to do with his current problems," he rejoined, annoyed that he had to justify himself.

"So, you *are* involved in something. You lied."

"No, I didn't. You asked if I lured Patrick into one of my schemes. I didn't initiate a thing and that's all I'm going to say."

The door opened again and the police officers came out. Tess and Jonas got to their feet. Patrick shook hands with the detectives, Noel August and his partner, a young, soft-spoken man named Gene Bardic.

"Thanks," Patrick said to the men.

"Like I said, exercise caution, Mr. Mayne, and you should be all right." August nodded to them as he and his partner passed by. "Take care, folks." The detectives descended the steps.

Tess turned to her son. "Well?"

"Not much to report," Patrick said. "They got a call while we were talking. They found the pickup downtown. It was stolen. The police impounded it, hoping to find some physical evidence. Is that the right term?"

"Yes," Tess said, looking unhappy. "So, it's business as usual? Forget what happened and move on?"

"They suggested I be careful, Mom, and that's what I'm going to do." He looked back and forth between them. "So, still want to go to lunch or should I run to the supermarket and pick up three steaks?"

"I may head for home," Tess said. "I've seen you and that's what I came to do."

"Don't leave," Jonas said. "You and Patrick talk while I go get the steaks."

"No, really," Tess insisted. "I'm fine now. My jitters are under control. You two discuss whatever…and I'll be on my way."

He knew he couldn't let things end on this note. "I don't mean to be pushy," he said, taking her arm, "but I think the three of us need to talk. Come on, Tess, let's go inside."

His assertiveness didn't please her, but it worked. Once they were in the front room Patrick gave Jonas a look, understandably perplexed.

"What's going on?"

"Your mother and I were having a parental discussion and I inadvertently let it slip that we have a business deal. And, knowing me as she does, she's alarmed."

"That's not true," she said. "I'm upset about these eco-terrorists, that's all."

"The concern, Patrick," Jonas said, "is my past. I defer to you in the matter, but I think we need to find a way to allay your mother's fears about our relationship."

"Honestly," she protested, "you're making more of this than I am. Let's forget it."

Patrick held up his hands. "I agree we need to talk. Please sit down, Mom. You, too, Jonas."

Tess took off her coat, laid it across the back of the armchair, then sat. She looked embarrassed and angry. Patrick dropped down on the sofa next to his father.

He cleared his throat. "Mom, Jonas and I have formed a company to develop and market something I discovered in connection with my research."

"You mean that's what these threats are about?"

"No, our thing has nothing to do with this. It's top secret. Very few people know about it. Nobody at the university. I don't even use their facilities. Save the Seed and others like them are unhappy with the things I do in my official capacity. I want to put your mind at ease about that."

"I don't see how a secret project is any better than any other kind."

"Maybe it isn't," Jonas said. "The point is I'm not pulling the strings. This is Patrick's deal."

"What *is* your role, then?"

"The financial side," Jonas replied.

She blanched. "I see," she said. "Okay."

But Jonas could see it wasn't okay. "I'm providing the seed capital," he said, hoping to put her mind at ease.

"Well, that's good for you both, I guess."

Jonas could see the past wasn't as much behind them as Tess had alleged. But resentment was what he would have expected, and she had cause.

"So, this is what I missed all these years," Patrick said, making light of it. "At least you aren't screaming at each other."

"And there's no reason why we should," Tess said. "Now, I really do think I should leave. No hard feelings, okay?" She got to her feet.

The phone rang. "Hang on, let me get this before you go," Patrick said, excusing himself.

After he was gone, Tess went to the front window with its gaping hole. Cool December air was flowing into the room and Jonas saw her shiver. She glanced at the Christmas tree and plucked something from a bough, dropping it into the cardboard box Patrick had gotten earlier for the debris. Probably a shard of glass.

Jonas wondered what she was thinking. If he had to guess, it involved what had happened between them. They'd never really talked about it. She'd retreated into her mother's protective custody and he hadn't been able to get through to her. It probably didn't matter. Tess had made her feelings clear. He could never be sorry enough.

Tess was sorry she'd come, but even sorrier that Jonas was there, that she had to endure all those reminders of that awful period she'd spent years trying to forget. The day their marriage collapsed seemed both a hundred years ago and yesterday. Except for Richard's death, it was probably the most difficult day of her life. She remembered it so clearly. Eight months pregnant at the time, she was lying in bed watching TV, feeling like a beached whale, Patrick playing soccer with her kidneys, when the doorbell rang. She struggled to the door and found a woman standing on the porch in a lavender business suit with a skirt that was too short and too tight, black patent high-heeled sandals, a cowhide purse slung over her shoulder, a bubble of golden-blond hair and a grimace on her face. She was thirty, give or take, pretty in a common way, but overly made-up.

Glancing at Tess's bulging stomach, she drawled, "'Scuse me, but do I have the wrong address? Jonas Lamb live here?"

"Yes, he does. May I help you?"

"And who might you be?" the woman asked.

"I'm his wife. Who are you?"

"Honey, you ain't his wife," the woman chortled, "because *I'm* his wife. So, unless the laws here in California are different from Texas, you're something else." She again looked at Tess's stomach. "I hate to think what."

An hour later, with the first and only Mrs. Lamb sitting on their as-yet-unpaid-for settee, Jonas came home to face a shit storm. He had the unenviable (and in the end singularly unsuccessful) task of trying to explain what the hell he'd done and how he planned to rectify it. Tess, suffering false labor pains, listened tearfully, then threw him out, but not until she'd slapped him, the only time in her life she'd ever struck anyone. Right afterward she went to her mother's.

In the ensuing weeks Jonas came by repeatedly, but she refused to see him. When Patrick was born, Jonas showed up at the hospital to see his son and managed to sneak by the nurses to visit her. All he accomplished was to provoke a crying, screaming fit, which didn't end until Security whisked him away.

Meanwhile her mother's attorney sorted out the legal tangle, putting her back to her circumstances ante-Jonas (except, of course for the addition of her ten-pound bundle of joy). She didn't see Jonas again until two months after Patrick was born. He had divorce papers in hand, but it made no difference. By then Tess could look at her putative husband with less emotion, knowing he was a flimflam man.

Glancing back across the room, she saw the Jonas Lamb of mature years, yet one so terribly reminiscent of that fellow who'd been seated on her mother's sofa twenty-eight years ago with such a contrite expression on his face, fingering his divorce papers as if they were some sort of magic bottle that would produce a genie capable of making their world right. There was no genie and there would never be.

"Sorry about that," Patrick said, coming back in the room. "It was the chancellor's office. They wanted to know if I'd attend a press conference tomorrow morning."

He said it with such easy confidence that Tess was alarmed. It almost seemed to her that Patrick regarded this business as a game, though that might be unfair. But it was his life and he was fully capable of making his own decisions. *She* was probably the one who'd lost perspective.

"So, Mom," he said, "can't we persuade you to stay and have lunch with us?"

"No, I'd really rather go, honey," she said. "Anyway, Walter and I have plans and I'd like to get back to the Bay Area before rush hour." Then she went over and took his face in her hands, just as she had when she'd arrived, and looked him in the eye. "I want your solemn promise you'll be careful, Patrick."

"I promise."

"I'm dead serious."

"So am I."

Tess hesitated before asking her next question, then decided there was no reason to censor herself because of Jonas. She and Patrick constituted the real family here. "Are you still planning on Christmas with Walter and me?"

"Sure, why not?"

"I'll call you this week." She kissed him on the cheek then got her coat, which Jonas took from her and held as she slipped it on. The man was still suave, the courtly gentleman, the charmer. And phony as a three dollar bill.

"Mind if I walk you to your car?" he asked.

She wasn't eager for further conversation, but neither would she be snippy about it. "If you like."

"I'll be back in a minute," he said to Patrick.

"Drive carefully, Mom."

The words came from a man, but she heard the thirteen-year-old who used to look after her so protectively. It touched her, but she only nodded, hurrying to the door before she teared up. Jonas opened the door for her. They went out, Tess buttoning her coat.

When they were midway across the street, he said, "I want you to know that my involvement in Patrick's project is nothing for you to be concerned about. I'm trying very hard to be a positive factor."

They'd reached the car and she turned to face him. "I don't care about your business deal," she said. "But promise me one thing."

"What's that?"

"Promise me you won't hurt him. I mean emotionally."

He looked into her eyes, which were swimming. "I promise."

"Thank you." She got her keys out of her purse, her hands trembling, and opened the car door.

Jonas didn't retreat until she started the engine and drove away. In the rearview mirror she saw him staring after her until she turned the corner. Once he was out of sight, she breathed more easily. Being around him was harder than she would have thought. Maybe it wasn't Jonas so much as the circumstances—Patrick in danger and all those terrible associations with Richard's death.

That night her husband died would always haunt her, a constant reminder of the fact that she hadn't been there. Tess visualized the sight of her husband's body in a pool of blood on the entry floor. Even now, a million visits to that terrible image later, she shivered. Walking into their home, disheveled, her chin raw from whisker burns, thinking Richard wouldn't be home from Mexico for at least another day, only to find him lying there. Tess knew with moral certainty that were it not for her affair, Richard would be alive today.

3:23 p.m.
TexasAmerican Petroleum Headquarters, Houston, Texas

Phillip Persons phoned his close friend, Albert Matheson, head of the thermodynamics laboratory at the National Institute for Petroleum and Energy Research in

Bartlesville, Oklahoma and asked if he'd heard anything about a super ethanol being developed in secret by GET, Inc., out in California. Matheson hadn't heard a thing about the project, and was flabbergasted when Persons recounted the rumored details. Certain something that big couldn't be kept quiet for long, he vowed to learn what he could, starting at the staff meeting he was about to convene. He told Persons he'd poll his associates and let him know if anything of interest came up.

4:16 p.m.
NIPER, Bartlesville, Oklahoma

None of Albert Matheson's associates had heard any rumors about the super-ethanol project, but the prospect of such a development intrigued Nigel Soames, a British national who'd been working at the institute for a year and a half. Though it was quite late across the Atlantic, Soames decided to risk awakening his brother-in-law, David Lawrence, phoning him at his home in Surrey. Lawrence was a fuel-additives expert at the Institute of Petroleum on New Cavendish Street in London and would be bloody astounded by the news. When he heard Soames's account of the rumored development, Lawrence was, as expected, excited and incredulous. He marveled that such a revolutionary development by an independent research firm like GET would have gotten that far without the American oil companies having saddled the technology. Soames speculated that that was likely to happen. Lawrence agreed, opining that matters might end in a bloodbath, considering not just billions, but trillions were at stake.

Jonas arrived home that evening to find an ambulance sitting in the circular drive, along with Melanie de Givry's Lexus. "Oh, shit," he thought.

He pulled up behind his stepdaughter's car, then got out and hurried through the wide-open front door. As he stepped into the entry hall he saw a couple of paramedics carrying Elise on a stretcher down the big circular staircase that wrapped around the ten-foot designer-perfect Christmas tree festooned with white porcelain and silk angels and huge red glass ornaments. Melanie followed behind.

Jonas hurried to the foot of the stairs. "What happened?"

Elise, hearing his voice, raised her head. "Oh, Jonas, thank goodness you're home."

From that angle he could see little more of her face than her fleshy jowls, her strong, slightly large nose and the blond-and-white swirl of hair atop her head. The paramedics stopped when they reached the bottom of the stairs, lowering the wheels of the gurney. Elise extended her hand to him, her dull gray eyes beseeching. "I had another episode, my heart again. The doctor thought it best if I go to the hospital for tests. As a precaution."

"Since there was nobody here I had to come over and take charge," Melanie intoned. She was on the other side of the gurney, looking perfectly willing to leap over her mother and throttle him.

Melanie de Givry was tiny, an elfin version of her

mother. She was blond and had a heart-shaped face that would have been pretty but for the grimace that was always threatening to break into a full-blown scowl. When she spoke, the ugliness of her tone and manner made it impossible to see any beauty. Jonas knew women, and his capacities for indulgence were more boundless than most, but in his book Melanie de Givry could be the poster child for congenital animus. She had her virtues, undoubtedly, but Jonas had seen pitiful few of them.

"Darling," her mother said, "that's not true. Charlotte was with me. And she did call the doctor."

"A responsible decision-maker should have been present," Melanie rejoined. "Not that there are all that many candidates in this house."

"Please," Elise said, giving Jonas's hand a feeble squeeze, "let's not squabble. Not now."

"I'm sorry I wasn't here, Melanie," he said. "My son was the target of a firebombing attack at the university this morning. I thought I should be with him."

"The son you haven't seen for twenty-eight years?"

"Please," Elise said again. "Jonas is here now. That's all that matters."

Melanie smirked. "Why don't we celebrate that joyful development at the hospital, Mother? No sense standing here discussing it with your health at risk. Come on," she said to the paramedics, "let's get her into the ambulance."

Elise gave Jonas another beseeching look. Only then did he realize she was wearing the bed jacket and gown he brought her from Hong Kong. It touched him, causing a lump to form in his throat.

"I'll ride in the ambulance with you," he volunteered.

"No, *I* will," Melanie said. "If you follow in your car, you'll have a way to get home. Wilson is meeting us at the hospital, so I can get a ride with him, if need be."

It sounded perfectly reasonable, but it was apparent Melanie's intent was to orchestrate things. Before Elise's illness had become so debilitating, she'd been more inclined to stand up to her daughter, but in her weakened condition, peacekeeping seemed to be a higher concern. Jonas, for his part, had decided that making things as easy for Elise as possible should be the object and he'd behaved accordingly, even at the expense of Melanie running roughshod over him.

He walked beside the gurney, still holding Elise's hand as the paramedics wheeled her to the ambulance. Fog had settled in and the night was damp. He pulled the lapels of his sport coat over his chest, shivering as he stepped away so they could load his wife into the back of the vehicle. Melanie came up alongside him.

"So, have a good time in Hong Kong?" she asked.

"It was a business trip."

Melanie glanced up at him, her eyes narrowing with disgust. "You're so full of shit, Jonas," she said under her breath. Then she climbed into the back of the ambulance with her mother. Once seated, she glared out at him.

The paramedics closed the rear door and went to the front of the vehicle. The engine started and the ambulance moved around the circular drive, passed through the gate and entered the street. Jonas stood motionless, feeling rooted to the ground as he watched the taillights disappear in the fog.

Pacific Heights, San Francisco

Tess sipped her cream sherry and observed her fiancé seated across from her in the parlor of his stately home. Walter's head lay back against his armchair and his eyes were closed as he listened to Verdi's *Aida*. He loved opera. And, in his case, it wasn't an affectation. Some of his favorite arias so moved him that tears would fill his eyes.

On the table next to him, his cigar rested in a crystal ashtray, the smoke curling up before being drawn toward the fireplace where logs blazed, filling the semidark room with a shimmering, warm glow. His cigars, smuggled to him from Cuba through a string of intermediaries, were his only vice.

Walter Bronstein was a patrician-looking man of seventy-one with high, wide cheekbones, a large, well-shaped nose and prominent brow. Heavy lids masked his nondescript gray eyes, his least attractive feature. His skin had a ruddy cast to it, which together with his thinning, slicked-back gray hair, betrayed his age. Even so, he had a strong, regal air of the sort associated with, say, a Roman emperor—a benevolent emperor, to be sure, one with a taste for the arts, as well as an appreciation of his own genius and powers.

Walter was a man whose sexuality was almost exclusively in his persona, more a spiritual phenomenon than a physical one.

At the moment he was wearing one of the plaid cashmere sweaters she'd picked out for him when he'd allowed her to redo his wardrobe. Tess had told him he needed to appear more with it if he didn't want people to take her for his third or fourth wife instead of his second. For years Walter had been wed to a shirt and tie, except on the rare occasions when he played golf or sailed. Otherwise, a nod toward informality meant taking off his suit jacket. Happily, he'd been a willing subject in her make-over program, even taking up an exercise regimen, which had in only three months reduced his paunch by fifty percent. "Keep this up, madam," he'd teased, "and you'll have the ladies lined up outside my box at the opera, just for a peek at this Eliza Doolittle of your creation."

Walter was a dear person, always upbeat and, with respect to her, admiring. She wasn't surprised when he'd admitted, some months after his wife's death, that he'd been infatuated with her almost from the beginning of their acquaintance. But to his credit, he'd never once, in all the years they'd worked together, said or done anything untoward, always respectful, always the perfect gentleman. So ingrained was his sense of propriety that she'd had doubts they'd be able to have a romantic relationship. Did pillars of rectitude actually make love? Their first kiss, she had to admit, had something of a teacher-student feel. It was as though he'd stepped out of his habitual role as an authority figure to steal a favor.

For whatever reason, Tess had decided she was ready for a man whose mood was more paternal. Perhaps it was her age, or maybe she was tired of the struggle and wanted to be taken care of.

The nice thing was she was confident of Walter's indulgence and understanding. But, like a dutiful daughter, she didn't want to disappoint him. That was why she hadn't yet found the courage to share with him the events, though earlier she'd left her place with that very intention.

As she watched Walter savoring his hedonistic (but harmless) pleasures, she drank sherry and thought of Jonas Lamb. Her ex was like an emotional cancer that wouldn't allow her remission, an unfortunate life choice, coloring everything that had followed. She'd continued debating whether or not to tell Walter about the encounter.

Restless, Tess went across the large room to the bay window looking out onto Broadway. It had begun raining as she'd driven over to have dinner with him, adding a touch of gloom to her mood. The rain was coming down harder now, streaking the windowpane, blurring the headlights of cars cresting the hill. She observed the passing traffic, wondering which bothered her more—what had happened to their son, or Jonas being in the mix.

"Verdi wrote this to commemorate the completion of the Suez Canal," Walter said. "Did you know that?"

Tess turned, looking back at him over her shoulder, seeing only the top of his head over his wing chair. "No, I didn't."

"Funny the way art and history intertwine, isn't it?"

She drained the last of her sherry and walked back to the seating group by the fire. Taking her place again, she put the empty glass down on the coffee table.

"Shall I have Sam pour you another?" he asked.

Tess was going to say no, then changed her mind. She drank very little as a rule, but felt the need for alcohol this particular evening. "Please."

Walter picked up the miniature walkie-talkie he used to communicate with his Filipino houseman, a handy device considering the vast proportions of the mansion. "Sam, would you bring us some more sherry, please?"

"Yes, sir" came the reply.

Walter put down the instrument, smiling benevolently at his wife-to-be. "You seem preoccupied, dear. Is it Patrick?"

"Yes, I guess I'm worried and distracted." Tess knew this was her opportunity to mention Jonas. She was vacillating, looking for the right opening, when Sam entered the room, carrying the bottle of sherry on a silver tray.

"Another glass for Mrs. Vartel, please," Walter told the houseman.

Sam had been with the Bronsteins as long as Tess had known them, but Walter and his domestic remained to this day on surprisingly formal terms, both of them referring to her as "Mrs. Vartel," when addressing the other. This was despite the fact that she often spent the night, even having her breakfast served in Walter's bed. On one such occasion, when Sam had been dispatched to fetch a special blueberry honey that Walter had brought back with him from a trip to Oregon, she'd asked her husband-to-be how he planned to refer to her after they were married. "Will I get promoted to Mrs. Bronstein?"

"Hmm," he'd replied, clearly not having considered the matter before. "That hardly seems right, considering that's what we called Rose. What would you like to be called?" His tone was surprisingly serious.

She'd shrugged. "Tess?" For the time being, though, she remained "Mrs. Vartel." (Gentlemen of a certain age, like old dogs, weren't easily changed.)

"Thank you, Sam," she said when the houseman had refilled her glass.

"May I bring you anything, sir?" he asked his employer.

"No, why don't you go on to bed. You've had a long day."

"The dinner was lovely, Sam," Tess told the retreating domestic.

"Thank you, ma'am." And he was gone.

Walter seemed to have tuned back into *Aida,* judging by the far-off look in his eye and the micro-movements of his head. Tess picked up her glass and gazed at the crackling fire.

"I'm sure Patrick will be fine," Walter said, coming back from his musical interlude.

She gulped some sherry, blinking as she mentally switched back to the thread of their conversation.

"Yes, I know," she said. "I guess it brought back that whole terrible tragedy involving Richard. I don't want to go through anything like that again."

"Of course you don't."

"It seems like there's always something that brings it back, though," she lamented. At that point, she could have said, "Like today for example..." But she just couldn't say the words to get herself started down that track. She drank more sherry instead, starting to feel the effects of the alcohol. "But let's don't talk about that, Walter. Tell me something about what you're doing. How are things going with your foundation? Have you had any interesting applicants for director?"

"Scads. This is a relatively big job as far as foundation work and nonprofit management goes. These kinds of positions are few and far between, and everybody is eager to move up. But there was one applicant who would interest you, if indeed you aren't already aware. He listed you as a reference. Jerry Tate. He was the director of the Poverty Center while you were doing volunteer work there."

Tess colored at the mention of the name. Jerry was one of those people in life whose path you hoped never again crossed yours. Like Jonas.

"Have you spoken to him lately?" Walter asked.

"No, I haven't."

"Well, he must have assumed you'd put in a good word for him."

"Probably."

"I take it he was competent."

"Yes, a very good administrator."

"Hmm."

She was relieved when Walter put his head back and closed his eyes, losing himself in the aria. *Jerry Tate,* she thought. God, of all people, why him?

Tate had been witness to one of the more embarrassing and, as it turned out, more devastating experiences of her life. Four years ago he'd come back to his office late at night, flipped on the light switch and found her naked on the couch, her legs wrapped around the bare ass of one of the center's more prominent board members, Gregory Hamilton. The poor man couldn't help but stare, mouth agape, before muttering "Sorry" and backing out the door. She'd about died, but it was nothing compared to the trauma she experienced when she'd reached home that night to find her husband had been murdered.

There was no connection between the two events except for the fact that had she not had her fling with Gregory, she'd have been home and available to aid her husband. The irony was that their dalliance was a chance thing. They'd both considered themselves happily married, but they simultaneously reached one of those junctures in a marriage where a touch of sadness and loneliness produced self-pity, which led to self-indulgence, which led to consolation, which led to sex. Yet, it was a sin, the only time in her life she'd slipped. And she'd paid for it dearly. Her punishment: having to live with Richard's death.

"I don't know much about the man," Walter said, obviously not as much into his aria as she thought, "but he's lined up an impressive list of references in addition to you."

"Oh?"

"Aaron Marks and Gregory Håmilton, to name but two."

"Gregory Hamilton?"

"The governor's nominee to the state appellate court. You know Hamilton, don't you?"

Tess felt a deep shame. "Yes, actually I do."

"He's a card-carrying member of San Francisco's legal mafia, WASP division," Walter added with a laugh, "so I'd think you would."

Her cheeks began to burn. Walter's eyes were still closed, his head back. Tess gulped some sherry.

"Do you know Gregory?" she asked, sounding as offhand as she could.

"Only to say hello."

She pictured Greg. He was the quintessential establishment lawyer—smart, attractive, a guy who had everything including a pedigree. He was the kind of man women dreamed of marrying but never found because they were the stuff of fantasy.

The man wasn't perfect, of course. Greg was a touch self-indulgent and a bit thin when it came to character. But that hadn't stopped Tess from living out her fantasy with him. It had been a brief assignation and as self-indulgent as anything she had done. It was weakness pure and simple, and it had been her downfall.

"References are nice," Walter said, "but all they do is get you in the door. Chemistry, as you know, is everything."

This seemed to be her day to face embarrassments from the past. First Jonas, and now Greg. And she had tried so hard to put those mistakes behind her. Maybe she needed to talk about it with Walter. He knew about Jonas, of course, but not Greg. Perhaps she didn't have an affirmative obligation to apprise Walter of all her sins, but neither did she want to be deceitful the way Jonas had been.

After Richard's death she'd seen Greg only once, a tense, guilt-riddled encounter in which he'd expressed his regrets and tried to assure her that God wasn't punishing her for being unfaithful—after which he'd gone home to his wife. Maybe Greg's true intent was to assuage his own guilt. It certainly didn't change her feelings of responsibility.

Needless to say, she never returned to the Poverty Center again. And, in a way, she considered it an insult that Jerry Tate, having witnessed her shameful act, would use her name in applying for a job with Walter.

The door opened then and Sam, still in his white jacket, entered. "Excuse me, Mr. Bronstein," he said, indicating the portable phone in his hand, "there's a call for Mrs. Vartel. It's Professor Mayne."

Tess practically snatched the phone from the houseman. "Patrick, are you all right?"

"Yes, Mom, of course. I'm calling to see if you're okay. You seemed pretty shook up when you left and I wanted to check on you."

"That's very sweet, honey," she said, pleased. "I'm fine. I appreciate the thought."

"Actually, it was Jonas's idea."

"Oh."

"He said he was afraid he'd upset you."

"Well, he didn't. It was the threats against you, the arson, that rock thrown through the window, that bothered me."

"Don't worry about me. I'll tell Jonas you're fine."

"Please do."

"I'll let you go, then. Bye, Mom."

"Good night, honey."

When she handed the phone back to Sam, Walter said, "Everything okay?"

"Yes, Patrick was just checking up on me."

"He's a considerate young man."

"Yes, he is."

It was yet another opportunity to mention her encounter with Jonas, but she couldn't. And she didn't even know why. Maybe she just didn't want to think about him, though that's exactly what she'd been doing most of the evening.

"Thanks, Sam," Walter told the man. The servant left the room.

Tess downed the last of the sherry. "Walter, I think I should go home. It's been a very stressful day."

Walter roused himself from his chair and went to her. Taking her hand, he pulled her to her feet and held her. Tess no sooner lay her head against his chest when the fire cracked loudly, making her jump.

"My nerves are shot," she said with a sigh. "I'm sorry to spoil the evening."

"Nonsense. But maybe you shouldn't drive. Let me call you a cab."

"No, I'm fine. I can handle a couple of glasses of sherry."

"How about if I drive you?"

"No, really."

"You sure, dear?"

"Yes. Just walk me to the door." She suspected he had thoughts of intimacy, but she just wasn't in the mood, more upset than she realized.

They made their way to the entry. Tess got her coat. Walter helped her on with it. She thought of Jonas helping her with her coat at Patrick's house. She thought about his words of apology for events that were decades old, realizing only now how much she still mattered to him.

Glancing up at Walter, she gave him a quick kiss on the corner of the mouth. "I'm sorry," she murmured, then headed for the door.

Pausing, she managed a parting smile, then out she went into the rainy night, hurrying down the stairs, running from her feelings as much as from Walter. She hoped to God her engagement wouldn't be yet another casualty of this terrible day.

SATURDAY
December 15

Ross General Hospital, Marin County

Jonas Lamb, who'd first developed a knack for patience in Kontum Province in the Central Highlands of Vietnam while waiting in ambush for Viet Cong and NVA, figured he ought to be able to outlast his ninety-eight-pound bitch of a stepdaughter, an adversary seemingly determined to discredit his commitment to her mother, whatever the cost. But Melanie didn't seem to appreciate the fact that she was up against a seasoned pro.

Jonas had learned that when you were engaged in a battle of wills, the trick was simply not to care how long it took to prevail, even if it meant sitting there the rest of your life. Hoping the other guy'd give in was the surest way to lose.

Shortly after midnight, Melanie de Givry threw in the towel. Kissing her sleeping mother, she took her purse and coat and left Elise's room at Ross General Hospital. She did not bother to say goodbye to Jonas. She simply walked out, presumably to gather up her brother, who was sacked out in the waiting room, so he could drive her home.

Once Melanie was gone, Jonas allowed himself the yawn he'd been stifling for the better part of three hours. Resolute about not showing weakness under duress, the past several hours he'd simply sat there, silent after Elise was asleep, either watching his wife or stepdaughter, who glared at him across the hospital bed that served, in effect, as a demilitarized zone.

Being the object of contempt was not a lot of fun. Not that he expected love or even respect. He'd had more than one difficult relationship over the years, but rarely had he engendered such hatred as Melanie showed. He hoped it had more to do with her than with him, though he understood why he was so unpopular. But, as his first father-in-law, Rae Lynn's old man, Boots Appleby used to say, "Sometimes the only way to get a mule to move is to piss him off." Jonas had never feared making waves. Relationships, like this one with Melanie, were sometimes the consequence.

His inner clock still a bit out of whack thanks to jet lag and sleep deficit, Jonas decided that he'd made his point and there was no need to continue the vigil. Elise's well-being was what mattered and there was nothing he could do for her now.

Even so, Jonas didn't want to leave on Melanie's heels, so he got up and stretched and yawned again, wondering if he should have a cup of coffee to facilitate the drive home. He'd spent most of the past few hours thinking about Patrick and Tess, Crystal and Jimmy Yee. The central players in his life at the moment were an odd assortment. Perhaps the most troubling character in the cast was the guy who'd had the run-in with the bus in Hong Kong, only to turn up alive and well in San Francisco.

Jonas had hoped to spend some time looking into that anomaly, but circumstances had intervened. One thing he hadn't done was check the answering machine at his office. With a few minutes to kill, he decided to do it now.

Taking his cell phone from his pocket, he dialed his office number and checked his machine. The first message was a solicitation, which he deleted. The next was from Crystal. The time stamp was late that afternoon.

"Jonas, I just got back from picking up Tammy at Dennis's place," she said, her voice on the edge of panic. "Somebody broke in while I was gone. It looks to me like the place has been thoroughly searched. At best I can tell none of my valuables were stolen, not even my new jade-and-diamond earrings that were lying in plain sight on my dresser. One thing *is* missing, though. That camera that Mr. Yee gave me, the one that belonged to the dead guy. It was in my cosmetics case in the bathroom. I'd already thrown away the disk, thank God. Tossed it in the bay, so my fat ass wouldn't be preserved for prosperity. I'm freaked, though. What the hell is going on? You have any idea? I don't know whether to call the cops or not. Give me a buzz when you have a chance."

Jonas looked at his watch. It was awfully late, but it was Saturday. And Crystal just might be lying in bed awake and scared. Once more, feeling wrenched in a couple of different directions at the same time, Jonas went to the bed and kissed Elise goodbye, then slipped quietly from the room. As he walked down the hall, headed for the elevators, he dialed Crystal's number.

She answered with a groggy "Hello?"

"It's me," he said. "I know it's late, but I was in Davis with my son all day and at the hospital with Elise tonight. Just got your message. You okay?"

"Huh? Yeah, I'm okay," she said sleepily. "What time is it?"

"A little after midnight."

"*Where* are you?"

"At the hospital. Elise had a heart episode."

"She going to be okay?"

"Yes. They mainly have her here for tests."

An elevator car arrived, and when the door opened, a nurse stepped out. Seeing him, she stopped, taking his arm.

"Sir, you can't use cell phones in the hospital. It can interfere with electronic equipment."

"Oh, sorry," he said, "I forgot." Then to Crystal, "They're making me turn this phone off. I'll call you back in two minutes."

The nurse acknowledged his concession and went on. Jonas stepped into the car. Descending to the ground floor, he wondered if he dare ask Crystal if she wanted him to drop by. She might like the company. God knew he could use some friendly affection after the day he'd had.

Once outside, he dialed Crystal again. She didn't

answer. A panicky feeling began to well. Did he misdial? As he hurried toward his car, he dialed again. Same result. "Christ," he muttered, thinking he'd better get to the marina as fast as he could.

Jonas was fumbling with his keys when he heard the roar of an engine. He looked back as a black Porsche 911 skidded to a halt on the damp pavement behind him. The passenger window slid down. Melanie de Givry, a sardonic look on her face, sneered at him.

"Hypocrite," she said with contempt. The window went back up and the Porsche sped away.

A few minutes later, Jonas was on Sir Francis Drake Boulevard headed toward the freeway. As he sped past the corner where he would have turned for home, he had visions of arriving at the houseboat only to find Crystal strangled or shot or something, her child crying helplessly in the next room. And, of course, it would be all his fault.

On 101, headed south toward Sausalito, he tried dialing Crystal's number again. This time, much to his relief, she answered. "Crystal, what happened? I called twice and didn't get a response."

"I know. I was in the bathroom and couldn't get to the phone."

"Jesus, you scared me to death."

"I'm okay," she said. "But whatever is going on, I don't like it."

"Me, neither."

"You still at the hospital?"

"No, on the freeway, headed for your place."

"Jonas, I don't think that's a good idea."

"Why?"

"I already told you. Besides, getting laid isn't going to help matters."

"Who said anything about getting laid?"

"Jonas, this is me you're talking to. I know you."

He was silent. And angry. This was the side of a woman he hated most. But like it or not, Crystal had moved into a philosophical phase. And once that happened...

"Okay, fine," he said.

"Look, call me in the morning. We still need to talk."

"Did you notify the police about the break-in?"

"No, that's part of what we need to discuss."

"All right. I'll talk to you in the morning."

"Jonas..."

"Yeah?"

"I'm sorry," she said. "I really am." Then she hung up.

12:35 p.m.
Black Boar Pub, St. John's Wood, London

During the lunch break of the Symposium on the Future of Fossil Fuels in Europe, David Lawrence had lunch with Sarah Godwin, a colleague at the Institute of Petroleum, and Dr. Amir Namvar, a petroleum engineer and visiting scholar from Iran, who was doing research at the University of London. Lawrence told his friends about the super-ethanol project under way in the U.S. Lawrence, who was into his second pint of ale, speculated that the Americans would be happy if they could break OPEC without any risk to their national security. Nobody had ever heard of GET, Inc., probably because the project was top secret. Dr. Namvar asked if Lawrence believed such a project was really under way. Lawrence, with a wink at Sarah Godwin, replied he had it on good authority. She explained to Namvar that Lawrence's brother was well placed at NIPER in Oklahoma and ought to know what was going on across the Atlantic.

Davis, California

In addition to Kenny Jarrett there were seven other "Seeds" gathered around the TV in Brad Kozik's off-campus apartment, watching the university press conference about the firebombing. Five of the eight Seeds were local—the Davis contingent. Besides K.J. and Brad, the others from Davis were Roger Lake, Kristy Ogawa and Tina Richter.

K.J., Roger and Kristy were all from farming communities in the Central Valley. Roger's old man was a foreman on a corporate farm near Visalia and Kristy's parents had a family farm in Solano County. Her dad had been born during World War II in a detention camp, an experience that hadn't radicalized him, but it had Kristy.

Brad and Tina were both from Southern California. His mother was a social worker in Orange County and had raised him and his sister to be liberal activists. Tina was not only K.J.'s fantasy woman, she had an interesting background. She was from Hollywood, her mother a not-so-famous Hispanic actress named Lola Ramirez. Her father, Hans Richter, was a director of photography who'd won an Oscar in the eighties. K.J. had asked about her life, but Tina hadn't wanted to talk about it much, though she'd once said, "If you think America is about money, you ought to go to Hollywood."

The other three Seeds had driven up from Berkeley to lend their support and expertise.

"What's with this jackass?" Robo, the leader of the Berkeley contingent, said.

"He's the chancellor," Brad replied, "what do you expect? He's the mouthpiece for the board of regents and they represent corporate America."

"It amazes me he can say that bullshit with a straight face."

"They've been doing it forever," Tina said. "These are the sons of bitches who clear-cut millions of acres of timber and crow about planting a few seedlings for future generations. It's bullshit window dressing."

Everybody nodded their agreement. K.J. glanced around, feeling the energy and determination. It was the first time he'd met the Berkeley group. They struck him as kind of arrogant. Robo was a tall guy with a crew cut, black T-shirt, black jeans and army boots—a Timothy McVeigh look-alike whom his friends deferred to as if he was some kind of military genius. The other guy had long hair, a beard and a beret, laughingly called himself "Che." The third was a woman who might have played middle linebacker on a women's football team, if there was such a thing. Her moniker was Baby Cakes. K.J. gathered they were too self-important to have regular names.

The Davis contingent pretended their names were

noms de guerre, but they weren't. They didn't use last names in the conversation, though, figuring that was enough of a nod toward discretion.

K.J. had staked out a spot on the floor next to Tina. The room was small and they were crowded close enough that when he took a deep breath he could smell her perfume.

"Fascist," Baby Cakes muttered at the TV.

The chancellor was waxing on while the group hissed "Pig!" "Corporate lackey!" "What about your crimes against nature, *asshole?*"

This was the first time they'd all gotten together since the operation and K.J. could tell his stock had gone up. When he arrived, Tina had given him a hug like he was some kind of war hero, which was totally cool. He was an insider now. Hell, why not? He'd pulled off the biggest blow against the corporate exploiters that Save the Seed had attempted. None of the others had ever thrown a rock through a window, much less burned down a building.

When the chancellor called Professor Mayne to the microphone, a silence fell over the room. K.J. felt his pulse quicken. When the camera zeroed in on Mayne's handsome face, K.J. wanted to heave a rock at the TV screen.

"Bastard," he said with contempt.

"I'd like to address my comments to those in the community who feel threatened by biologically engineered crops," Mayne said. "We know there are people who feel uneasy about the notion of tampering with nature and that's understandable, especially when the work we are doing is so poorly understood. But I want to say this, those in the community who understand the value of bioengineering shouldn't lump our critics in with those who committed those crimes yesterday morning. Reasonable people can differ and debate is desirable, but there's no excuse for violence."

"So, why you trying to destroy the planet, dickhead?" Che shouted.

"Let me just comment on the objectives of bioengineering," Mayne continued. "It's not that different from, say, inoculating your children against disease. When we inoculate we inject organisms in the body that help it become resistant to viruses. Similarly, when we make subtle changes in the gene structure of a plant, the object is to make it more robust, perhaps resistant to infestation by pests. Why? One reason is to reduce the need for pesticides that can be both costly and dangerous to the environment. Other reasons are to make foodstuffs less perishable or more nutritious. People have been engaged in such activities for thousands of years. The difference is that we now employ more refined techniques. The goal is the same, the ultimate result more advanced, but not that different from what we've always done."

On screen the chancellor stepped forward again and said, "Now we'll take your questions."

"You know what?" Brad Kozik said to the others. "They're making Mayne the poster boy for genetic mutation. They think a pretty face and a smooth tongue will make their lies fine with the public. This guy's their Goebbels."

"Their who?" K.J. said.

"Goebbels, kid," Che said. "Don't you know anything about European history? Ever hear of the Nazis?"

"Sure," K.J. replied, turning red, "I just didn't know about him."

"K.J.'s a science major," Tina explained, "give him a break."

Everybody laughed, which only embarrassed K.J. more, though he wanted to believe Tina had intended it as a kindness. But when she tousled his hair, his blush deepened.

"Don't sweat it, man," Che said. "Everybody was green once."

K.J.'s temper flared. "How many buildings have you burned down?"

"Huh?" He looked at the others. "Is this the guy who did it?"

"Yeah," Tina said, "our own K.J."

"Hey," Robo said, "knock off the bullshit. Let's listen."

The guy clearly considered himself in charge. He was a veteran of campaigns going all the way back to NAFTA, the World Trade Organization demonstrations in Seattle—where he was arrested—and countless environmental campaigns before that. People said his mother had blown up an ROTC facility at a university in the Midwest during the Vietnam war and that protest was in his blood. On paper he probably was the best qualified person in the room. Nobody was challenging him.

On the TV, Patrick Mayne was asked a question about Save the Seed. Everybody in the room leaned forward.

"I think their intentions might even be laudable, though misguided," Mayne said. "But the ends don't justify the means. I call on everybody in the community to take a deep breath, step back and discuss this issue openly and intelligently. There's one thing we can agree on. This is about the future of the planet."

"This is the guy you people put out of business?" Robo said.

"Seems to be a slow learner," Baby Cakes added.

"Apparently the cocksucker didn't take your warning seriously," Che said sarcastically. "Seems to me you need to escalate."

Kristy, who was normally real quiet, spoke up. "You mean kill him?"

A hush settled over the room. Only the TV could be heard.

"Apparently you're the man in this group," Robo said to K.J. "What do *you* recommend?"

K.J. thought for a moment. "I don't know. I guess I'd have to think about it."

"Why don't you do that. Meanwhile, seems to me unless you shut these people up, they've won."

The others shifted uneasily.

"Okay, here's the deal," Robo said. "After Christmas break we meet again. We come up with a plan to turn your professor into the poster boy for contrition."

"Meaning what, exactly?" Brad asked.

"Meaning you've got to expose the bastard for what he is, a storm trooper for corporate greed."

The Davis group looked at one another.

"But how?" Kristy asked.

"You've got Wonder Boy on your team," Che said, reaching over and giving K.J. a friendly slap on the knee. "He'll come up with something, won't you, tiger?"

"I can work on it," K.J. said.

"We will, too," Robo said. "At the next meeting we'll compare notes."

K.J. felt vindicated. The trouble was now he had to come up with some brilliant idea. But what?

2:45 p.m.
Embassy of Iran, London, England

Dr. Namvar used the office of the absent science attaché to draft his dispatch to Dr. Mahmoud Farbood, president of the Research Institute of Petroleum Industry in Tehran. Namvar was the former head of the International Affairs and Scientific Information Group at RIPI and a close friend of Farbood. He considered the intelligence he'd received at lunch that afternoon to be of the utmost importance to his country. Farbood was, of course, in constant contact with Mansoor Saleheen, the oil minister of the Islamic Republic of Iran and chairman of the board of trustees of RIPI. Farbood would know what to do with the information.

Corte Madera, California

He was in a booth in Myron's Coffee Shop waiting for Crystal. She'd suggested they meet there, rather than at the houseboat, without explaining why. (The fact that the place didn't have beds and therefore no opportunity for immediate sexual gratification, could be a factor, he reasoned.) She was late.

Jonas had gone to the hospital early, knowing they'd be starting Elise's tests first thing. As it turned out he only had a few minutes with her before an orderly came to take her away.

"You don't have to stick around, dear," his wife had said. "I'll be fine. I'm sure you have things to do. If they let me go home, Melanie said she'd come and get me."

"I'll leave my cell phone on, so have them call if you need me for anything. In any case let's plan on having dinner together tonight."

"That would be nice. And, Jonas...one other thing..."

"Yes?"

"I know it's hard for you, but don't be too upset with Melanie and Wilson. You bite your tongue a lot and I appreciate the fact. The things they say and do have no bearing on my feelings for you, the respect I have. I want you to know that."

Jonas had kissed her, then he'd left. Melanie was entering the parking lot as he drove out. He was glad she knew he'd beaten her to the punch. He wished he could be as forgiving as Elise, but he was more convinced than ever that his stepdaughter was a dangerous person. The evil in some people radiated like plutonium.

He checked his watch. Crystal was now twenty minutes late, which wouldn't give them much time.

She had to open her shop up at ten. Jonas had ordered a bran muffin, a glass of orange juice and coffee. The coffee had been in front of him for a couple of minutes. The waitress brought the juice and muffin.

"Would you like anything else?"

Jonas saw Crystal come in the door just then. "My friend is here. Bring her some coffee. I doubt she'll want anything to eat."

The waitress left. He waved until Crystal spotted him. She was in green, her skirt short. The put-upon expression was not a good sign.

"Sorry I'm late," she said, slipping off her jacket and laying it on the banquet as she scooted into the booth. She did not make eye contact with him, also not a good sign.

"You okay?" he asked.

She did look at him then. "Yeah. I had baby-sitter problems and an uncooperative child, but what else is new? You?"

"I'm fine."

"How's Elise?"

"She doing okay under the circumstances. When one thing goes wrong, there seems to be a domino effect."

Crystal shivered. The waitress put a coffee mug in front of her.

"Care for anything to eat?" the woman asked.

"No, thanks. Coffee's fine."

The waitress left. Crystal picked up the mug, wrapping both hands around it, as though trying to warm them. She peered into his eyes in a wary, cautious way.

"So what's with the break-in?" he asked.

"I don't know. I was hoping you'd have some ideas."

"Wish I did."

"Is there anything I should do?"

"You can have the police come out, but burglaries are a dime a dozen. I don't know how excited about it they are likely to be."

"That's pretty much what I thought. I went ahead and cleaned the place up, so any evidence is probably gone."

"It saves you needless hassle," he said, trying to be encouraging.

Crystal sipped her coffee. Jonas drank some juice.

"Want half a muffin?" he asked.

"No, thanks." She shifted uneasily. "So, we just forget about it?"

Jonas shook his head. "Under the theory the break-in is somehow connected with what happened in Hong Kong, I'll follow up on Chuck Haggerty. Maybe I'll get some answers from him."

Crystal nodded thoughtfully. "I don't know how to say this, Jonas, but I'd like to back out of this thing…you know, not be involved anymore."

"What do you mean by 'this thing'? Me?"

"Not exactly. Well…sort of maybe."

"That's pretty specific."

"I guess what I'm trying to say is you're involved in some secret business having nothing to do with me, but I seem to be getting sucked into it, anyway, and...well, I don't need the headache."

"I can certainly understand that. I hope you realize that I had no idea any of this was going to happen."

"Oh, I'm not blaming you," she said. "I know that. But as I explained the other night, this might be a good time for me to sort of...move on, I guess." She looked pained.

Jonas took another drink of juice. "Getting dumped this particular way is a first for me," he muttered. "And coming on the heels of what seemed like a real nice getaway trip, a fun time...I...well, I'm obviously disappointed."

"I've been thinking about it," she said. "We did have a good time. You were very generous, very sweet. But to be honest, I think this feeling has been building for a while and I just didn't realize it."

"How long?" Jonas was not new to rejection. Plenty of women had given him the old heave-ho. That's what happened when you played the game.

"Jesus, I don't know," Crystal said. "Relationships are never...what's the word?... always the same."

"Static?"

"Yeah, static. We're coming off a nice long run. Hong Kong was sort of the last big hurrah. Now I need something different."

He understood. At a certain point getting your rocks off wasn't enough. For women especially. Crystal knew he'd be a widower soon. That kind of change wasn't necessarily good for the "other woman." Whether or not she had designs on him for something more serious, he couldn't be sure, but her gut instinct told her to make him hungry. That was the way women handled these things. If he had to guess, she figured time and distance apart would be good for them both. Then later, when the dust settled, she'd give it another look. Meanwhile, the danger scared her. He'd become a liability. It was as simple as that.

"Okay," he said. "I understand where you're coming from. And I don't blame you a bit."

"But I do feel shitty about it."

"Hey, sweetheart, you know me. I've had more wives than many women have had orgasms. You don't need to worry. I'd rather you miss me than worry about me, to be honest."

"Oh, I *will* miss you. I already do."

The logic of that totally escaped him, though it was vintage feminine thinking. Yet that's the way they did things on Venus. He also knew there was but one course of action—give time a chance to do its thing, for better or for worse.

He munched on the muffin. Crystal looked at her watch. That time thing.

Another gulp of coffee and she said, "I've got to go."

"You want me to keep you informed about developments, or do you prefer to sail along blissfully in the dark?"

"Let me know, Jonas, *if* you think it's important."

"Ball back in my court."

She patted his cheek and left.

He sat staring at the coffee stain on the tabletop.

He'd been soundly thumped by not one, but two women in the last twenty-four hours—Tess and Crystal. And that's not even counting getting kicked in the balls by Melanie. Some lives, it seemed, were simply star-crossed. At least those little Black Sheep were alive and kicking.

10:03 p.m.
Tehran, Iran

Mansoor Saleheen, Minister of Oil, escorted Dr. Ali Bin Sa'ad, president of the King Fahd University Petroleum and Minerals Research Institute in Saudi Arabia, from the ministry banquet room where they'd had dinner, to his private cabinet. Dr. Sa'ad was head of a peace and cooperation delegation dispatched to Iran by the kingdom, one of the first high-level contacts of its kind between the two states. The emphasis of the talks, which had been cordial, was oil.

After an exchange of pleasantries, Saleheen told his guest that his government was distressed to learn of the American efforts to disrupt world oil markets through the development of new technologies and he wondered if the Saudi officials felt any concern about the super-ethanol project being conducted in secret by GET, Inc., in California. Sa'ad told the minister he had no knowledge of the project, but doubted sinister motives on the part of the Americans, not with respect to international markets. Stability, Sa'ad noted, was the American watchword. Saleheen conceded the point, but observed that an additive capable of a tenfold increase in the energy yield of petro-

leum fuels would make world markets all but irrelevant to the Americans. Perhaps, Saleheen added, it's nothing but a rumor.

Sa'ad told his host that if the rumor was true, the project had to be in the early stages of development. If it was ready for market, someone would be preparing to make his fortune, independent, in all likelihood, of American government and, for that matter, the American oil companies who stood to lose as much as anyone. Saleheen agreed, saying the fellow behind GET, Inc., was at once the most fortunate and unfortunate man alive.

San Francisco

Jonas Lamb unlocked the front door of the world headquarters of Global Energy Technologies, Inc. At the moment it consisted of roughly five hundred and fifty square feet of office space, a suite of two rooms with two desks, one filing cabinet, a small sofa, five chairs, two wastepaper baskets, a framed photograph of Elise de Givry and one thirsty ficus. In, say, nine or ten months it was slated to become the nerve center of one of the world's major energy sources, assuming things went according to plan.

Jonas began by watering the ficus.

The office suite, having been closed for a week, had a funny smell. Jonas traced the origins to the remnants of a ham-and-cheese sandwich in the wastebasket by his desk. He disposed of it in the trash bin in front of the building, then returned to his desk. He'd been at work only three and a half minutes and already two pressing problems had been solved. He moved on to item number three: Chuck Haggerty.

Jonas began with the yellow pages, but found no listing for Haggerty (Chuck, Charles or Chas. or C.) under private investigators. There were no private investigators named Haggerty at all. He tried the white pages. There he found eleven Haggertys, no Chucks or Charleses, though there was one C. Jonas dialed the number and got a machine. The voice was young and female. "You called Cynthia's number, but guess what, you got me, her machine. Bummer. But we love getting messages. So when I beep, start talking…." Jonas decided to pass.

What did he do now? Thinking another P.I. might know of Haggerty, he turned to the yellow pages and began to call, starting with the agencies that had placed the biggest display ads. He got machines. The fourth attempt yielded a meat person. Apparently.

"Yeah?"

"Uh…hi," Jonas said, "I'm trying to locate an investigator named Chuck Haggerty and—"

"This is Chuck Haggerty."

"*You're* Chuck Haggerty?"

"Yeah, isn't that what I just said? What can I do for you?"

Jonas glanced down at the ad. He'd called City Investigative Services on Geary Street. "Uh…I was making random calls to see if somebody knew you and—"

"Who is this?"

"Oh, my name is Jonas Lamb," he said. "I wanted to talk to you."

"Regarding what?"

"I was in Hong Kong a few days ago, and while I was there I had a rather unfortunate encounter with a private investigator from San Francisco named Chuck Haggerty...or so I thought."

"Oh, that deal again. You're the second person who's talked to me about Hong Kong."

"Yes, I know. The first was an associate of an associate of mine."

"Look, Mr. Lamb, the guy in Hong Kong wasn't me, all right? It's a stolen identity thing. I've had this problem before and frankly it's pissing me off."

"I can understand that. But if some guy's running around the world claiming to be you, there's likely some sort of connection."

"If so, I don't have the vaguest notion how, or who, or what."

"Is your passport missing?"

"I don't have a passport. But look, much as I sympathize, you shouldn't be talking to me, you should be talking to the guy in Hong Kong."

"I'm afraid that Mr. Haggerty was run over by a bus. He's dead."

There was a brief silence, then, "Well, I guess that means I won't be getting any more of these calls, then, don't it?"

"Perhaps, but the fact remains that a private investigator from San Francisco using the name of Chuck Haggerty committed a crime in Hong Kong a few days ago. Breaking and entering. A number of people are eager to find out why."

"Well, it wasn't this Chuck Haggerty, Mr. Lamb. Now, if you'll excuse me, I've got things to do."

The phone went dead.

Jonas pondered Haggerty's unhelpfulness. Was it the man's personal style? Or was there more to it?

11:36 p.m.
Tehran, Iran

Mansoor Saleheen stood at the entrance to the ministry building, watching his guest enter his limousine and drive away. He smiled to himself, knowing that Dr. Sa'ad, who was close to the Saudi royal family, couldn't get back to his country fast enough. Saleheen knew that Sa'ad might be simply out of the loop, but he doubted it. The Iranian intelligence services had a lot of work to do in order to get to the bottom of things, but if his intuition was correct, Saleheen felt certain the Saudis would be engaged in the same battle, and what's more, they would be leading the charge. Of all the players in the Muslim world, they probably knew best how to jerk the Americans' chain. Allah willing, and with luck, this super-ethanol business would be sent to an early grave.

San Francisco

With not a lot to do in the office, Jonas wondered whether he should have an early lunch or head back to Marin. Elise might appreciate his company. Or he could go by the offices of City Investigative Services and find out if Chuck Haggerty might be a little more forthcoming in person. That was the problem with being king of the world in waiting. So many choices, so little time.

He opted to let fate decide. He phoned Ross General and learned that his wife had been released. Jonas saw no point in hurrying back to Kentfield for a glaring match with Melanie. He'd join the evening commute like every other working stiff and have dinner with his wife. Meanwhile, he'd head for Geary Street and pay Haggerty a visit.

City Investigative Services was located on the ground floor of a little office building that looked as though it had been converted from an apartment house. It was a couple of steps down from Global Energy Technologies, Inc., though Jonas wasn't one to feel smug. Haggerty, given the clutter in his shabby outer office, at least appeared to have things to do with his time.

With no secretary on duty, Jonas stuck his head in the open door to the private office in back, getting quite a start in the process. There, sitting behind a desk that looked too small for the guy, was the very same ex-marine who'd done the photo layout of Crystal's rear end. That was Jonas's initial impression, anyway. A closer look revealed that maybe it wasn't the same guy. A darned close facsimile, though.

Haggerty glanced up from his paperwork and saw Jonas at the door. "Oh, sorry, didn't hear you come in."

"Didn't mean to sneak up on you," Jonas said apologetically. He was still in a minor state of shock. The two Haggertys could have been brothers. They even had the same haircuts.

"May I help you?" the San Francisco version said.

"My name's Lamb," Jonas replied. "I spoke with you on the phone earlier."

"Hong Kong," Haggerty said with obvious annoyance. To punctuate the point, he threw down the pencil he'd been using.

"I was in the neighborhood and thought I'd just stick my head in the door."

"Look, mister, I don't mean to be a hard-ass, but I really don't have time for this."

"I appreciate that, but can I just say one thing?"

Haggerty leaned back in his chair, clasping his big hands behind his head, looking like a former weight lifter, a guy who'd lost some tone, but not bulk. "What?"

"You look enough like the guy who burst into my hotel room in Hong Kong to be his brother."

"And what's that suppose to mean?"

"Don't you think that's interesting? I mean, same name, same appearance."

"Interesting no, strange yes."

"Could we discuss 'strange,' then?"

"Look, I'm finishing up a report here and a courier is going to be walking in the door any minute to pick it up. I gotta finish it."

"I'm willing to wait, if you won't be too long and you wouldn't mind me sitting in your outer office while you work."

Haggerty thought for a second, then said, "Okay, whatever."

Jonas retreated, taking a seat in a 1950s-era chair

with a curved chrome tube instead of legs, the kind that you could rock. He glanced around at the clutter. Chuck Haggerty and his office were both a curiosity.

For the next fifteen minutes Jonas occupied himself paging through issues of *Field & Stream*, paying special attention to the gun ads. He wondered whether, given recent events, he shouldn't consider some Charlton Heston–style protection.

Amid his ruminations, the outer door opened and a bike courier—a lanky girl in spandex and a bike helmet—walked in, bringing the outdoor air with her. She was freckled, long-faced and had a skinny ass. A canvas pouch was slung over her shoulder. She gave Jonas a nod but didn't say anything, going right to the door of Haggerty's private office.

"Hi," Jonas heard the P.I. say. "All I have to do is seal the envelope."

A few moments passed, then the girl came back out and was gone. The P.I. appeared at the door. He leaned against the frame, folding his arms over his chest, his expression uncompromising.

"The guy in Hong Kong, the imposter, was not on a lark," Jonas said. "I figure somebody hired him to embarrass me or worse. I'd like to know who."

"I don't see how I can help you."

"Have you had lunch, Mr. Haggerty?"

The P.I. shook his head.

"Will you be my guest? Maybe we can chat over a sandwich."

Haggerty shrugged. "Whatever."

He got his jacket, locked up and they went outside. A cold wind greeted them. Jonas held the lapels of his jacket over his chest. Haggerty glanced up and down the street as though looking for something.

"So, where do you want to go?" he asked.

"It's your turf."

"There's a coffee shop down a couple of blocks and around the corner. The soup's good."

"Fine."

They started walking.

"So, tell me about yourself, Mr. Lamb. What do you do?"

"I'm an entrepreneur." Jonas fished one of the business cards he'd had made at Kinkos out of his pocket and handed it to Haggerty.

"Energy technologies, huh? High-tech stuff?"

"Sort of."

"Proprietary?"

"Yes."

"What were you doing in Hong Kong?"

"Meeting with an investor."

"And what happened, exactly?"

Jonas gave him a vague account of events, neither discussing Patrick's Black Sheep nor mentioning either Jimmy Yee or Crystal by name.

"Well, if they got a body, they've got prints, dental records, that kind of stuff. They should be able to make an ID."

"You'd think so. The fact that it's international may be slowing things down. Meanwhile, I thought I'd learn what I could."

They were passing an art gallery and Haggerty stopped to look in the window. "Will you look at this shit? And the prices they get for it are incredible."

Jonas was surprised by Haggerty's interest. "You into art?"

"No, I'm checking something out. Keep looking at the art and talking," he said, putting a hand on Jonas's shoulder and pointing in the window.

"What's going on?"

"I'm checking out your tail. Did you notice anybody following you to my place?"

Jonas felt his heart go blip. "No." He gestured toward the window. "Somebody's following us?"

They continued walking down the street. "I think so."

Jonas had to fight the urge to turn around and look back.

Haggerty said, "Maybe we should find out who. What do you think?"

Jonas was befuddled, but at the same time calmed by Haggerty's reassuring manner. Then it occurred to him he shouldn't be so trusting. After all, he didn't know Haggerty from Adam.

"You want to find out who she is or not?"

"She?"

"Yeah, little blond woman. Thirtyish."

"Could be my stepdaughter. We've got issues."

"It's up to you, Mr. Lamb."

"Well, okay, let's check it out."

There was a parking garage on the corner. Haggerty led the way to the door accessing the stairwell. Once inside, they stepped behind the door, the P.I. gently pushing him against the wall behind him.

"Let's hope she follows," Haggerty whispered.

They waited. A minute passed. Haggerty was poised, ready to pounce. Jonas began to wonder what he'd gotten himself into.

Then the door slowly opened. With Haggerty's broad back blocking his view, Jonas couldn't see much, but the next thing he knew the door slammed shut and Haggerty had a woman wearing jeans and a windbreaker by the arm. She screamed and tried to jerk free, flailing like a fish on a line. As Haggerty swung her around, Jonas got a good look at her. It wasn't Melanie. It wasn't anybody he knew.

Haggerty, who had to be more than double her weight, shoved her against the door and pinned her by the throat. The woman's eyes bulged as his huge hand closed tight. She looked terrified.

"Who the fuck are you?" the P.I. roared. "What do you want?"

The woman opened her mouth, but only made a gurgling sound. Jonas was afraid Haggerty was going to kill her. He was about to tell him to let her go, when Haggerty relaxed his grip. She gasped for air.

Just when Jonas thought they'd be getting an answer, the blonde with spiky hair brought her knee up abruptly, driving it into Haggerty's groin. The big P.I. doubled over and the woman gave him a two-handed rabbit punch to the back of his neck, dropping him like a sack of potatoes. Jonas, who was sure he was next, backed away, but she only gave him a scornful glance, yanked the door open and went out.

It had all happened so fast that Jonas was stunned. He looked down at Haggerty, who groaned, opening his eyes. He looked up at him. Jonas bent over, putting a hand on the big man's shoulder.

"You all right, Chuck?"

"Christ," Haggerty said, slowly rising to his hands and knees.

Jonas helped him to his feet. "Surprise attack," he said.

Haggerty rubbed his neck. "No kidding."

"Well, we were outnumbered," Jonas said, trying to make light of it.

"I take it that wasn't your stepdaughter."

"No."

"You recognize her?" Haggerty asked, working his jaw as he brushed himself off.

Jonas shook his head.

"Me, neither."

"What do you make of it?"

"You tell me, Mr. Lamb. You seem to be the one attracting interest."

Kentfield, California

Elise had fallen asleep, her meal only half finished. Jonas, seated in the easy chair next to the bed, got up and removed the tray, which he carried into the hall, putting it on the floor by the door for Charlotte's weekend replacement to pick up in the morning. The

TV tray he'd used for his own meal he'd already set aside. He took that out into the hall as well.

Returning to his wife's bedside, he took the TV remote control and turned off the set. As he pulled the covers up over her chest, Elise stirred.

"What happened?" she murmured, blinking awake.

"You dozed off, honey."

"Oh, my," she said, rubbing her face. "I'm not even good company anymore."

"Don't worry about it, you had a rough day."

"That's no excuse, Jonas. They're all rough days."

He sat on the bed next to her, smiling at her and brushing her cheek with the back of his fingers. "Rotten luck," he said.

"I feel badly for you."

"Ah," he said, dismissing the comment, "my only problem is your suffering. I wish there was something I could do about it."

"Being here for me is an awful lot," she replied, her eyes shimmering.

Her words made his heart ache. She put her hand to his face.

"I'm sorry about Patrick. Things like that are so difficult for a parent."

"He's got spunk like his old man. He'll be all right."

"Well, at least you won't have to worry about me much longer."

"Elise, don't talk that way."

"It's true, Jonas. And it's best you realize it. I'm not sure I'll make it to the New Year."

"Of course you will."

She smiled with sad amusement. "I want to minimize the unpleasantness that's likely to happen after I'm gone, but I'm not sure what to do."

"That's the last thing you need to worry about."

"No, Melanie's going to make life miserable for you, I know. And I'm sorry. It's not fair."

"Elise, let's try to make the time you have left as pleasant as possible. Worrying about others won't help. I can take care of myself. And I promise you I won't add fuel to the fire with your children."

She wiped a tear from the corner of her eye. "I know," she said hoarsely.

"Now, I think you need to get some sleep."

She nodded. She looked exhausted. Jonas gave her a kiss, turned off all but her night-light and slipped from the room. When he reached his suite he heard his cell phone ringing. It took a minute to find it in his jacket pocket in the closet, but he got there just in time. It was Jimmy Yee.

"Thought you should know, old man, with the help of the police in California, the authorities here have information about Chuck Haggerty."

"I'm listening."

"The fellow had several identities. They think his real name is Steve Williams, a former navy SEAL, former small-time cop and former ex-convict—assault with a deadly weapon. At best they can determine he's been working as a mercenary."

"A mercenary?"

"Yes. He has a history of taking on difficult, perhaps illegal assignments for hire."

"Any idea who he was working for?"

"None whatsoever. And I don't believe there'll be much additional effort on this end to find out. Essentially, the case is closed. Whether you wish to pursue it from there is up to you. Perhaps a little of the cash I gave you could be used for that purpose."

He could tell Jimmy was feeling skittish. Jonas tried to put his mind at ease. "Yes, I intend to look into it," he said.

"I'll fax what documentation I get to your office."

"Thanks. And again, thanks for your hospitality, old buddy."

"It was my pleasure. Do give my regards to your young lady."

"I'd like to, but Crystal and I are in a cool-down phase. It may be over."

"Oh? Sorry to hear that, old bean."

"I'd suggest you send her a ticket, but I don't think you'd fare much better than I."

"Why's that?"

"She's into craftsmen, Jimmy, not financiers like you and me."

Yee laughed appreciatively. "Strange bird, that one. But magnificent breasts."

"On that note I think I'll crawl off to my lonely bed."

They both laughed and said goodbye. Jonas put down the phone, wondering if the prize awaiting him would be enough. His whole life he'd been convinced that the big score was what it was all about. Until he figured out something else, though, king of the world would have to do.

SUNDAY
December 16

Ocean Beach, San Francisco

Though it was Sunday, it was also mid-December, so the beach was mostly deserted. The drizzle and icy wind weren't likely to bring out the crowds. Even so, there were a handful of fishermen and a few people walking on the firm, moist sand left behind by the receding tide.

Jonas parked the Mercedes with the passenger side overlooking the gray-green sea. The window was down and Elise, bundled up in a sweater and coat with a knit cap, drew the salt air into her lungs. "Thank you," she said. "Thank you for this, Jonas."

That morning she had awakened in good spirits and came down to breakfast with the help of the weekend aide, a rawboned woman named Mitzi. While they were having their poached eggs, Elise told him she wanted to see the ocean. "I don't know why, but I have a strong urge to see the water and smell the salt air."

"Would you like to drive over to Stinson Beach?"

"I'd love to, but with these meds I'm taking, I'm not sure I could take the twisty road without getting carsick."

"How about Ocean Beach in the city? No twisty roads to get there." And so they'd settled on San Francisco.

Elise took his hand as she continued to gaze out at the ocean and overcast sky that met on the gauzy horizon. "Are those the Farallons out there?"

Jonas looked past her, barely able to discern three gray bumps at the farthest extreme of sea and sky. "They are unless Japan drifted over to our side of the pond during the night."

"Silly goose," she said, squeezing his fingers.

He was aware that his wife was partial to the ocean, she and her first husband having had a cottage near Duxbury Point in Bolinas when Melanie and Wilson were small. Elise told him she and the children would spend much of the summer in Bolinas, she reading romance novels and writing little poems while the kids flew kites and played in the sand.

"Incredible to think this may be the last time I ever see the ocean," she said, sounding more wistful than sad.

"We can come back tomorrow, if you want to."

She laughed.

"I'm serious."

"We'll see. It all depends on how I feel. But I think this is it, Jonas. I'm grateful for the opportunity, though."

They sat for another twenty minutes watching the

gulls soar and a big black dog frolicking at the water's edge, chasing tumbling balls of sea foam and barking at the surf. Then Elise rolled up her window, dabbed her nose with a tissue and said, "Okay, we can go now."

"Anything else you'd like to see or do while we're out?"

"I've never seen your office."

"It's not very exciting."

"Could we at least drive by the building?"

"Sure."

Jonas headed for downtown via Golden Gate Park, Park Presidio and California Street. When they passed the Fairmont Hotel on Nob Hill, Elise leaned forward to look up at it and murmured, "Oh, my." She didn't say more, but he knew she was thinking about their wedding night, which they'd spent at the hotel before flying off to Tahiti. It choked him up a little, too. They shared the unspoken moment, then descended the hill, toward the Financial District.

But when they reached Grant Avenue, Jonas, following an impulse, made a left turn, so they could drive through Chinatown, which he knew she also enjoyed. Their excursion was taking on the character of Elise's farewell tour of the city where she'd lived most of her life. Neither of them spoke, though Elise dabbed her eyes from time to time. This was the first death of consequence for him since his mother had passed and it was proving to be more difficult than he expected.

"I don't believe in public mourning," she said as

the traffic stopped, waiting for a delivery truck off-loading in the narrow street. "I hope when I'm gone you won't feel the need to go through the motions. I'd prefer you go on with your life."

"This is not the time to think about that."

"Yes, it is. And I don't want you to worry about what my children think. I've told Melanie I don't want any of you to put on a show, so she's aware of my desire for you to pick up where you left off before we met."

"That must have gone over well."

"Never mind what Melanie and Wilson think."

"I'm curious what she said."

"You don't want to know and I don't want to tell you."

It wasn't hard for him to guess. Knowing his stepdaughter as he did, she'd come back with something like, "Don't worry, Mom, Jonas will be cruising the pickup bars before you're in the ground."

It bothered him a little that Elise's children had taken his petty sins and twisted them into crimes against humanity. Half-truths were worse, in ways, than lies.

"I'm sorry you have to deal with the unpleasantness," Jonas said. "I don't know what I could have or should have done differently."

"Nothing, probably."

"Then it's the fact that you married me."

Elise sighed. "That's partially it."

"What else?"

"Do you really want to discuss it?"

"Unless you don't."

"Let's just say Melanie's convinced you're a womanizer and that the only thing about me you care about is my money. I've tried to tell her she's wrong."

"Has she said anything specific?"

"This is silly," Elise said. "We shouldn't even be discussing it."

"If I can dispel your doubts," he said, "I will. I can tell it bothers you."

"Oh," she said with a sigh, "when you were in Hong Kong, Melanie said she was sure you were with a woman, that it was in keeping with your character. When I told her you were with Patrick, she laughed. Nothing I can say will change her mind. She's just convinced."

Jonas, feeling miserable about his stupid slip, could see that Elise was more troubled than she cared to admit. The very last thing he wanted was for her to suffer unnecessarily. "Maybe I haven't been as forthcoming as I should have been," he said. "And not as truthful as you deserve."

"Please, let's just forget it. This has been a nice day and I'd rather not ruin it."

It was obvious she doubted him and he didn't want things ending with her hurt and suspicious. "No," he said, "I want you to know the whole story. When I said Patrick went with me to Hong Kong as a tourist, I was fibbing. The truth is that Patrick is involved in my company. In fact, he's responsible for the scientific discovery that's made it all possible. I'm really just the front, and because of the sensitivity of the subject matter, we're keeping his role secret. Not even his mother knows."

"Then GET and the trip to Hong Kong was really for Patrick's sake?"

"I did it for him, yes, but I admit I'd like to make a few bucks myself along the way. If everything works out as we hope, it could be very, very lucrative for us both."

"I feel so much better," she said, smiling. "I must admit that business about Patrick being a tourist didn't ring true."

"I probably should have told you right from the beginning, but secrecy really is of paramount importance, Elise. I don't even know the details of his discovery myself, only the broad outlines."

"I'm glad that what you're doing is for your family's benefit and that Melanie is wrong about you. That's all that matters to me."

He reached over and took her hand, feeling better in one way, but worse in another. His disparagement of Melanie and her half-truths were coming back to haunt him—hoisted by his own petard. His stepdaughter had been right about him, technically speaking, but wrong in the philosophical sense. The best he could hope for was that he'd lightened Elise's burden.

The traffic again began to move. Elise peered out at the crowds. "There's the shop where I get my fish pots," she said, a lightness in her voice. "Mr. Shu always gave me a deal, even though I could afford his asking price. That's why I always went back to him."

"Smart retailer, Mr. Shu."

She was silent for a while, then wiped her eyes. "You know what the oddest part of dying is? It's knowing that everything will go on as though nothing happened. The world won't take notice."

"Not the whole world, Elise, but your world will."

"Are you trying to tell me you'll miss me?"

"I will miss you."

"You're a dear man, Jonas, for hanging in with me. Not all men are strong enough or honorable enough to do that, you know. Some would run off just to spare themselves the anguish...or the trouble."

"It's the least I can do."

"I won't be changing my will, regardless of what you do or don't do. I don't believe in coercing people, so don't fear your honest feelings."

"I never do, Elise, though if I had I'd probably have had a more normal life."

"Then you wouldn't have been you and the world would be the poorer for it."

He was touched by her appreciation, especially knowing it was genuine. "You're far too generous."

"I know your faults, but I like to focus on the positive."

"It's getting warm in here," he said with a grin. "Let's change the subject."

"What shall we discuss?"

"I don't know."

"You don't often talk about your company. Here I am an officer and I haven't the vaguest idea what you do. I know it's all a big secret, but are things going well?"

"We're in the very early stages, but so far, so good."

"I'm happy for you, Jonas. I hope it's a big success."

"Your generosity will have been a major factor. When we build our world headquarters, we'll name the building after you, Elise."

"How thoughtful."

"The Elise de Givry Plaza will be known throughout the world."

"With people saying, 'Who the hell was she?'"

"It'll be there long after they're gone."

"Jonas, you're such a romantic. That was one of the things that attracted me to you, you know."

He was aware of that. They'd met at a charity ball. Jonas was one of the few men who'd been able to tango and Elise loved to tango. She thought him passionate with a Latin temperament, despite being of Northern European background and relatively fair. Thank God for that job as an escort he'd taken with the cruise line after his fifth marriage. The dance lessons had paid off handsomely.

After winding their way through North Beach and Telegraph Hill, they arrived at the northern section of Montgomery Street. He pulled the Mercedes up to the curb in front of the three-story brick building that housed the temporary world headquarters of Global Energy Technologies, Inc., though it only warranted a simple engraved plastic plaque in the directory.

"It's very nice," Elise said.

"But modest inside."

"I won't go in."

"You know, come to think of it, I'm expecting a

fax," he said. "Would you mind if I run in to see if it's arrived?"

"No, of course not."

"I'll only be a minute."

Jonas went into the building, having to let himself into the lobby since it was the weekend. His offices smelled better than on his last visit. He found the fax machine blinking because it was out of paper. There was a transmission in memory, so he resupplied the paper cartridge and the machine began to click out a fax from Jimmy Yee. It contained more particulars on Steve Williams, aka Chuck Haggerty. The information included a last known address in Tamalpais Valley, which was in Marin, just off the Redwood Highway.

He returned to the car, where he found a homeless guy leaning on a shopping cart piled high with his possessions, talking to Elise, whose window was halfway down. The guy had a gray beard and dreadlocks sprouting from under a stocking cap. He was so thin he was gaunt, practically swimming in the fatigue jacket he wore.

When Jonas came up to them, his wife said, "Jonas, this is William. He was in the army in Vietnam, like you."

"That right?" Jonas said to the guy.

"Yeah, man. 1st Cav. Duc Pho, '67. How 'bout you?"

"173rd Airborne. Dak To, '67."

"Hey, we practically brothers, man. Same time in country. Welcome home, bro."

"You, too."

William looked at Elise, then back at Jonas. "Man, I hate to ask, but maybe you can spare a little bread for a brother, you drivin' a Mercedes and all."

"Sure." Jonas took out his wallet and gave the man a twenty.

"Hey, bro, you a saint sure enough. Thank you, man. Thank you."

William gave Jonas the black handshake and they parted as former comrades in arms, Jonas going around to the driver's side. As they drove off, she touched his arm.

"It still affects you, doesn't it?"

"I'm trying to remember if anybody ever said 'Welcome home' to me before."

"You're kidding."

"People wanted to forget what you'd been doing for a year, and they wanted you to forget, too. But when you've taken a trip to hell, it's not easy to pretend it never happened. On the other hand, maybe it's better than embracing it. I don't know the answer."

Elise's eyes were full of compassion. "I wish we'd talked about things like this more. We should have known each other better, Jonas. It must be one of the biggest mistakes people make in marriages."

"Marriages? Hell, Elise, there are people who'd rather not know themselves."

As they approached the Golden Gate Bridge he asked if she'd mind another quick stop on the way home. "There's an address in Tamalpais Valley I need to check out, assuming you aren't too tired."

"It's on the way, I don't mind."

The traffic over the bridge wasn't bad, but on the way down the Waldo Grade, a light rain began to fall. They exited at the Shoreline Highway where Jonas pulled over and checked his map. "It's half a mile in," he said. "It'll take maybe ten minutes."

"I'm fine. Don't worry about me."

The place was just off Highway 1 on a side road, a modest, somewhat run-down house, probably two bedrooms and one bath, that in most parts of the country would be considered a shack. In Marin, fixed up, it would sell for more than half a million. But this place wasn't fixed up. The picket fence was in shambles, the house needed paint and a new roof, though a string of multicolored Christmas lights over the door added a festive touch. The front "garden" consisted of a plot of foot-tall grass and a few shrubs badly needing trimming. As they paused in the street, a woman in sweatpants and a parka came out the door.

He parked and got out of the car as the woman reached the gate. She was in her late thirties, tall, a bit on the heavy side, no makeup, glasses, her ordinary brown hair pulled into a ponytail.

"Excuse me," Jonas said, drawing a wary look. "I'm trying to find Steve Williams and was given this address. Does he live here?"

"Who told you that?"

"A business associate."

She studied him. "Stevie used this address for some things, but he didn't stay here much. What's it about?"

"Are you a relative?"

She thought before answering. "Sister."

"Then perhaps you know what happened."

"You mean that he's dead?"

Jonas nodded. "Yes, I'm sorry."

The rain came down a little harder and the woman pulled up the hood of her parka. "He was my brother, but he didn't do me any favors. Why you coming here?"

"Before Steve died we had...let's say an encounter...and I never was able to find out what it was about. I thought maybe—"

"Look, mister, I don't know a thing about my brother's business, so you're wasting your time asking me. I didn't even know he was in Hong Kong. Now I'm left with the problem of burying him."

"Could you give me a name of somebody to talk to about his work? Did he have an office, associates? Anything?"

"If so, I didn't know about it."

"Are there friends or other relatives I might talk to?"

"Maybe his ex-wife, Penny, knows something, but I couldn't say for sure. We don't talk anymore."

"How can I reach her?"

"I don't know her current address or number. But I think she still tends bar at a place called Kelly's in the city, the Mission District. That's all I know. Now I've got to go," she said, moving past him toward the old Chevy Nova parked nearby.

Jonas watched her get in the car, then he returned to the Mercedes.

"Did you get what you were after?" she asked.

He turned down his collar, brushing the moisture off his shoulders. "Not really, but it wasn't a total washout, either."

"In keeping with the secrecy of your business, I guess I'm not supposed to ask and you're not supposed to say anything."

"A man with whom I had a brief encounter in Hong Kong was subsequently killed in a traffic accident. I never got the chance to find out what he wanted from me."

"That all sounds terribly mysterious."

"I don't know a lot more than that," he said, feeling disingenuous.

"I married a man with an interesting life," she said. "I'll content myself in that."

If she only knew. "Now for a truly important question, Elise. Can I interest you in a chocolate sundae or a banana split?"

"On a rainy day in the middle of December?"

"Sure, why not?"

"Okay," Elise said, her pale lips making a smile, "as long as you're paying."

Telegraph Hill, San Francisco

Jonas made coffee, then sat at his desk, drinking it and eating the Krispy Kreme he'd bought on the way into work. Not an artery-friendly breakfast, but he hadn't time for anything sanctioned by the American Heart Association. He wanted to get an early start, even though it had been a bad night. In addition to anguishing over Elise's failing health, he'd thought a lot about Steve Williams, tormented by the fact he didn't know what the guy had been up to, and at whose behest he'd acted. And so Jonas had hit the freeway before first light, heading for the City by the Bay.

It was too early to pay a visit to Kelly's in the Mission, though first thing he'd done was get the address of the place. On the off chance that the guy was an early riser, Jonas decided to give the real Chuck Haggerty a call as well.

He got an answering machine and left a message. "Chuck, it's Jonas Lamb, your friendly Hong Kong connection. I got your alter ego's real name and thought you might be interested. Give me a call. I'm at—"

"Christ, you're at it bright and early," Haggerty said, coming on the line.

"Hi, Chuck. Nice to see you've still got that resonant baritone."

"Very funny, Lamb. So, who's my cousin?"

"Fella named Steve Williams." He relayed the information he'd gotten from Jimmy Yee, ending with, "Ever heard of him?"

Haggerty only took a moment. "Not that I can think of, no."

"Well, if Williams was the one who'd done this to you before, I guess you won't have to worry anymore. Just be thankful he wasn't running up your account at Sears."

"That's true. So, how are things with you, Mr. Lamb? Seen any more of that little blond spitfire with the lethal knee?"

"If she's been following me, I'm not aware of it. I don't suppose you've seen any more of her."

"No, I think her only interest in me was the fact I'd had her by the throat. You were the one she was following, no doubt in my mind about that."

"Yet another mystery unsolved."

"Well, if you need a good detective to help you find out who might be behind this, you've got my number."

They ended the conversation and Jonas took the Krispy Kreme wrapper and started to toss it in the trash when he noticed a dab of frosting on the paper.

He wiped it off for a final guilty taste. The sweetness made him think of Crystal and how much he missed her. He'd been repressing the desire to give her a call under the theory the ball was in her court.

As Jonas reflected, he realized it was one of those situations where a woman either succumbed or she didn't. There wasn't much he could do at this point short of breaking down and proposing marriage, a course of action he'd tried to excess in the past, with less-than-sterling results.

Anyway, a vacation from women was not only desirable, but proper. He owed that much to Elise, though God only knew what he'd do if Crystal gave him a jingle and said she had the hornies. Forcing the subject from his mind, he consulted his watch and calculated how long before he made a run out to the Mission.

The Financial District, San Francisco

Tess was not accustomed to wrestling with her conscience. Most problems and choices she'd faced in life were clear cut. There always seemed to be "the right thing to do." But Jerry Tate applying for the job of director of Walter's charitable foundation put her in a quandary. Was Jerry trying to take advantage of embarrassing information he had on her, and if so, did she tell Walter? It would mean coming clean about her affair with Gregory Hamilton.

Tess sat at her desk in her corner office, unable to concentrate. Ironically, Stacey Kellogg, the headhunter Walter had retained to find a director for his foundation, had come in that morning to review the applications with him. Tess hadn't been invited to participate in the discussions, but when she walked past Walter's office on the way to get a cup of coffee he called to her.

"Stacey wanted to know what you thought of Jerry Tate, Tess."

"I'd just like your general impression," the girl said. She was young, but had a manner that was mature for her years. Moderately attractive, Stacey had a nice image, professional and understated.

Looking back and forth between them—Stacey young, earnest, trying hard to be everything she herself had become after years of hard work and honest dealing, Walter mellow, accepting, content—Tess realized she was on the hot seat and was uncertain whether to blurt out the truth or dissimulate. But she just didn't have it in her to do a mea culpa. Not here, not now, not under these circumstances. "Jerry did a good job," she said evenly. "He was competent and he got results."

It was true. She'd have said that whether Jerry had something to hold over her head or not.

"If the decision were yours, would you hire him?" Stacey asked.

"Based on my experiences at the Poverty Center?" She hated herself for doing this. It was like honoring the letter of the law, but not the spirit.

"Yes," Stacey said, "based on what you saw of Mr. Tate at the Poverty Center."

The image of herself naked on Jerry Tate's couch flashed in her mind and she felt nauseous. She glanced at Walter, feeling the weight of his big diamond on her finger. She girded herself and said, "Yes, I would."

Stacey said, "That's certainly a positive recommendation."

Tess nodded, feeling corrupt and miserable.

"Thank you, dear," Walter said, giving Tess leave to crawl back to her office.

At her desk once again, she searched her heart. Was she within her rights to withhold embarrassing personal information? How was this different from, say, Jonas withholding from her the fact that he'd had a prior marriage? True, the consequences of Jonas's perfidy were greater, but in a moral sense wasn't it just as wrong to hide a small embarrassment as a large one?

It was easy to rationalize. Walter wouldn't care about any transgressions that predated him, so why humiliate herself unnecessarily? And there was probably nothing she could say about Jerry Tate that would induce Walter either to hire or reject him, if he was inclined to go a different direction. Besides, she didn't consider Jerry unqualified. In other words, no harm would be done if she simply let things unfold naturally.

And yet, she felt guilty. Maybe the easiest thing would be to get it off her chest. After Stacey left, Tess got to her feet to go to Walter's office to confess all, making it as far as the door before she stopped herself. Just because forgiveness was virtually assured, why put herself and, for that matter, Walter, through an ordeal? What purpose did it serve apart from unburdening her conscience? Maybe doing a mea culpa was more selfish than minding her own business. She returned to her desk and sat down again.

Walter had resolved her immediate dilemma when he stuck his head in the door to say he had a luncheon appointment with his lawyer. "I'd invite you along," he'd said, "but one of the items on the agenda is our prenuptial agreement."

"You best talk to Howard alone," she'd quipped. "I might spike your guns."

His grin was full of appreciation. "Let's go out to dinner this evening," he offered.

"Good idea," she said. "There's something I want to discuss with you." There, she'd said it. Planted the seed.

"I hope that's not an ominous look in your eye."

"No, Walter, of course not."

"Sure?"

"It's about business, sort of about business, I mean."

"Guess I'll have to wait until evening to find out what's up, then."

He'd winked and left. Tess had spent the next minute with her head on the desk, wishing she'd never met Gregory Hamilton. She also wished she could vanquish the image of Jonas Lamb sitting in the corner, chuckling at her hypocrisy.

10:15 p.m.
Washington, D.C.

Harmon Shelbourn, CEO of TexasAmerican Petroleum, Wally Hodges, chairman of Delphi Oil International, Brock Stuart, CEO of Continental Consolidated Petro-

leum and Laren Ogelthorp, chairman of the South-Western Energy Group, met in Shelbourn's suite at the Hays-Adams Hotel to discuss the implications for the industry of the rumored super-ethanol discovery by GET, Inc. out in California. All four had attended a daylong symposium on American energy policy at the American Petroleum Institute, but it was apparent to Shelbourn that super ethanol was what was on everybody's mind. The rumors had been pervasive, and he felt certain that the matter was best dealt with collectively.

After they'd exchanged impressions and expressed their concerns, Shelbourn summed things up, saying the problem was that they were in the dark and it wasn't clear that the government knew a whole lot more. Shelbourn said he had been able to determine through high-placed friends in the administration that an overseas capital source, unrelated to the industry, could be involved, which meant there might be an effort to corner the market. That could mean disaster for everybody in the room.

Ogelthorp wondered if they didn't need to find out more about the technology itself, whether it was viable and therefore a genuine threat. Hodges told the others that he'd tried to do exactly that, but was unable to learn much. They agreed that it was in all their interests to find out what they were up against as soon as possible and they agreed further that rather than working at cross purposes, a collective effort—one that was highly discreet—was the best way to go.

Brock Stuart, who'd spent many years in Europe and the Middle East, said he knew some people abroad who might be helpful in such an endeavor. If discretion was *the goal, there were extracurricular methods that were efficient, effective and safe, but also expensive. The others pledged financial support if Stuart was willing to make the arrangements. Considering the world as they knew it could be at stake, the men agreed they had little choice but to press ahead.*

The Mission District, San Francisco

Kelly's, Jonas learned, was a workingman's bar by day and a lesbian hangout at night, the dinner hour, more or less, being the transition point. The liquor was the same, although the drinks of choice varied, the two pool tables were in use day and night and the concrete floor remained covered with sawdust. What changed was the nature of the colognes and the size of the boots.

Jonas had made his first appearance at Kelly's that afternoon when the ascendant combination was ponytails and mustaches, hairy chests and body odor. When he returned for his second visit (having been told that Penny worked the night shift), work shirts and leather now covered breasts, and the excess body fat had shifted from beer bellies to thighs and asses. Both incarnations of Kelly's manifested an equal number of buzz cuts and pierced body parts. The ultimate difference came down to the postprandial absence of the Y chromosome.

Upon his return, it only took Jonas five seconds to realize he no longer belonged. When he stepped through the doors, there was a momentary lull in the background noise, which included a spirited choral rendition of "Frosty the Snowman" on the sound system. If glares could kill, he would be dead before he got halfway to the bar.

There were two bartenders, one butch, the other not. Jonas headed for the end where the more feminine woman presided. She had a Rudolph with a blinking red nose pinned to her top, above her left breast.

"Yeah?" she said, sounding like she expected to be asked for change for a parking meter rather than a drink order.

Jonas offered neither. "I'm looking for Penny," he said. "That you?"

She was smallish and thin but well-scrubbed and wiry-looking, the sort of woman who wasn't afraid of men or horses. She checked his hands, perhaps thinking he was a process server with a summons. "Yeah, that's my name. What do you want?"

"Some information about Steve Williams," he said, keeping it ambiguous by not using the term "husband," which, for all he knew, could be a mark of shame in the present company.

She gave a half laugh. "Small world."

"Pardon?"

She checked her watch. "Whatever you need, you can get it from him. He should be rolling in anytime."

Jonas blinked. "Steve Williams—" he leaned closer, lowering his voice "—your ex?"

"Yeah, that one. Isn't that the guy you meant?"

"Maybe one of us is confused," Jonas said. "Are we talking about Steve Williams the former military guy, the former cop, the former ex-con, the sort of free-lance detective?"

"Yeah," she said with what's-with-you-anyway amusement. "I don't know any others. Do you?"

"Have you been contacted by police the last few days?"

Penny's lighthearted, bemused expression turned sober. "No, why should I?"

"Hey, Penny," somebody down the bar shouted over the din, "quit flirting with the boy and serve some brew. How about it?"

"Hang on," she said to Jonas, "I got to take care of my customers."

Penny was gone a couple of minutes, giving him time to ponder his confusion. She obviously hadn't heard that her former husband had been killed. But what was this business about Williams coming in to see her?

Finally, she returned. "Sorry about that. By the way, who are you?"

"Jonas Lamb."

"So, what's with you and Steve?"

"Penny, I'm hoping we're talking about two different guys. The one I'm referring to was killed in a traffic accident in Hong Kong a few days ago."

"Huh? Are you shitting me?"

Jonas shook his head. "My Steve Williams was on some kind of job and he was using the alias 'Chuck Haggerty.'"

A silence, then she muttered, "Haggerty? Oh, fuck." She looked ashen.

"What's this about Steve coming to the bar?" he asked. "What gave you that idea?"

"That's what my boss told me when I got here. She said Steve had come in this afternoon looking for me. But obviously somebody's got his head up his ass."

"Does she know Steve?"

"She's seen him. He comes in every once in a while." Penny seemed shaken. "He was really killed in a traffic accident?"

"Yeah."

"Jesus. So, why are you here?"

"Because I'd like to find out as much about him as I can."

Penny stared in the direction of the entrance and, still looking a bit dazed, suddenly blinked. "Wait a minute, I think I'm beginning to understand."

Jonas turned and saw that another gunslinger had stepped into the bar, and damn if it wasn't Chuck Haggerty. Or, Steve Williams, aka Chuck Haggerty. Or, maybe a goddamn ghost. As Chuck/Steve made his way to the bar, parting the crowd like Moses in the Red Sea, Jonas realized the schizophrenic arrivee was neither the would-be paparazzi in Hong Kong nor a ghost. It was the proprietor of City Investigative Services.

The gumshoe, recognizing him, reacted like somebody who'd just found a banana growing on a peach tree. Then his surprise morphed into an oh-shit-what-now expression.

"What are you doing here, Chuck?" Jonas asked.

Haggerty stared at Penny for a second or two, then said, "After our conversation, I got curious."

"Welcome to the club, big guy."

Penny said, "I've got a cigarette break coming. Maybe we should go outside."

They trooped out. Penny wore a knit tank top and jeans, but the cold air didn't seem to bother her. She leaned against the building and lit a cigarette.

"How about one of you tell me what's going on," she said.

"Do we need further introductions, or am I to assume you two know each other?" Jonas asked.

"We met a couple of years ago," Chuck explained. "And became friends."

"We screwed for a month or so after Steve and I split," Penny said dryly. "Why be coy? I was looking to get laid."

"Did you notice the resemblance between Chuck and your ex?" Jonas asked.

"Yeah, but it wasn't so obvious as you might think. At the time Steve wore his hair in a ponytail and it was darker. He also had a goatee and mustache. Chuck looked like Mr. Clean in comparison. When it really hit me was recently, when Steve changed his image and started looking like this. I sure as hell noticed then."

Jonas turned to Haggerty. "How about you? Didn't you notice Steve resembled your long-lost brother?"

"I never saw the guy, just heard about him from Penny—mostly what a shit he was. And her last name wasn't Williams, so when you called this morning, I didn't make the connection."

"I've always used my maiden name, Klein," she explained.

"But after we talked," Haggerty continued, "I started thinking about you saying Williams's ex was a barkeep and that her name was Penny. That's when I got curious and decided to check it out."

Jonas said to Penny, "So, when your boss saw Chuck this afternoon, he assumed it was Steve because now Steve looks...or *looked* like Mr. Clean, too."

"I guess."

"Mystery solved."

"But what's this about Steve getting killed?" she asked. She glanced at Haggerty. "And what's this got to do with you?" She extended her lower lip and blew smoke upward, past her nose.

"Seems your ex has been using my identity. And not just in Hong Kong."

"You apparently weren't aware of that," Jonas said.

"No," Penny replied. "I see Steve occasionally, but it's not like we have a relationship."

"Did you know he'd gone to Hong Kong?"

"The last time I saw him was maybe two weeks ago. He came by the bar to pay back the five hundred he'd borrowed. I about dropped my teeth. I asked him if a rich aunt had died or if he'd started layin' down the hustle. He said he got a big job and would be leaving the country soon. But he didn't mention Hong Kong specifically."

"Big job," Jonas said. "What did you take that to mean?"

"I didn't give it a thought. He was paying off a debt, that's all I cared about."

"What can you tell us about his work?"

"Very little. He did stuff that normal investigators wouldn't do. He didn't even have a license as far as I know."

"Did he work on his own?"

"I think mostly, but my impression was people would use him regularly, licensed P.I.s who had dirty work they didn't want to do themselves. Steve liked the adventure." She took a deep drag on her cigarette.

"I'd really like to know who hired him to go to Hong Kong," Jonas said.

Penny coughed out a lung full of smoke. "Don't expect me to tell you because I don't have the foggiest."

"Was there anybody he worked for on a regular basis?"

"Seems to me there was a woman. I'd say good-looking by the way he talked."

Jonas and Haggerty exchanged glances.

"A little blonde?" Haggerty asked, his jaw working.

"Don't know. Never saw her and Steve never said what she looked like."

Jonas said, "How about a name?"

Penny thought, rubbing her goose-bumped arms, the dwindling cigarette wedged between her fingers. "You know, he might have mentioned her by name once. Seems to me it was a goddess name. Daphne or something like that. Yeah, Daphne seems right."

"No last name?"

Penny shook her head. "Look, boys, this has been fun, but I'm getting cold and my break's over. About a third of the time I work a day shift. Why not drop by then, have a beer on the house?" The last was directed mostly at Haggerty, who nodded vaguely.

After she went inside, Jonas and Chuck Haggerty looked at each other, neither quite smiling. Jonas said, "Do you think you could find Daphne for me?"

"Sort of like to find her myself if she's who I think she is."

"The recruiter for the Vienna Boys Choir, you mean?"

Haggerty flushed. "Yeah, her."

"Any idea what it might cost?"

"I could be lucky or it could be expensive. I'd eat some of it, though."

"What would, say, a grand buy me?"

"A serious preliminary effort, minimum."

"Let's start with that," Jonas said, offering his hand.

Haggerty took it and they shook. "Done."

Part TWO

TUESDAY
January 15

Paris

He had a choice of three different apartments when he came to Paris, but the one he favored was the most modest, the one on the rue Mouffetard in the Latin Quarter. Though Alfred Le Genissel was neither academic nor plebeian, as were his neighbors, he was a man who valued his neck and took comfort in anonymity.

After arriving at the Gare de Lyon the previous afternoon, Le Genissel, dressed as a migrant worker, had gone to Châtelet by taxi, where he'd entered the maze of the Métro, losing himself in the crowds. Boarding a "seven" train headed in the direction of Villejuif L. Aragon, Le Genissel rode four stops to Censier-Daubenton.

Disembarking from the train, he had waited for the other half dozen passengers to leave the platform, taking careful note of each. None was of a suspicious appearance, but Le Genissel took nothing for granted. He'd been at this long enough to know that no one could be trusted and everyone was suspect. That didn't make for the most genial existence, but he had no aspirations for a social life. Le Genissel did what he did for the money.

He'd been very successful. So successful that it had taken a very large sum—ten million American dollars, to be precise—to bring him back to France, where he was already wanted for two deaths. The figure was more than five times the amount of his previous largest fee. Almost too good to be true.

Though satisfied he wasn't being followed, he hadn't gone directly to the apartment, stopping first at a café near the église St. Médard, where he had a beer, leaving afterward through the delivery entrance at the rear. He found the apartment secure, the small armoire full of suits, shirts and ties, just as he had left it three months earlier.

Le Genissel awoke that morning after a less-than-comfortable night on the narrow bed to find the rooftops of the city glazed with frost. Errant snowflakes drifted past his window from the leaden sky. Were he a poet, some aesthetic thought might have tripped through his brain, but Alfred Ahmed Le Genissel was a French Lebanese mercenary and assassin, known by Interpol and national police and security services around the world as the "Gazelle." What he saw out the window was gray and cold slush.

Le Genissel put a pot of water on the hot plate to make coffee, then went to shave in the phone-booth-size bathroom. Having successfully entered France undetected, he was free to dress more suavely, so he donned a crisp white shirt of Egyptian combed cotton, a deep purple merino wool sweater and dark blue hand-tailored Italian suit. The shoes were Italian, as well.

Le Genissel drank his coffee and left the apartment, walking the four or five blocks to the Panthéon. He was hawkishly handsome, swarthy enough to be mysterious, attractive to both women and men, though he had no sexual interest in men. His primary interest in people was to the extent they could be helpful with the task at hand. His face was not unknown to the authorities, but on the streets he was in little danger of being recognized. Such was the reality of life in the ethnically diverse urban cities of the West.

Overhead the cloud cover had begun to break up and patches of blue and sunlight appeared. The Gazelle did not wear a topcoat, content with a heavy scarf (expensive and, what else, Italian), which was wrapped once around his neck with one end thrown over his shoulder, the other tucked under the lapel of his jacket.

Alfred Le Genissel was a quietly prideful man who revealed his thoughts and feelings to no one. Or, almost no one. His mother and grandmother, who lived in a villa outside the Lebanese town of Sidon, overlooking the Mediterranean Sea in the home he provided for them, were the only people on earth he talked to about himself, though his work was never discussed. The Gazelle believed that to feel too much was dangerous. He was always careful with his thoughts. Always. His survival depended on it.

Le Genissel stopped in a café on rue Soufflot, where he had two croissants, strawberry jam, butter and another coffee. From there it was a short walk to the Jardin du Luxembourg where he was to meet Gaston de Malbouzon.

He bought a paper at the newsstand, crossed the boulevard St. Michel and entered the garden. He found a bench and sat down to read his paper, though in fact he was observing his surroundings. It appeared he was being neither followed nor watched. So far, so good.

At nine o'clock, the sky even clearer than before, he walked nonchalantly across the garden. On the far side, near the rue Guynemer, Le Genissel spotted the *comte,* a man of thirty-seven or eight, going on eighteen. Comte Gaston de Malbouzon was perhaps the most bizarre human being Le Genissel had ever met—a nobleman from an ancient French family that went back to the Crusades (reason enough right there for the Gazelle to hate him), plus he was a homosexual, a cultural and intellectual snob and a great admirer of the "American experiment," as he called it (another good reason to hate him). But de Malbouzon was also a genius, a man who had mastered both the technical and political worlds, a man with incredible resources and a willingness to do anything for money, especially if it had the effect of tweaking the establishment. De Malbouzon was reading *Le Monde,* a briefcase at his feet.

Perrin, as expected, was sitting on a bench twenty meters away. Seeing Le Genissel, Perrin spread his arms along the back of the bench and crossed his legs. It was the all-clear signal. Le Genissel strode over to the bench where the *comte*, dressed in worn corduroy pants and a bulky sweater, his wiry hair going every which way, pretended to read his paper. Le Genissel sat down on the other end of the bench.

"Turned out to be a nice day, after all," Gaston de Malbouzon said in English. They both were fluent, though de Malbouzon, who'd spent two years at the Massachusetts Institute of Technology before being kicked out, spoke idiomatically correct English, albeit with a rather pronounced accent. Despite being French, he preferred English for business "because it was so much more precise" and French for pleasure, especially sex, "because it was so much more effective." These were details Le Genissel would rather not know, but de Malbouzon had been intent on sharing such tidbits whenever they met, probably because he knew how much it annoyed him.

In response to de Malbouzon's comment about the weather, Le Genissel said, "Yes, very nice. Chilly, though." Le Genissel had less of an accent, though he hadn't mastered the English idioms and colloquialisms as well as the Frenchman.

"So, my little Gazelle, let's cut to the chase, as my friends in America are wont to say. What do you have for me, eh?"

"I need intelligence and a woman."

"Intelligence and a boy would be more down my alley."

"I do not mean a woman for me, I mean for a mission."

"*Tiens,* you should have been clearer, my good man. *That* kind of woman I can provide, no problem. Who are we seducing?"

"I am thinking a good choice for the job would be Carly Van Hooten," Le Genissel said, ignoring the question. "Is she working again?"

"I think I'm the best judge of who would be suitable from my stable, *mon ami.* Give me your requirements."

"I need to learn the business secrets of an entrepreneur. He must also be dispatched."

"Dispatched as in killed?"

"Yes."

"Alfred, you've been spending much too much time at the movies. You want the contents of the gentleman's brain and then you want him removed from the scene permanently."

"Precisely. But you should not worry about the killing. It is my department."

"See how easy this is when we keep things simple?"

Le Genissel couldn't help a contemptuous glare, but de Malbouzon seemed not to notice or care.

"Tell me about your pigeon, Alfred. What age?"

"Late fifties."

"I see. Nationality?"

"American."

"Ah. In Europe?"

"No, California. San Francisco."

"Indeed. That makes things somewhat more challenging. Entrepreneur, you say?"

"Yes, a small company that has developed revolutionary technology."

"And your sheiks want the technology along with our American's head on a platter."

"I said nothing about sheiks," Le Genissel protested.

"You didn't have to, Alfred. I know who I'm dealing with. I'll give you odds it's energy related. Probably oil, possibly nuclear. Your sheiks don't care about electronics except to buy it." De Malbouzon hesitated, thinking. "Good God, don't tell me somebody's perfected hydrogen fusion."

"The details are unimportant," Le Genissel said.

"It *is* hydrogen fusion." But then, after reflection, de Malbouzon said, "No, can't be. I would have known before you."

"All I can tell you, Comte, is that the project is still in the experimental phase. I need to find out everything there is to know about it, including who is aware of its existence. Eventually, all persons connected must be eliminated."

"Present company excepted, of course."

Le Genissel couldn't help smiling. De Malbouzon was so mad he was amusing. "We will be permitted to live, absolutely."

"There's no absolutely about it, Alfred. You're the boys who perfected the art of suicide bombers, need I remind you. Thing is, forty virgins do me no good. I run a cash business."

Alfred Le Genissel did not appreciate the condescension, but he was in no position to complain. There were very few women in the world suitable for the mission and de Malbouzon had access, if not control, of the most qualified candidate available. "Point taken."

"Can you share a few more details about our mark?" de Malbouzon asked. "What makes you think he would be susceptible to a woman's charms?"

"He has been married six times and has had numerous other women, during and between marriages. His current wife is terminally ill."

"Say no more. You're right, Carly's the one. There is a small problem."

"Yes?"

"She's been on extended holiday since…well, since the tragedy. I'll have to chat her up and see if she's up to it."

"And if not?"

"There are other candidates, of course, but American men don't appreciate the subtleties of the European female. They do much better with their own kind. It's like ducks and chickens."

"I defer to your superior knowledge in such matters, Comte. But I will need your reply soon."

"I may want Carly to speak with you, Alfred. Do you have photographs of the chap, biographical particulars?"

"I do, indeed."

"Very good. Then all that remains is to settle our

fee. In negotiating with Carly, I have to know what's available."

There was a whistle just then and Le Genissel quickly glanced in the direction of Perrin, who gave a hand signal indicating danger. Farther along the walkway Le Genissel saw a young couple approaching.

"Someone is coming," he said to Gaston de Malbouzon. "Read your paper."

"Alfred, Alfred," de Malbouzon said under his breath, tsking, "you have the nerves of a man wanted for a dozen murders."

"Do not make a joke of it, Comte."

"We *have* abolished the death penalty here in France, need I remind you. Unlike your Saudi cousins, who are likely to hack off a finger or a toe for an illegal left turn." With that, de Malbouzon lifted his newspaper and began humming the "Star-Spangled Banner."

"Please, Comte, I beg of you."

Le Genissel was relieved when de Malbouzon fell silent, wondering if it was worth dealing with the guy. But irreverent or not, there was no denying he got results. It didn't come cheaply, though. That was why when Le Genissel had taken the assignment from the Saudi secret operative, Abu Saiid, he'd told him it was an extraordinary challenge and that the fee would have to be commensurate. The Gazelle was beginning to think he'd understated his case.

Casually glancing in the direction of the young couple, he subtly sized them up. They were both quite tall and slender. Attractive, as well. They didn't appear sly enough to be agents in the Bureau of Internal Security, but you never could tell. The young woman was speaking in an animated fashion, her words becoming clearer the closer they came.

"*Serpants, serpants, serpants,* Sylvain. Snakes, snakes, snakes. Is that all you can think about?" She spoke in French, but with a discernible American accent. It wasn't British, Le Genissel knew the difference.

"*Sybil, ce n'est pas juste,*" the young man pleaded, his voice fading as they moved along the walk. He was indisputably French.

Le Genissel watched them closely. Neither of them had so much as glanced his way. He continued watching them until they moved out of sight, obscured by some trees.

The pretty American girl had gotten him to thinking about Carly Van Hooten again. On the train he'd thought of her a great deal, wondering if she'd be available. Le Genissel had worked with her once before, back when Antoine was still alive and she was untouchable. Not that he hadn't fantasized about her since. Carly had intrigued him, tempting him as no other woman could. She was a spectacular beauty and she was fearless—alluring yet contemptible, like America itself.

Le Genissel had kept his distance from her, knowing that with Antoine in the picture, pursuing her would have been fruitless. But now that was no longer a problem. And so he'd fantasized, even as he'd satisfied his needs with the services of prostitutes.

The passing couple now out of sight, Le Genissel said, "That girl was American."

"So? They're everywhere, Alfred. You should be here in August. Paris is nothing but Americans, waiters, taxi drivers and pickpockets, my dear boy."

Le Genissel was by nature paranoid, but in his case with good reason. It was impossible to be too careful. Gaston de Malbouzon slapped his paper against his knee.

"But we digress, *mon ami*. I believe we were about to discuss money."

This part of his work Le Genissel disliked most. But it came with being in charge. "Indeed, Comte," he said. "Your fee."

"What are you prepared to offer me for my services?"

Le Genissel did not hesitate. "Two million, U.S."

"Two million, eh? Hmm. That means you're prepared to settle for four, which tells me they've offered you ten or twelve, that's a hundred-percent markup plus wiggle room."

Le Genissel stared at him blankly, hating the bastard. "You find my offer insufficient?"

"Considering I would be doing all the difficult work and you would be taking all the glory, yes. Plus, I will have others to pay. You've told me very little about the mission, but from what you've said, I can see there will be need for much research and preparation. It will not be an easy task. Of that much I am certain."

"You will not have full responsibility, Comte. In fact, I insist on being heavily involved. I am already. I have men in the field as we speak, gathering intelligence. My payroll is already large. You will be but a piece of the puzzle." Le Genissel continued to stare into his eyes. "Let's get right to the bottom line, my best offer. Five million. Not a penny more. But with a condition, Comte. Carly van Hooten is in the deal."

De Malbouzon smiled. "For your benefit, Alfred, or your employers'?"

"For the good of us all."

"That's what I like—a man willing to fuck for his country. But in fairness, I must tell you, my friend, only in your dreams. But I'll talk to Carly and let you know."

Le Genissel nodded. "I understand the money is, for you, foremost," he said, "but be assured, the fee is incredibly large for a reason. The danger is considerable. Much of the world community is already engaged. My men in California have determined that foreign intelligence services are conducting operations. And for good reason, my friend. We are talking about global economic dislocations, if that gives you an idea. This is big."

"Is it cold fusion?"

"You will learn the answer when necessary. I'll say this—the threat must be eliminated and quickly. We have little time."

"How little?"

"Seven or eight months. The longer we wait the more people will become involved and the list of potential targets will grow. There is one other thing," the Gazelle said. "Your actions must be virtually invisible."

"Meaning?"

"It should be done in such a way that no one will get suspicious of what we are doing until it is too late.

It would be best if the gentleman and his associates disappear without anyone knowing why since we can't draw attention to their work."

"*Dis moi,* Alfred, out of curiosity, what is so magical about eight months?"

Le Genissel rolled his tongue through his cheek, then said, "It is the growing season, Comte."

San Mateo County, California

A steady rain fell on the congregation of mourners, the water drops beading on the shiny casket and running down the side and into the grave. The large, black umbrella Patrick held partially obscured the gray sky, but not the muted hills that undulated down to the Pacific. On a clear day you could see the ocean off to the west and Mount Diablo over in the East Bay, but not today.

It wasn't the first time Jonas had been to Skyline Memorial Park, situated atop the coastal mountains separating Half Moon Bay from the towns ringing San Francisco Bay. On the prior occasion—a windy, but bright and sunny summer afternoon—he and a ragtag band of middle-aged warriors from the old outfit had buried a Vietnam War buddy, saluting nostalgia as well as their departed brother, while Old Glory snapped overhead and a trio of navy jets roared across the sky in a ceremonial flyby. Jonas had watched the jets that day until they disappeared over the Pacific, images of Vietnam flickering in the back of his brain like the tattered fragments of an old newsreel.

But there was no sun on this dismal day, which also

happened to be his and Elise's wedding anniversary. His poor wife was being laid to rest under a rain cloud that hugged the mountaintop with blustery vengeance, pissing on everyone—family, friends, detractors, cynical vultures all. Or nearly all.

Jonas knew that while Elise's battle with cancer was over, his battle with her children was just beginning. Melanie, hidden under an umbrella a few feet away from him and his son, was sobbing quietly. Wilson, beyond her, was probably doing the same. Neither of the de Givry progeny had spoken with him since Elise's passing three days earlier, though, like Jonas, they'd been at their mother's bedside. Once she was gone, they'd spent a few tearful minutes with her, then left without so much as a nod in his direction.

At long last the minister, a punctilious man even by clerical standards, began winding up the oratory that had kept them hard to the grave. And none too soon. Jonas could almost hear his late wife, who had little patience for tedium, muttering in her coffin, "Come on, Reverend, get on with it."

With the crowd of mourners heading for their cars, Jonas, who was not without civility, turned to his stepchildren, prepared to offer words of condolence. Melanie lifted her umbrella to hug lingering relatives and friends and express her thanks to the minister. Jonas, having received expressions of sympathy and handshakes himself, waited until his stepdaughter finally turned his way, her expression telling him she was fully prepared to do her worst.

"I'm sorry, Melanie," he said. "I truly am."

"Sorry for what?" The word *what* on her lips had that acerbic quality known only to a woman in the full blush of contempt.

He refused to take the bait. "The loss. I know how close you and Elise were."

"Save your breath, Jonas. It's yourself you should feel sorry for. You've lost your protectress and benefactor. Be warned. It's a new ball game."

"I beg your pardon?"

"It's me you're going to have to deal with from here on out, and I'm not impressed with big blue eyes and pseudo manly virtue. It's not what you say but who you *are* that counts in my book."

He cleared his throat, glancing back and forth between Melanie and her brother before continuing. "I was hoping that with Elise's passing we might—" He got no further.

"Well, it's not going to happen," Melanie snapped, cutting him off. "You'll be getting served papers soon, but I'll forewarn you out of courtesy. Wilson and I expect you out of our house by the end of the month, and I insist that you return the money you squeezed out of Mother while she was dying."

Melanie's words didn't surprise him so much as the context in which they were uttered. Though most mourners had already left, Jonas couldn't help but be embarrassed, though as much for his stepdaughter's sake as his own. As he gathered his thoughts, debating between frontal assault and strategic withdrawal, he glanced first at his son, then at Elise's coffin, reminding himself of the occasion.

"She can't help you now," Melanie said bitterly.

That was it. A dagger in his manhood. Forbidden territory for any woman. "Look," he shot back, bristling, "I have every intention of cooperating fully with you and Wilson, but I don't like being bullied. Your mother told me I could stay in the house up to a year, but she was being overly generous. I don't need that long. And as for money, none was offered while Elise was dying and none asked for."

"I know about the hundred thousand you pried out of her for your company, so don't try to con me. Your flimflam might have worked on Mother, but it won't work on me."

"That money was a loan and it was made months ago," he rejoined, taking another sideward peek at his son.

"Yeah, I know, in exchange for stock that's probably worthless," Melanie intoned.

"Worse-case scenario, when her estate is settled the advance will be deducted from what your mother left me."

"Wrong," she replied. "I've got news for you. We're going to contest the entire bequest, which means you'll have to pony up the cash."

"On what grounds?"

"You inheriting the million was conditioned on your fidelity, or did you forget that clause in the prenuptial agreement? The prenup was incorporated by reference into Mom's will, so, guess what, lover-boy? You'll be getting nothing and you'll be paying back everything you've taken."

Jonas hoped to hell the color he felt rising wasn't visible. Though he'd never asked Elise, he had assumed the vow of fidelity was strictly between the two of them. Apparently he was mistaken. Melanie had decided to make it her business and was either ignorant of the dispensation Elise had given him, or chose to ignore it. The reason was apparent. Money.

Gazing at his stepdaughter with righteous but wobbly indignation, Jonas knew there was no way the truth would fly. Who'd believe that Elise had told him he could have his fun as long as he was discreet? There could be no justice, he realized, without prevarication. So he waffled. He bobbed. He weaved. He lied.

"Our marriage was solid and satisfactory to us both," he proclaimed, looking Melanie hard in the eye. "I was never unfaithful to your mother, and I resent you impugning my integrity." Well, that part was true, anyway.

"Resent all you want, Jonas," she rejoined, "Mother may not have had detectives on your ass, but we did."

The revelation was a shock, though it shouldn't have been. It never occurred to him that Elise's children might use the fidelity issue against him. Slowly it began to sink in. Melanie had been plotting this for months. She might even have been responsible for the people who'd been following him. There'd been that blond fireball, Daphne, who they'd never been able to track down. Hell, maybe even Steve Williams!

Those photographs. Sure. Pictures of him in bed with Crystal would have suited Melanie's purposes. The irony. And all along he'd thought it had to do with Operation Black Sheep. Everything was about Melanie and Wilson wanting to deny him the million-dollar bequest.

"You want proof?" Melanie continued when Jonas failed to respond. "You told Mother you'd been married twice before." She held up five fingers. "Five is the correct number, Jonas, counting the mother of your son here. We know about your bankruptcy and your middle-of-the-night departures from whatever town you were running your scam. And, yes, we know about your women."

Jonas glanced at Patrick and was relieved to find him more annoyed than shocked. Fortunately Melanie's disclosures weren't radically out of line with the facts of which his son was already apprised, only the way she characterized them.

"By the way, I'm not your only problem," she went on. "The FBI is on to you."

"What are you talking about?"

"They came to see me after Mother died, wanting to know about you and your so-called company. Naturally, I told them exactly what I thought of you."

"That's bullshit," Jonas shot back.

"Oh? Well, guess again. As executor of my mother's estate, I control the stock she held in your company, and I'll use it as I see fit to get back the hundred thousand. I told the FBI everything." She grinned with cynical glee. "I hope I'm not upsetting any applecarts, but being a fraud and a phony has its consequences, even *en famille*."

Jonas was reduced to diversionary jabs. "You're completely transparent, Melanie. You picked today for the funeral because it was your mother's and my anniversary, didn't you?"

"Yes, in addition to burying my mother, I wanted to bury this sham of a marriage."

Low blow. He seethed. What the hell, he decided, a cathartic broadside would be good for his soul. "Melanie," he said, through gritted teeth, "for your sake I hope your problem is self-delusion, because I'd really hate to think you're a liar in addition to being a snotty little bitch."

Her eyes rounded.

Jonas continued. "Look, why don't you honor your mother by going home and grieving instead of attacking me? Maybe when you've calmed down we can have a polite, adult conversation and work out our differences."

She glared. "Oh, you'll be seeing me, all right, Mr. Lamb. *In court*." With that, she turned on her heel, nearly knocking over her brother as she stomped away, waving her umbrella in the wind as though doing battle with Mother Nature.

Jonas again looked at his son, who raised his brows as if to say, "Golly, that was certainly a show."

"Sorry about that," Jonas muttered. "The lesson, if there is one, is that in-laws are part of the package."

Patrick's expression remained sober. "Was that all bluster or do we have problems?"

"Mostly bluster," he said, taking his son's arm and heading toward the parking area. "There *is* a problem, but you don't have to worry about it."

"You mean the FBI?"

"No, I don't know where that came from. Nobody's committed any crimes. I think it's a matter of her doing anything she can to keep me from inheriting from Elise's estate, not that she and Wilson would miss it. They'll each be getting ten times what their mother left me. It's mostly posturing, certainly no reason for you to be concerned."

"I hope you're right."

They'd come to Jonas's car. He unlocked the doors and they both got in.

"Maybe I'm paranoid," Patrick said. "I've been feeling funny the last few days, like I'm being watched and followed."

Jonas had been feeling the same himself. He'd assumed it was connected to the Steve Williams/Chuck Haggerty mystery, which was now starting to look like a Melanie de Givry mystery. Could she have taken it so far as to snoop on his son? He'd told Elise of Patrick's involvement in the company and it was possible Elise had mentioned it to Melanie.

"Could be that I've had too much free time, considering I'm on sabbatical this quarter," Patrick said. "When you're busy it's hard to find time for paranoia."

"You never know," Jonas said. "But just to be safe, it might not be a bad idea if we keep each other informed."

Jonas started the engine and turned on the windshield wipers. His gut was in turmoil. Melanie had done a number on him. But she hadn't specifically mentioned Crystal. Was that because she didn't know about her, or because she still needed hard evidence? If Steve Williams had been working for her, that would be an indicator she was still trying to make her case—which meant trouble, particularly if she got to Crystal.

It had been the better part of a month since he'd spoken to his erstwhile mistress. He hadn't called her because he'd decided the first move was up to her, and also because he'd been preoccupied with Elise. But now that Melanie had openly declared war, all bets were off.

Jonas had been around long enough to know that remaining cool under fire was as important as being well armed. He also knew that he'd be well advised to get to Crystal before Melanie did—if it wasn't already too late.

Paris

Carly Van Hooten stared at the ceiling, fascinated by the pattern of cracks. They could be found in practically every bedroom in Paris, it seemed, the face of eighteenth- and nineteenth-century France in microcosm—old and venerable, greater than the present, greater than the petty concerns of today and tomorrow. In Europe, the past was more important than the future, if only because the future couldn't be trusted. Maybe that's why she liked it so. She'd never had much faith in what lay ahead.

Carly held up her wrist to catch the fading light

coming in the tall window. According to her watch, she had only forty-five minutes to get to Gaston's place, including a half hour ride on the Métro.

Kissing Anook on the cheek, she slipped from the bed and began to dress in the semidarkness, the floor and the thick walls cold yet somehow poignant. They'd been witness to a million yesterdays, the room a stage for a thousand actors come and gone, none counting for much, just filling the time they occupied the place.

There was a certain *tristesse* about the apartment, the building, the street, the city that appealed to Carly. The ugliness here and there didn't matter. History, after all, was ugly, too.

Anook moaned, but her eyes remained closed. Carly glanced at her friend as she pulled on her panties. The sheet lay across Anook's belly, leaving her large breasts exposed to the chilly air. Carly stepped over and pulled the sheet up so she wouldn't get cold and awaken. The sleeping woman looked like an Italian Renaissance painting, her dark corkscrew curls splayed Medusa-like across the pillow.

Anook was an exotic beauty, the first woman for whom Carly had ever felt sexual attraction. After men, it had been odd at first, but then she'd come to realize it was simply a different course in the larger feast of human sexuality. Not that she needed philosophical justification. Carly Van Hooten had always done what she wished.

One thing she liked about Anook was that she was easy to talk to. They could discuss sex without the least embarrassment. "If you had your choice between only men or only women," Carly had asked her once, "which would it be?"

"*Ça, c'est facile.*" That's easy. "*Moi, je préfère les femmes.*" I'd take women. "Maybe it's just easier with another woman because of the tenderness. *Et toi?*"

"I don't know," Carly replied. "I want whatever pleases me at the moment. Who can predict what it will be?"

"But I please you now?"

"You please me now."

Carly had always been unafraid of her desires, even as a child when she was still Caroline Howe. Nor did she lack courage. The first twenty-eight years of her life had been one daring adventure after another, always crossing the bounds of convention when given the opportunity, preferring the forbidden and the unexpected simply because they were forbidden and unexpected.

Sex wasn't what mattered, though. Love mattered, and that was because she didn't understand its causes and its boundaries or what it did to her heart. There was a time when she thought she had that all figured out. Now she wasn't so sure.

Did she love Anook? In ways she did, of course. But mostly what they shared simply happened. Carly continued to notice men, but felt no need to connect with them. The uncomplicated was better. She'd known love and she suspected she'd never experience it again, at least not in the same way.

And so she lived for the sake of experience, because

that was the best way to feel alive. With love out of the picture, adventure was her only passion. Danger her currency. Criminality her game.

It was about feeling something. It had come down to a very simple dichotomy—life and death. Wasn't that what had always moved the world? Heaven and hell. Good and bad. Life and death. If that's what it was all about, why not embrace it?

"Tu t'en vas." You're leaving, Anook said, stretching in the bed, her arms extended to the cold wall above her head, her breasts once again uncovered.

Carly hadn't noticed she'd awakened. *"Oui, il faut que j'y aille."* Yes, I have to go.

"To do what?"

"I have an appointment."

"Another of your mysterious rendezvous," Anook said with disapproval.

Carly pulled her turtleneck sweater over her head, running her fingers back through her long blond hair to free it. *"Oui, c'est juste."*

"It's with a man, isn't it?"

"Oui."

"Un amoureux?" A lover?

"No, Anook. Business."

Carly looked at her ghostlike image in the cloudy mirror above Anook's old-fashioned dressing table. Her beauty was undeniable. In America as a child she'd been a photographer's model, having made sufficient money by the time she was eighteen to become financially independent and free of her mother's obsessive control.

Whim had taken her to Paris, where she'd hoped to have a modeling career as an adult. But nature had been unkind to her in one important respect. While her beauty had matured, she had stopped growing when she reached the height of five feet, three inches. Though blessed with a lovely figure, and positively irresistible in four-inch heels and a miniskirt, she knew this was not the look the fashion industry craved.

Grousing, Anook propped herself on her elbow. "I don't understand you, Carly."

"There is nothing to understand. I am who I am."

"You revel in your secrecy."

Carly put her hands on her hips. "Would you prefer that I don't come here anymore, Anook?"

"No, of course not. I love your visits."

"Then please don't question me."

Anook watched her get her suede coat from the chair. "I didn't believe you when you told me you'd once killed a man. But now I do."

That amused her. "Why? Because I seem evil?"

"No, I meant that you're so unafraid," Anook replied, "sometimes it frightens me. Your fearlessness, I mean."

Carly zipped the coat. "You have nothing to fear."

"I don't mean in that way. I mean because I don't know your heart and I'm afraid I never will."

"How can you know what I don't know myself?" She went to the door.

"Carly?"

"Yes?"

"It's all because of Antoine, isn't it?"

Carly left the apartment without answering the question. As she made her way down the dank stairwell, she wondered if the time hadn't come to end things. Anook was almost too female in her attitudes and outlook. Besides, if Carly ended up taking the job Gaston wanted to talk to her about, she could be abroad for weeks, even months. This could be the perfect time to end the affair. Too bad for Anook. But then, that was life.

San Francisco

By the time they reached San Francisco the rain had stopped and the sun had begun breaking through the overcast sky. Off to the right of the freeway there was a partial rainbow over Candlestick Park. "Suppose that's a good omen for us or the 49ers?" Jonas asked his son.

"Let's hope it's us," Patrick replied. "The 49ers can take care of themselves."

"You've got a point."

They'd talked just enough during the drive up the Peninsula to keep the silences from being overly long. Hanging over them was the uncertainty of how much trouble they were in because of Melanie. Jonas was really bummed to think the little bitch had been fucking with him all this time—spying, intruding in his personal life—just to screw him out of his inheritance. More ominous still was her remark about using Elise's stock in GET as a weapon. The last thing they needed was to jeopardize Operation Black

Sheep. It just went to show you couldn't take anything for granted.

Jonas had nobody to blame but himself, though. He could have kept his pants zipped. On the other hand, he'd always abjured the notion of living less than fully and the only way to do that was to take chances. Of course, when you took chances, sometimes you lost.

But it was no time to become faint of heart, not with the world virtually at his feet. "You know," he said to his son, "maybe you and I ought to take a trip to Hong Kong sooner rather than later."

"To pick up some money?"

"In part, but mostly to shore things up with Jimmy Yee."

"He getting wobbly?"

"No, but if you leave a buyer alone too long, he might find something else to get excited about. I had a call from him last week and he asked how things were progressing. I said everything was fantastic." He looked over at Patrick. "Did I lie?"

"No, everything's on course. Mostly things hinge on the experimental field, which is still a few months away. The proof is in the pudding, as they say."

"You mean there's a chance we could get weeds instead of super corn?"

"No, but sometimes nature can throw you a curve. Look what happened to Calgene and their Flavr Savr tomato that was genetically engineered to slow-ripe. Crop yields were disappointing and the damned things were so fragile that they got mashed in the packing and shipping process. The company almost went under and finally sold out to Monsanto. Point is they didn't conquer the world."

"Patrick, is that calculated to give me a lift on the day I buried my wife?"

"No, sorry. It's not my intent to be negative. All I'm saying is that nothing is a sure thing because Mother Nature is both clever and stubborn."

"I'm glad you didn't say, 'God is both clever and stubborn,' because I may be in His doghouse right now."

Patrick laughed. "I can cite examples where genetic engineering has worked to perfection, if that would make you feel better."

"I'll take your word for it."

They came around Hospital Curve and the skyline of San Francisco loomed ahead, the tall buildings bathed in sunlight. Jonas wondered if it was really that important for a guy to be able to look at a sight like that, pick out a sparkling gem rising toward the heavens—the Transamerica Pyramid, for example— and be able to say, "That baby's mine." He'd have to ask Jimmy Yee about it the next time he saw him.

"So, you want to go to Hong Kong," Patrick said, his mind having gone back a few steps.

"Yeah. It doesn't have to be tomorrow, of course, but I figure it wouldn't hurt if you give some thought to a presentation to wow Jimmy. Something calculated to loosen the purse strings, technical enough to be persuasive, but still intelligible for a generalist."

"I'll get started on it."

Patrick had left his car in a Financial District parking garage. He was meeting his mother for a late lunch. The plan was for Jonas to drop him off at her office. As they left the freeway, Jonas's thoughts shifted to Tess as they had on several occasions over the past few weeks. The dead of night—while all the world slept, except for him and guys working the graveyard shift—seemed to be the most common time for her to put in an appearance. He'd wondered about that, thinking it bizarre that he should become fascinated with a woman he'd been married to nearly thirty years before.

He ventured a question about her, keeping his tone offhand. "How's your mom doing, anyway?"

"She's been distracted. Not her usual self at Christmas. And she hasn't seemed to have gotten over it, whatever is bugging her."

"She's got a lot on her plate, sport—career girl, a son besieged by eco-terrorists, an impending marriage."

"I've tried to put her mind at ease regarding my safety," Patrick said. "I think she's finally calmed down about that."

Based on prior conversations, Jonas was already aware the police hadn't been able to identify specific suspects in the firebombing. The pool of people they were looking at was large and the situation was complicated by the fact that the perpetrators weren't necessarily from the university community.

"Have Tess and the old guy set a date?" Jonas asked.

Patrick was amused by the question, being aware of his father's less-than-enthusiastic ("disapproving" was too strong a term) reaction to Tess's choice of husband. "Nothing official as far as I know, but they're thinking late spring or summer, I believe."

"Tell me, Patrick, does Walter know how lucky he is?"

"I think so. He's always adored Mom, even when they were just friends."

"That I understand. It's the other way around I have trouble with. One of the fringe benefits of having money is being irresistible, I guess."

"Not to get personal or anything, but did money figure into *your* relationships?"

"Were my wives and girlfriends after my considerable fortune, you mean?" Jonas said with a laugh.

"Well, you obviously had something that would make six different women want to take the plunge with you."

"Six, hell, it could have been thirty just as easily."

"So, what's your secret?"

"You want to know the truth? Optimism. Women groove on it. A little technique between the sheets doesn't hurt, either," he added with a wink.

They were on Montgomery Street now, nearing Tess's building. Jonas pulled the Mercedes up to the curb.

Clasping Patrick's arm, he said, "Thanks for holding my hand today. It meant a lot that you were there for me."

"Sure. Glad to do it." Patrick opened the passenger door to get out.

"Say hi to your mom for me."

"I will."

"What happened to us was *the* major regret of my life, you know."

Patrick, one foot out the door, paused. "She know that?"

"I tried to get the point across back when, but she didn't believe me. Or didn't want to hear it. One or the other."

Patrick digested the remark, thinking God knew what. Jonas was as sorry as he'd ever been in his life.

"Take it easy, son. And have some fun now and then. It's good for the soul."

To get to the Golden Gate Jonas had to drive across town to Van Ness Avenue, then north to Lombard Street, Richardson Avenue and Doyle Drive. But while he was negotiating the downtown traffic, contemplating how he'd deal with Crystal, he started fulminating again over Melanie and her damned detectives. Too bad Chuck Haggerty hadn't strangled that little blond spitfire, or at least cowed her into submission. It would have been nice to get a jump on Melanie. Of course, Jonas still didn't know for sure that either the blonde or Steve Williams were in Melanie's employ, though it certainly looked that way from where he sat.

Which reminded him that he hadn't heard back from Haggerty, though over the past week he'd left three or four messages on his machine. Right after the first of the month Haggerty had phoned him with a preliminary report. "I've talked to the licensing authority," he'd said, "and I may have turned up a possible Daphne out of L.A. If I get a chance, I may go down there and check it out."

That was the last Jonas had heard. When he didn't get a return call, he thought maybe Haggerty was in Southern California, but a week was on the long side to be gone. Since he'd be within a couple of blocks of Haggerty's office, Jonas decided to swing by on the off chance he'd find the P.I. at his desk.

Lady luck smiled when a parking place opened up only a few doors down from City Investigative Services. Jonas had just maneuvered the Mercedes into the spot when who should come waltzing up the street but the little blonde who'd flattened Haggerty in the parking garage. Daphne, or whatever her name was, didn't notice him as she'd walked past wearing jeans and a leather jacket. An even bigger surprise came when she turned and entered Haggerty's building.

What the hell was going on? Did she want another piece of the guy?

Jonas wasn't sure what to do. Rush to Haggerty's aid? The two of them ought to be a match for the girl. If nothing else, he'd sure like to know what she was up to.

Entering Haggerty's office a minute later, he found the two of them sitting on opposite sides of the gumshoe's desk, each with a steaming cup of coffee in front of them. They showed equal surprise at the sight of him.

"Well," Jonas said, "did my invitation get lost in the mail or am I being snubbed?"

Haggerty looked embarrassed. Not a good sign.

The woman slowly got to her feet. "I'll leave you to deal with this, Chuck." Then, not so much as giving Jonas a glance, she pushed past him and went through the outer office and out the door.

Jonas turned his attention to Haggerty. "So, the lady's gone from ball-breaker to best buddy. What gives, *Chuck?* Or, would you rather have your attorney present before you answer that?"

"I've been intending to give you a call."

"I think Benedict Arnold said the same thing to George Washington."

"Look, I did what you hired me to do," Haggerty said, showing annoyance. "This is something different."

"Yeah, fraternizing with the enemy isn't quite the same thing as fighting them, I grant you that. How about we skip the semantics and get right to the bottom line. What the fuck is going on?"

"That was Daphne Miles. She and Steve Williams were working together. Actually, she hired him to follow you to Hong Kong."

"Who's Daphne working for?"

"I'm not at liberty to say."

"The hell you aren't, Haggerty. You've got an obligation to me, one that you've breached in violation of some goddamn rule. Don't ask me which, but I know it exists. If the state isn't interested in your lack of fidelity, I know my lawyer will be. So cut the crap and answer the question."

Haggerty stood. "Look, Mr. Lamb, your interests haven't been compromised. I didn't know anything about you that would be helpful to them. They just wanted me off the case, that's all."

"All you had to do was ask, Chuck, and I'd have canned your ass." Jonas tried to think what he'd told the guy. He was sure he'd never mentioned Crystal by name. Even so, he was going to do what he could to protect himself. "You might think that's all there is to it," he said to Haggerty, "but I don't. To walk away from this, I want three things. First, I want my money back. Second, I want to know who you and Daphne are working for, and third I want to know what, if anything, Steve Williams reported back. If you don't give me satisfaction, I'll have your balls...what's left of them, that is."

Haggerty flushed with anger. "All right," he said, pulling a check ledger from a drawer and opening it. "Daphne works for your stepdaughter, Ms. de Givry."

Jonas was not surprised, but it was always good to know you were paranoid for a damned good reason. "What about Williams?"

"I honestly don't know what he might have said because they didn't tell me. But, for what it's worth, they wanted to know what you told me."

"And you said?"

"I told them I wasn't at liberty to say."

"Chucky, if you think I'm going to believe that, I've got a big bridge a few miles from here I'd like to sell you at a very reasonable price."

Haggerty grimaced, but not having much in the way of bargaining power, quickly gave in. "All right, let me finish writing this check." A few more moments and he tore the check out, then closed the folder. "I told them that Williams broke into your hotel room while he was in Hong Kong posing as me. I said you didn't know who he was working for and that you'd hired me to find out. That's all you told me, so that's all I could say."

Jonas considered that, figuring it was plausible, though uncertain because of his faulty memory. Thank God it was his mind going, not his sex drive. He tried to reason things out. Melanie was so emotional at the grave site that it seemed to him she'd blurted out exactly what she was thinking. In all probability she had circumstantial evidence against him, but no smoking gun. If her case was iron-clad, she'd have been making different sounds. The trouble was, he couldn't be sure.

"What about the FBI?" Jonas said. "What's their role in this?"

"The FBI? I didn't know they were involved."

"According to your new employer they are."

"It's the first I heard about it."

Jonas studied him, realizing there was no way to know if he was lying or not. "Okay, fine, Haggerty," he said. "But if you're fucking with me, I'll show no mercy."

"I've told you everything, Mr. Lamb."

Picking up the check, the P.I. extended it toward him. Jonas took it, studying it for a moment or two. Then he put it back down on the desk.

"Tell you what, Chuck. Why don't you keep this?"

"Huh?"

"All I ask in return is that you get on the horn

every once in a while and keep me informed what's going on over on this side of the Maginot Line. That shouldn't be too tough for a man of your character and experience."

Haggerty shook his head. "No, I've already flip-flopped enough in this deal."

"What's the difference between double-crossing Melanie and double-crossing me?"

"I dunno," Haggerty said, shaking his head. "Four thousand bucks, I guess."

"She gave you *five* grand?"

The other nodded.

Jonas snatched up the check. "Whore," he said, and headed for the door.

Paris

It was late by the time the taxi came to a stop in front of the eighteenth-century town house situated just off the avenue Bosquet in the Seventh Arrondissement. Carly Van Hooten looked up at the venerable old house. It always appeared a party was in full swing. Gaston entertained a lot, and when he didn't have friends in, he kept the house lit up like a Christmas tree, with music filling the air. And, of course, there were always his companion and his cats to keep him company.

Gaston was thirty-seven years old and estranged from his father, Julien, Comte de Malbouzon, who resided at the family's ancestral country estate in Angoumois, outside the town of Barbezieux-St. Hilaire (Charente). Part of the old man's "arrangement" with his son was that Gaston got the pied-à-terre in Paris, provided he kept his "troublemaking" to a minimum. Julien didn't give a lick about his son's business and political activities. It was Gaston's social *bêtises* that concerned him.

Carly had known the younger *comte* for five years, but Gaston never ceased to amaze her. She had no idea if he was typical of the French nobility, but she doubted it. Surely, even with all the inbreeding, the French couldn't produce that many eccentrics. There was no question, though, that Gaston eschewed his own kind, having said as much. "Stuffy, pompous, arrogant nitwits, who can't wank without the assistance of a servant" was the way he'd put it.

Carly paid the driver, got out and went up the stairs. She knocked on the solid oak door that had replaced its more flimsy antecedent that, according to legend and Gaston, had been knocked down by an angry mob during the Reign of Terror, sending Jean-Patrice, Comte de Malbouzon, the title-holder at the time—and the great-great-great-great-grandfather of Gaston—scurrying out the back door, dressed as a scullery maid. (It was either that or be carted off to the Bastille to be, in due course, separated from his head.)

Moments after she knocked, the heavy door swung open and Charles, Gaston's lover from the Ivory Coast, shirtless as always and wearing a headset, his rail-thin body swaying to the rhythms of unheard music— probably calypso, which he adored—grinned sweetly and said, *"Carly, c'est toi! Viens. Entrez. Je t'en pris."*

Charles, his skin as black and smooth as polished

ebony, took off the headset long enough to buss her on each cheek, though his body never stopped undulating to the music. He replaced the apparatus then, grinning at her in a manner that was both sweet and exuberant, chirped in English, "How are you, anyway?"

"Fine, Charles, how are you?"

He grinned again and nodded, obviously not having heard a word. Closing the door, he said, "Gaston is having his bath. I'll tell him you're here." He danced his way back toward the large spiral staircase at the rear of the entry, curling a finger over a shoulder as if to say "Follow me." He stopped at the base of the stairs and, indicating the sitting room, said, "Make yourself at home. I'll get you something to drink in a minute. And maybe something to eat. Are you hungry, love?" He started up the stairs without waiting for a reply, bumping and rocking. "By the way, there's cocaine in the gold box on the coffee table, if you're so inclined."

Actually she was hungry. She'd hoped to grab a bite on the way, but was running late and didn't have a chance, though she did buy a chocolate bar at a kiosk near the Métro.

Carly unzipped her coat as the room had to be at least eighty degrees (Gaston and Charles preferred a tropical environment). She tossed the coat on a footstool and sat in a Louis XVI armchair, having first chased off one of the half dozen Persian cats (all named "Poof" and all declawed for the sake of posterity) that occupied the premises along with Gaston and Charles.

The music on the house sound system was classical. A string quartet. She listened. Either Hayden or Mozart, she wasn't sure which. (She'd once done a little job for Gaston involving a cultured man who was into the performing arts. In preparation for the liaison, Gaston had given her a crash course in classical music, some of his insights having stuck.)

The sitting room was decorated in antiques and fine reproductions from the era of Gaston's ancestor, Jean-Patrice, the aforementioned forebear to whose guile all the subsequent *comtes* owed their very existence. The house had been occupied continuously by de Malbouzons for more than two hundred years, except for the period between the revolution and the restoration when it served first as a soup kitchen and later as officer's quarters for Napoleon's Imperial Guard.

Carly had met Gaston through her lover, Antoine Laurent, who'd been a longtime friend of the *comte*. Antoine and Gaston's friendship was ironic considering Gaston was of noble birth and gay, whereas Antoine was the son of a petty criminal and a high-wire artist of Gypsy blood, and anything but gay. Teenagers at the time (though Gaston was a few years older), they'd met in jail, of all places—Antoine had stolen a car that he took for a joyride; Gaston was charged with indecent exposure for strolling unclothed through a country fair, high on cannabis. The *comte*, his father, managed to get the more serious charges dropped and, at Gaston's insistence, sprung Antoine from the slammer at the same time.

Entertainment value aside, Carly treasured Gaston neither for his excesses nor his eccentricities, but rather for the fact that he was her principal source of employment. The man was a genius, a true Renaissance man. Though he'd never gotten his degree from MIT, where he'd pursued "higher education and lower morals," he was knowledgeable of everything from Greek philosophy and modern art to cybernetics, systems theory and quantum physics.

The *comte* was so fiercely independent that he was willing to play both sides of the street ("morality being relative"). Though he'd done consulting work for both the French national police investigative services and Interpol, he was thoroughly corruptible, having an affinity for intrigue, crime and decadence. He professed to be "philosophically Buddhist, but nonpracticing." Gaston was, in essence, a crime boss.

"So, Carly," Charles said as he entered the room, his headphones now around his neck, "what can I get you?"

"Water would be nice. And something to munch on. Nuts or something."

"Vittel?"

"Fine."

Charles went off to the kitchen, returning after a few minutes with a bottle of Vittel, a Baccarat tumbler, a plate of hors d'oeuvres and a huge bowl of cashews. "So how's Anook?"

"She's fine."

"I adore that woman's hair. I'd give my soul for it," he effused. Charles, like Gaston, spoke flawless English, though with something of a British accent, having spent several years in London where he'd worked as a musician before being deported after a drug arrest.

Carly, perspiring from the heat, poured some water and took a few sips. "So, how are things here?" she asked, quickly downing a couple of canapés. Her question was not vacuous. Developments in the household were, if nothing, unpredictable.

Charles laid a finger aside his cheek. "Let me see...oh, of course! Birthday pictures!" He ran from the room, only to return a few moments later with a large silk brocade photo album. Setting it on her lap, he opened it. "The little *comte* had his fourth birthday last month and they sent pictures. Isn't he just adorable?"

Carly, her hand moving between the cashew bowl and her mouth, glanced at the photos of the little Comte Patrice de Malbouzon in his pageboy and silk sweat suit with "Vive le Roi" embroidered across the chest.

"Ah, Carly, *ma chérie*, how are you?" It was Gaston in a silk-and-satin dressing gown, and apparently nothing else. He was barefoot, his dark wet hair pulled back in a stubby ponytail, his hairy barrel chest framed by the shiny satin lapels of the robe. He carried one of the Poofs under his arm. "So good of you to come, *mon angelet*."

"Hi, Gaston."

Carly stood as he made his way to her and they brushed cheeks three times, Gaston pursing his lips and kissing the air with each pass. He bent over and deposited the cat on the huge Oriental carpet that dominated the room, then drew himself up and peered into Carly's eyes.

"I still see the pain, my love. And you must see it in mine, as well." He brushed away the tear that hadn't quite formed. "Life will never be the same without him. You know, of course, he was the love of both our lives. *Sans aucun doute.*"

The gloppy sentimentality was the side of Gaston that Carly least admired. But, over the top or not, it was sincere. Carly knew how much Gaston had loved Antoine. It was a love they both shared and, in a way, what bound them together now. His death had left a huge void, which was all the more conspicuous when Carly and Gaston were together. That probably explained why they hadn't seen a lot of each other these past difficult months.

"Yes," she said to Gaston, "I know."

He glanced down at the album. "*Tiens,* I see Charles has already shared with you the most recent joys of the fruit of my loins, preserved for our unborn descendants in living color."

Somehow even the most crude comments sounded just fine in a French accent. "Yes, he's adorable, Gaston."

He took her by the arm and drew her to a love seat, taking the album from her and opening it on his lap. "We've edited out Papa Julien," he said, pointing to a creatively snipped photo. "The bastard. But there are some precious shots, nonetheless."

Together, they studied the Kodak moments *à la francaise.*

"He's adorable," Carly said.

"Impregnating his mother was one of the most gratifying coups of my life, though not for the usual reasons, as you well know."

Carly had heard Gaston recount the family saga on more than one occasion and knew the story well. Sometime in the fourteenth or fifteenth centuries a gentleman soldier by the name of Guy Malbouzon was ennobled by royal grant and given lands entailed to his male descendants. To preserve the family fief, Gaston's father, Julien, like all the de Malbouzons before him, had dutifully produced a son. Unfortunately soon after impregnating his wife, Julien promptly became sterile, which meant when Gaston's preference for boys became clear, the family faced a crisis—*pas de seigneur sans terre, pas de terre sans seigneur,* which, loosely translated, meant no land without a lord and no lord without land. Upon Gaston's death, everything would be lost.

Julien was not only eager to have his name and bloodline endure, but, being a monarchist and an enemy of the Republic, he considered it his noble duty to ensure France's nobility would live on in perpetuity, not an easy task, considering the road to perpetuity went through Gaston. Julien's solution was to offer Gaston the house in Paris and a comfortable income if he would take a wife who would bear a son. Julien agreed to raise the child and support the wife, which meant that Gaston's only obligation was to go through the civil process (a ten-minute ceremony at city hall) and provide the fertility clinic with the necessary DNA.

Julien cleverly chose his mistress, Clotilde de Neeser, "Cleo" for short, as the vessel of de Malbouzon posterity. (Vivienne, Julien's wife and Gaston's mother, had perished in a train wreck in Greece many years earlier.) Cleo, a comely young woman with child-bearing hips and remote family connections to the Duke of Orléans, was, apart from her regard for Julien, impelled to enter into the arrangement because of her family's indigence and her own paucity of employment skills. It was an arrangement made in heaven or, as Gaston liked to say, "out of need, greed and my old monarchist fart of a father's stupidity." He couldn't sign the contract quick enough.

Though it wasn't a condition of the deal, Gaston, with Charles in tow, made an annual pilgrimage to the family château to see the boy. Cleo, who was something of a traditionalist in the mold of her father-in-law/lover, felt enough of a wifely obligation to send Gaston the annual birthday photos. Now happily installed as head of the Parisian branch of the family, Gaston was wont to say, "Never has the act of masturbation been so rewarding and guiltless."

"*Bien,*" he said, closing the album, "another year in the books, so to speak." He turned to her. "Now down to business. As you are aware, *chérie*, I wish to enlist your services. A very big job has come up, and quite frankly, I need your assistance."

"What sort of job is it, Gaston?" she asked.

"Your part of it would be a seduction, but it's a complex mission, requiring multiple talents. Before it's over the chap will be killed and others as well." He looked deeply into her eyes, searching, she knew, for steel. One needed a taste for this work to do it successfully.

In a way Carly was disappointed it was a seduction. Not that she wasn't up to seducing a man. That she could do without effort. It was best, though, to fall naturally into the spirit of things, and she was more in the mood for something adventurous and dangerous, anything to shake her from her lethargy.

"I detect doubt," Gaston said.

"I was hoping for something I could do with my clothes on."

"It's too soon? *Est-ce que c'est ça?*"

"No, it's not that."

Gaston took her hand. "What is it, then, *chérie?*"

"I'm in the doldrums," she said, "and I guess I feel the need for something exciting to get me going again. A seduction seems like more of the same."

"One goes where their talents take them, Carly. But be warned, this job is anything but routine."

"Tell me about it."

"For starters your cut will be a million."

Her brows rose. "Who am I to seduce? The president of France?"

Gaston smiled. "Lovely thought, that."

"Well?"

"An American gentleman, one residing in America."

"Oh."

Carly had never worked in her own country before. Not doing this. It had been an unwritten rule. She liked Europeans, preferably the French. She had a love-hate thing about their arrogance. The quality appealed to her at one level, but she also liked giving them their comeuppance. How often she wished she could see her mark's face when he awoke and found her gone, along with the jewels, the bonds, the incriminating evidence, the trade secret, the classified documents or whatever.

"Is it a problem?" Gaston asked.

"You know I don't want to do this work back home."

"Let's talk about that."

"It's nothing very mysterious. Here it's playacting, it's Disneyland. There it would be more like sleazy crime."

"A million, Carly."

She ate another canapé, some nuts, then sipped some water from the Baccarat tumbler. "Okay, tell me more."

"Our mark, it seems, is intent on changing the world and our job is to stop him."

"Change the world?"

"He's got technology that will potentially reduce the demand for fossil fuels by a thousand percent. We need to get our hands on the technology and everybody who knows about it."

"I'm beginning to understand the million," Carly said, warming to the notion. "Where in the States?"

"California. San Francisco. The gentleman is in his fifties, but a rake. I suspect a rather charming chap, though my information is sketchy. The situation is complicated. This will test you, Carly. I promise you that."

Gaston was a master at selling a job. But it wasn't his words that were convincing. It was the money. If she was being offered a million, the operation had to involve many millions more. Perhaps tens of millions. The prospect had gotten her engine going.

Gaston observed her. "Is that color in your cheeks an encouraging sign, my dear, or is it the temperature?"

She fanned herself. "It is warm, but I admit you've piqued my curiosity. Who's our employer?"

"That's the interesting part."

"Oh?"

One of Gaston's diabolical grins creased his face. "Why don't we withdraw to the war room and discuss this further?"

Setting the photo album aside, Gaston snatched a passing Poof from the floor and ambled toward the entry hall. Carly followed. They went up the grand spiral staircase, passing another Poof on her way down. At the top of the stairs they entered the master suite through a set of double doors. Gaston had remodeled the upstairs, knocking out walls and completely modernizing the place (a sacrilege in some quarters). His explanation—"Anything good enough for Napoleon's officers couldn't possibly be good enough for me."

After dropping Poof on the unmade bed, Gaston led the way into the master bath, making a hard right turn into the huge walk-in closet—"large enough to accommodate a couple of lieutenant colonels and maybe their horses"—where he pushed a button hidden under a shelf. The back wall of the closet began to pivot, revealing a tiny chamber with a tight wrought-iron staircase. They went up the dimly lit shaft, which was deliciously cool compared to the rest of the house, until they reached an upper floor. Under the mansard roof, lit during the day by two small dormer windows and a skylight—now black with the night—was Comte Gaston de Malbouzon's war room, a showplace of the latest technology available anywhere on the globe. He'd once told Carly he had the megs and the horsepower to run the U.S. government, if they'd let him, "though probably not the French government...not without first killing a hundred thousand bureaucrats and emptying their files."

Gaston went to a twenty-four-inch flat computer screen on one wall, pulled up a chair for Carly, then sat in the Aeron chair he'd brought back with him from New York on the Concorde. Pushing a button, he brought the screen to life, tapped a few more keys, hunt-and-peck style. After a couple of moments the picture of a mature, nice-looking man appeared on the screen, though the photography wasn't the best.

"That our boy?"

"Yes," Gaston replied. "Monsieur Jonas Lamb of Kentfield, California, a suburb of San Francisco, photo courtesy of the Department of Motor Vehicles, Sacramento. I thought you'd like a preview."

"You hacked their computer system?"

"A dear friend of mine in the Ukraine did the honors. I prefer to avoid detection wherever possible.

My hacking days are at the essential minimum, *chérie*. It's mostly surrogates now." Gaston pushed his chair back from the table and swivelled to face her. "Three days ago I was hired for a job by an American industrial-security guy representing some U.S. corporate interests. The job was to investigate Jonas Lamb and his company, Global Energy Technologies, Inc. The chap did not disclose who his employers were, but naturally I determined that it was a sub-rosa consortium of oil company CEOs. My assignment was to liberate Mr. Lamb's technology. I was offered a substantial sum for my services.

"Then yesterday I got a call from Alfred Le Genissel. You remember Alfred."

Carly nodded, unable to repress a shiver. She'd never liked Le Genissel, mainly because she didn't trust him. There was also something kinky, maybe sick, about him.

"Yes," Gaston said, reading her thoughts. "I feel the same. Anyway, Alfred asked for a clandestine meeting in the Jardin du Luxembourg early this morning. We met and Le Genissel offered to hire me to debrief Mr. Jonas Lamb."

Carly's mouth opened. "The same guy?"

"Yes."

"Did he know the oil companies had already hired you?"

Gaston flicked his eyebrows a couple of times. "No, that's the beauty of it, Carly. Neither knows about the other. I've got two prospective employers unwittingly hiring me to perform the same task, though the oil companies did not ask for Lamb's head on a pike. You Americans are a touch more civilized. But only a touch. If they decide Lamb has to go, I suspect they'll hire a hit man at the appropriate time—off the books, of course. Our work for them is exclusively intelligence gathering."

"Who does Le Genissel represent?"

"The Saudis and their Arab cousins, of course. OPEC light."

"So the oil producers and the oil companies both want Lamb and they've both hired you for the job, neither knowing about the other."

"Remarkable, eh? Never has happened to me before."

"You aren't going to do it, are you? Work for both of them at the same time, I mean."

"Why ever not, *alors?* They're allies, more or less...I wouldn't be working at cross purposes, I'd simply be collecting two paychecks for a single job."

"Gaston, you're unscrupulous."

"What do scruples have to do with it? I don't see it as an ethical issue. I see it as a challenge. And bloody good fun!"

Carly hated to admit it, but Gaston's scheme was growing more appealing by the moment. It would be like seducing a man at the behest of his wife *and* his mistress.

"There are a few wrinkles," the *comte* added. "Le Genissel made your participation a condition of the job. He'd also like to meet with you before we get started."

Carly felt her spirits dwindle.

"I know how you feel, but the fee he's offering is considerable. We've got to keep him happy."

"Does my cut reflect the double fee?"

Without hesitation Gaston said, "Perhaps it could be adjusted upward a bit. Shall we say a million and a half?"

To Carly it didn't make a whole lot of difference as long as she was well paid. She could rely on Gaston to be fair, and squeezing out a few more dollars would do more harm than good. But Alfred Le Genissel was another matter altogether. He was the principal downside to the mission.

"Maybe I should talk to Le Genissel before giving a firm commitment," she said. "If he wants to interject a deal-breaker, we might as well know going in."

"Naturally he'd like to fuck you, Carly. There isn't a straight man in the world who wouldn't. But I don't think he'll press you. He lives to kill, not fuck. He's the predator in the food chain."

"I don't like your food chain analogy, Gaston. Where does it leave me?"

"In my care, of course. And, as you know, I'm God."

"Still, I think I need to talk to Alfred," she said.

"I agree. Shall I arrange a meeting?"

"Yes, if you would. Assuming everything goes through, what's our time frame?"

"I figure a week of intense research at most, then we head for California. You'll need a shtick, but that's more your department than mine. If whatever you choose has technical content, I'll have to school you." He grinned. "Ever have the urge to become a wiz at genetic engineering, my love?"

"In a week?"

"If I had a month, I could make you Albert Einstein."

"Let me work on a strategy," she said.

"I'll call you in the morning after I talk to Alfred."

"Okay." She got up and Gaston did, as well. Having decided to end things with Anook, she had lots of personal business to take care of, and little time. "I'm going to run along, then," she said.

"Want me to call you a taxi?"

"No, I think I'll walk for a while, then catch a cab. I need the air."

They retraced their steps down to the foyer where Gaston helped Carly on with her coat. As she turned to leave he said, "I've selected your code name for the operation, by the way. Little Bo Peep. Clever, eh?"

She smiled. "But she lost her sheep, Gaston."

"Ah, in the end they came home, though, *n'est-ce pas?*"

Sausalito, California

If Jonas had his druthers, he'd have gone directly back to Kentfield. This was not a day to be playing Philip Marlowe. It was a day for sober reflection, but he didn't have the luxury of grieving. He had to find out whether or not his erstwhile lover had gone over to the enemy like Chuck Haggerty. A million bucks, minimum, could be riding on it, and if Operation Black Sheep worked out, it could be a whole lot more.

There was no reason why Melanie would have

waited until today to dispatch her minions to suborn Crystal, but Jonas needed to satisfy himself that she was still on the team. This visit also had the corollary benefit of providing him with a plausible excuse for contacting her. Who could say? Maybe all they needed was a little impetus to rediscover the wonders of togetherness. God knew he could use some affection. It had been a rough couple of weeks.

Unfortunately, he found himself in the teeth of the rush hour, first creeping over the bridge, then up the hill to Rainbow Tunnel. And, of course, his eagerness to see Crystal made it all the worse.

Jonas originally thought he might catch her at her shop, but at the rate he was going she'd have already gone home. He dug out his cell phone to let her know he would be dropping by, but the damned battery was dead. Then the traffic came to a complete halt. Shit.

The longer he sat parked on the freeway, the more anxious he became. Melanie was a formidable opponent. She'd bribed Chuck Haggerty. What would keep her from doing the same with Crystal?

But even if Crystal remained devoted to him, Melanie could always subpoena her at trial. Unlike some women he'd known, Crystal had principles. He didn't think she'd lie for him. No, his best bet was to gain her allegiance now, before Melanie got to her.

But how?

Then it hit him. The "M" word.

Actually, the notion wasn't as far-fetched as it might seem. He liked Crystal. They always had a good time, and not just in bed. He'd married for less compelling reasons. Hell, on at least one occasion, he'd taken the plunge with little more to go on than a hormonal litmus test. If financial security was reason enough to take wife number six, wouldn't preserving that hard-won security be reason enough to take Crystal as wife number seven?

Jonas knew he was engaged in a mental diarrhea of the sort commonly afflicting commuters. Marrying Crystal was just one of those silly ideas that came with free-form brainstorming. And, though he'd lost his marital virginity long ago, Jonas knew that if he were to retain a shred of respectability, he had to become more conservative henceforth. No, he wouldn't actually marry. Not unless his situation grew really, really, *really* desperate.

At long interminable last, Jonas reached the marina. The houseboats—some of which (though not his) cost more than a fifteen-room mansion in places like, say, Omaha or Muncie—were tied up on a grid of finger docks, floating on the brackish water of Richardson Bay, a sort of aquatic Levittown for the peacock-feather set.

Over the course of the last twenty minutes or so a cloud had pushed its way over the mountain, subjecting Marin to a slow drizzle. Darkness had set in. The marina was aglow with lights and muted music could be heard, giving the place the air of a floating Gypsy camp.

Jonas had an ominous feeling. Melanie's loathsome countenance hung over him like the perfume of a polecat on a breathless night. He was afraid Crystal would tell him he was too late, that the cat was already out of the bag.

Jonas moved quickly along the dock, perspiration on his lip and brow despite the coolness of the air. When he reached his little houseboat, appropriately named *Lamb's Croft,* with its tiny deck just big enough for a pair of patio chairs and a few potted plants, he saw the warm glow of lights inside and heard the sound of the country-and-western music Crystal favored.

Crossing the boarding plank onto the deck, he was brought up short by the sound of a man's voice coming from inside. And worse—Crystal's giddy laughter. *Shit,* he thought. *What now?*

Friend, neighbor, brother (Crystal had two), father (one) boyfriend (God knows), appliance repair man, detective, cop—the possibilities reeled through his mind. It was no time, he concluded, to be faint of heart. So he stepped over to the door, under the second-floor overhang where he was protected from the rain, and knocked.

"Finally," he heard Crystal say from inside.

Through the gauze of the curtains he saw a figure move toward the door. It opened. Crystal in a scoop-neck, satiny chartreuse dress that screamed "serious date," her red hair swept back in a careful chignon, looked out at him, her expression going from expectation, to surprise, to dismay in a sort of domino progression that ended with a glare.

"Jonas!" she hissed. "What are you doing here?"

This was the woman to whom (if need be) he was prepared to become betrothed? This was the woman with whom he was willing (if circumstances warranted) to enter into holy matrimony? This was the woman he was actually considering making the seventh Mrs. Jonas Lamb?

No, this was an insult, that's what it was!

Jonas set his jaw as he tried to see past her at what was going on inside. "I need to talk to you, Crystal."

She half glanced over her shoulder. "This is not a good time."

He couldn't help being a prick. "Why not, pray tell?"

She stepped onto the deck, half closing the door behind her. "Because it's not!"

He realized antagonizing her would do no good. He mentally shifted to a more constructive frame of mind. "I tried calling, but my cell phone is dead. It's important that I talk to you and it won't take long."

"I said this isn't a good time." Her tone was very insistent.

Jonas could hear Garth Brooks inside, but not the mystery guest. He searched for a strategy. Pique was all that came to him. "Christ, Crystal," he blurted, "what's it been, three weeks? And I've already been replaced? It's not like I was out playing golf. Elise was dying. I had things on my mind, responsibilities."

"Jonas," she said, lowering her voice, "we ended it, remember? A month ago. Anyway, wasn't your wife's funeral today?"

"Yeah."

"Well, what are you doing here, for crissakes? Isn't

that kind of disrespectful? I mean, I know I'm not exactly Miss Goody Two-shoes, but Jesus…"

"Look," he said, recovering, "you don't understand. I'm here on business. Important business."

"You are?" She looked disappointed. Even crushed.

That threw him for a loop. Could it be that her pique was just posturing? Maybe underneath the show of anger she was thrilled to see him. "Crystal, what did you think?"

"Nothing," she said, her lips tightening. She gave her head that little shake that was meant to inform that "nothing" really meant "everything God considered holy."

"Crystal, *what?* Don't play games with me."

"Forget it, Jonas!" she snapped.

"No, I won't forget it. Tell me!"

"Okay, it's my goddamn birthday! Satisfied?"

In two seconds he went from Mr. Hard-ass to a puddle of piss on the floor. And Crystal went from the prospective Mrs. Jonas Lamb VII to just another woman wronged. *Christ, he'd forgotten her goddamn birthday!*

"Jesus, Crystal," he said, his voice tremulous with regret, "I'm sorry. I truly am."

She seemed to revel in the affront.

"Actually, I didn't so much forget as I was preoccupied," he explained. "I thought of it a few days ago, then with Elise and all…"

"Forget it. It's not important. It doesn't matter."

He gave her his most sincere look of remorse, taking her hands. "Happy birthday, sweetheart."

"Thanks." A touch embarrassed, she extricated her hands from his, indicating she'd wanted her due and, having gotten it, they were now free to resume hostilities. This seemed to suggest that there were good reasons and bad reasons for him to show up at her door, and as far as she was concerned, he'd blown it.

"I do have something very urgent to discuss with you," he said with all the contrition he could muster.

Crystal rolled her eyes. "Why does everything have to go wrong at the same time?"

"What do you mean?"

"The goddamn baby-sitter hasn't showed! I think the little bitch stood me up. And I've got a date!"

"Oh," he said with mock surprise, "so that's what this is about." He indicated her attire. "Somebody's taking you out for your birthday."

She gave him a dirty look. Then she brightened. "Wait a minute. I've got an idea. Jonas, are you busy tonight? Are you doing anything?"

"You mean besides wishing you happy birthday and grieving for my dead wife?"

"Yeah."

"No. Why?"

To his surprise, she grabbed him by the arm and pulled him through the door. Seated in the big easy chair, where Jonas normally liked to watch TV and have sex with Crystal, was a big jocular-looking fellow of thirty-six or eight. He was holding pajama-clad Tamara, bouncing her on his knee, their mutual glee abating when he saw Jonas. The guy, whom Crystal promptly introduced as Bob, wore a dark, ill-fitting suit and white tie with cute red hearts on it. His haircut, only hours old, had the look of assembly line precision. His shoes were spit-polished, military-style. In short, Jonas was seeing the guy in his Big and Tall, Sunday best. And he'd have bet the family farm Bob was a craftsman.

Being a quick study, not to mention a man of keen observation, Jonas took in the scene. A box of chocolates on the table, a vase with a dozen red roses, a matching blush of red on Bob's cheeks—it was obvious. True love. Birthday love. Jonas could only marvel. Three lousy weeks and the big guy had slipped in under the radar, undetected. It was all because of that goddamn fortune-teller in Hong Kong.

"Bob," Crystal chirped, "this is my uncle Jonas."

Jonas about choked.

"He came by to wish me happy birthday and he's agreed to stay with Tamara until Cindy arrives," she went on. "That way we can keep our dinner reservation. Isn't that nice?" Then she looked at Jonas, her eyes hardening. "You owe me," she said under her breath.

Jonas did his best to ignore the fact he was surely as red as Bob, though for a very different reason, of course. *Uncle* Jonas?

Bob had put Tamara down, lifted his large frame from Jonas's TV-and-sex chair and ambled over to greet him, a big arm extending toward him like the boom on a backhoe. Pipe-fitter, stevedore, ironworker, it hardly mattered what. Odds were the guy drove a brand-new four door, four-wheel drive, forty-thousand-dollar Ford pickup and was taking in four grand every two weeks. All that was missing was a tattoo on his forehead that said, "Craftsman."

Grinning, Bob said, "Nice to meet you, sir."

Jonas refused to wince as the guy's paw clamped down on his, smiling as the amiable oaf shook not only his hand, but his arm, his shoulder and his torso. "Same here," he said through his rattling teeth.

"I'm sure Cindy will be here anytime now, Uncle Jonas," Crystal effused, "so you won't have to stay long. But even if she doesn't show up, we won't be late. Bob has to be on the job bright and early."

"That's certainly good to know. But, Crystal dear, I do have family business to discuss with you, if I could have a few minutes before you two lovebirds skedaddle."

She hesitated, then said, "Sure." Taking his arm, she pulled him toward the kitchen. "Bob, will you excuse us for a minute?"

"No problem," he said, tucking his head earnestly.

Once they were in the other room and Crystal had closed the door, Jonas said, "Uncle Jonas, huh? Nice touch, Crystal. Before you sat him in my chair did you tell him what we do in it? The incest, I mean?"

"Jonas," she said through gritted teeth, "that's all in the past, remember?"

"Tell me," he said, "I'm really curious. Has been forgetting me been that easy? I mean, here today, gone tomorrow, like I never existed?"

She clenched her jaw. "Dammit, Jonas, we had an agreement."

"Okay, I concede the point. But *Uncle* Jonas? Wouldn't *Cousin* Jonas have worked just as well?"

"Keep your voice down," she said, glancing toward the door.

"Well?"

"Is this the family business you want to discuss?"

Jonas sighed. "No," he replied, somewhat chastened.

"Then what?"

He braced himself. "Look, Crystal, I'm in a pickle. Some private investigators are on my ass. Elise's daughter, Melanie, sicced them on me."

"The bitch?"

"Yes, the bitch. Anyway, she's decided to make a federal case out of us."

"Us?"

"Well, my infidelity."

Jonas was watching her closely to see if she'd betray fore-knowledge. When dealing with duplicitous women, a guy had to be more duplicitous by a turn. He'd never met a woman who couldn't lie like a champ when her back was to the wall. Only the most astute observer had a chance of seeing through the smoke.

Crystal put her hands on her hips, looking very annoyed indeed. "Oh, great! That's just wonderful!"

For a second he was confused. Then it occurred to him that his news might be just as unwelcome for her as for him, especially if "Ford-tough" Bob meant more to her than just a three-pound box of chocolates, a dozen long-stemmed roses and dinner at a white-tablecloth joint. "So what do you want from me, Jonas?"

That was Crystal. Cut right to the chase, babe.

What did he say? Where did he begin? Their comfortable little arrangement was as dead as Jimmy Hoffa. Melanie de Givry aside, that was not an easy pill to swallow. He looked into her eyes, realizing that not only was marriage beyond the realm of possibility, but reestablishing a sexual relationship would be as problematical as the Mid East peace process. How was it that a kick in the balls always seemed to be followed in short order by a kick in the ass? He cleared his throat.

"I need to know, Crystal, has anybody ever approached you wanting information about our relationship?"

"No."

"Nobody?"

"Jonas, I said no."

"You haven't noticed anybody suspicious hanging around, nobody who..." Then it hit him—he'd forgotten about the houseboat being burglarized. It completely skipped his mind. "Oh, my God. That break-in. When they got the camera..."

"What about it?"

"That was Melanie. Or her hirelings."

"You think?"

"Yeah, it all adds up. Since I last talked to you, I've uncovered enough evidence to keep Ken Starr busy for a year—with the taxpayers paying for it, maybe two years."

Crystal started getting impatient. "Jonas, what the fuck are you talking about? Who's Ken Starr?"

He waved off the question. "Never mind. It was before your time. The point is, Melanie's definitely zeroed in on us. I think all they're missing is hard evidence. They probably followed me here on a number of occasions and tailed us to Hong Kong. That was why Steve Williams broke down the door in the hotel to get those pictures."

"Steve Williams? I thought his name was Haggerty."

"Sweetheart, it's a long story. By the time I explain everything Bob's erection in there would be but a distant memory. I assume his staying power isn't commensurate with the size of his biceps."

"Are you through?"

He was having trouble determining whether she was being curt for purposes of evasion or because she was pissed. The deepening grimace on her face indicated the latter. She took an impatient breath.

"Because if you aren't, *I* am!"

"Hang on, babe. I just want a clear understanding between us. Melanie's never contacted you, right?"

"Don't you think if she did, I'd have mentioned it?"

"We haven't exactly been in daily contact, Crystal."

"Well, I'd have called you."

"Would you?"

"*Jonas!* This is getting ridiculous. Bob and I are going to lose our dinner reservation if we don't get going."

"Promise me if she or anyone associated with her contacts you, you'll put them off until you've talked to me."

"Okay, fine."

"Promise?"

"Yes, goddamn it, I promise. Now, whether you like it or not, I'm leaving."

He followed her back into the front room where Bob waited, umbrella in hand. He seemed a bit anxious.

"All set," Crystal said, breezing past him, headed for the closet to get her coat.

Bob helped her with it as Jonas watched, feeling as avuncular and ancient as Mr. Rogers. After sweeping up curly-topped Tamara and giving the child a kiss, Crystal waltzed over and deposited her in Jonas's arms.

"Half an hour, Uncle Jonas, then it's off to bed."

The couple headed for the door. Jonas, watching them go, felt like Methuselah.

"You two kids have fun," he muttered. "And happy birthday, Crystal!" But they didn't hear. They were already outside and headed for Bob's truck.

Tamara put her arms around his neck. "How come Mommy called you Uncle Jonas?"

"Because big girls like your mommy are very sneaky. They have a talent for tricking boys."

"What does that mean?"

"It means you've got a lot to learn, but you'll get there soon enough."

Jonas put the little girl down and went to the window. He pulled the curtain aside and peered out into the darkness for a few moments, then let the curtain drop. He shook his head, feeling exhausted, suspended somewhere between disappointment and relief. A mild form of panic was in the mix, as well.

But then, it occurred to him. He'd never told Crystal he stood to inherit a million bucks from Elise. He was glad now he hadn't. She might decide that if his interests were pecuniary, there wasn't any reason she shouldn't develop pecuniary ambitions of her own.

Then, too, Melanie could shit-disturb and tell Crystal everything. The question was, would he be better off telling Crystal himself, hoping she'd hang in there for the sake of auld lang syne, or let nature take its course and deal with the consequences when they arose? Christ, nothing was ever easy. It was times like this when a couple hundred thousand in FDIC insured bank accounts and a nice pension check sounded pretty good.

Davis, California

Tina Richter stood at the window of her upstairs flat in a house out near Chestnut Park, off Pole Line Road, watching the rain pound against the dark glass as she waited for K.J. The old lady who lived in the lower flat was vacuuming again, something she did day and night. The old crow was loony, but no more than Tina's parents.

During Christmas break she'd gone home to L.A., which was a downer. Her mother bitched about her botched face-lift and her father, blissfully uncommunicative, was obviously having another of his affairs.

Tina had surprised herself by developing an obsession of her own—with Professor Mayne of all people. The worse part was that it had a sexual dimension, which made no sense because the whole point was to knock him on his ass. The Berkeley Seeds would be coming up in a few days, and Tina and her friends had to have a plan ready. Fortunately, she'd hit upon an idea—one that had come to her over break while she was lying out by the pool in the smoggy air of L.A., thinking about the professor, feeling all twitchy.

There was only one problem. Their little gang of eco-warriors was more eco than warrior—with the exception of K.J. Which was why she'd decided to enlist his support. She'd run into him at the Student Union soon after the winter quarter started and invited him to come to her place to discuss her idea. He couldn't agree fast enough. But she'd made him wait a few days, claiming she had a paper to do, just to make sure he was good and primed.

About then she saw K.J. pull up to the curb out front. He was on his bike. The poor little bastard had to be soaked to the bone.

Tina had put on her tightest pair of jeans and a clingy sweater, figuring K.J. would be appreciative. In her experience, it never hurt to have control of both a guy's cock *and* his mind. She went downstairs to let him in.

"Hi," she said, swinging the door open wide.

K.J. just stood there, water running down his face, his lower lip sagging open. God, he wasn't even a challenge. Tina led him up the stairs, giving him a nice view of her ass. After he took off his jacket she gave him a towel to wipe his face and dry his hair. A few minutes of pleasantries followed, then she asked if he wanted to share a joint. He did.

Tina got out her stash, which she kept in a plastic sandwich bag in her tiny refrigerator. She didn't have much. Maybe a bee, including an already rolled ace.

"Mexican brown?" K.J. said, showing his stuff.

Tina smiled. "I have no idea. I always got it from my boyfriend."

He looked devastated. "You got a boyfriend?"

"I did. We split before the break."

The kid's joy was palpable. It gave her a sense of power.

They sat on the love seat. It was worn, but she'd draped a colorful cloth over it to improve the looks. She'd put two water glasses filled with wine on the wooden box that served as a coffee table. There was a single candle on it. She used it to light the reefer, leaning over him so her leg pressed up against his.

After taking a drag, she handed the joint to him, sort of moving her leg away, but not completely. She picked up her glass and took a sip of wine while he took a puff of the dope. Tina studied him, reaching over after a while and pushing a lock of wet hair back off his forehead.

He took a puff of the joint, then handed it back to her. Tina took another drag, then said, "Since we're not only comrades-in-arms, but friends, maybe we should have sex. What do you think?"

K.J.'s jaw sagged open.

"Only if you're interested, of course," she added.

"Sure," he said. "I liked you right from the start, you know."

"Well, I've got to be honest with you, K.J. I've got

mixed motives. I'm attracted to you, but I also want your support for my plan for Professor Mayne."

He shrugged. "Sure."

"Don't you think you should hear about it before you agree?"

"Yeah, what I meant was, I'm open."

She took a slow drag, handing the joint back. He took a quick draw, choking a little. Tina saw the bulge in his pants. "You proved how brave you are when you burned down that building," she said, "but I'm wondering if you've got the guts for something really daring."

"Like what?"

She ran her hand up to his bulge and let it rest there. "What do you think of the idea of kidnapping Professor Mayne?"

He gulped. "Kidnap him?" he said, his voice cracking. "For money?"

"I was thinking mostly for the propaganda value. We've got to awaken people's indignation. Publicity is what it's all about, K.J. That's the only way we'll ever make the world aware of what corporate America is doing to the environment."

"God, Tina, that's awesome. Brilliant. But it would take more than the two of us."

"Yes, but it starts with us. You and me." She put her hand on his crotch again. He looked like he was going to burst. "Are we agreed, then?"

"Definitely."

"Good. So, let's fuck."

WEDNESDAY
January 16

Kentfield, California

The best thing about working for yourself, Jonas decided, was that you didn't have to call in sick if you didn't feel like facing the old grindstone. You just blew it off. He awoke late and didn't bother getting out of bed except to pee. Fortunately the old prostate was holding up well, and if he limited his intake of fluids in the evening, he could get through the night without a latrine call. (One small victory over Father Time, though a pyrrhic victory because no matter how many times you prevailed in battle, the old man always won the war.)

Ensconced back in his warm bed and gazing out the window, Jonas was happy to see the sun peeking through the broken clouds. He needed a little sunshine. Yesterday was among his least favorite of the 200,000 plus days he'd spent on earth. Burying Elise was harder for him than he would have thought when they married. Over the months she'd become aware of his flaws, but she'd also seen his virtues. Her faith in him had meant so much, and he'd always be grateful to her for that.

When he'd gotten home the night before, he'd discovered a neighbor had left a casserole dish and a sympathy card. Seeing it had put things in perspective and he'd gotten choked up.

Some of his tears might have been for Crystal, as well. No, not so much *for* her as *because of* her. It had finally sunk in that Crystal was history. Which left him not only without wife and mistress, but also hanging out to dry. The vultures were pecking at his carcass, one named Melanie in particular.

When the doorbell rang, breaking his self-absorbed reverie, Jonas's first thought was more bad news. He checked the clock. It was a few minutes after nine. Too early for a casserole delivery. It had to be trouble.

He got out of bed, having nothing on (sleeping nude was a time-saving habit that dated back to Rae Lynn), and put on his robe and slippers. As he descended the stairs, the bell rang again. "Coming, coming," he called.

Opening the door, he found himself face-to-face with Tess. She was in a business suit, looking smart, professional, lovely and fresh as a crisp leaf of lettuce. He flushed with regret, wishing he'd at least brushed his teeth.

Coming up the walk behind her was a man in a tweed sport coat. She was about to say something when she heard footsteps behind her and turned. The guy, unfamiliar to Jonas, but having an official air about him, didn't hesitate to intrude.

"Mr. Lamb?" he said.

"Yeah?"

The guy reached into his inside coat pocket and produced some folded documents. "These are for you." After handing them to him, he turned on his heel and retreated.

Jonas, half knowing what it was, took a peek. As expected, it was a summons and complaint. He glanced down the page until he saw the name "de Givry," folded it again and slipped it into the pocket of his robe. Without his reading glasses he wouldn't have been able to read the damned thing, anyway. (Not that he was eager.) He looked at Tess and smiled. "What a pleasant surprise."

She seemed confused, glancing over her shoulder, then back at Jonas. "I...don't know who that was. I didn't..."

"No, that's okay," he said, waving her off. "It's nothing. Legal papers. I was expecting them."

"Oh, well, sorry. I guess we happened to arrive at the same time. I didn't..."

"Not a problem." He beamed even though he felt like a sloth. Bed hair. Rumpled. Unshaven. Certainly not the *GQ* poster boy for fastidious grooming. But what the hell, this was one of the low points in his life, he might as well get all the shit out of the way at once.

"I apologize for showing up uninvited," she said, "and I know this is a difficult time for you, but Jonas, we need to talk."

"About what?"

"May I come in?"

"Oh, sure. Sorry. I just woke up and I'm a bit discombobulated. Still not a morning person," he added with a laugh.

Tess was too preoccupied to react to his feeble attempts at making the best of a bad situation. Jonas, his slippers flopping, led the way into Elise's sitting room.

It was probably the nicest house in which he'd ever lived, though Sonia, having married him at one of the financial high points in his life, had created a home for them that was as expensive as it was tasteless. But Elise had had taste. And a good decorator. The sumptuousness of his digs were reason to be proud, though the credit belonged to Jean de Givry, not him.

When Tess sat down on one of the silk sofas, Jonas said, "Would you like a cup of coffee? It'll only take a second."

"No thanks. I won't be staying more than a few minutes."

He dropped into the armchair across from her, the legal papers in his pocket bending awkwardly as he hit the cushion. Removing them, he nonchalantly tossed them on the table between him and Tess. The gesture was a bit too cavalier. She stared at the documents for a moment then looked hard into his eyes.

"Jonas, what the hell is going on?"

"Oh, I'm in a pissing match with my stepchildren. It's no big deal."

"No, I'm not talking about *that*," she said, indicating the legal papers, "I'm talking about Patrick."

"What about him?"

She sprang to her feet and began pacing. "Patrick and I had lunch the day before yesterday," she began, "and he spent most of the time lying to me. My own son. How do you think that makes me feel?"

"Give me a little help here, Tess. What was he lying about?"

But she was in a dither, her words of explanation turning into a rant. "He was never like this before. Patrick and I had our disagreements, but he was always truthful. Until..." She stopped talking and stopped walking, her eyes falling on him.

"Until I showed up again?"

She resumed her pacing. "Yes."

"Tess, forgive me, but I don't know what the hell you're talking about."

"You know what it reminded me of," she said ignoring him, her voice rising, her turns more abrupt. "It reminded me of some of the conversations I've had with you! It was Jonas Lamb all over again!"

"Oh, God," he muttered, squeezing the bridge of his nose between his fingers. He was eternally damned.

"I can't tell you how upset I am," she said, almost in tears. "This is the worst thing that could have happened and you sit there like you could care less."

He glanced up. "I'd really like to be helpful, Tess, but until you explain what the hell you're talking about, there's not a damned thing I can say."

She stopped again, her hands on her hips. "The FBI, that's what I'm talking about!"

"The FBI?" He hadn't expected that. But then he

recalled Melanie having made reference to the FBI during their showdown at the funeral. What the hell was going on?

"Oh, don't act so goddamn innocent," Tess snapped. "You've gotten Patrick involved in something criminal and I want to know what it is."

He got up so abruptly that the tie of his robe came undone. He quickly fastened it again but not before she'd gotten a glimpse—a sight which she undoubtedly considered more an affront than a treat. "Listen," he said, "I don't know where you got this idea, but Patrick and I are not involved in anything remotely criminal. And I certainly don't understand why the FBI would be interested. Where is this coming from, anyway?"

She spun around. "I'll tell you where it's coming from. On Monday Walter got a call from Llewellyn Schumacher, a close friend who also happens to be on the board of regents of the University of California. Llewellyn told Walter that the FBI is investigating Patrick."

"Investigating him for what?"

"I don't know. That's the point. Nobody seems to know."

"It's undoubtedly in connection with the firebombing."

"No, the FBI is not involved in that. It's something else. All we've got is rumors at this point, because the agents didn't disclose what they were doing except to say it was a background check."

"A background check..."

"Yes. But that's just police-speak, like 'routine investigation,' et cetera, et cetera. All that means is they won't say."

"And you think *I* know what's going on?"

"When I asked, Patrick gave me a bunch of double-talk. He was clearly hiding something."

"Forgive me, Tess, but it could be because he doesn't consider it any of your business."

Her expression went stony, her eyes accusing. "Patrick and I do not have secrets. Not like this."

"You're naive if you believe that. He does have a life of his own, Tess."

She stood seething, censoring her thoughts, he could tell. Finally she said, "Is that the answer, then? It's none of my business?"

"No, I'm trying to help you to understand Patrick's vagueness."

"*Vagueness.* Oh, so that's what you call it. Isn't 'bald-faced lies' genteel enough? When you've flim-flamed your way to the top, it becomes *vagueness.*"

Jonas, angry now, glared back at her. "What's the point of even discussing this? You've already made up your mind that I'm a criminal and that I've turned our son into one. In your view it has to be my fault because I'm ultimately responsible for everything that goes wrong in your life, especially anything related to your son. I'll bet that kid's never done a thing you didn't approve of that you didn't find a way to blame on me."

She stood very quiet, not moving. Thirty seconds passed, then she said in a quiet voice, "What should I think instead? In my shoes what would you have done?"

"The fact is, I don't know. I'd wonder, I guess. I'd ask questions, maybe. But I *can* tell you this, I don't have the vaguest idea what the FBI is doing. I'm sure of one thing, though. It's not because of criminal activity I'm involved in."

There was another long pause, then she said in a soft voice, "Are you at all concerned?"

Jonas ran his fingers through his hair. "Yes, I'm worried it might have something to do with our business venture, though don't ask me how. Like I told you the last time we spoke, this is Patrick's deal, not mine."

"Now we're back to being mysterious again. The FBI must have *some* reason to investigate."

"Tess, business deals can be sensitive without being illegal. And when they're big enough and important enough, when lots of money and power are at stake, people can do very strange things to protect their interests."

"Is that calculated to put my mind at ease?"

"Your son's a grown man, Tess. Trust him."

She studied him. "You know, it's absolutely amazing how convincing you are. You've got a gift, Jonas, you really do."

"Somehow I don't think that's intended as a compliment."

"The truth is I'd like to believe you, but…"

"But what?"

"I'm afraid to."

"Because you trusted me once and got burnt."

She lowered her eyes. "Yes, I got burnt."

Jonas nodded. She continued to avoid his eyes. The chasm between them was wide as ever.

"I'll talk to Patrick," he said, "to be sure that I haven't caused any problems unwittingly. And if I learn anything that might assuage your fears, I'll let you know."

She looked up at him. "That's very generous. But I want to know something. Are *you* worried?"

"I'm hoping that Patrick applied for a federal research grant that requires a security clearance...maybe something he's completely forgotten about."

"But you don't think that's what it is, do you?"

"Would you rather I be honest or reassuring?"

"Honest."

He shook his head. He was concerned all right—if only because of Melanie's reference to the FBI—but he still didn't know what was going on and there was nothing to be gained by adding to Tess's anxiety.

She nodded. "I suppose it could be innocent."

"Patrick is a good person, Tess. He's got your virtue and your integrity."

Her brow furrowed, her eyes filled and she quickly looked away. It wasn't the reaction he expected.

"I've got to go," she said. "I've invaded your home, hurling accusations, attacking you, and here you are mourning your wife. I've done enough damage and I'm sorry."

"Don't apologize. It's enough if there can be peace between us."

She wiped her eye with a knuckle and took a calming breath. "I'll go now. I'm sure from your point of view that's the kindest thing I could do."

She headed for the door.

"No, as a matter of fact I always enjoy seeing you, Tess. Even if our discussions get a little heated."

"Liar," she said over her shoulder

"No, it's true," he called after her. But the front door had closed, cutting off his final words.

Paris

La Brebis Noire was a French and Moroccan restaurant located in the Fifth Arrondissement between St. Germain and the Seine, a casual place with rough-hewn beams overhead and Berber rugs on the walls. Le Genissel arrived early, ordered a carafe of red table wine and sat sipping it in a rear booth while he awaited Carly Van Hooten's arrival.

He was uneasy about the woman. She was good at what she did, or had been at one time. But how was she now? Alfred Le Genissel did not like having to worry about such things.

There was a time when he'd worked alone. It was so much easier. And even though his résumé read like a chronicle of international assassination, to succeed at an operation such as this, he needed people like Gaston de Malbouzon and Carly Van Hooten. He needed to trust not only them, their abilities, but also their emotional state.

Would Carly be the same without Antoine Laurent? He'd discussed that with de Malbouzon. "She's fine," the *comte* had assured him on the phone. "Do you think I'd trust her with something as important as this, if it weren't so?"

Le Genissel had doubts all the same. Carly Van Hooten and Antoine Laurent were legendary. The Gazelle had worked with operatives more technically proficient, but he'd never known a pair as daring and fearless. If they weren't helping de Malbouzon track down a corporate blackmailer, or entrap a corrupt politician, they were skydiving in Belgium or hang gliding off the cliffs of Gibraltar. They were equally at home at the opera in Milan or breaking into a warehouse in Southwark. Above all, they were seducers *par excellence,* a talent that had first brought them together when they found themselves on opposite sides of a marital dispute between a prominent French banker and his wife—Carly as the husband's mistress and Antoine as the wife's paramour. It was sad in a way that such talent, such brilliance, should be totally unknown to the world at large.

The Gazelle was pouring his third glass of wine—an overindulgence rare for him—when Carly, an angel with flowing blond hair, entered the restaurant. From where he sat he could see the rosy glow of her cheeks. A more beautiful face he'd never seen. She stirred him and that was not good.

Le Genissel waved and she spotted him, smiling as she made her way toward him in stiletto-heeled boots. The light of melting candles added to the poetry of her graceful image. He rose to greet her, the rich aroma of lamb, cinnamon, olive oil and wine embellished now by the soft fragrance of her perfume. They kissed on each cheek in the French manner.

"Alfred, you bastard, Gaston tells me you've been neglecting us."

His brows rising, he helped her off with her coat, which she threw onto the banquette before sliding onto the bench opposite him. He took the carafe and poured her some wine.

"This makes me a bastard?" he said.

"No jobs, no money. Not even a Hanukkah card this year."

Despite himself, Le Genissel flushed. Carly threw back her head and laughed, exposing her white throat and her white teeth. Her eyes twinkled.

"Alfred, you're so easily teased."

Only then did he realize she was playing with him. The scamp. What a woman. "You are making a joke of my heritage."

"I'm doing no such thing. I'm letting you know how displeased we are that you've been out of touch."

"The world is not the same place as before," he said, fingering his glass. "There is distrust everywhere. The work is no longer the same, either. And personal lives have changed as well, *n'est-ce pas?*" He picked up his glass, looking at her meaningfully over the rim as he sipped wine.

"If that's a subtle reference to Antoine, I accept your condolences."

"*Bien entendu.* Like everyone, I was saddened by the news."

"Thank you."

"But one's first concern must be for the living. The important question is how are *you*, Carly?"

"I won't deny it's been difficult." She took her glass. *"Santé."* After a quick sip, she continued. "But I must go on with my life. What other choice do I have?"

"Are you the same person as before?"

"Of course not. But that isn't really what you want to know. Can I do the work? That's the question."

"Perhaps."

"I suppose we'll find out, won't we?"

"Needless to say, I am not keen on experiments."

"Nor am I, Alfred. Not with my life on the line. But change cannot be avoided. There was a time when you worked alone and trusted no one. Now you undertake large tasks involving many people. How were your employers to know you were up to the challenge?"

She was very clever. One had but to talk to her to understand the reasons for her success. It was more than cleverness that made her special, though. He stared at her mouth, horrified at the realization that he coveted it.

"If along the way you have doubts," he said, "you will be forthright about it, I trust. Honesty is essential, Carly."

She looked into his eyes with unflappable certainty. Le Genissel couldn't help but be admiring, perhaps of Antoine Laurent as much as Carly herself. What a man he must have been to have won her heart.

Antoine had disappeared while mountain climbing in the Alps during an unexpected blizzard. Everyone who knew Carly was aware that those first months after the accident had been unbearable. The fact that Antoine's body hadn't been recovered for six months had been a curse. Against all logic, Carly had clung to the hope he was hiding out for reasons she didn't understand and Antoine hadn't been at liberty to tell her. Le Genissel had gotten all this secondhand, of course, but her suffering was easily understood.

And yet, one merely had to look at her to appreciate her powers. *How could she possibly fail with Jonas Lamb?* the Gazelle asked himself. She couldn't. Not if the man was human.

"I hope that's not skepticism I see on your face, Alfred," she said.

"No, to the contrary."

"Well then?"

"If we're of a mind," he said, "and I believe we are, I have one additional piece of business to discuss with you before we dine."

"Okay."

"I assume the *comte* has given you a general idea of the nature of the operation."

"Yes."

"I have details here," he said, touching one of the two briefcases beside him. "Once we have concluded our business, you can take the information to Gaston. But I have a second case." He lowered his voice. "Inside is a quarter of a million euros, cash. This case is not for the *comte*. It is for you."

"For me?"

"That is correct."

She ran a red-tipped nail under the soft collar of her sweater in a subtle but sensuous way. "What is it for?"

"The operation is complicated with many persons interested in what Lamb is doing. I must know everything that is going on at each moment of the operation. I do not have to tell you of Gaston's eccentricities. He does things in his own way, insisting that results, and results alone, are what count. And for the most part he is right. But for me, minute-to-minute information is essential."

Her eyes narrowed. "You want me to spy for you, betray Gaston."

"Not betray, Carly. I merely want to know everything he does. I want my own person on the inside. I want it to be you."

She abruptly grabbed her coat and slid from the banquette. "This conversation is over, Alfred. Goodbye." With that she headed for the door, weaving her way through the crowded tables.

"Carly!" he shouted. *"Attends!"* But she was already out the door.

Le Genissel, cursing under his breath, grabbed both briefcases as the waiter rushed over.

"Monsieur?"

Exasperated, Le Genissel put down the cases and took out his wallet. "We can't stay, I'm sorry." He handed the man thirty euros, picked up the cases and pushed past him, hurrying to the door.

Once outside, he peered up and down the street. There was no sign of Carly. Then he spotted her climbing into a taxi at the corner. Another taxi was coming down the street. Le Genissel leaped into its path, forcing the driver to slam on the brakes. The vehicle skidded on the frosty pavement and the bumper hit his shins, causing him to fall over the hood. But he quickly recovered and, limping, jumped into the rear seat.

"*Ce taxi là-bas.* That taxi there. Follow it. Don't let him get away. Quickly! *Allez! Vite!*"

The taxi lurched ahead, skidding around the corner in pursuit. Le Genissel saw that the driver was Algerian, so he switched from French and started giving instructions in Arabic. Once they reached St. Germain, they nearly lost Carly's taxi in the traffic, but caught up with it at a light.

From then on they were able to keep pace, crossing the Seine at the Pont de la Concorde, through the *place* and up the rue Royale, past the Madeleine to the Gare St. Lazare. Skirting the station, the taxis proceeded north up the rue d'Amsterdam to the Eighteenth Arrondissement. There, on a little street between the Cimetière du Nord and the Sacré-Coeur, Carly's taxi stopped. Le Genissel had his driver stop a hundred feet back. He handed him twenty euros and got out.

She'd wondered if he would follow, strangely undecided if she was happy about it or not. Normally, Carly took pleasure in manipulating men, but Alfred Le Genissel was a creature unto himself.

She pretended not to see him limping up the sidewalk as she rummaged through her purse for her keys, then gave a little jump when he said her name.

"Alfred, what are you doing, following me?"

"You left before our conversation was finished."

"As far as I'm concerned, it was over."

It would have been all right with her had he shrugged and walked away. Yet part of her was intrigued—not by the man's appeal, which was negligible at best, but rather by the darkness and danger in his soul. Perhaps it was the challenge he posed.

He glanced up at the dark apartment building. "Can we go inside?"

"No."

"All right, then, if you prefer, I will explain here on the pavement."

The street was empty and dark, the shadows obscuring his face. She'd been dead inside for so many months that, ominous and disgusting as Alfred Le Genissel might be, he made her feel alive by virtue of her need to resist him.

"The money I offered," he said, indicating the case, "was a test."

"What do you mean, a test?"

"I had to know the depth of your loyalty. If you were willing to betray the *comte*, you might have easily betrayed me."

"I don't believe you."

"There is always a higher bidder."

"That is true whether I'd taken your money or not," she said. "I don't see the point of this charade."

"Perhaps there is no point, except that I want very much to know you. My life, our lives, perhaps, will depend on it."

"Don't you think I'm aware of that?"

"I am trying to say I do not want this to jeopardize the mission. Please. Here is the intelligence data my people in California have been gathering. It is for Gaston," he said, offering the case. "Take it to him and say nothing of what happened between us this evening."

"If I take him the briefcase, I'm going to tell him everything," she said.

"All right, if you must, then tell him. I can see your loyalty is unfailing."

Carly took the case, aware that he was drawing her scent into his lungs, savoring her like a predator its prey.

"Carly," he said, "please do not hold this against me." He inched closer, making her muscles tense. "Let me be perfectly honest. I know of your absolute commitment to Antoine, the trust between you. I only hoped for the same between us."

She stopped breathing, knowing that any second it would be too much—*he* would be too much. Then he pounced. Before she knew what was happening, her face was in his hands and his mouth was pressed hard against hers.

For a second she didn't react, but then she slammed the case against his back and twisted her mouth free, shoving him away. She dropped the briefcase at her feet. When he reached for her again, she swung, catching him on the side of the face, stunning him.

"Never try that again, Alfred, or I swear I'll kill you!"

He blinked with surprise, perhaps stunned as

much at his own compulsive act as her reaction. She kicked the briefcase toward him. "I don't see how this can work. I'm going to tell Gaston I'm out."

"No, please don't. I apologize. It is...well...testimony to your powers. Keep it," he said, picking it up and offering it to her. "Take it to the *comte*. I beg you. It will never happen again."

"Why should I believe you?"

"I acted without thinking," he lamented, his eyes on the wet pavement.

Even his contrition was insincere. She could tell. But there was satisfaction in knowing she'd forced the words from his mouth. The only thing she didn't know was which he wanted more—her services, or her.

"I have some advice for you, Alfred. Take the money you tried to give me and spend it on a woman who is willing to accommodate you." She milked the moment a bit longer, then took the case. "I'm going to forget this happened, Alfred, but don't cross me again. If you must communicate, talk to Gaston. I'm going inside now. *Bon soir.*"

Taking her key, she let herself in the door, confident he'd given up, even knowing he'd like nothing better than to force his way in and have his way with her, if only to prove he could. It was a dangerous game, but what other kind was worth the effort?

Telegraph Hill, San Francisco

The streets were tied up with emergency vehicles, their lights flashing, when Jonas arrived at his office.

Most likely a robbery or somebody had a heart attack. In any case, it was clear he wouldn't be parking anywhere nearby. Finding a space a few blocks away, he started walking back toward his building.

Having received Melanie de Givry's little present that morning, Jonas was not in the happiest frame of mind. On his way to the office he had gone to see an attorney by the name of Braxton Weir to discuss Melanie's lawsuit, there being little chance of him enjoying a quiet day at home, anyway. Weir had been recommended by Don Ehrlich, who was Elise's attorney. Jonas had called Ehrlich right after Tess had left.

"Jonas, I'd like to help you," Ehrlich said, "but I've had so many dealings with the family I'd have a real conflict-of-interest problem. You're going to have to see somebody else. I'd be happy to give you some names, if you like."

Jonas had been inclined to go with Braxton Weir because he happened to be Ehrlich's brother-in-law and Jonas knew Don Ehrlich hated Melanie. They'd fought constantly over Elise's legal affairs, plus Melanie had her own attorney handle the probate, thus denying him a nice piece of business. Weir was more likely than anyone to get unofficial help from Ehrlich, which further prompted Jonas to go with him. Weir had some time before law-and-motion court that morning and told Jonas to bring by the papers.

Watching the attorney look over the complaint, he'd had a feeling the news would be bad. The complaint, Weir explained, contained several causes of action. As executor of Elise's estate, Melanie wanted the return of the hundred thousand, alleging fraud and duress, plus she asked the court to invalidate the bequests in Elise's will in favor of Jonas, specifically the million dollars and the stock in Global Energy Technologies, Inc. The complaint prayed further that the assets of GET be impounded until the disposition of the stock was determined by the court. The request for the invalidation of the bequests was based on failure of condition—namely his fidelity.

"And there are some lesser causes of action involving the house," Weir told him.

"She's trying to evict me, right?"

"Since you're not a holdover tenant or a putative owner of the property, a statutory eviction wasn't necessary. In her view you're essentially a squatter. The cause of action was unlawful detainer. They're also asking for an injunction to keep you from removing anything but your personal effects from the premises. They're asking for an immediate hearing on the injunction and will probably get it. But this stuff is nickels and dimes compared to the probate matter."

"I know."

Braxton Weir was a big, husky man with dark hair, thick bushy eyebrows and a heavy beard that started showing five o'clock shadow around ten in the morning. For a big guy, he had a gentle manner. The rosy cheeks also gave him a benevolent air.

"I'll have to study this more carefully, of course, but offhand it looks to me like it all comes down to whether or not you violated the terms of your premarital agreement, which has been effectively incorporated into Mrs. de Givry's will as a condition precedent to the gift."

"Meaning if Melanie can prove I screwed around behind Elise's back, I won't inherit anything."

"Correct. The result being that Ms. de Givry and her brother would get the million dollars and they'd end up splitting the ninety percent of your company that was owned by their mother."

That was enough to give Jonas an ulcer on the spot. "Shit," he muttered. "Things were already bad enough without this."

"The million in cash speaks for itself," the attorney said. "But a corporation is only worth of value of its assets, including goodwill. Does GET, Inc. own anything of value?"

"We've only been in business a few months. The office space and furniture are leased. The hundred thousand I got from Elise is what I'm using to cover expenses."

"And the plaintiff wants that back."

"Am I going to have to pay it, assuming I get screwed out of my inheritance?"

"We could argue that the hundred thousand was in effect a capital investment in exchange for stock. So long as the money was used for legitimate corporate expenses, the amounts already spent wouldn't have to be reimbursed, though presumably they would be entitled to ninety percent of the remaining capital in the event the corporation was dissolved. But there are a lot of ifs, Jonas, and we're getting ahead of ourselves. The first concern is how vulnerable you are on the infidelity issue."

Jonas had thought for a long moment and said, "Let's put it this way, Melanie has her suspicions, but she can't prove anything." He hadn't said it to Braxton Weir, but an additional word had gone through his mind—the qualifier, *"yet."* Even before he'd walked out of the attorney's office, Jonas realized that everything—his inheritance, his company, his future, his destiny, the works—was in the hands of Crystal Clear.

Driving to his own offices, he'd considered what he might expect from her. The hell of it was, he couldn't be sure. Last night, when he'd been promoted to honorary "uncle," she'd promised to put off Melanie until after she'd spoken with him. He figured he could trust her to do that as a minimum, but what happened after she'd alerted him was anybody's guess. Jonas could see he had to tend to his garden. It was also apparent that Ford-tough Bob having arrived on the scene would make things that much more difficult.

If Melanie hadn't done enough to ruin his day (never mind his life), he also had the FBI to contend with. Unlike Tess, he wasn't worried about criminal wrongdoing, but he was concerned about unwarranted snooping. Right after phoning Don Ehrlich, he'd tried to reach Patrick at the university, but all he got was his voice mail. He'd left a message to call him at the office.

When Jonas finally reached his building he was surprised to find yellow police tape strung around the entrance. There was a small crowd of onlookers staring at two browny-red pools of what appeared to be blood on the patio area outside the door. The pools were outlined in chalk in the shape of bodies.

Jonas recognized a secretary from the architectural firm next door standing in the crowd. "Hi," he said, coming up next to her, "what happened?"

"A gun battle, apparently," she replied. "Two guys shot each other."

"When?"

"Early this morning, they think. Somebody coming to work found the bodies. The coroner's already carted them off."

"Who were the victims?"

"I don't know. Somebody said one guy was Chinese and the other guy dark, maybe Hispanic. When I got here the bodies were already covered."

"A street crime, maybe," Jonas said.

The woman shrugged. He noticed that access to the building was blocked off.

"Are we locked out?"

"No, you can get in through the delivery entrance in back. I'm on a coffee break and came out to watch."

Jonas nodded. "Guess I'll go inside. See you."

He went around back where a uniformed officer was ensuring that anybody wanting access had a reason to be in the building. Jonas showed the cop his business card and driver's license and was waved through.

Once in his office, Jonas checked his messages.

Patrick had tried to reach him. Jonas immediately returned the call.

"What's going on?" Jonas said. "I had a hysterical visit from your mother this morning. She was ready to indict me for shooting both Kennedys and Martin Luther King, as well as corrupting you."

"Lord. Maybe I should have expected it."

"Care to clue me in?"

"I don't think we should discuss it on the phone. I'll be finished here in a couple of hours. How about if I come to see you?"

It was Patrick's tone that gave him pause as much as anything. "Fine."

"Oh, and Jonas?"

"Yes?"

"Have you ever had anybody do a security sweep of the office?"

"No, it never occurred to me. As you know, GET is still in gestation."

"Well, I'm getting the feeling somebody would like to see it stillborn."

"Why do you say that?"

"We'll talk when I get there. But to pique your curiosity, I had a security specialist go over my house first thing this morning. It was bugged and the phone tapped."

"By whom?"

"I don't know. But I've probably already said too much. I guess my point is, stay on your toes."

Jonas hung up. He felt a migraine coming on. Melanie, Crystal, the FBI, now this. Where was God's compassion?

Bugs and wiretaps didn't seem like Melanie de Givry's style. After that business in Hong Kong with Steve Williams and her open declaration of hostilities, he'd been so preoccupied with Melanie that he'd never considered other threats. Could the FBI be responsible for the funny business? Or maybe somebody else more pernicious?

He thought of the pools of blood in front of the building, wondering if that crime was somehow connected with their problem, or was that being completely paranoid?

"Hello? Anybody here?" The voice was coming from the outer office.

Jonas got up just as a man in a rumpled suit appeared at the door.

"May I help you?"

"Hi, I'm Inspector Arverson of the SFPD." He flashed a badge. "Do you have a minute?"

"Sure. Have a seat."

"And your name, sir?"

"Jonas Lamb."

Arverson offered his hand in a perfunctory manner. They shook hands. "This your company, Mr. Lamb?"

"Yes, it is."

"I assume you're aware of the homicides that took place outside this morning," Arverson said, sitting in the chair across from Jonas. He was an affable-looking fellow with a big moon-faced grin and squinty eyes that seemed to be smiling, too.

"Yeah, I just got here a while ago and one of the other tenants told me."

"We're polling the occupants of the building to see if there might be a connection between the incident and any goings-on inside. The assumption is a street crime, but we want to cover all the bases. What sort of business is Global Energy Technologies?"

"Investment in energy-related technology."

Arverson grinned. "Makes sense. So, you do business abroad?"

"Yes, why do you ask?"

"Where?"

Jonas shrugged. "Actually we're a new company, in operation for only a few months. We don't have established relationships, but we're happy to take investors where we find them."

"How about China?"

Jonas tried not to blanch. "Sure."

"Contacts there?"

The line of conversation was making him uncomfortable. "We've had conversations with an investor out of Hong Kong."

"Who?"

Jonas hesitated. "No offense, Inspector, but would you mind if I had another look at your badge? Our work is highly confidential and I'm reluctant to—"

"No problem," Arverson said, getting out his badge again. He extended it across the desk.

Jonas, not having his reading glasses on, couldn't make out a thing, but the cop's forthright manner was reassuring enough. "Thanks."

"Always pays to be careful. We were talking about your contact in Hong Kong."

"Yee Industries is the name."

"That a big company?"

"One of the largest real estate investment firms in the world."

Arverson got out his pad and jotted down a note. Jonas didn't like this, and though he knew he had no obligation to answer the questions, neither did he want to arouse suspicion. With a subpoena, the cops could tear the place apart. That sort of attention he did not need.

"Anybody else?"

Jonas wished he could throw out another name for balance. "Well, we've had preliminary conversations with Royal Dutch Shell."

"They're European, right?"

"Yes."

This time the detective did not make a note. "Anything you know of that might explain what happened outside? Notice anything strange, suspicious people hanging around, any business or personal problems that could be related, that sort of thing?"

"No, Inspector. Not unless they were bringing me a suitcase full of money." He chuckled. Arverson did not. The inspector looked like he was prepared to wrap up the interview, but Jonas was too curious to let things go at that. "The gal next door in the architectural firm said one of the victims was Chinese," he said. "Is that why you asked about China?"

"You got it, Mr. Lamb," Arverson said, his grin returning.

"You know who he was?"

"Neither guy was carrying ID. Judging by appearance and attire, we've got them both pegged as foreign nationals."

"I see. The other guy Mexican?"

"No, Arabic, it looks like. Maybe Pakistani. One of those countries. Our lab guys and the feds will probably figure it out soon enough. Don't suppose you've got any contacts in that part of the world?"

"Not yet, but we're trying."

"Well," Arverson said, "the guy on the sidewalk this morning's not a good prospect, I can tell you that." He gave Jonas a happy face. Then, rising, he handed him a business card. "You think of anything else, give me a call, okay?"

"Sure, Inspector."

The officer offered a casual salute, not bothering to shake hands, then walked out.

As soon as Jonas heard the outer door close, he picked up the phone and started to dial Crystal, then he remembered Patrick's warning about electronic surveillance. Instead he got his cell phone and went out into the hallway. He reached the girl who'd once been mistress of his dreams at her shop.

"How's it going?" He'd almost added "sweetheart," but decided at this stage of the game overfamiliarity might engender contempt.

"Jonas, I've got customers. This is not a good time."

"I was hoping you'd have a minute for your old uncle, honey, the sweet old guy who baby-sits for free and eats a big chunk of rent every month."

"Okay, what is it?"

"First, let me say Bob is a real nice guy, a terrific guy, and I'm happy for you both. Sincerely."

"Thanks."

"Second, have you heard from Melanie, had your place burglarized again by the bitch, anything like that?"

"Jonas, I promised I'd put her off and talk to you first, and I will."

"Thank you, Crystal, that means a great deal to me...your consideration and loyalty, I mean."

"Anything else?"

He did not like her perfunctory tone. "One last little thing. Melanie's putting pressure on me to move out. Which means I'll be needing a place to live. Now, I'm not pressing you or suggesting anything, but I was wondering how long you'd be needing the houseboat. I mean, maybe Bob has a beautiful house that puts *Lamb's Croft* to shame."

"We aren't exactly to that point yet, Jonas."

"No problem. Stay as long as you like. In fact, if things are a little tight with the looming expense of a trousseau and all, feel free to skip a month's rent...or two, for that matter. Consider it my wedding present to you."

"Jonas, Bob and I aren't even engaged. And forgive me, but you're sounding desperate. It's not very becoming."

"You always could see right through me, couldn't you, kid?"

"That it, then?"

"Just thanks for your understanding, that's all."

"Talk to you later," she said, and hung up.

Jonas leaned against the wall, his shoulders sagging. The opportunity of a lifetime was beginning to feel like the trophy fish that got away. He glanced up as Arverson walked by on his way to his next interview. They exchanged nods.

Jonas returned to his troubles, ruing the day he'd discovered sex. How simple life would be without it. How remarkable that so many woes were directly attributable to the urge to copulate. And all in the name of perpetuation of the species. Somebody, somewhere, wasn't clear on the concept.

Back in his office, Jonas dug out the phone book and started looking for security firms.

The Financial District, San Francisco

Tess peered out at the bay from her office window, unconsciously wringing her hands. She'd been up and down two dozen times since Walter had given her the news right after she'd gotten back from Marin.

"I got another call from Llewellyn," he'd said. "This time the information is even more bizarre."

She'd been almost afraid to ask. "What did he say?"

"That he believes the investigation has national security implications."

"*National security?* Patrick isn't doing anything remotely connected with national security."

Walter had shrugged. "I can't explain it. But, Tess, please don't forget Llewellyn was doing me a very big favor passing this along. It would probably be best not even to mention it to Patrick. The only reason I'm telling you is because you were worried about it being a criminal matter."

"I'm not sure which is better, to be honest."

"This is totally outside my realm of expertise, I'm afraid," Walter said. "But I'm sure it will all shake out in the end. Try not to worry."

Tess knew her fiancé meant well, but the new twist only added to her anxiety. She hadn't told Walter she'd gone to see Jonas. Now she wondered if that had been a mistake. Her lies and deceptions were dragging her deeper and deeper into the morass. And if things hadn't started out badly enough already today, on top of everything else Walter and Stacey Kellogg were interviewing Jerry Tate. Worse still, Walter had asked her to sit in on the interview.

For the better part of a month she'd been struggling with her perfidy, silently watching the selection process move forward, relieved, yet in another sense horrified, as Jerry passed each hurdle. Ironically, the man hadn't said a word to her. Their only connection, if she could call it that, was his using her name as a reference. Yet she felt that he was taking advantage of his secret knowledge of her past. She either quietly advanced his candidacy or she assumed the risk of being humiliated.

And when she wasn't worrying about Jerry, her thoughts were on Jonas. He'd been smooth as silk that morning, deflecting responsibility, making her feel like a fool for even suspecting him of wrongdoing. She'd left his house chastened, still not knowing if one word he'd uttered was the truth. God knew, their marriage had been one grand misrepresentation, but could she claim to be any better? The primary reason for her silence about Jerry Tate was to keep Walter from finding out about her affair with Gregory Hamilton. The way things were shaping up, she would be damned whatever Walter decided. Either Jerry would get the job and she'd feel vile because of her complicity in the fraud, or Jerry wouldn't get the job and choose to punish her for not returning his favor.

Wendy rapped on the door. "Tess, they're ready for you. Mr. Tate is here."

Tess girded herself and went to Walter's office. He sat at his desk, looking over some papers as Stacey Kellogg, chipper, intelligent, confident—everything Tess had once been and had taken as her due, status earned by hard work and virtue—stood nearby. *You wait, Stacey,* she thought, *you'll screw up somewhere along the line and the world won't be yours anymore.*

"Morning, Tess," the headhunter said, her smile pretty and diplomatic. "So, your candidate made it to the finals. You must be pleased."

"Jerry is hardly my candidate, Stacey. We worked together and my name was used as a reference, that's all. I'm sure Walter will make his decision based on what he thinks, not what's implied by any of that."

"To the contrary, my dear," he interjected. "I value

and respect your views and insights to the fullest."
Then he smiled as if to say his true objective was to
compliment her, not disagree. They both knew he
was his own man.

"And if I say you should hire somebody else instead of Jerry?"

"Then I'll do as I choose."

She gave Stacey a see-that's-my-point look,
which gave her a bit of pleasure, though it didn't
solve her dilemma. Irrational as it probably was,
Tess was beginning to see this crisis over Jerry Tate
as a metaphor for her relationship with Walter. If
nothing else, it was forcing her to ask herself who
she really was. On that point, the jury was still
out.

"Well," Walter said, putting the file down on the
desk, "let's get Mr. Tate in here, shall we?"

She was just about finished transferring her things
from her desk to the second of the two boxes Wendy
had brought her when Walter came in. She glanced
up and, seeing him, said, "The interview over already? I apologize for walking out in the middle, but
I couldn't stay and listen."

"Why? Tess, what are you doing?"

"Cleaning out my desk."

"What for?"

"Wendy's typing up my letter of resignation."

"What?"

"Wendy is—"

"Yes, yes, I heard you, but *why?* What's happened?"

"I realize that I can't be a constructive force around here so I'm doing both of us a favor and I'm leaving."

"Is this because of Tate?"

"No... Well, yes, but it's about a lot more than just him."

Walter came over and sat on the corner of the desk, his gray eyes sad and earnest. "Would you care to explain?" he asked, his voice soft and patient.

Tess leaned back in her big, high-back desk chair and looked up at him, her eyes beginning to swim. "I've failed you," she said, her voice cracking.

"How so?"

She knew the time had come to unburden herself. "I wasn't completely forthcoming about Jerry. There was something I should have told you and I didn't."

"If you mean his attempt to use you to sway me, I ignored it. The fact is I'd pretty well made my decision before today's interview. Jerry Tate is third of the three finalists, Tess. A distant third. I'm offering the job to Lena Ramirez."

"I'm glad," she said.

"Why?"

"Because he never should have listed me as a reference."

"It might have been a bit heavy-handed, but it wasn't unethical."

"Walter, the point is I'm not the saint you think I am and Jerry Tate knows it. He's privy to some very embarrassing information and may have used me as a reference thinking I'd do everything in my power to remain in his good graces."

"Are you saying he blackmailed you?"

"No, we've never even spoken about his application. In fairness, it may be my imagination."

Walter shook his head. "I'm totally confused."

"I made a terrible mistake several years ago, Walter, a mistake that Jerry Tate was a party to, or at least knew about." She lowered her head, fiddling nervously with her fingers. "I was unfaithful to Richard."

Walter was obviously not expecting so damning an admission. "With Tate?"

"No. With someone else. But Jerry knew about it. Witnessed it, actually."

"I must say I'm surprised by your admission. But I think you know me better than to believe I'd hold something you did in the past against you. If I'm disappointed, it's that you didn't trust me enough to come to me with this earlier."

"I knew you'd be understanding," she said through shimmering eyes. "I never doubted that."

"Well, then, what's the problem?"

"In the course of this process I discovered something about myself I'm not particularly proud of. I am not the woman you wish to marry, Walter."

"That's absurd. I know you, Tess. You're human. You make mistakes like everyone else, including me."

"I can't tell you how much I appreciate and respect that," she said. "But your feelings aren't the issue. It's what I've learned about myself."

"Will you share?"

"The first order of business is for me to figure out who I am."

Walter Bronstein stroked his chin as he studied her, looking weary. "You're having some sort of midlife crisis, aren't you?"

She stepped over to him and kissed him on the cheek. "I need some time to think. But even if I do get my head together, I'm not sure I should continue working for you."

"You're my right arm."

"Walter, there are thousands of eager young people out there. Frankly, I think I'm ready for something else. I don't know what, but I do need to look at my options."

He caressed her face. "Well, a little time off never hurts anyone. Maybe you do need a rest. And afterward things might not look so bleak."

She didn't want to tell him there was a strong possibility she wouldn't return—not just to the company, but to him. But she didn't want to hurt Walter any more than she already had. "Thank you," she said, giving him a kiss.

"So, what are you going to do?" he asked. "Or is that a secret?"

"I have to figure that out. Having some time alone is what matters right now."

"Okay, if that's what you want, I'll support you, Tess."

She gave him a big hug. "You're a fine human being, Walter Bronstein," she said.

He took her by the shoulders and looked into her eyes. "I love you, Tess."

She wanted to say the same thing back, but realized to her shock and dismay that she couldn't.

Ted Myers was gathering the classified documents on his desk to secure them before going home when his section chief, Ken Kellerman, rapped on his door. Kellerman told Myers he hoped it wasn't his wife's birthday because there'd been a new development in the Jonas Lamb/GET, Inc., case. Kellerman said he was heading for a meeting at FBI headquarters and that it was probably a good idea if Myers threw his GET, Inc., files in his briefcase and came with him.

Ted Myers asked what was up and Kellerman explained that early that morning two men were found dead outside GET's offices in San Francisco, apparently having shot each other. One was an MSS operative, a top agent in the Foreign Affairs Bureau named Zhihuan Tung, who had arrived in the States from China twelve days before with the title deputy trade attaché at the embassy in Washington. The other was believed to be Maarouf Khoury, a Lebanese-born soldier of fortune with ties to various Middle Eastern national security agencies and terrorist organizations. How he'd entered the country and how long he'd been here was unknown.

Myers asked if they had any idea what had happened, and Kellerman told him he understood Khoury was in possession of burglar tools when the bodies were found. Myers could see that the little piece of intelligence he'd culled a month ago was pointing to a much bigger conflict than first appeared. Jonas Lamb, it seemed, had become a bone of contention between warring security agencies. The FBI might know more, but that was Myers's guess. The question, of course, was how much did Lamb know and to what degree was he pulling the strings?

Kellerman told Myers the FBI had turned up something else, as well. They'd found out the source of Lamb's technology. It was his son, a biologist at the University of California at Davis. Myers was amazed. The world was on the brink of economic revolution and all because of a little family enterprise.

Aquatic Park, San Francisco

Jonas and Patrick sat side by side on a bench watching a couple of long-distance swimmers churning their way across the cove, headed for Municipal Pier. It was a clear, sunny afternoon, but the water temperature had to be in the fifties, cold enough to freeze the gonads off a seal, assuming they had gonads. Jonas shivered at the thought, folding the flap of his coat collar over his chest.

Behind them the bell of the Hyde Street cable car clanged and Patrick, who'd been jumpy, glanced over his shoulder. "Having the FBI on your ass would be enough to make the Pope paranoid," he said.

"The question is how the hell it happened."

It was a continuation of the conversation they'd started when Patrick picked him up at the office. Jonas had been waiting in front of the building, within sight of the dried pools of blood still protected by the yellow police tape and two uniformed officers. "Not only was the office phone tapped," he told his son upon jumping in the car, "but the security guy found two bugs."

They agreed not to involve the police because that would put Operation Black Sheep in jeopardy, not to mention the fact that the feds could be responsible or otherwise involved. Patrick's news had been just as grim. A friend who was a personnel clerk at the university confirmed what Jonas already knew—that the FBI was investigating him. When Jonas told him about the two foreign nationals that had shot each other outside the office, Patrick speculated, as did he, that it wasn't a coincidence. Clearly, they were squarely in the midst of a shit storm.

"I can understand that you and the company would come to people's attention," Patrick said, "but how did they figure out I'm involved? You haven't told anyone, have you?"

"No, not a soul. Not even Jimmy Yee." But then it hit him. "Hold on. I did say something to Elise."

"That still doesn't explain why the FBI is investigating me."

Jonas considered that. "Melanie could have mentioned you."

"But why are they involved at all? Unless some kind of a leak came from Jimmy Yee's end."

"If so, it surprises me, first because the guy deals in sensitive stuff all the time and is discreet, and second because he's hurt by this as much as we are."

Patrick said, "There's no point in worrying, I suppose. We've got to hold things together until we can make our deal. That's got to be our focus."

Jonas had been wondering just how much he should tell Patrick about his legal woes with Melanie. There was no point in going into it now—not when he still might beat her at her game. Down the road that might change.

"So, where are we?" he said to his son. "What do you propose?"

"I'm leaving from here to make the necessary provisions to plant the experimental field."

The bell of the cable car clanged again and a group of pigeons nearby took wing.

"Is there anything constructive I can do while you're off farming?" Jonas asked. "That is, apart from drawing enemy fire."

"Why don't you drop out of sight, relax for a while, take a minivacation."

"And go where?"

"Anywhere."

"I shouldn't go back to Hong Kong, at least not with empty hands."

"I agree," Patrick replied. "But I will have something for us to show him in two weeks at the outside. Maybe sooner, if I can get things moving with the field."

"Sounds good."

"I've got an idea," Patrick said. "Why don't you go up to the Tahoe cabin?"

"What cabin?"

"Mom's and mine...well, hers and Richard's before

he died, but I use it more than she does. It's a family place. That's where I went to write my dissertation."

"I don't think Tess would be thrilled at the thought of me there. I'd be about as welcome as Yasser Arafat at a bar mitzvah."

Patrick laughed. "Mom wouldn't know. And it's a cinch she won't be using the place. The only time she goes up to the lake is in the summer. I've got the key right here in my pocket."

Jonas was tempted. With Melanie, the Chinese, the Arabs, the FBI and God knew who else after him, a little downtime would be nice. "Maybe I could be persuaded."

THURSDAY
January 17

Beaumesnil, France

It was late morning by the time they reached the village. Gaston was a terrible driver, but he was fast and they'd gotten there in good time. Carly, in the passenger seat—her only nod toward common sense, the seat belt she wore—should have been in fear of her life, but she gave in to the experience. Antoine had also driven fast, but at least he had been skillful, a man whose sexuality showed when he was behind the wheel. *Maybe that was true of Gaston, as well,* she thought with a touch of whimsy.

"Well, here we are," he said, setting the handbrake.

They'd stopped in the square across from the church. It was a brisk, windy day. A few leaves left over from autumn tumbled across the cobbled pavement. Carly, feeling a bubble of emotion, looked out at the poetically bleak scene, the gray stone of the church and surrounding buildings, the naked, black branches of the trees against the slate sky.

When last she was here, it was to bury Antoine. It had been a warm summer day, the trees fully leafed and casting dark shadows on the villagers, who stood in small groups around the square, curious about the *comte* and the foreign woman who'd bribed the priest to allow the outsider—a mountain climber, of all things—to be laid to rest in their sacred ground.

When Antoine's body had been found in the Alps, Gaston and Carly assumed responsibility for the burial. But they weren't sure what to do as Antoine had never discussed his desires with Carly.

It was then that Gaston had recounted the time years ago when he and Antoine had been on their motorcycles and stopped in Beaumesnil. After a couple of beers in the café on the square, Antoine had told Gaston that when he died he wanted to be buried in the graveyard of a small village. "In fact," he'd said, "this would be the perfect spot. I like this place." Gaston had asked why, and Antoine couldn't explain except to say he'd never belonged anywhere his whole life and every Frenchman ought to have someplace to call his own.

Gaston had remembered the conversation and so he and Carly made a pilgrimage to Beaumesnil to make the arrangements. The priest had said that burial there was impossible, though a hundred thousand francs donated to the parish coffers had changed impossibility to a done deal.

Carly remembered the day of the funeral as the most poignant of her life. The priest did his thing in a perfunctory manner, then left them to say their goodbyes. As Carly sobbed, Gaston had done a rambling monologue about Antoine, a sort of homily which he ended by lifting outstretched arms to the heavens and uttering, "God, bless the soul of our friend, Antoine Laurent, and save us all from those who believe in You." And then they'd gone home to Paris.

Today was the anniversary of Antoine's disappearance. Carly and Gaston had decided to make this pilgrimage before heading off to America—Gaston because it appealed to his sense of theater and Carly because she sensed the end of an era.

She and the *comte* got out of the car and walked across the square to the church where they entered the cemetery through the gate. There, under a huge, naked chestnut tree, wedged between a hero of the Great War and one M. Augustus Molliard, 1817—1883, a wealthy burgher judging by his headstone, lay Antoine Laurent, child of a petty thief and a Gypsy. But he was also a son of France, consecrated by the church on holy ground and made a true respectable Frenchman for all time.

Carly had come to say her final farewell, just as she had said goodbye to Anook a few days earlier. Her first priority had always been to be free, gamboling about like a butterfly, landing for so long as it pleased her and no more. She had been at rest on the blossom that had been Antoine for a very long time. But he was gone now and she, by her nature, had to take wing or die.

"Let's walk, Gaston," she said.

They left the village on a narrow lane that ran along the ridge line separating the Charentonne and Risle river valleys. There, amid fallow fields running to patches of woods, a hedgerow or a stone farm-house huddled under the pewter sky, Carly told Gaston she was certain anything they got from Alfred Le Genissel would be hard-earned.

"*Alors*, that I already know," Gaston said. "But I like challenges."

"So do I," she replied, "but I think we'll end up in a crossfire. I have a bad feeling about this, Gaston."

"What are you saying? That you have cold feet?"

"No, the opposite. I love danger. But you do have a tendency to be cavalier. My point is we must be very careful and plan well."

"Carly, I agree. I talked to the Gazelle this morning. He's already lost one of his men. Apparently the guy ran into some opposition and there was a gun battle."

"Wonderful. That's going to make our job that much harder."

"Yes, I told Alfred that. He agreed to back off once we're in California, but if he senses things are out of control, the bastard's going to step in."

"In other words, he's going to be looking over our shoulder."

"*Malheureusement*." Unfortunately.

Carly tossed her hair, her eyes watering from the bite of the wind. "I don't like it."

"We're being well compensated, *chérie*. And I especially like it that we have two employers, each ignorant of the other's existence. By the way, I've come up with a name for the operation. Brebis Noire."

"Like the restaurant?"

"Yes. When Le Genissel had called to set up the appointment the other day, I jotted the name down on a slip of paper. When I saw it this morning, it hit me. Jonas Lamb, Little Bo Peep, Brebis Noire. It's perfect."

"Whatever. Personally I'm more concerned about our plan."

"Mr. Lamb's trousers are your department, Carly. Have any ideas?"

"Yes, preliminarily. From what's in the file, my guess is Lamb's a knight-errant type. I think I'll let him rescue me."

"That'll work?"

"If I have him pegged correctly."

Gaston looped his arm in hers. "Well, when it comes to straight men, you know best, *mon angelet*."

"I may need your help initially."

"Me?"

"Yes, you can pretend to be straight for a day, can't you?"

Gaston frowned. "What do you have in mind?"

"Don't worry, it doesn't involve sleeping with me. But you might have to slap me around a little."

"*Mon Dieu!* How curious. This is supposed to elicit the fires of passion?"

"In Mr. Lamb, of course. Not you."

They came to the high point on the road and stood staring off to the west and the fields that rolled away from them until they met the somber sky. Just beyond seeing was the channel. Beyond that the Atlantic. And America. This would not be the return to her native land that Carly had envisioned. But it was the one she had chosen and it would have to do.

Crystal Clear, a woman newly in the blush of love (or a reasonable facsimile, thereof) had gotten Bob a cup of coffee, given him a peck on the cheek and settled him in her tiny office at the back of the shop, when the bell over the front door tinkled. "Excuse me, honey," she said, "got a customer." She went out front.

An odd-looking threesome had entered, two women and a man. The women, both short and blond though very different types, approached the counter. It was the sight of the man, though, that was arresting. He looked just like that guy in Hong Kong who'd burst into their hotel room. Obviously, it had to be the guy Jonas told her about, the one whose identity had been stolen.

Crystal turned her attention to the women. The one who appeared to be in charge wore a designer suit and an expensive gold watch and had the bearing of a drill sergeant. The other had short, spiky hair and was dressed informally in pants and a leather jacket. Neither of them smiled.

Crystal was wary but said hello with shopkeeper cheeriness. "May I help you?"

"Are you Crystal Clear?" the one in the designer suit asked.

Crystal didn't care for her officious tone. "Yes," she said, waiting.

"My name is Melanie de Givry," the woman said. "And this is my associate, Daphne Miles. That's Mr. Haggerty, back there. We'd like to talk to you about Jonas Lamb."

Crystal had that all-too-familiar, oh-shit-what-now feeling.

"Excuse me," Crystal said, going back and closing her office door, happy to see Bob with his nose in the *Chronicle* Sporting Green. She returned to the counter, aware of the stern expression on the grim little face of Jonas's stepdaughter, aka "the bitch."

"What *about* Jonas?" she said, with a brief glance at the other woman, Daphne.

"I'll be direct," Melanie said. "Ms. Miles and Mr. Haggerty are private investigators. Daphne's been watching Jonas for several months. We know the two of you are lovers. I'd like to discuss that with you."

"My personal life is none of your business."

"Unfortunately your involvement with Lamb does make it my business. You see, Ms. Clear, Jonas Lamb swindled money out of my mother. He conned her into marriage and into providing him an inheritance in her will. You're in a position to prevent further injustice simply by telling the truth."

"What makes you think Jonas and I were lovers?" Crystal said.

"Look, we know he came by your place a couple of times a week, often staying late into the night. You were having an affair, Ms. Clear. It's obvious."

"Jonas was very fond of my daughter and he babysat her a lot. And he also did maintenance on the houseboat. We were friends."

Melanie gave her an indulgent smile. "Crystal, we *know* what was going on, so don't bother denying it. But rest assured, my purpose isn't to make trouble for you. Just the opposite. By telling the truth, you can do me a very great favor. You see, I've sued the bastard, and one of the principal issues will be whether or not he was faithful to my mother. You'll be called as a witness. I don't think I have to tell you what the consequences of lying would be. Perjury is a serious offense."

"I don't need any lectures from you, Ms. de Givry."

"Fine. But remember it would be much easier for both of us if you don't fight me on this," Melanie warned. "It could even be beneficial for you. Let me put it this way—cooperate with me and you'll come out way ahead. Stay in bed with Jonas and it could get real messy. I don't think a spectacle would give your friend, Mr. MacDonald, a very good impression. I'm sure you don't want that."

"Are you threatening me?" Crystal shot back.

"Not at all."

"Well, you leave Bob out of this. It has nothing to do with him."

"There are two ways to proceed, Crystal. Quietly and not so quietly. Which way is up to you." With that, Melanie de Givry opened her purse and took out a business card, which she laid on the counter. "You'll be served for purposes of a deposition. It's the same as testifying in court with respect to the perjury statute. You can expect that to happen in about two weeks. So, if you have a lawyer, you might like to have him or her get in touch with us. The smoother this goes, the less painful it'll be. Remember, all we ask is the truth."

Crystal glanced down at the card.

"I'm sure in the end you'll choose to do the right thing," Melanie said. Then she said goodbye and, glancing at her companion, tossed her head and retreated toward the door, which Haggerty opened for them. All three left the shop.

Crystal was numb. This was the worst thing that could happen. Now she could see why Jonas was so pushed out of shape. Melanie de Givry was not just a bitch, she was a bitch pit bull.

Crystal felt sorry for the guy, sure, but she wasn't going to let this fuck up her life. She had a daughter to think of, after all. Her palms wet, she glanced toward her office door, which opened just then. Bob, filling the door frame, gave her an inquiring look.

"Everything all right, sweet stuff? Sounded like some pretty heated conversation going on out here."

She looked into his eyes, wavering between a lie and the truth. In the end, she settled on compromise. "It was some people inquiring about Uncle Jonas," she said.

"Jonas?"

"Yeah..." She hesitated for only the briefest second. "He has a tendency to get into financial difficulty and people come asking questions. This is not the first time this has happened." Crystal said it with aplomb because telling a man what you wanted him to know was not only natural, it was essential. (They never understood the truth the way it needed to be understood, anyway.)

Bob sauntered over and put a big arm around her shoulders. "Family can be a pain in the ass," he said with compassion. Then he noticed Melanie de

Givry's business card on the counter and picked it up. "A lawyer, huh? Jonas must be in a real pickle."

"He'll be okay. The guy has nine lives. Always lands on his feet."

"Hmm," Bob said, giving her shoulders a squeeze. "Well, don't give it a second thought." His tone suggested that she was in his care now and there wasn't a thing to worry about. Then, turning Melanie's business card in his fingers like a card shark, he casually slipped it in his shirt pocket. "How about if you close up shop a little early, we go pick up Tammy and I take you both to dinner?"

Crystal gazed up at the big lug, disconcerted that he'd taken the card without asking, though she wasn't about to make an issue of it. Every reading she'd done for Bob had come up stellar, though health issues seemed iffy. Over all, however, his readings were as good as Jonas's had been bad. "I can't," she said. "It's too early."

"I don't mean now. Say in an hour. I've got things to do on the phone. Materials to order, deliveries to arrange and stuff like that."

"Okay."

Bob kissed her temple, then headed back toward her office. He stopped at the door. "You think I should maybe talk to Uncle Jonas for you?"

The question caught her by surprise. "Why?"

"His business is his business, but when it starts being a problem for you…"

"Honey, it's nothing," Crystal said, dismissing the suggestion. "Trust me."

Bob shrugged and went inside the office. Crystal sighed, her shoulders sagging. Her guy had Melanie de Givry's business card in his pocket and Jonas was sitting out there somewhere like a ticking bomb. That wasn't good for her future or for her. She had a nose for trouble and that's what she smelled. Trouble.

Lake Tahoe, California

As he'd made his way up the mountain, Jonas had started thinking he'd have been better off to go somewhere else. It had started snowing at about the five-thousand-foot elevation and it had gotten worse as he climbed and night fell. His had been among the last vehicles to go over the pass before they'd closed the highway.

Descending into the Tahoe Basin on Highway 50, he'd felt like Moses returning from the wilderness. But he did have a sense of respite. Elise's final days had not been easy. Much as he hated to admit it, he was tired and needed a blow. But even the wilds of the Sierra Nevada contained potential dangers, and he wasn't just thinking of the elements. Faceless bad guys could be lurking anywhere.

Jonas had watched his rearview mirror from the time he left home. Several times he'd seen the same car behind him, sometimes two cars back or in the next lane, but then it would disappear for miles at a time before popping up again. He wasn't sure it represented a genuine threat or if it was a trick his mind was playing on him.

Tess and Patrick's cabin was located on the California side of the lake at Tahoe Pines. When Jonas reached the junction of 50 and State Route 89, he stopped for gas and a cup of coffee. It was after 10:00 p.m.

"What's the condition of 89?" he asked the girl behind the counter in the convenience store.

"I got no idea," she said, popping gum in response. "If it's closed, they'll let you know. I heard there're blackouts on the North Shore because of the storm."

Jonas bought half a dozen donuts, two bags of chips, four candy bars, three apples, plus a quart of milk and a carton of orange juice—in case he ended up in a snowbank. Between extra clothes and a car blanket he wasn't going to freeze to death on the road, but needless hunger could be avoided with a little forethought. Patrick had said the cabin was well-stocked with canned goods, but that he'd better pack in anything fresh. Given the hour, he wasn't going to hunt down an all-night supermarket.

As he headed out of South Lake Tahoe, he was behind a tow truck, which was either a stroke of luck or a bad omen. There were two or three other cars in the convoy, making the going easier.

At Meeks Bay the tow truck stopped to assist a car in the ditch, leaving Jonas in the role of advance scout. It had begun snowing harder, and without those big taillights in front of him, the going was tough. At times he almost stopped because of whiteouts.

He noticed there were no lights in Tahoma, so the convenience store girl's intelligence seemed to be accurate. When he reached Tahoe Pines, he discovered it, too, was without power, meaning he'd be dining by candlelight. As he searched for the landmarks Patrick had given him, Jonas slowed to five miles per hour and still had one vehicle behind him. Finally he came to the turn. A parking area had been cleared, but not the side road. There were two other vehicles parked there and three more strung out along the shoulder on the other side of the road. He pulled over and the car behind, perhaps confused, stopped as well for a moment or two before continuing down the highway.

His engine off and the car's headlight extinguished, Jonas couldn't see a thing. Fortunately he had a flashlight in the glove box. Considering he wasn't suitably dressed—no parka or gloves, just jeans and a heavy jacket and running shoes—getting to the cabin would be an adventure. His feet would be wet and his hands frozen, but Patrick had said there was plenty of dry firewood. Fire and a warm bed would seem like heaven. Jonas got his suitcase and the sack of provisions from the back seat. After locking the car, he shone the flashlight around, identified his route and began trudging up the side road. There were no footprints in the snow so he couldn't tell if other residents were around, and with the power off, there were no lights to indicate which cabins might be occupied, if any.

He'd gone maybe forty or fifty yards when he thought he heard the sound of a vehicle on the highway. He turned, but could see nothing. Was that a car door slamming he heard, or a branch crashing to the ground? He couldn't believe anyone had followed him. No, it was paranoia.

Jonas concentrated on finding the cabin. According to Patrick's map it should be just ahead, but nothing was visible but trees and snow-covered boulders. Just as he began to fear he may have missed the place, he saw a dark shape off to his right. A few more steps and he spotted a building. Seeing what looked like a sign nailed to a tree, he waded through a drift, put down the suitcase, brushed away the snow and saw the name "Vartel." Eureka!

His fingers frozen, his feet starting to feel like a couple of blocks of ice and his pant legs wet from the knee down, Jonas stumbled up the front steps of the cabin. By the time he got to the door he was shivering, his ears freezing. But he'd made it.

He put down the groceries and the suitcase, fished the key out of his pocket, inserted it in the lock as the flashlight slipped from his numb fingers, hit the deck, went out, and rolled off the porch into a snowbank. "Shit," he muttered.

There was no point in trying to look for it now. Feeling for the door in the darkness, he found the key in the lock, turned it and the bolt slid clear. He was in.

The air inside felt warm by comparison, thank God, but it was darker than hell. Dragging his stuff in with him, Jonas closed the door, then felt his way toward what he perceived to be the fireplace, stumbling once and banging his frozen toes against the leg of a chair.

"Damn," he muttered.

Maneuvering around a long dark object that had to be a sofa, he approached the fireplace and was shocked to see the faint glow of coals. What the hell?

Fumbling along the hearth, he found a box of matches. His fingers were so stiff it was a struggle, but he managed to remove a match and strike it. At the same instant he was hit in the face by a stream of liquid fire. He dropped the match and let out a howl, his eyes burning. Amid his pain, Jonas realized he wasn't the only one screaming.

The next thing he knew he was shoved to the floor and a club crashed down on his skull, mercifully putting him out of his misery.

As he regained consciousness, Jonas was aware of three things: the searing pain in his eyes, the throbbing in his skull and the damp coolness on his forehead. He groaned, opening his eyes just enough to see a blurry light.

"Thank God," she said, "I thought I'd killed you."

He strained to see through the blur, unable to make out anything in the dim light. "What...who... Jesus, what the fuck happened?"

"Jonas, I'm so sorry. I didn't know it was you."

The voice he recognized. "Tess?"

She took the cloth from his forehead and lightly dabbed his eyes, holding a candle in her other hand. "Yes, it's me. What are you doing here?"

He couldn't see her face clearly. "I thought it would be a fun place to die," he mumbled.

"Did Patrick give you a key?"

"Yes, he said you never come here in the winter," Jonas muttered, his head throbbing, "so what you didn't know wouldn't hurt you." He flexed his aching neck. "Obviously, it was a slight exaggeration."

"Well, I don't come in the winter normally, but these are not normal times."

"That I can agree with. What did you do to me, anyway?"

"I zapped you with pepper spray and hit you over the head with a piece of firewood. I thought you were an intruder."

"I am."

"A stranger intruder, I mean."

"Tess, what's stranger than a former husband?" He tried to lift his head but it was too difficult. Blinking repeatedly he was able to make out the general contours of her features. "Hey, you're pretty even under these conditions."

"What conditions? Your blindness or your delirium?"

"Both, I guess."

"I really am sorry," she said, pressing her cool hand against his cheek. "You deserved it, of course, walking in unannounced. Why did you come, anyway? Surely, you aren't here to ski."

"No, I was just seeking a few quiet evenings alone by a fire. I hadn't anticipated it'd be flat on my back and in pain. So, what's the story? You heard somebody breaking in and went into action?"

"I was dozing on the sofa when I heard you fooling with the lock. I was scared, so I got the pepper spray out of my purse and when you struck the match I fired, figuring it would be my best chance."

"You figured right."

"Jonas, you don't look very good. Maybe we should get you to the hospital."

"And spoil a perfectly lovely evening with my favorite wife?"

"It's not a joking matter."

"I'm delirious and figure I can get away with saying anything."

"Well, you're wrong. Maybe you should get up off the floor and out of those wet pants before you get pneumonia on top of everything else."

"God, I never dreamed I'd ever hear you tell me to take off my pants again."

"Jonas, stop that before I pitch you out into the snow. See if you can sit up."

He managed to, but only barely, the room taking a slow spin as he tried to adjust to an upright position. Tess supported him with her arm and knee.

"Do you think you can get to the sofa?"

"I'll try."

He made it with only minor difficulty. His vision was improving. He checked Tess out. She was in long johns and looked cute as hell.

"Let's get off your coat," she said.

"Where's Walter?"

"He's not here." She tossed his coat on the chair, then added wood to the fire.

"You mean we're alone?"

"Yes, but I've still got the firewood handy, so don't get any cute ideas."

"Nice to know you still trust me."

"I'm not finding this conversation amusing, Jonas," she said, giving him a stern look. "Now, can you take off your pants alone or do you need help?"

He decided to play it straight. "I can do it, I think."

"Patrick keeps some clothing here. I'll find you something to wear." She left, taking a candle.

Jonas got his pants off and was sitting on the sofa in his shorts, his head feeling like a balloon, when Tess returned. She'd slipped on a pair of ski pants and a sweater. With scarcely a glance in his direction, she tossed him a sweat suit.

"I'm going to get an ice bag for you." As quickly as she'd come, she was gone.

He sat for a moment, contemplating this unexpected turn of events, wondering if it was an act of beneficence or just another complication destined to add to his misery. But before he could decide which Tess returned with an ice bag, which he gingerly applied to the lump on his skull. No sooner had she dropped into the armchair close to the fire when the lights suddenly came on, followed almost an instant later by a crashing sound outside, perhaps on the porch.

"What was that?" Tess said, alarmed.

"I don't know." But he remembered the feeling of being followed. "Maybe I should check." He got to his feet, a bit unsteady, his brain too foggy perhaps to properly register fear.

"Are you sure you're up to it?" she asked.

"All I'm going to do is look out the door."

Tess handed him the can of pepper spray. "Here, take this. It's very effective."

"No kidding."

Jonas went to the door, ready to inflict blindness. Tess was behind him, the chunk of firewood in her hands. The suggestion of fear beginning to register in his muddled brain, he turned the bolt and, taking a deep breath, yanked the door open.

The front of the cabin was lit now by a porch light. He peered out, catching a glimpse of a figure disappearing into the trees down the road. It wasn't his imagination, after all.

"Do you see anything?" Tess asked.

He shook his head and said, "No," intending his untruthfulness as an act of kindness.

They returned to the fire, Jonas trying to decide what the hell he should do besides keep the pepper spray handy. Was someone just spying on him or did they intend him harm?

"Head injuries can be dangerous," Tess said. "I really think you need medical attention."

"I'm fine."

"I want you to go to the hospital."

He studied her, noticing again how pretty she was, how, after all this time, she still did it for him. "Is it a medical issue, or do you want me out of your hair?" he asked.

"I'm concerned for your health. But beyond that, I find this very awkward. Don't you?"

He considered saying no, but she was already uneasy. There was a ringing sound and Tess jumped.

"Is that a cell phone?" she asked.

"Yes. It's in my coat pocket. Would you mind handing me the coat?"

He got the phone out of the pocket, wondering who'd be calling at this hour. Patrick? Jimmy Yee? The FBI? He pushed the button. "Hello?"

"Jonas, it's Crystal. I know it's late, but we've got a problem. I would have called earlier, but Bob just left. Something's happened."

He considered the irony of receiving a call from his disaffected mistress while sitting by the fire with his wife (four times removed). "What's happened?"

"Your stepdaughter came by the shop today."

"And?"

"She's going to make me testify against you."

"Oh, God," he moaned, his head starting to throb still more. He glanced at Tess, who'd sat on the hearth to poke at the fire. "What exactly did she say?"

"That she knew about us and that if I didn't tell the truth, she'd send me to the slammer for fifty years—you know, basically ruin my life."

"And you said?"

"I told her we were friends. Which, of course, was true."

Jonas decided not to ask if she'd chosen the past tense intentionally. He opted to be assumptive. "We're *very* good friends. Way to go, girl."

"Yeah, but, Jonas, I'm going to have to give a disposition in a couple of weeks. *Under oath.*"

"Crystal, you've done beautifully, just hang in there with me a bit longer."

"What's the point? I'm going to have to tell the truth eventually. I've got myself to look out for. And Tamara. Things are getting serious between Bob and me. I can't screw that up to save your butt."

"Listen," he said, glancing again at Tess, who pretended to pay no attention, "I'll find a way to work this out. And if you give me the chance, a little time, I'll make it worth your while. I promise."

"Yeah, sure."

"I'm serious. You know the scope of the deal I'm working on."

"No, I don't, Jonas. Besides, this isn't about money. It's about my future. I can't afford to screw that up. The bitch is threatening to blackmail me with Bob."

"She said that?"

"In effect."

"So, how was it left?"

"I'm going to be served, which means getting a lawyer and all that shit, I guess."

"I'll cover your expenses."

"That's not kosher, is it?"

"If no strings are attached."

"Still, it doesn't look good, no matter what you say."

"Okay," he said, "just give me until the deposition. That's all I ask. And if she comes back, stonewall her. There's nothing she can do before then."

"Except fuck up things with Bob."

"She wouldn't do that."

"Oh, yeah?"

"Call me if you have a problem, all right? Meanwhile, just sit tight."

"Easy for you to say."

"Actually, it's not. But I appreciate you giving me a heads-up."

"Until the disposition, Jonas." (Crystal could be stubborn about her malapropisms.)

"Yes, just a couple of weeks. I'll be in touch." He put down the phone.

Tess's demeanor was neutral, as if to say she was politely minding her own business.

"My stockbroker," he said.

"The market opened early today."

He chuckled. "Actually, it's about that lawsuit. No big deal."

Tess put another piece of wood on the fire. "Jonas, it's no concern of mine, except maybe to the extent it adversely affects Patrick."

He could see there was no point in pursuing it. Tess already had made up her mind about him.

"I believe we were talking about you going to the hospital," she said.

"Tess, I spent a lot of time at hospitals lately with Elise and, frankly, I've had my fill of them. Anyway, it's a take-two-aspirin-and-call-me-in-the-morning situation." He could see he'd hit on a winning formula. She looked like she might back down.

"That noise on the porch earlier," she said. "You told me there was nobody out there, but there was, wasn't there?"

He nodded. "Yes, I didn't want you to be upset. It's also another reason I don't think I should leave you here alone."

"I don't think I'm the one in danger...except to the extent I'm with you."

"It's not that kind of situation."

"Who was it?"

"I really don't know."

"Then how can you say it's not dangerous?"

"God, you are a lawyer, aren't you?"

"Jonas, I don't consider this a game. It's about whatever you and Patrick are doing, isn't it?"

"Possibly."

"And it involves a national-security problem."

"What makes you think that?" he asked, surprised.

"Walter's friend, the regent, told us."

"You're referring to the FBI investigation."

"Yes."

He considered that, wondering how things could have gotten to this stage without warning. It was obvious Tess wanted an explanation. "The thing is international in scope, but I honestly can't say it involves national security."

She seemed concerned. He felt her frustration.

"Look," he said, "let's deal with this in the morning. Keep the pepper spray by your bed and tomorrow things won't seem so grim. Where do I sleep, by the way? On the sofa?"

"There's another bedroom upstairs next to the master."

"Maybe it's better if I stay down here."

She seemed to appreciate that. He felt better for having scored a point.

He took her hand in an avuncular way. "I'm sorry to have ruined your stay."

"I'm sorry to have assaulted you," she said, removing her hand from his. "I think I'll go to bed. Need anything before I go?" she asked.

He cast about for something to say. "I could use some legal advice."

"Is it that serious?"

"I could lose a million bucks or so."

Tess shook her head, perhaps more with pity than sympathy. "How about we discuss it at breakfast?"

"Sure."

She hesitated, then giving him a small smile left the room.

Alone, Jonas gazed at the fire, which was what he'd come to do. But it wasn't enough. He had yet another problem to contend with. He was falling in love with his second wife all over again.

FRIDAY
January 18

Hong Kong

Jimmy Yee knew something was up when his father's old friend, Zhang Jintao, invited him to come by for a drink at 10:00 p.m. on a Friday night. Zhang was one of those indispensable individuals unique to eastern cultures—particularly the Chinese—whose value was in his ability to make the system work more smoothly. In the West there was no direct equivalent. He was neither a powerbroker nor a *consiglière*, not a godfather nor an *agent provocateur*. *Consultant* was perhaps the best description, though one with considerable status. Zhang simply knew how to get things done, and people on all sides of an issue came to him for advice.

The British had consulted Zhang about dealing with the communists. The communists consulted him about dealing with the nationalists. Industry consulted him about dealing with the government. The government consulted him about dealing with foreigners. It was said that there were men who even consulted Zhang Jintao about how best to handle their wives, though Zhang always denied such rumors as foolishness. He was a modest man and that was a major reason for his effectiveness.

Jimmy Yee knew little about Zhang's personal life and background except that when he spoke it was always with authority. With the takeover of Hong Kong by the PRC, Zhang's status may have, if anything, increased, because the communists knew they were at a disadvantage in the larger world and valued a man who could get them results. Which was not to say Zhang promoted a particular cause or ideology. He worked for all parties to an issue. He was an honest broker.

Yee's previous encounters with Zhang Jintao had taken place mostly at the request of the Crown Colony and had involved sensitive business matters that had import for the government. Mostly Zhang had greased wheels that were squeaking and reduced the friction to the satisfaction of all concerned.

What was unique in this instance was the fact that Jimmy had no idea what Zhang had in mind. He couldn't even say with certainty who the party behind the scenes might be. Of late, Zhang's communications with the business community were more often than not at the behest of Hong Kong's new political masters, but as regards which of Yee's endeavors might be at issue, he had no idea whatsoever.

Jimmy Yee left his home with his usual entourage of bodyguards in his Mercedes limousine. Zhang Jintao lived in an old Victorian house on the lower slope of Victoria Peak, a substantial home but hardly an ostentatious one. If it was remarkable it was for the high brick wall that surrounded the house and garden.

When the limo pulled to the gate, a hunched little man stepped out of the guardhouse, bowing as the limo rolled past the gate and up the gravel drive to the front portico. One of the bodyguards opened the car door and Jimmy stepped from the vehicle, taking a deep breath of the fresh air as he glanced up at the evening sky.

A bright star caught his eye, which, when he looked closely, appeared to be moving. It wasn't a plane and it was traveling too slowly to be a meteor. It occurred to him then it was the International Space Station. The West and its technological marvels. The Japanese had gotten in on the act, of course, but most of what they did was derivative. The Chinese had always been stoic, even dismissive of the technological successes of the foreign devils, but when satellites from across the seas filled the firmament it was much harder to be cavalier. China may still be the center of the world to the Chinese, but it certainly wasn't the only part of the globe that mattered.

The huge front door of the house opened and Jimmy Yee turned to see an old *amah* in traditional dress bowing and smiling. "Welcome, Mr. Yee," she said. "Please come in."

Jimmy went inside the big Victorian, which was furnished in the classical Chinese style with Western touches. Oddly, it reminded him of the home of the provost at Oxford, a stately manse with Gothic overtones. He had gone there on one less-than-felicitous occasion to explain the falsity of the complaints that had been lodged against him by a comely young woman of dubious character. Oddly, he had a somewhat similar trepidation coming to see Zhang Jintao.

"Please come this way, Mr. Yee," the *amah* said as she padded along the ebony-stained hardwood floor, overlaid with a dark red Oriental carpet.

The woman, in her sixties, reminded him of the *gan sun,* the nanny, he'd had as a child, a woman of quiet firmness who'd played as great a role in molding his character as his parents. The *amah* opened a set of double doors and gestured for him to enter.

Zhang, who'd been sitting in one of two matching Ming chairs by a burning fire, rose and came to greet Jimmy. He smiled, extending his hand.

Zhang Jintao was slender and tall for a man of his generation. Though it had been a while since they'd seen each other, and though Zhang had aged considerably in the interim, the old man had the same quiet energy as before. He was a bit stooped now, his hair thinning and whiter than Jimmy's, but he still had the look of a man of influence, his prominent eyebrows and the dark circles under his eyes reminiscent of the first premier of the PRC, Chou En-Lai.

"Welcome, Jimmy," he said, bowing, then shaking his hand vigorously. "Thank you so much for coming."

"It is my pleasure, Honorable Zhang."

"Please come sit by the fire. It's a cold night. The fire is warm."

Zhang wore a modified Mao jacket and matching trousers. He might have been a middle-level official in some provincial town; he certainly didn't have the appearance of someone who'd played a role, albeit a minor one, in Nixon's rapprochement with the People's Republic of China.

"What would you like to drink, Jimmy? Scotch?"

"That would be fine. Please."

"Neat?"

"Yes, thank you."

Zhang gave instructions to the *amah* and sent her on her way. The men settled into the chairs in front of the blazing fire.

"I think often of your father," Zhang said. "He was a very fine man."

"Thank you. He spoke of you with reverence, Honorable Zhang."

Zhang Jintao bowed his head politely. Jimmy, glancing around, noticed the book on the small table between them. It was Sun Tzu's *The Art of War.*

"I hope this is not the subject of our meeting," he said, indicating the book.

Zhang laughed. "Hardly. Since the fall of the Soviets, the world is much more interested in money than conflict—except, of course, in the usual hot spots, which are most dangerous in their own way."

"Yes, that's true."

"What the Americans fail to understand is that commerce, like politics, is a form of conflict that can be as dangerous as war, unless husbanded properly."

"But a conflict of acceptable proportions."

"Perhaps," Zhang said.

The English tall clock in the corner began to chime and Jimmy took a quick peek at his watch.

"Don't worry," Zhang said, "it's slow. Like me."

"You are more formidable than ever, from what I'm told."

"You are one of the foremost businessmen in the world, Jimmy. I won't try to keep up with you."

The humility was part of the ritual. Jimmy Yee still hadn't the vaguest idea what this was about.

The *amah* arrived with their drinks and a small bowl of rice crackers. Zhang picked up his glass as the old woman left the room, silently closing the door. Then he tapped Jimmy's glass with his own, Western-style, and said, "Cheers," in English.

"Cheers."

They each drank and Zhang Jintao stared for a long moment into the fire. Then he said, "I'm sure you're wondering why I invited you here this evening, so I won't keep you in suspense. I've had conversations with the Third Bureau."

Jimmy knew that he meant the Third Bureau of the Guojia Anquan Bu or the Ministry of State Security, the security agency of the PRC. The Third Bureau of the MSS had operational responsibility for Hong Kong, Macao and Taiwan, all of which were near and dear to the hearts of the boys in Beijing. Matters with security and intelligence components often were handled by the state body responsible for espionage, if only because the MSS had had agents on station for long periods who were well established in the communities in which they operated. In brief, they knew their way around.

Jimmy was well aware of this, of course, and had had several meetings with officials from the MSS, both before and after the takeover in '97, when sovereignty of the colony was ceded back to China. The communists had looked to people with economic influence, men like Jimmy Yee, to shore up the credibility of their "one country, two systems" policy, which promised a continuation of capitalism, Chinese-style. And so, like it or not, to do business in Hong Kong, Jimmy and others like him had to be cognizant of the desires and interests of the Chinese rulers in Beijing.

"Obviously, the conversations were about me."

"Indeed."

Jimmy waited.

Zhang sipped his drink. "You have had conversations with an American named Jonas Lamb about his technological breakthrough, some sort of substance to enhance the efficiency of petroleum, a biological agent, I believe. You'll have to forgive me, I am ignorant of the details."

Jimmy remained calm, turning his glass slowly as he maintained eye contact with his host. "Most impressive. My compliments to the Third Bureau. How did they do it?"

"I do not know, Jimmy. They never discuss their methods, only their desires."

"Of course."

Now it was Zhang who waited.

"So, what are their desires?" Jimmy asked.

"They see opportunity. Mr. Lamb's discovery could change many things in the world economy, as you very well know. Certain interests and certain economies will have great advantages because of it. Beijing wants to know with certainty that China's interests will be served."

"What is it they want from me, Honorable Zhang?"

"Your cooperation."

"In exchange for…"

"Assurances that Yee Industries will control and market the product."

"This is within their power to grant?"

"I am told that they have already been working in your interests, Jimmy. The Guojia Anquan Bu is combating hostile foreign threats to Mr. Lamb's person and interests to ensure that the technology will eventually come under your control."

"Are you saying other foreign governments are involved?"

"Yes. And our friends in Guoanbu believe the goal of these elements is the destruction of Mr. Lamb and his technology."

Jimmy realized this investment opportunity of Jonas's had wider ramifications than he'd thought. While he was horrified to think that the MSS was involved, it was also an indication of the credibility of what Jonas was doing. The question was whether or not his old pal was two-timing him. Jonas had to be talking to others if the national-security agencies of other countries were involved.

"Jonas is my friend," Jimmy said, "but I have no control over him."

"My clients would like to see that change. They encourage you to press ahead."

"I understand they want me to be successful and that China benefit from the undertaking. What specifically do they want from me beside assurances of cooperation?"

"The National Defense Science, Technology and Industry Commission would like to become your silent partner in the enterprise, Jimmy."

"They want me to be the front, in other words."

"And become even richer in the process. Considerably richer."

Jimmy could see the pie was being cut into ever-smaller pieces, but he could also see that for one man to control something so important to the whole world was unrealistic. A hundred percent of nothing was still nothing. He knew that, Zhang Jintao knew it, and the boys in Beijing most certainly knew it. They were counting on his common sense and good judgment.

"There is no way I can take on the world's security agencies and win," he said. "Not without help. Who better to have on my team than the Guoanbu? Please be kind enough to tell your clients that I am agreed in principle, Honorable Zhang."

Zhang Jintao bowed his head. "They will be most pleased, I'm certain."

"What's the next step?"

"Someone from the office of the minister in charge of the National Defense Science, Technology and Industry Commission will contact you about entering into a commercial agreement. Meanwhile you should make arrangements to provide Mr. Lamb with the resources he needs to complete the deal, including security personnel."

"They want me to send bodyguards?"

"The MSS will provide the personnel, but they will go under the auspices of Yee Industries. Someone from the Hong Kong office of the Third Bureau will contact you about particulars. They want you to work it out with Mr. Lamb. It's important that he not know anything about Beijing's role in this. My clients made a special point of this."

That was easily enough understood. It seemed unlikely to Jimmy that the FBI and CIA were totally in the dark about Jonas's operation and the MSS wanted to hedge its bets. In fact, it was possible Jonas was secretly working with the American government, though to what end Jimmy couldn't imagine. The point was, in an operation this sensitive anything was possible. Jimmy knew his best bet was to buckle his seat belt and go along for the ride.

"There's one other thing," Zhang said. "It's a question I was asked to put to you."

"Yes?"

"My clients are under the impression that Mr. Lamb is very fond of the ladies. Is this a fair assessment?"

"I would say so, yes."

"They would like to know then, is it your judgment that, in selecting an agent to assign to the case, a woman would be the best choice?"

"I would say so," Jimmy replied. "Preferably young, attractive and Westernized."

"I will pass that on," Zhang Jintao said. He drained his glass. "May I offer you another drink, my friend?"

"Please," Jimmy said, draining his glass as well. "I could use one."

Zhang summoned the *amah* with a little bell. Once their drinks had been refreshed, he said, "May I propose a toast, Jimmy?"

"Certainly."

"To your friend, Jonas Lamb," he said, bowing his head slightly. "And to China's friend, as well. May we prosper together."

Lake Tahoe, California

Jonas awoke to the smell of bacon, toast, coffee and the happy thought of being alone in the cabin with his favorite wife. He repaired to the bathroom. When he came out, improved but well shy of peak condition, he went to the kitchen, where he found Tess looking bright and alert and pleasing to the eye.

"There you are," she said. "I wasn't sure if I should wake you or not. Breakfast?"

"Sounds wonderful."

"Sit down and I'll pour you some coffee."

Jonas didn't exactly stagger to the table, but he wasn't his usual graceful self.

"How do you feel?" she asked.

"Awful, to be honest."

She poured coffee into a mug. "I feel terrible about what happened."

"That's all right, I like it when you're beholding."

"Guilty I might be, beholding I'm not." She brought the mug to the table and put it down in front of him.

"Did I overplay my hand again?" he asked, looking up at her, offering a smile.

"You've been overplaying your hand since the day I met you," she said, retreating to the counter.

"At least I'm consistent."

"Eggs?"

"Please."

"How do you want them?"

"The usual."

"Jonas, it's been nearly thirty years."

"It was a test."

"Well, I failed."

"Scrambled."

"Fine."

She broke some eggs into a bowl. He checked out her body. She glanced over at him, catching him in the act.

"I don't mean to be antagonistic," she said, "but I find this very uncomfortable."

"You said that last night. Does it mean you're trying to convince me of the fact, or are you trying to convince yourself?"

"What's that supposed to mean?"

"I don't know, I guess I'm just trying to understand."

"My point is we need to talk about it."

"Okay, but can we defer negotiations until after breakfast? When my stomach's empty, I'm easily outwitted."

"I wish I'd known that before I agreed to marry you."

"Didn't you wonder why I never showed up until after lunch?"

She gave him a look.

The more he saw of her, the more Jonas remembered the way things had been—not just the bad stuff, mostly the good stuff. Watching her, he almost felt like the goofy, besotted twenty-nine-year-old he'd been.

Tess carried over a plate of toast, bacon and a jar of jam. "Want some of the juice you brought?"

"Sure."

She got the carton from the refrigerator and poured some in a glass and set it in front of him. He continued to admire her.

"I don't recall you being this domestic."

"I'm not. It's the circumstances."

"Feed me and get me out of the house?"

Her silence was her response. She did not seem receptive to the notion of a rapprochement. What did he expect? That after a smile and a few quips she'd be head over heels in love with him again?

She brought a plate of eggs, then sat in the other chair with a coffee mug of her own. "You know what the worst part of this whole thing is?"

"Define 'whole thing,'" he said, picking up his fork.

"Patrick, you, the FBI, everything."

"If I had to guess, I'd say me." He took a bite of eggs.

"The worst is I'm beginning to think you and Patrick are in over your heads."

Tess was a smart woman. "You could be right."

"And there's nothing to be done about it?"

He knew it was a serious question. "Sometimes you go down a road and find there's no backing out, regardless of your desires. Hasn't that ever happened to you?"

She stared at her coffee cup. "I'm in a situation like that right now, as a matter of fact. I made a serious mistake a few years ago and now I'm paying the price."

He waited for further explanation but, seeing none was forthcoming, said, "I can relate to that."

"If you're talking about us, Jonas, you seemed to have gone on."

"I'm still suffering."

"I don't believe you."

"What I mean is I never fully recovered from losing you, and my life since has been a long attempt to compensate."

"That's not very flattering to your wives."

"Oh, they had their virtues and I had my motives. It was a combination that produced six marriages."

"I feel sorry for you. And for them."

"Don't. Everybody did the best they could. Seems to me that's what matters."

"No regrets?"

He took a couple more bites of egg. "No. I may be a fool, but to live you have to take chances. Maybe I don't have a lot to be proud of, but I'm not often bored."

"Or boring," she said.

"Was that a compliment?"

"Yeah."

They looked into each other's eyes until Tess picked up his plate.

"I've got to clean up the kitchen," she said, carrying the plate to the sink.

Jonas watched her; she was absorbed in what she was doing but, seemingly, with an extra bit of color in her cheeks. He got up to pour himself more coffee when he heard his cell phone in the other room. "That will be for me."

Jonas went off to find the phone. It was Jimmy Yee.

"Good to hear your voice, *Jimmy*," he said louder than was necessary.

"I've got news."

"I'm all ears."

"Word of your project seems to have spread around the world."

"Funny, I've been coming to the same conclusion."

"You could be in danger, old bean."

"I've got news for you, my friend. It's a documented fact. Dead bodies and mysterious strangers have started showing up at every turn."

"How about if I send you a security expert and some cash to reinforce the castle?"

"You're *that* worried, Jimmy?"

"I'd hate to lose an old friend and a fabulous fortune."

"In that order, undoubtedly."

"You know me, Jonas."

"Care to share the source of your information?" he asked as he moved toward the bathroom, beyond Tess's hearing.

"My tentacles spread far and wide."

"You think your security guy can keep me from being separated from my head?"

"Security girl. Her name's May Li and she's the best."

"Knowing you, Jimmy, she's probably the fastest gun in a miniskirt," he said, closing the bathroom door.

Yee chuckled. "Competence is the first consideration."

"When does your girl arrive?"

"In a day or two. She'll have a few associates and a check with her for a hundred thousand."

"Lord, you must be more worried than I thought."

"We go way back, my friend. And I'm as ambitious as ever. When will you be coming to Hong Kong, by the way?"

"As soon as we wrap up preparation for the experimental field. My best guess is a week or two."

"I'm jolly well looking forward to it. Meanwhile, do whatever May tells you."

Jonas laughed. "Jimmy, you make me blush."

"I thought the idea would appeal to you."

He thought of Tess, realizing he was feeling a new sobriety as regards his addiction to women...or, at the very least, a lull in his usual passions. It was still difficult to tell if the inciting cause of his attraction to Tess was nostalgia or something more. "To be honest, Jimmy, I may be entering a more puritanical phase."

"Surely you jest."

"Life can be sobering at times. Death even more so."

They ended the conversation.

When Jonas left the bathroom, he found Tess at the front door talking to a woman standing on the porch. They were just saying their goodbyes and Tess closed the door.

"Who was that?" Jonas asked.

"A neighbor. She's headed to the store and stopped to ask if I needed anything."

"That was considerate."

Tess leaned against the door, looking a little shook up.

"What's wrong?" he asked.

"That wasn't all she said. Last night her son arrived late from the Bay Area and encountered a man down at the road. The guy had been up here somewhere and her son was suspicious since he looked foreign, like he didn't belong."

"It could have been the guy we heard on the porch."

"That's what I was thinking. But that's not all. This morning the highway patrol pulled a car out of Emerald Bay."

"You're saying it might have been the same guy."

"Jonas, he was carrying a Jordanian passport and he had a gun."

Solano County

They drove south on Highway 113, through the town of Dixon, until they reached Highway 12. The land was flat and low, only a few feet above sea level.

To the south and east was the Sacramento Delta, once a vast marsh that had been turned into a network of sloughs and levies that formed "islands" of reclaimed land sitting below water level, always vulnerable to the ravages of Mother Nature.

Kristy Ogawa's parents owned a large farm on the northern bank of the Sacramento River, south of Birds Landing, between Collinsville Road and Montezuma Slough. Most of the Ogawas' land was farmed by tenants, but Kristy's parents still lived in the big house and managed a small truck-farming operation. She was not taking her friends to meet her family. She was showing them the old fishing boat her grandfather had once operated, which was now moored to a rickety dock on the slough. It was the place, she'd told Tina, where she and her high school boyfriend had lost their virginity.

K.J., who had more or less ascended to the post of chief of field operations of Save the Seed, and Brad Kozik, who still ran the Davis chapter, had come to check the place out. Tina was along mostly because she and K.J. had become the alpha female and male of the pack. The four were in Brad's old VW van. Because it had been Tina's idea to kidnap Mayne, she and K.J. were in charge of the operation. They were a team, and the fact that they were screwing didn't hurt. He'd all but moved into her flat.

They'd turned onto Dutton off Collinsville Road and had gone a mile or so when Kristy told Brad to slow down because the gate they had to enter was coming up soon. She had a key to the padlock.

"You sure nobody ever comes here?" K.J. asked.

"Only me. My father doesn't get much farther from the house than his vegetable garden, not since his stroke. And my mother never goes out."

"What about the farmworkers?"

"They have no reason to come here," Kristy said. "And the tenant farmers stick to their fields. Anyway, they're hardly around in winter. The fishing boat is off-limits. It's a family shrine and I'm in charge of it."

"What about people seeing lights at night?" K.J. said. "The land here is flat enough to see forever."

"There's the levee along the slough and there're trees, too. Anyway, our house is a mile and a half away. No neighbors in sight. The only thing we have to watch out for is somebody coming up the slough by boat, but there's very little traffic this time of year."

"I guess you'd know."

"Believe me, K.J., if I can have half my high school class here for a beer and pot party in June without anybody finding out, we'll be safe hiding one professor here for a week in January."

"Yeah, makes sense."

"That's the gate there, Brad," Kristy said, pointing to the spot ahead.

He turned into the drive. Kristy got out and removed the chain and padlock that secured the iron gate. After she swung it open, Brad drove through and she secured the gate. Then she got back into the van and followed the gravel ruts that ran to the levee. When they reached the slough they stopped at a second gate, also locked. Kristy got out and repeated the drill. The barbed-wire fence secured the section of levee where the boat was moored, but they couldn't see it because of the height of the levee.

"Jesus," K.J. said, looking at the high fence, "this is like a concentration camp."

Tina, who was sitting next to him, poked him in the ribs with her elbow.

"Not funny," Kristy said. "My father was born in a concentration camp for Japanese Americans. They accused his father of spying on the munitions plant across the river in Pittsburg, for no reason except that they were Japanese."

"Sorry," K.J. said, "I didn't mean nothing."

The four got out of the van, climbed over the levee and down the other side to the dock where the old boat was moored. It was larger than K.J. expected.

"Hey, this is cool. Does it run?"

"No, it's a floating museum. My father couldn't get rid of it, so we do what we have to do to keep it afloat."

"But it has electricity?"

"Yes. And water and a propane stove."

"God," Brad said, "maybe we should set up headquarters here."

"Keeping the prisoner here for a week or two is plenty," Kristy said. "I'm already taking a chance of dishonoring my parents. They'd kill me if they found out."

"It's for a good cause," Tina said. "Anyway, nothing bad's going to happen."

"Yes, that's what I tell myself."

They toured the boat. Kristy had said that the hold

would make an ideal cell for the prisoner because the iron door could be locked and there were ventilation ducts, but no portholes. The only disadvantage was that it didn't have toilet facilities, but the head was right next door and a bedpan could be provided.

Tina and K.J. had decided there'd be two Seeds guarding the prisoner at all times, which meant lots of shifts. When she saw the double bed in the main cabin, she glanced at K.J. and they exchanged smiles. She could tell what he was thinking of doing when the two of them stood guard together.

And that was fine. K.J. was no Don Juan, but he was young and enthusiastic and Tina enjoyed the sex. But in the back of her mind what she looked forward to was seeing Patrick Mayne up close and personal. And having power over him. *That* was a turn-on.

"So, what do you think?" Brad asked. "When do we do it?"

"Mayne is out of town," Tina said. "He's supposed to be gone a week. As soon as he gets back we'll strike."

South Lake Tahoe

Tess asked for a room on one of the top floors with a lake view, partly because the vista was wonderful, but also because she felt safer higher up. Jonas had convinced her to stay at one of the casinos long enough for him to divert the attention of the bad guys. He'd decided to head back to the Bay Area.

Entering the room, Tess went over to the picture window and opened the sheer curtains. The entire Tahoe Basin was frosted white except for the large patch of cobalt-blue water in the middle of the lake that hadn't yet frozen over. It was dazzling in the sunlight.

Jonas handed the bellhop a five and sauntered over next to her. "Quite a view," he said.

"There *is* beauty in the world," she replied. "Lot's of it."

She could feel his eyes on her and could almost read his thoughts. Incredibly, it was as if the last thirty years hadn't happened. He was still enamored with her, still able to look at her with lovesick eyes. She wasn't sure why, unless it was an unwillingness to accept the impossible, to dream on in the hope of undoing history. Or, simply to pretend. As she knew all too well, Jonas was a great pretender.

Growing more uncomfortable by the moment, Tess decided to deflect him with conversation. "Last night you said you wanted to discuss your lawsuit," she said. "I'm not in active practice, but I'd be glad to point out danger areas, whatever."

"I appreciate that, Tess."

"I assume you're getting an attorney."

"I already have one. Braxton Weir. Ever heard of him?"

"No, but that doesn't mean anything. There are thousands in San Francisco."

"He's in a small firm with a couple of other lawyers. Less overhead, lower fees for the clients."

She nodded. "Sounds like you're in good hands. I'm sure there's nothing I can add."

"There is something I'd like to discuss with you because you're affected in an indirect way."

"Me?"

"Through Patrick. You see, our company has gotten sucked into my lawsuit with my stepdaughter. Elise put up the capital and I was supposed to inherit her stock, but now Melanie is contesting the will, which puts her in the middle of things."

"The problem, in other words, is control of the corporation," Tess said.

"Basically Melanie is a shit-disturber. She doesn't know what GET does, she's just happy to have an opportunity to make life miserable for me. It's an annoyance more than anything because we essentially have no assets. If Melanie gets control, we'll just form a new corporation. My question is more personal than legal. Patrick's aware I'm in a pissing match with Melanie and her brother, but I haven't told him about the threat to the company for a couple of reasons. First, it's my fight, not his, and second, he doesn't need the worry. Managing things is how I'm earning my keep. Do you think that's all right, or should I tell him everything?"

Tess started to say, "I believe honesty is always the best policy," but then thought of her recent dilemma over telling Walter about her affair. She'd rationalized not telling him until the eleventh hour; how could she tell Jonas he'd be wrong to do the same? She went over and sat on the bed.

"I guess it's a question of whether Patrick needs to know and whether he'd be hurt by you keeping him in the dark."

The way Jonas looked at her, she knew what he was thinking—about his failure to tell her about his first marriage and the tragic consequences. "I would rather not repeat my mistakes," he said, "but telling the truth isn't always the kindest thing, is it?"

"I guess it's something each of us has to decide for himself."

Jonas shook his head. "Good intentions hardly matter, do they?"

Tess realized that in her dilemma with Walter her good intentions had mainly to do with sparing herself, even if it impacted him to some degree. But where did one draw the line? "Maybe the question is whether the other person needs to know, if only to protect themselves," she said.

As he stared at her it was hard to know if he was thinking of thirty years ago, or if he was thinking of their son. "I guess I can tell Patrick I've decided to form a new corporation because Melanie's messing up GET."

"That sounds reasonable."

Jonas seemed pleased. Tess was glad, too. But then a thought occurred to her.

"Wait a minute. You said your company doesn't have much in the way of assets. What about Patrick's discovery?"

"That's not an asset, is it?"

"Well, it depends. Is there a patent?"

"We did the paperwork."

"Is it in Patrick's name or the corporation's?"

"Since the whole thing is top secret we put it in

the name of the corporation, to keep his name out of it."

"That's all well and good, Jonas, but putting it in the corporation's name means the corporation owns it. Wasn't your attorney concerned about that?"

"We didn't discuss the patent."

"Maybe you should."

Jonas blanched. "Christ," he said, "are you suggesting Melanie could end up owning ninety percent of our fortune?"

"Does she know you've got a valuable discovery?"

"No, she thinks I'm a flake." He glanced at her. "The woman's obviously delusional."

Tess chuckled. "No comment."

"Seriously, Tess, we're talking major tragedy here. A billion-dollar tragedy. We'd better transfer the patent to a new corporation before Melanie gets wind of things."

"That may not solve your problem. If she finds out you ripped off a valuable asset, she can sue your new corporation to get it back. You could end up paying her, anyway. I think you need to sit down with your lawyer."

"What about Patrick?"

"What do you think, Jonas?"

She saw that faraway look in his eye. "I'd better tell him. With luck I might be able to work out something with Melanie and spare us all a lot of grief."

She nodded approvingly. Jonas's smile was a bit sad. "I'm a slow learner, Tess," he said, "but I get there eventually."

There was a warmth to his tone and she became very much aware of his proximity. Uncomfortable, she got up and returned to the window. She knew he was watching her.

"Are you really going to marry Walter?" he asked without fanfare.

"Of course," she replied, continuing to stare out the window.

"There's no of course about it."

She turned to face him. "Walter and I are engaged."

"You don't have on the ring."

"I didn't want to travel with it." She colored, not feeling comfortable with either his questions or her less-than-fully-truthful responses. "But we *are* engaged."

"That's not the same thing."

"What are you suggesting?"

"That maybe you won't marry him. Or shouldn't."

"What could possibly make you say that?"

He got up and walked to where she stood. He searched her eyes for uncertainty, a sign of hope, then plunged ahead. "Because you don't love him."

The audacity annoyed her. "How would you know?"

"I sense it, Tess. You don't belong with the guy."

"Do all your misadventures with marriage make you an expert?"

"Actually, failure is a good teacher."

"Then maybe you *are* an expert."

When he said nothing, she realized she'd hurt him. "I'm sorry, that was unkind."

"But understandable."

"Look," she said, "we're both under a lot of stress, on edge..."

"If you're trying to explain away our mutual attraction, it won't work, Tess."

Her eyes flashed and he laughed. Then he took her into his arms and kissed her. Though she resisted momentarily, she kissed him back. But then she changed her mind and wedged her hands between them, easing him away. "That was not at all considerate," she said, "taking advantage of me that way."

"You wanted to kiss me."

"Even if true, it's not very gentlemanly of you to say so."

"The point is you did."

"No, the point is I did something I shouldn't have done. It's not the first time, need I remind you. I slipped. That's all there is to it. Now, can we please leave it at that?"

"I think you're in denial."

"Please, Jonas," she said. "Go."

"All right. I'll respect your wishes. But I've learned something important, Tess. I never stopped loving you."

She couldn't believe he actually said that. "Your wife has only been dead a few days. How can you say such a thing? It's an insult to me as well as her."

"I've really only had one wife, Tess, and I lost her a long, long time ago."

Part THREE

WEDNESDAY
January 23

Berkeley, California

The big, black, armor-plated limo left I-80 at University Avenue and headed toward the campus, which lay at the foot of the mist-shrouded Berkeley Hills. Jonas Lamb, ensconced in the back seat, had some knowledge of the town and its inhabitants.

Before marrying Elise he'd briefly dated a psychology professor at the university, a forty-six-year-old divorcée named Rachel Bauman, a woman hell-bent on cramming twenty years of sexual experience—and possibly a child—into the few years she had left before menopause. Her husband had been asexual, and she a devout Jew who believed—even at the cost of painful self-abnegation—in fidelity. With divorce, all bets were off.

The candid sort, Rachel (stark naked and under the influence of a little hemp) had provided Jonas with a full account of her sexual exploits, which ran the gamut from her department chair to a minor rap artist from East Oakland, a twenty-four-year-old stud "with a cock like a fence post." Jonas had been her "nonacademic WASP businessman" whom she'd considered a possible contender for the honor "father of my child," until she got wind of his bank account.

Fun and games were about the furthest thing from his mind at the moment, however. Jonas was so focused on his upcoming meeting with Patrick that he was only half aware of the bare legs protruding so enticingly from the little miniskirt of May Li, his security chief, seated next to him. His son was attending a scientific conference of some sort on the Berkeley campus and they were meeting for lunch at the Faculty Club to catch up on developments with respect to Operation Black Sheep and to plot their next step. Over the weekend Patrick had returned from his "planting trip." They'd spoken briefly on the phone to set up their meeting.

Jonas was warm and lowered the window for some air.

"Sorry, Mr. Lamb. Best to keep window up," May, who looked angelic but was as lethal as a smart bomb, said to him. "You hot, we put on air conditioner."

May, using the intercom, barked out orders to the driver, a skinny little black guy who promptly made an adjustment to the climate-control settings. Jonas dutifully raised his window.

"Thank you very much, Mr. Lamb," the girl said, bowing her head respectfully. (He was "Jonas" when the context was positive and "Mr. Lamb" when decorum or apology were called for.) Using the intercom again, May gave Curly, who was riding shotgun, instructions in Chinese. The man nodded and said something that sounded like "Hey!" but based on Jonas's observations the past few days, surely meant something like "Yes, ma'am."

Curly was one of May's three sidekicks whom Jonas had nicknamed the Three Stooges because of superficial resemblances to their namesakes. None spoke much English and May's was closer to pidgin than either the queen's or the American variety. Curly, Moe and Larry (whom Jonas believed were actually Tang, Shu and Fan, but were perfectly content being addressed by their "American" names) rotated shifts, and at least one of them was with May and Jonas at all times.

"I suppose better safe than sorry," Jonas said to May as he checked out her legs.

"My job to worry, Jonas."

He had to smile because May's speech pattern was such that she made it sound like she was saying "My job is to worry Jonas," without the comma. Though tough as nails, the girl was actually endearing. Whenever he expressed concern about something, or even asked a question, she would invariably say something like "Mr. Yee say don't worry about nothing."

He'd come to appreciate the fact that Jimmy worried about very little that could be addressed with money. But having a sugar daddy—a unique experience for Jonas—had as many disadvantages as advantages, he'd come to discover. It had only been five days, but life with May Li was proving to be remarkably ritualistic, even the flirting and sexual come-ons, which had been growing in intensity the past couple of days.

May had a nice figure, though her legs were slightly bowed, beautiful black silky hair and a pretty face. She hadn't been through Jimmy Yee's breast enhancement program, but she wasn't exactly deficient, either. In her own way she had fire, even a trace of a sense of humor, but she lacked genuine desire. Jonas had been around the block enough that he could distinguish between a woman's libido and her devotion.

The bottom line was, May was as accommodating as she was attractive. Jonas was convinced she'd as readily give him a blow job as bring him a cup of coffee if that was what he wanted. God knew he was tempted, considering his most recent sexual encounter had been with Crystal in December.

It was safe to say he was horny, but he'd been slow to avail himself. Maybe it was because of his preoccupations. Or maybe it was Tess once again who tore at his heart, the time spent with her at Tahoe having set back his recovery program thirty years. It was almost as though Gloria, Sonia, Alice and Elise had never happened. All those years of compensating, of learning how to forget, undone.

The driver turned left on Oxford Street, then right on Hearst, and up the north side of the campus. The Faculty Club was across the road from the stadium and situated in a wooded grove, a fine old wooden structure that had the feel of a national park lodge.

The driver pulled into the parking lot above the club. Curly, who was round of face, had a crew cut and was larger than his compatriots, thus earning him the moniker, got out and surveyed the scene before opening the passenger door. May slid out, followed by Jonas.

They made their way to the front of the building in a foggy mist, Curly walking ahead (presumably to take any rocket-launched missiles) and May half a step behind Jonas, which was a woman's place evidently, even one trained to kill. He found the care and attention flattering in a way, but definitely tedious—enough to convince him that an incarnation as president, Mafia don or rock star should be avoided. Becoming king of the world was odious enough.

Patrick was waiting in the lounge, where a fire burned cheerily in the large stone fireplace. They greeted each other, shaking hands as May and Curly moved discreetly to the entrances to the room (presumably ready to pounce if some seventy-five-year-old classicist was cheeky enough to try to slit Jonas's throat).

"Who are your friends?" Patrick asked.

"A walking life insurance policy sent from China, courtesy of Jimmy Yee."

"Is our situation growing that dire or just that bizarre?"

"I think both, son."

"The dining room's pretty crowded at the moment," Patrick said. "I thought maybe we could sit here by the fire and chat for a while."

"Fine."

As they sat down on a leather sofa, Jonas glanced at May's bare, if delightfully bowed, legs and wondered if the radicals from the sixties would have imagined that a Maoist invasion of the People's Republic of Berkeley would have come in such a serendipitous package. Funny how life played its little tricks.

Jonas decided to defer the bad news and asked Patrick about his trip. "Get those Black Sheep in the ground?"

"They'll be going in soon. Everything is ready."

"Excellent."

"I understand Tahoe wasn't as restful as you'd hoped," Patrick said.

"You've talked to your mother."

Patrick looked sheepish. "Yeah. Sorry about that. I had no idea she'd be there."

"It wasn't a total disaster. I got to see your mom in her skivvies."

"My impression was she wasn't as pleased by the whole thing as you." His expression sobered. "She told me about your Jordanian visitor, by the way. Makes me think these bodyguards aren't such a bad idea. Do you suppose the bad guys are on to me, too?"

"It didn't take long for the FBI to make the connection between us."

"That's what has me befuddled," Patrick said. "Is it what we're doing, or is it the attention we're getting from abroad?"

"God only knows. With the oil companies owning the guys in the White House, anything's possible. I guess what it means for sure is that Operation Black Sheep is growing less secret by the hour and we'd be well advised to put things on a fast track."

Patrick nodded, looking thoughtful as he gazed into the fire. Jonas was not eager to share his top news. Apparently Tess hadn't said anything, which was a sign of respect, if nothing else.

"Maybe I should get the bad news out of the way first," he said.

"There's worse?"

"I'm afraid so." Jonas gave him a rundown on developments with Melanie de Givry's lawsuit. "Your mother spotted the problem—the fact that we made the mistake of putting everything in the corporation's name. My attorney confirmed Tess's suspicions. Melanie and Wilson could end up owning ninety percent of the technology, as well as ninety percent of the company itself. And it's my fault for not seeing it. I fucked up royally, Patrick, and I owe you an apology."

"Let's not worry about who's to blame. We're in trouble only if the de Givrys win their lawsuit, right?"

"Yes. Everything hinges on whether they can prove I was unfaithful to Elise, and that, in turn, hinges on whether they can get Crystal to testify against me."

"Will she?"

"Crystal is very moral in an odd sort of way. Plus she's devoted to her daughter and she's got a boyfriend she hopes to marry. She's concerned about her future and she's not about to screw up her life by risking perjury."

"We're talking about hundreds of millions of dollars, Jonas."

"I know, but we can't put a gun to her head. And while she's genuinely sympathetic, there are limits to her devotion to an old beau."

"Well, let's make her a partner. I mean, what's ten or twenty percent in the greater scheme of things?"

Jonas considered that. "I honestly don't think money's the issue with Crystal."

"Are you saying she wouldn't deny having an affair for, say, fifty or a hundred million dollars? I mean, there are a lot of women who'd deny it for pride's sake alone, never mind a fortune."

"Crystal's not your everyday, garden-variety female."

"Have you asked her what it would take? Have you mentioned money?"

"Not in so many words."

"I think you should."

"It's your deal and your money, Patrick, so I didn't feel at liberty to make any offers without your concurrence."

"Feel free now."

His son was dead serious. And what was remarkable was that he wasn't pissed. Jonas had been dreading telling him because he knew it was his fault this had happened, and Patrick had every reason to be livid.

"We're under some time pressure," he told the boy. "Crystal's deposition is set for January 30, a week from today. According to my attorney, it's the ball game, the Super Bowl, the championship, the works. January 30 is our D day."

"Then you'd better get on it. Anything else we need to worry about?"

"I think we need to pay Jimmy a visit as soon as possible. When can you have a package together?"

"I worked on it over the weekend. It's pretty much ready."

"Great! How about if we go to Hong Kong next weekend? That'll give me time to deal with Crystal and make travel arrangements."

"Perfect."

Jonas felt better, taking a moment to enjoy the warmth of the fire. He recalled that campfire in the Sierra when Patrick had set his life on the road to fame and fortune. The "king of the world" thing still set his blood to racing, but there had been another benefit, the quieter joy of renewing his acquaintance with Tess—not that it had been all that fruitful. But it had been eye opening.

Whether or not it was unrequited love, Jonas did worry about his former wife. He decided this was an opportunity to address at least one problem. "Patrick, it's none of my business, but if you can find a way to allay your mother's concerns about the FBI, it might not be a bad idea."

"Yeah, I know. I plan to talk to her. I didn't want to do it on the phone so I've been waiting for her to get back."

"Where is she?"

"Home now, but she's been in Mexico. She said she needed some sun."

"She go with Walter?"

Patrick gave him a knowing smile. "No, she went alone."

Jonas brooded for a few moments, then said, "I really don't think she should marry that guy."

"I know you don't. As a matter of fact, I told her you felt that way."

"You did?" Jonas wasn't sure he was glad to hear that or not. "Would it be a breach of confidence to tell me what she said?"

"She said, 'Patrick, your father is a self-centered egotist, albeit a charming one.'"

"At least she said 'charming.'"

"Don't get too excited. She finds you attractive, but wants nothing to do with you."

Jonas wasn't surprised. Tess had made that patently clear—after she'd kissed him. That had been his one small victory, though evidently a Pyrrhic one.

Patrick checked his watch. "We'll probably be able to get a table now. Hungry?"

Jonas might have said yes, or he could just as easily have said no. When a man was in his fifth decade and everything that had ever mattered to him was on the line—win or lose, all or nothing—how did he think about his stomach? "I could eat a horse," he said. And then he laughed.

6:18 p.m.
The White House, Washington, D.C.

The president, vice president and the president's chief of staff, Morton Case, were in the Oval Office with the secretary of state, the attorney general, the directors of the FBI and CIA, the national security adviser and a few aides. The president had been briefed on the developing situation out in California concerning the super-ethanol project, which had attracted the growing attention of the international intelligence community.

The director of the FBI told the president agents had been tracking the activities of the principals of GET, Inc., and had been monitoring the actions of several known intelligence operatives active in the area. No one was able to answer the president's questions concerning the actual viability of Jonas Lamb's discovery or his intentions. The president was alarmed to learn that a suspected PRC intelligence operative was working closely with Lamb.

The president asked if there was a basis for bringing charges against Lamb. The attorney general told him that Lamb hadn't broken any laws they were aware of, though it was possible a pretext could be found for questioning him. It could backfire, however, and end up being counterproductive. The president asked if they had anything on Lamb that could be used against him. The director of the FBI said that there had been a recent development of interest. Agents in San Francisco learned that Lamb was involved in a legal dispute with his in-laws regarding an inheritance. Interestingly, control of GET, Inc., was at stake. Jonas Lamb could end up losing control of the company.

The vice president asked the director if control of the technology was at stake as well. The director said he wasn't sure. The president and vice president exchanged looks. The president told the director to make finding out the answer to that question a top priority. With that, he closed the meeting. The others left, but the vice president and the chief of staff remained in the Oval Office with the president.

After an assistant handed the vice president a glass of Scotch and left, the president asked his good friend about the feelings of people in the industry. The V.P. told him that the industry was intrigued, concerned and befuddled by the reports of Lamb's genetically modified organism. It seemed to have caught everyone flat-footed.

The president wondered aloud if the guy might be playing everybody for the fool. Morton Case noted that an awful lot of people were taking it very seriously. Usually when there was that much smoke, there was fire.

The president noted how frustrating it was that the country virtually had to be mugged before the government could do anything about it. The V.P. said it was fortunate that private interests weren't under similar constraints. Raising a brow meaningfully, he noted that there were people in Houston and elsewhere who were taking the matter very seriously and were rumored to have already taken steps to ensure that the U.S. economy wouldn't be cut off at the knees because of one man's greed.

Morton Case observed that the oil people might benefit if they were aware that Jonas Lamb may not hold all the super-ethanol cards. It could be just as important for them to have Lamb's in-laws in their pocket as the man himself. The president and vice president nodded their agreement. Lamb may control the technology at the moment, the V.P. said, but perhaps not forever. How fortunate there were concerned citizens who cared as deeply about the consequences for the country as anybody in the room.

THURSDAY
January 24

Marina Green, San Francisco

She'd arrived from Cleveland the previous night, taken a room at a cheap downtown hotel a few blocks from the Tenderloin, had a muffin and a cup of coffee for breakfast at the café on Geary Street, then taken a taxi to the yacht harbor by Marina Green. It had been raining lightly all morning.

Carly Van Hooten opened her collapsible umbrella and walked to the bench nearest the entrance to the yacht club and sat down. For ten minutes she watched the boats bobbing in the marina, the pigeons strutting back and forth on the sidewalk in front of her, and she thought nostalgic thoughts of Paris and Antoine. Carly didn't wallow in *tristesse* often, but she was in a kind of limbo—the hiatus between preparation and action, like the actress in her dressing room, not yet in character and waiting to be called.

Gaston de Malbouzon arrived in a Yellow Cab ten minutes after she did. As he emerged from the back seat with a huge black umbrella in hand, Carly got a glimpse of the pretty boy with high cheekbones and bleached platinum hair who accompanied him. The boy stayed in the taxi and Gaston strode over to the bench. He was in a tweed sport coat and wore an ascot and an amiable grin.

"Carly, you're the picture of loveliness. Even more alluring on your native shores, if improving on perfection is possible."

"Please, Gaston, I already have a headache," she said, lowering her umbrella.

After taking out his handkerchief and brushing away the beads of water on the seat, he sat beside her, kissing her on each cheek as he held the big umbrella over the two of them. "I kid you not," he said, the colloquialism sounding particularly amusing in his French accent.

She looked past him at the taxi, which waited. "I see you haven't wasted any time getting into the swing of things."

"That's Reece. I'd forgotten how much I adore San Francisco." He glanced over his shoulder at the taxi, then turned back to her. "So, Little Bo Peep, have a good trip?"

"I'd forgotten how much I hate winter in Ohio."

"Get everything done? Work history, references?"

"Yes, I'm ready to roll."

"Excellent."

"Everything set here?" she asked.

"I'm happy to say Operation Brebis Noire is underway. I've gathered considerable data on our little lamb. Le Genissel informs me the FBI has a heavy presence, which complicates things. But I've asked my people in Texas if there's a way to get the feds to stand down. Considering their influence in Washington, I'm hopeful."

"That would be nice."

"There is bad news, though. Le Genissel has been up to his usual butchery, *alors*. He lost another man."

"Wonderful. I'll be stepping over bodies to get to my mark."

"And, I'm afraid, past the palace guard, as well, *chérie*. Alfred tells me Lamb has a security team in place. All Chinese, possibly PRC-sponsored, he isn't sure."

"I can deal with that."

"Not if one's in the bedroom."

"A woman?"

"A comely lass, I'm told. She seems to be in charge and may be entertaining our little lamb after hours. Alfred thinks they may have beaten us to the punch and he's bloody pissed. Gave me hell for taking so long to get here. I told him not to count Little Bo Peep out just yet because there's more to seduction than tits and pussy." Then Gaston added drolly, "I'm not sure he considers me a credible authority in the matter, however."

Carly thought. "This does complicate things."

"Alfred spoke in terms of eliminating the competition to clear the way for you."

"Sounds like there are enough corpses already. At some point the police are going to notice, and I don't want to have to work around them, too."

"*Bien sûr!* I told Alfred that, but you know assassins. They think there's a bullet for every occasion." He shook his head. "I'll tell you what the modern world is lacking, Carly. Finesse. It's gone the way of savoir faire. And you know why? Every peasant has a TV and a cell phone, that's why. They think that makes them part of the ruling class, but all they've done is brought their *bêtise* with them to the halls of power. I know I sound like my dear old papa in saying this, but it's no accident that the Gazelle's ancestors herded goats."

"Class politics isn't going to solve our problem, Gaston."

"You're right. And I hate myself for siding with my father, *le comte*. On *anything!* I must say, though, Le Genissel tries the patience. He's what the world can expect if there's another Saladin. Almost makes you want to become a Zionist."

"It makes me want to get Le Genissel off our backs."

"*Oui, je suis d'accord.* So, what do you think? This is a woman thing calling for feminine guile. Frontal assault? Attack the flank? Double envelopment? He's your sheep, Bo Peep."

"I won't know until I see them together. But Le Genissel might as well know it could take a while. Tell him to back off. If he wants to be constructive, that's the best thing he can do."

"You can tell him yourself. He has some videos of Lamb he'd like you to see."

She groaned. "Is it necessary?"

"Carly, I share your disdain, but Alfred does sign the checks. Indulge him."

"When does he want to do this?"

"He'd like to come to your hotel room tonight, *mon angelet.*"

"Tonight's fine, but it's got to be *your* room, Gaston. And you'll be there."

"He won't be pleased."

"Fuck him."

"And meanwhile?"

"Meanwhile, ditch the boy and take me to lunch."

Gaston de Malbouzon's brows rose.

"Preferably wherever Jonas Lamb is dining," she explained.

"I don't know that he has an established pattern, but perhaps we'll get lucky. I just hope that if he does go out, he chooses a place that serves some of that scrumptious sourdough bread."

Sausalito, California

Jonas had decided to drop by Crystal's shop unannounced—he didn't want her to have time to think before they spoke, nor did he want her conferring with Ford-tough Bob. His best chance was to be with her one on one, where he could look her in the eye and give her his best shot. Patrick was right, he decided. This would require every bit of skill he'd acquired over the years, and in a sense, it would be even more critical to their success than his negotiations with Jimmy Yee. There were always other investors, but there was only one witness to his infidelity.

They were parked across the street from Crystal's shop. Opening time had come and gone. Crystal had a tendency to be approximate about such things, but Jonas feared that she wouldn't show at all. For all he knew she'd decided to tank her business, knowing that she'd soon have a husband who was a bread-winner, par excellence.

May Li, curled up in the seat as far from him as she could get, gave a heavy sigh. Jonas knew the sound. It was the universal sign of displeasure, common to every female of the species, regardless of her culture or the language she spoke. May was pissed and the object of her displeasure was him.

May had come to breakfast that morning in a lit-tle silk robe that revealed a lot of thigh and some cleavage. She clearly had something on her mind.

"Jonas, please tell truth. I not please you. You think I not so pretty."

"What? Of course you please me. And you're very pretty, May."

"Then why you act this way?"

He'd read the problem instantly. May had been alerted to the fact that he was a randy old fart, and not getting the attention she expected, she was con-cerned she wasn't up to his standards.

"May," he'd told her, "I've got a lot on my mind. It has nothing to do with you."

That was true, but also not true. Jonas had always been a man who could screw no matter what. (Well, with a few minor exceptions, perhaps, to wit, Crys-tal in Hong Kong.) Normally, though, he could be on death row and would opt for sex as his last meal. But being horny wasn't enough anymore. The last thing he wanted, however, was to make the girl feel badly. His assurances at breakfast hadn't exactly fallen on deaf ears, but he knew she wasn't convinced. There hadn't been time to sort it out because talking to Crystal had been his top priority. But with the Closed sign still hanging in the shop window, it appeared he had time to mend fences with May.

He glanced over at the girl. She was in a Chinese-red-leather miniskirt and black turtleneck. Her black-booted feet curled under her as she stared out at the drizzling rain.

May Li was childlike, but she was also steely. Between the show of innocence and the pidgin English it would be easy to take her lightly. Jonas had little doubt she knew what she was doing, though. A couple of days earlier he'd found her going through the file drawer of his desk.

"Lose something, sweetheart?"

"Looking for bug," she replied, making a show of checking under the desk. "So far okay."

He'd found that strange, but couldn't think of a nefarious motive for snooping. There wasn't much in the drawer apart from the papers regarding Melanie's lawsuit. Then it occurred to him that his difficulties with Melanie might be of interest to Jimmy Yee. After that, Jonas had kept the file drawer locked.

The topic of the moment, however, was employee morale. "Hey, sugar," he said, "why don't you sit closer to me?"

May turned her head. "You cold, Mr. Lamb? You want maybe they put on heat?"

"No, I need to get my blood flowing and you can accomplish that just fine."

May scooted closer, seemingly relieved as much as she was pleased—possibly because a bonus was at stake and his rectitude (or age) was standing in the way of a happy new year for the Li clan back home. Love wasn't everything, he told himself, and Tess had made it clear she wasn't interested in him. Besides, comfort sex was the best palliative to a broken heart known to man.

Jonas pulled May up against him, then put his hand on her bare knee. She cooed and when he drew his hand up her leg until his fingertips slid under the hem of her skirt, he elicited a smile.

"Maybe you like me after all," she said, beaming now. She lightly played with the hair on his wrist, perhaps never having been intimate with such a hairy Caucasian before.

"I do like you, May."

"You want maybe I come to your room tonight?"

So much for Asian subtlety. "That would be nice," he said.

"You still very much safe because my men keep watch," she said.

Jonas understood her to be assuring him that the rest of the palace guard would be on their toes while the captain of the watch was busy raising the master's spirits. May was the only one who slept in the house, occupying the downstairs bedroom. One of the Three Stooges was always on duty, as well. Jonas wasn't sure, but he suspected the boys occupied the small hours watching infomercials, *Maverick* reruns and the farm report. (No reason not to soak up a little American culture while visiting the Golden Mountain.) "I'm not worried, May," he said.

She lifted her pretty mouth toward him and kissed him on the chin. "You think about it today," she said in a coquettish tone. "I think about it, too. Maybe tonight we see what happen."

"Being a big believer in the art of seduction," he said, "may I suggest we have a nice romantic lunch? Just the two of us."

"No Curly, Moe or Larry?"

Jonas chuckled. "No, just you and me. I'll take you to my favorite spot."

"You're boss, Jonas."

It was a nice thought, but only half true. Man, he'd long since learned, was servant to his needs and desires. It was simply the way people were built. Rather than fight it, sometimes the thing to do was give in to it. After all, what was the worst thing that could happen?

About then a crackling warning came over the intercom in Chinese. Moe, the Stooge of the hour, was alerting them to something. May peered past Jonas toward the shop across the street.

"Maybe the lady come," she said.

Jonas looked. There was a woman at the shop door, all right, but not Crystal. It was a well-dressed matron of about fifty with yellowy-blond hair holding an umbrella. "No," he said, "that's not her."

The woman peered in the shop door and checked her watch. An anxious customer, apparently. She paced until a white pickup truck pulled up in front of the shop, blocking their view. Jonas recognized the driver—Ford-tough Bob. The woman leaning across the cab to kiss him goodbye was, of course, Crystal Clear.

The truck pulled away and Crystal went to the door, where, if body language was any indication, she was gushing apologies to the matron. The two went inside the shop.

"You go now?" May asked.

"I'll wait until the other woman leaves."

"You say when, and Moe make sure safe."

"You and Moe can stay in the limo," Jonas said. "If I get killed walking across the street, it's going to be by a bus, not some fanatical Arab. And the lady inside probably has as much interest in assassination as I have in needlepoint."

"Jonas, you say very strange things."

"It's called early senility, sweetheart."

"I better go with you."

"No," he said. "You sit here and think about tonight."

When the customer didn't reappear, he decided to go inside, anyway. "Hold down the fort," he said, climbing out of the limo. "I shall return."

Successfully crossing the street without a hostile encounter with a bus, Jonas entered Crystal's shop, feeling even more desperation than when he'd first darkened her door some ten months earlier. This promised to be the seduction of his life, and it didn't even involve sex.

The bell over the door rang as he entered, but the shop appeared to be empty. Then his erstwhile lover appeared at the door to the small office in back. She was in a green sweater and matching skirt that showed off her dynamite figure to good effect. No, to perfection.

"Jonas, what are you doing here?"

"I came to have my cards read."

"Well, it's not a good time. I'm doing a reading now, as a matter of fact."

"Can I wait?"

She did not appear to like the idea but, saying neither yea or nay, returned to the office, closing the door behind her. Anxious and impatient, Jonas moved about the shop, picking up things, reading covers, labels, the information on packaging and wondering what Crystal would do with fifty million dollars. Open Crystal Clear shops all around the country? Buy an island in the Caribbean? Build a home for unwed mothers? Or, would she simply content herself cooking fancy meals for Ford-tough Bob?

Come to think of it, what would he do with *his* piece of the pie, once he'd bought his yacht and fancy house? Donate to political campaigns? Buy a baseball team? Make a movie? Running around in limousines with compliant young women would probably be unavoidable for a guy with his predilections, but at the same time another, still more vivid and compelling image came to mind. Jonas saw himself sitting at the kitchen table and being served scrambled eggs by none other than his second wife. He heard himself asking Tess whether she'd rather plant petunias or take a walk in the woods. Maybe that was the success his mother didn't believe him capable of achieving.

The door to the little office opened and out came the blond matron. She looked distraught.

"I'm sorry, Ellen," he heard Crystal say.

"It's okay. It's okay," the woman said as she hurried out the door, tears running down her cheeks.

There was silence then. Jonas looked at Crystal and vice versa. She leaned on the counter, staring him down. It seemed to him a hundred years since they'd made love.

"I hope it was the cards, not the mood of the swami," he said.

"What do you want, Jonas?"

"Actually I would like to take a look into the future."

"I did your reading the other day, as a matter of fact. It's essentially the same. You're in for some rough times."

"I could have told you that," he said. "But out of curiosity, why are you reading *my* cards? Aren't I past tense?"

"Yes, but I still have to deal with you, don't I? I was hoping for some insight."

"I gather I should get to the point."

Crystal nodded.

Jonas walked over to the counter and stood across from her. He looked at her with all the profundity he could muster. "Do you believe there's a difference between what's true and what's just?"

Crystal blinked. "I don't know. I never thought about it."

"If you were on a jury and the facts said the guy should go to jail, but you knew in your heart the guy didn't deserve to go to jail, that in a moral sense he was innocent, what would you do?"

"We're talking about you and Melanie."

"Yeah."

"It's not my fight," she said.

"There are hundreds of millions of dollars at stake, Crystal."

Her brows went up.

"That's right, *hundreds* of millions of dollars. This is no routine family pissing match. Melanie's trying to keep me from getting back my stock in my company, the stock Elise willed to me. There's a million-dollar inheritance involved, but frankly, that's only a drop in the bucket. Either I get what Elise wanted me to have or Melanie steals it from me by using you. It all comes down to whether or not by having an affair with you I broke my agreement with Elise. I say I didn't, but what matters is what you say, Crystal."

"They're going to ask me if we had sex. What do you expect me to say?"

"I had Elise's consent. Her only conditions were that it not be among her circle of friends and that I be discreet. I respected that to the letter."

"But they aren't going to ask me that."

"It's true, though. The question is what I deserve."

"That's not the way it works, Jonas. However you cut it, you want me to lie."

"Do I *not* deserve my inheritance, my stock? Is it right to deny me that?"

"That's not what they'll ask me."

"It's in your power to do justice, Crystal. Isn't justice really what we all want?"

"Easy for you to say. I've got to live with the consequences."

"I don't expect you to do it for nothing. I'm asking a lot, so I'm prepared to share the fruits of justice. Here's my offer. At your deposition give them the moral truth. Tell them I'm innocent. If you do that, *Lamb's Croft* is yours."

"Jonas…"

"I know you're going to marry Bob and maybe you'll want to live in his house. But why not have a little security? The houseboat makes a great rental, as you know."

"You're trying to bribe me."

"I'm asking you to take a risk to do justice. You should be rewarded for that. And if my company makes it big, you deserve a piece of that, too. Because only you can make it happen. How about ten percent of the company up to fifty million dollars?"

"Jonas, what have you been smoking? Fifty million dollars? You aren't serious."

"Did Jimmy Yee strike you as a frivolous person?"

Crystal sat on the stool, just as she had the previous April. He'd been intent on seducing her then;

he was intent on seducing her now. But the objective and consequences were light years apart. Incredible to think the destiny of the world was hanging in the balance. Incredible it should be happening here and now in Crystal Clear's New Age trinket shop in Sausalito, California, on a rainy day in January.

Crystal looked at him hard, her mind turning in slow loops. He could see it all on her face. She was out of her league. Hell, *he* was out of *his* league. Yet, this was the whole ball game.

"I'm going to have to think about it," she said. "Jeez, talk about a decision." She shook her head as though it was too much to contemplate.

"Fifty million, Crystal. Think what you could do for Tamara. For Bob."

"Please, my head's already spinning." She bit her lip, scrunching up her face. "Maybe you should go."

"All right. Should I call?"

"I'll call you."

He didn't like the sound of that, but what choice did he have? He'd given it his best shot for God and country, for Patrick, for himself, for a lifetime of struggle, for redemption. Maybe for redemption more than anything else.

Jonas headed for the door, but even before he was out of the shop, Crystal headed for her office and—he suspected—for her cards. Looking up at the rainy sky, Jonas was sorry for every bad word he'd said about the occult. Now, of all times, he needed the beneficence of the tarot gods.

* * *

After Uncle Jonas left and the limousine pulled away, Bob MacDonald got out of his truck and walked up the street to Crystal's shop. He was seething. The sonovabitch was harassing her again. Bob was determined to put a stop to it, once and for all.

Russian Hill, San Francisco

Tess's condominium was on the fifteenth floor with both a northern and a western exposure. From her front room she could see the Golden Gate, the Presidio and Pacific Heights. Using binoculars she could make out part of Walter's rooftop. He'd telephoned several times, but she hadn't yet found the courage to return his calls.

From her bedroom, where she was now, sitting on her bed, she had a perspective of Fisherman's Wharf, Telegraph Hill, Alcatraz and Marin across the bay. Jonas was out there somewhere doing his thing. Upon her return from Mexico, she'd been tempted to phone him, but she was too proud, too bitter, too afraid. Yet Jonas didn't frighten her. It was her feelings that scared her.

Several days of lounging in the warm sun, and several sensual nights alone, had nearly stripped her of common sense, rendering her almost as helpless as she'd been at nineteen when that "Texas" cowboy turned her life upside down. There were differences between now and then, of course. Jonas was no longer a mystery, his feet of clay were obvious. But then, so were hers. And, as a result, there was no wonder in his love for her anymore, only an understanding of its relentless, dogged certitude.

When her buzzer sounded, Tess jumped. She had no idea who'd be coming to her door in the middle of the day, but she hoped it wasn't Walter. She went to the intercom, anyway, debating before she finally pushed the button.

"Yes?"

"Mom, it's me."

Tess was relieved. Thrilled. Once a mother had let go, any and every overture from her kid was cause for joy, especially when she was worried, especially when she was alone. "What a nice surprise," she said. "Come on up."

Tess, who was in sweats and walking shoes, having gotten back from a five-mile walk only half an hour earlier, ran a brush through her hair and greeted her handsome son at the door. Patrick looked more pensive than pleased. She knew that something was wrong, especially after noticing he had a briefcase in his hand.

"The shit has sort of hit the fan," he said. "I need a favor."

"Come in."

Once seated on her sofa, Patrick launched into his story. "As you know, I've been trying very hard to keep you out of things…for your own protection," he began, "but the situation has gotten out of hand. I want to tell you everything."

"Is this your idea or your father's?"

"He's been as concerned about you as I am."

"Okay, I'm all ears."

He explained what had been going on, then waited for her reaction. She'd expected Jonas to have been a more negative factor, but she could see he'd behaved honorably—though she was also sure his participation wasn't completely selfless.

"I feel badly for the way I've treated your father," she said.

"He's been taking a lot of heat. My great fear is that something's going to happen to him because I got him into this."

"Your father wouldn't do anything he doesn't want to do. My sense is he's in his element—wheeling and dealing."

"This isn't kids' play, Mom. The worst part is neither of us know exactly what's going on and why. Somehow the Chinese and the Arabs are on to us…or, I should say, on to Jonas. At best I can tell they haven't figured out my role yet."

"Then why is the FBI investigating you?"

"We haven't figured that one out, either."

"Patrick, I think you should take your data to the government, lay it on the table and announce your discovery to the world. Once you do, these people have no reason to come after you."

"Mom, if my goal was to play it safe, I wouldn't have gotten involved to begin with."

"Well, things have gotten serious. People have died."

"Anyway, you're assuming the FBI is on our side."

"Surely you don't think they're up to no good."

"Look who's in the White House, Mom. Behind that smile there's billions of dollars of oil money and a foreign policy centered on energy. You think Enron was an anomaly?"

"But won't most of the world benefit from your discovery?"

"Sure, but some powerful interests will lose big time," Patrick said. "And there will be disruptions of major proportions. Governments, superpowers in particular, want stability. How important are Jonas and I in the greater scheme of things?"

"You must have known all this when you got started."

"Yes, to some degree. I didn't fully appreciate the implications, but our plan was to come in under the radar. Somehow things leaked before we were ready. Now it looks like everybody's scrambling to get their hands on our Black Sheep."

"Black Sheep?"

"That's our code name for my GMOs."

"Patrick, I'm a lawyer not a scientist."

"Genetically modified organisms."

"The things that change the way ethanol works."

"Yes."

"Okay, so what are you going to do?" she asked.

"That's the other reason I'm here. The world economy is up for grabs. With that hanging in the balance, how many people can I trust with my research? You're it, Mom. I can't think of anybody I'd trust more."

"Is that what's in the briefcase?"

"Yeah."

Tess glanced down at it. It hit her that what her

son had brought to her home could impact lives as much as almost any scientific or technological development of the twentieth century. Its importance was almost incalculable.

"I don't know what to say, Patrick."

"I'd like you to keep this stuff for me, but having it puts you at risk. You need to know that." He opened the briefcase and removed two file folders, a large one and a small one. "This thick file contains all my basic research, test data, lab reports and so forth. There's a subfolder inside that contains information on the test field that will be planted in the next few weeks. The people doing the planting think it's a new variety of feed corn. It's very important the location remain secret. I suggest you don't even look at this stuff." He took out the other folder. "This smaller file contains the materials I put together for Jimmy Yee."

"Jonas's billionaire friend in Hong Kong."

"Yes, the one who's financing our venture. The package is not as thorough as I'd have liked, but it'll have to do. Jonas and I will be taking it to Hong Kong sometime in the next several days. I figured it would be safer with you in the interim than with either of us. Unlike the research materials, you should be able to put your hands on this smaller folder quickly."

Tess looked into the eyes of the young man who'd once been her baby, the child who'd listened to the bedtime stories she'd read, the adolescent who'd made every choice an adventure. It had all come to this. Never in a million years would she have thought that she, that phony cowboy she'd married thirty years ago, and their child would be standing at a turning point in history.

She watched Patrick put the folders back into the briefcase. He reached over and put it at her feet. The briefcase, she realized, contained the key to everything, the future for millions of people, perhaps. She touched it, trying to get perspective.

"Mom, you aren't going to like hearing this, but if anything should happen to me and Jonas—" Patrick paused "—if we should be killed or disappear, then take everything to the press and put it in the public domain. Just don't give it to the government. I don't trust people who sell themselves to big oil to attain power. The average voter may figure it doesn't matter who butters the president's bread, but I do."

"So, why wait? Let's take it to the press *now!*"

"Mom, the game's not over. I'd rather play it out my way."

"Patrick, this is *not* a game!"

He drew a long, slow breath, then said, "There are those who do and those who watch. I can't sit on the sidelines."

Hearing those words, Tess saw it all clearly. For the first time it hit her, *really* hit her. Patrick was Jonas Lamb's son.

Cow Hollow, San Francisco

The limousine stopped in front of a place called the Balboa Café and Gaston told the driver of the taxi, an Indian in a turban, to continue up the street a ways before stopping. "Would you care to dine at the Balboa Café, *mademoiselle?*" he asked Carly.

She glanced back through the rear window, taking a good look at the restaurant. It was airy and light with big windows in the front and running down the side. "It doesn't look very intimate," she said. "I wouldn't want him to notice us together. Not here."

"*Tiens,* I suspect Mr. Lamb is capable of looking right through me," Gaston said. "Not true of you, however."

"I can make myself inconspicuous," she said, opening her purse. She took out a rain hat and a pair of large sunglasses. Twisting her long blond hair into a knot, she tucked it under her hat, which she pulled down snugly on her head, then slipped on the glasses and looked at him.

"Garbo," he said. "I *adored* that woman. So much I almost wished I was straight. That was during puberty, but I soon wised up. You want to go have lunch or not?"

"I think I should go alone, Gaston. And I might not stay, depending on the setup."

"This is your department, *chérie.*"

"Wait here for me, okay?"

"And if we get hungry?"

"Find a convenience store and get yourself a candy bar and a bag of chips."

"*Oui,*" Gaston said dryly, "*nous sommes bien en Amérique.*" We're in America, all right.

She got out of the taxi and walked back to the Balboa Café. As she drew near, she saw Jonas Lamb and the Chinese woman at a window table halfway down the side. She entered, happy to find the place crowded, meaning she'd be less conspicuous. She was struck by the aroma of wine, pasta sauces and perhaps fish. It was more reminiscent of Italy than France.

The café and bar were in a single long room with the bar to the left along the wall opposite the side windows. Tables were strung along the bar section, with quite a few more in back. The dark paneling and crisp waiters gave the place a European flavor but with American overtones—more, perhaps, a product of the clientele than the physical place. In public Americans were more open, like children in a playground, whereas each Frenchman seemed an island unto himself, aloof to his surroundings, disdainful of the fact the world had to be shared.

Lamb's table was at the midpoint of the bar. He faced the entrance, the Chinese woman looked toward the rear of the establishment. Every bar stool was taken except for a couple at the back in the section that wrapped around, facing the front. She'd have an ideal perspective from there. And it was good she'd be able to see the woman's face. That's where the important clues were to be found. As long as she could observe his body language, she'd get a decent reading of their relationship.

The bartender, slender and fair with a wispy mustache, put a cocktail napkin on the bar in front of her. "What would you like?"

"Can I eat at the bar?"

"Sure."

"A bowl of soup and a glass of wine. What's your best merlot?"

"The Martin Ray is very nice. It's a California wine."

"That's fine." Carly's eyes settled on the woman.

The first thing she noticed about her Chinese competitor was that she was very much aware of her surroundings, her attention only half focused on Lamb. She smiled a lot, but her eyes were cold. Physically she was attractive, but she was a peasant in city-girl clothes. Her hands weren't bad, but they lacked grace. Carly's wine arrived and for the next three or four minutes she observed the couple, concluding the woman was a piece of ass and not a very enthusiastic one at that. Not a classical seductress. Her demeanor was that of a very young woman married to a very old man.

Lamb, for his part, seemed to be going through the motions himself, like a man who felt obliged to make conversation with women—even hookers—though that was mostly speculation on her part. She'd have to hear their conversation to be sure. There was no chemistry that she could see. The interplay between them screamed need and accommodation. Carly felt better.

They brought her a bowl of soup and a chunk of bread. The food smelled good.

She began to eat, not noticing him approach until he slipped onto the stool next to her and, leaning close, said in French, "I'm going to kill her. That will solve the problem."

Alfred Le Genissel, wearing a San Francisco 49er sweatshirt, jeans, athletic shoes and a baseball cap, smiled at her with his lips, but not with his eyes.

"Alfred," she hissed, "you're going to fuck up everything!"

"What do you accomplish, watching them, Carly? He is fucking her, what else do you need to know?"

"For starters, that I'm not being second-guessed."

"I told you, the solution is to eliminate her. I'll take care of it."

"Look," she said, effecting an outwardly serene demeanor, though her tone was harsh, "I'm the one dealing with Lamb. Unless you'd rather I pack my bags and go home, leave before she spots you talking to me. You're about as blatant as a miniskirt in Mecca."

He growled. "Why do you always do that? You think that endears you to me?"

"I don't give a damn what you think, Alfred. Now you either walk out of here this minute or I will. And, I'm not coming back."

The bartender, perhaps sensing tension between them, drifted down and put a cocktail napkin in front of Le Genissel. "What'll you have?"

"Nothing," he grumbled, "I am leaving." He got up and headed for the door.

As he walked along the bar, the Chinese woman noticed him. Then she looked in Carly's direction. Carly, cursing under her breath, spooned some soup into her mouth and pretended to be oblivious. The peasant calculated. The peasant was a pro.

It was very early Friday morning and raining hard as Jimmy Yee's limousine pulled up in front of the noodle shop per Zhang Jintao's instructions. They were no sooner at a stop when Zhang, wearing a topcoat and Western-style felt hat, emerged from the shop and slid into the back seat next to Jimmy.

"Good morning, Honorable Zhang," Jimmy said, bowing his head.

The old man returned the compliment. "It's very good of you to meet me at such an ungodly hour."

"You said it was urgent."

The chauffeur drove on through the narrow streets in the pouring rain.

"A problem in San Francisco has come to the attention of my clients," Zhang said. "They believe a quick decision is required, and that because of your familiarity with Mr. Lamb you could advise them."

"If I can, certainly."

"It seems Mr. Lamb has serious legal problems with the son and daughter of his late wife. Wilson and Melanie de Givry. If they prevail in a lawsuit, they may gain control of GET, Inc."

Jimmy was astonished. "Is this true?"

"How serious the matter is remains uncertain. My clients are concerned that the de Givrys may prevent Mr. Lamb from transacting his business with you. The intricacies of the American law are unclear to me, but it appears the matter turns on whether or not Mr. Lamb was unfaithful to his wife. Don't ask me why this is of importance, but apparently in America it is."

Jimmy thought of Jonas's girlfriend, the redhead with the large breasts. "Is a woman by the name of Crystal Clear involved in the lawsuit?"

"This I do not know," Zhang replied.

Jimmy nodded. "So tell me, Honorable Zhang, what do your clients want?"

"They consider this development to be of the utmost importance. Nothing will be allowed to thwart the interests of the state. They will spare no effort, even if it means lives. But the proper course of action is not clear. What is your counsel?"

Jimmy could see Jonas had gotten himself in a pickle. The poor bastard had to be feeling the pressure. "When is the trial?"

"I believe not for many months."

"Perhaps addressing the matter is not urgent, then. Jonas is coming to Hong Kong in a few days. I will find a way to explore the issue with him."

"Excellent," Zhang said.

"I agree that the situation must be closely monitored, though. The de Givrys could prove to be a great danger to us all."

"They could be eliminated, but there is another alternative," Zhang observed. "Sometimes the best way to deal with those who are dangerous is to make them your ally. Unfortunately, though, the de Givrys could have many suitors."

"This is true," Jimmy Yee replied. "It is also true that with Jonas we have an inside track. And, at present at least, he controls the technology." He gazed out at the driving rain. "There is no right and wrong in a situation like this, is there, Honorable Zhang?"

"No, my friend. There are only winners and losers."

The Financial District, San Francisco

Bob MacDonald had left the job site in San Rafael before the end of the workday, heading down the freeway for the city. Not that anybody would be giving him shit about it. He was boss and that was one of the privileges. Besides, he didn't care. The whole day had been ruined for him after what had happened that morning. He and Crystal had had their first major fight and it had been a doozy.

Maybe he'd come on too strong, demanding to know what the hell Uncle Jonas wanted, but Crystal hadn't helped matters by getting so pushed out of shape. "It's none of your damned business," she'd said. "And what are you doing spying on me, anyway?"

"I wasn't spying," he'd told her. "I got concerned when I saw that big limo full of people parked across from your shop. So I parked up the street to find out what was going on. Then when I saw Jonas get out, I knew something fishy was in the works."

"It's not fishy."

"Then why won't you tell me?"

"Look, Bob," she'd said, "let me worry about my relatives and you worry about yours. Okay?"

"You're hiding something, Crystal. What does that say about you and me?"

"All right, I'll tell you this. It's a business deal, okay? Lots and lots of money is involved. Millions. That's all I'm going to say."

That pissed him off, but there was more than one way to skin a cat. He'd been thinking about talking to that lawyer, anyway, and this gave him a good excuse.

For a while now he was convinced something wasn't quite right about Jonas. He wasn't even so sure he was an actual relative of Crystal's. Once, about a week or so ago when he was reading Tammy a story that had a nice old uncle in it, Jonas's name had come up. "He's not my real uncle," the little girl had said. "He's my pretend uncle." Bob hadn't said anything to Crystal about that, but it had got him to thinking. And seeing Jonas at the shop this morning had put him over the edge.

When he reached the Financial District, he parked in the garage of Melanie de Givry's building. He knew he was taking a chance coming without an appointment, but on the phone it would have been easy for her to put him off. After all, who was he? As it was, he'd probably just seem like a jealous boyfriend.

And maybe that's what he was. But if he and Crystal were going to get married, which was his plan, there had to be trust between them. Crystal, he figured, had lied about Jonas. And her story about a business deal worth millions didn't make sense. She probably said that to shut him up.

When he got to Melanie de Givry's floor, the receptionist in the big fancy waiting room said, "May

I help you?" hardly giving him a glance. Maybe because he was in work clothes.

"I'm here to see Melanie de Givry."

"You have an appointment?"

"No, my name's MacDonald. Tell her it's about Jonas Lamb."

The girl got on the phone and passed his message along.

In about three minutes a little blond lady who looked like a sixth-grader except for her fancy clothes and grumpy face, came out. Standing in front of him, she said, "Are you Mr. MacDonald?"

Bob, who'd sat on one of the sofas, got to his feet. "Yeah, that's me."

"What about Jonas Lamb?"

"I want to know what he's up to."

"I beg your pardon?"

"A while back you came to the shop of my fiancée, Crystal Clear, to talk about her uncle's financial problems, and I'd like to know what the hell is going on. She's upset and doesn't want to talk about it, but I'm not letting this problem screw things up for us. Since you're the lawyer on the case, I figured you'd know what the deal is and who I need to talk to to straighten things out."

"Wait a minute. You're Crystal's fiancé?"

"Yeah, well, it's only semiofficial, but we're pretty much agreed to do it." He was embarrassed. "Actually, I was thinking maybe Valentine's was when I'd officially pop the question. But don't say anything if you talk to her, because I'd sort of like to surprise her.

Point is, that's where we're headed, which is why I'm getting involved."

"Did you say Crystal's *'uncle'*?"

"Yeah, her uncle Jonas. I'm not so sure he's an actual relative, though."

Melanie de Givry got a funny little smile on her face. "Mr. MacDonald, why don't you come back to my office."

Bob followed her through the rabbit warren of hallways. Melanie's office was not super fancy, but it had a window and nice furniture. In Bob's experience, that put her somewhere in the middle of the pecking order. She went around her desk and sort of hopped up in her chair, making him think of a kid playing grown-up. But her steely expression told him she wasn't playing a game. He figured that when she was doing her thing she could be a real pain in the ass.

"Mr. MacDonald," she said, setting aside the bottled water in front of her, "why don't you tell me what happened that made you think you needed to talk to me?"

"Crystal told me that her uncle has financial problems and is always getting into trouble. I suggested she tell him to leave her out of it. And I thought that's what happened, but this morning he went to her shop. I don't know what they talked about for sure, but Crystal said it was about a business deal worth millions."

"What? She actually said that?"

"Yeah, but I don't think it's true. I figured you could tell me if Crystal's in some trouble I should know about. Is Jonas using her? Is she mixed up in something bad?"

"I'd like to say she's not in danger, but I can't. Your instincts are correct, Mr. MacDonald. Jonas *is* using her and he's a very unsavory character."

"How so?"

"I take it you really love Crystal and you want to help her."

"Yes. Definitely."

"Then I suggest you tell her that we've spoken, that I sympathize with your concerns, but that she should be the one to explain things to you."

"I tried, but basically she told me to butt out. I want to know why."

"I would tell you, Mr. MacDonald, but the last thing I want is to get Crystal mad at me. That's why I'm being vague. If you tell her about our conversation, I think she'll appreciate that fact. What I want her to know is that in me, she's got a friend."

"Can't you give me a hint about what's going on?"

Melanie de Givry hesitated, then said, "I'm involved in a lawsuit against Jonas Lamb and I'd like her help in prosecuting the case."

"Is he a criminal?"

"To be honest, I am considering criminal charges. Fraud and theft."

Bob flushed. "But not Crystal. I mean, she wouldn't get dragged into it."

"Not if she's smart, Mr. MacDonald. Not if you advise her to do the right thing."

"Which is what?"

"Jonas Lamb is a con artist and I'm sure Crystal's protecting him out of fear. And if he's talked to her about money, it could be because he's trying to bribe her. You might tell her that taking bribes is a serious offense."

He felt his pulse quicken and got to his feet. "Maybe I just ought to wring the son of a bitch's neck and save everybody a lot of trouble."

"I certainly can understand why you feel that way," Melanie said, rising, "but trust me, there are better ways of dealing with Mr. Lamb."

7:37 p.m.
TexasAmerican Headquarters, Houston, Texas

The building was locked for the night, so a security guard escorted Brock Stuart, CEO of Continental Consolidated Petroleum, to Harmon Shelbourn's office, where the head of TexasAmerican Petroleum waited with his administrative assistant. Shelbourn greeted his guest and the men exchanged pleasantries while Shelbourn's assistant served them drinks. Once she'd left the room, they got down to business.

Shelbourn told his friend that there was a new wrinkle in the GET saga. He'd learned from his sources that Jonas Lamb was in jeopardy of losing control of both his company and the super-ethanol technology, that his stepchildren, Wilson and Melanie de Givry, appeared ready to wrest everything away from him. Stuart, shocked, asked where that left them. He told Shelbourn he had people in place in California, ready to go into action against Lamb. Did this mean they had to switch to a new target?

Harmon Shelbourn suggested that such an action was probably premature, though they might be well advised to prepare for any contingency. If the undercover operation was not successful, they could end up in negotiations with both Lamb and the de Givrys. But there was another issue to consider, Shelbourn said. The stepchildren seemed to be unaware of the importance of GET's assets. Did that work in the interests of Shelbourn, Stuart and their friends, or against them? The de Givrys might be easier to deal with than Lamb, who was already in bed with foreign interests. So, did they take sides in the lawsuit or did they stay neutral?

The two men sipped their drinks and pondered the problem. Then Brock Stuart got an idea. He suggested they focus on appropriating the technology from Lamb as their primary option. Failing that, they would buy the technology from the de Givrys, which meant informing them that they had something of considerable value. The problem was that could drive up the price.

After some discussion, they settled on a strategy. They would alert the de Givrys of the potential value of their GET stock, if only as a means of putting pressure on Lamb. Then they'd wait to see how things settled out. If the de Givrys ended up in control then they would negotiate with them. Either way, their group would come out on top, and Jonas Lamb would be left out in the cold.

Stuart told Shelbourn that his people in California found the FBI's presence inconvenient, making their mission much more difficult. Was there a way to get them to back off their surveillance of Lamb and GET? Shelbourn promised to have a word with his high-ranking friend in Washington.

As Harmon Shelbourn went to fix them another drink, Brock Stuart noted that it certainly paid to have friends *in high places, friends who understood that the business of America was business.*

Kentfield, California

Considering that his sex life the past few weeks consisted of little more than watching "G-string Divas" on HBO, Jonas Lamb concluded the prospect of screwing May Li was a godsend, even if his heart wasn't in it. If he didn't owe it to himself to have sex with her, he reasoned, maybe he owed it to May Li, who, after all, was only trying to do her job.

And so Jonas lay naked under the covers waiting for May Li to knock on his door. Off and on during the day he'd pondered this encounter, but the sad truth was he'd spent more time thinking about Crystal and Tess. With regard to Crystal, the question had been what the hell would she decide to do? With regard to Tess, the question had been what the hell would she decide to do? Would Crystal lie for the sake of justice? Would Tess lie to Walter for the sake of some misguided notion that love didn't matter? Crystal owed him a lie. Tess owed him the truth. Why was he the only one who could see that?

Just then there was a rap on his door. Was it the mountain come to Muhammad? "Come in!"

May, in silk pajamas, her shiny black hair up, was carrying a tray with a bottle and a glass on it. He hadn't thought of it before, but it occurred to him then how compelling the notion of a woman's service and devotion could be. He felt a stirring in his nether regions.

"Jonas," she said, "you want maybe a night cup?"

"Night *cup*, huh? That's very thoughtful."

She grinned and made her way to the bed, setting down the tray with one hand.

"Only one glass?" he said.

May beamed, presenting a second glass she'd been holding behind her. "I hoping you ask," she said. She climbed on the bed and sat facing him, cross-legged. Then she turned the bottle so the label faced him. "Cream sherry okay?"

"A tab of Viagra dissolved in a spritzer might be more effective, but sherry could work, too."

"We have viger and spizer?" May asked, butchering the pronunciation. "I go get."

"Never mind, this is fine."

As she poured sherry, Jonas stared at the nub of the girl's nipples under the silk pajama top. He thought of the millions of Chinese servant girls who accommodated their masters over the centuries, submitting because it was expected. That might be the way May looked at it, but could he?

May handed him a sherry. They touched glasses, then she said, "I so happy to work with very important man."

Jonas wondered if, in China, that was considered a prelude to an erection. "I'm happy to work with a very beautiful girl."

May batted her lashes demurely. "Is it true you very happy with me?"

"Yes, indeed. You're very good at what you do."

"Jonas, you only see some of what I do. There is much more. You want to see?" she asked.

"How could I say no?"

May put down her glass and whipped off her top, quick as a flash. She beamed. The sweet little mounds of her breasts beamed. She was at once waiflike and toned as a bantam-weight prize fighter. Thin, taut muscles covered her bones. Jonas wouldn't have been surprised if she sprang from the bed and ran up the wall and across the ceiling like the girl in that *Crouching Tiger* movie.

It was then he saw a silvery scar across one shoulder. "What happened there?" he asked.

"A man with a very big knife," she replied, almost sounding amused.

"You're young, but I think you've lived a very interesting life."

"Very fortunate life."

He wondered how she defined *good fortune*. Coming to America all expenses paid to kill or be killed? Having sex with a round-eye foreign devil so her loved ones back home might prosper? Jonas knew what was happening, why he was torturing himself. Vietnam.

This was the psychological version of shingles, the moral equivalent of post-traumatic syndrome. Oh, the Vietnamese girls he'd screwed—waifs submitting their thin little bodies and somehow managing to seem pleased. Pretending. As much for themselves as for him. War by different means. On both sides.

May, go home to your mother or your lover, he wanted to say. *Your smile is killing me.*

She took his glass from him, put it on the tray and the tray on the floor. Then she pulled down the covers. "Oh," she said, drawing her hands down his matted chest and smiling. "You like a big bear, Jonas."

He didn't believe her pleasure. He didn't believe *her.*

Leaning over, she kissed his mouth with precision.

Jonas started to get hard. Then May, who knew her stuff, reached her hand down between them to encourage the newfound life in his stalk. When she'd inspired him enough, she climbed on and began riding his cock. She was an enthusiastic little thing, and when he finally came, it was more than release. His manhood had been reaffirmed. He was whole.

But fate wouldn't let him enjoy the afterglow for long. The doorbell ruined the moment.

May, who was lying on his chest, raised her head, whipping it toward the door.

"Who this hour?" she said.

That was indeed the question. May uncoupled from him and moved from the bed with the willful single-mindedness of a ninja warrior. She went to the door and listened, while downstairs their first line of defense, one of the Stooges, investigated.

Jonas saw May form a karate fist as she opened the door a crack. The sound of angry voices drifted up.

May hopped back to the bed in three strides, snatched her top and had it on before she'd made it back to the door. "Stay here, please, Mr. Lamb." And she was gone.

How quickly a man could be demoted from God to mister.

Sensing the master of the house might be called upon to intervene at some point, Jonas got out of bed and put on his robe. He went to the door and, like May, listened.

"Just tell the sonovabitch to get his ass down here," a man said. "I don't care how late it is."

Jonas decided that was his cue to enter. Cinching the belt of his robe, he strode from Granny's room to uphold the household's honor. From the top of the stairs he saw Bob and Crystal. There seemed to be trouble in paradise, and Jonas's instincts told him they'd come looking for fuel to throw on the fire. He also sensed the hope he'd so painstakingly constructed that morning wobbling like a drunk on stilts.

When Bob saw him descending the stairs, his verbal fury abated. His beefy hands remained clenched in a fist. Larry, his topknot of permed black hair barely coming to the height of Bob's shoulder, along with May, who was shorter still, were in a blocking position between Bob and the staircase. Crystal, her red hair flying every which way, her cheeks streaked with tears, had hold of Bob's arm, trying to restrain him. This wasn't the Bob with little hearts on his tie, this was one pissed-off bull elephant.

"Well, *Uncle* Jonas," Bob sneered, "I didn't think you'd have the guts to face me."

Crystal, who hadn't said much that Jonas had heard, moved around in front of him, along with

Jonas's security detail. "The 'uncle' business wasn't his idea, Bob, so drop it, okay? Now, will you please let me handle this?"

By this time Jonas had reached the bottom of the stairs. "Good evening," he said. "What brings you kids to my door in the dead of night?"

"To beat the shit out of your worthless ass!" Bob shouted, the spittle flying. He was obviously drunk.

"Goddamn it, Bob, will you please shut up!" Crystal shrieked. "You promised me."

She turned to face Jonas, rolling her eyes as only a woman could when dealing with boyish excess and an overabundance of testosterone. "This evening Bob and I had a big argument about you," she said, her voice shaky.

"I see," Jonas said, looking back and forth between them, feeling more like Arthur Dimmesdale than king of the world in waiting. "Let's repair to the drawing room, shall we?"

"No, let's just talk here," Crystal said. "We aren't going to be staying long."

"Just long enough for me to kick the bejesus out of you!" Bob roared.

May looked back at Jonas with inquiry on her face, as if to say, "You want me to dispatch this shit-eating dog?"

For two cents Jonas would have sicced his little hundred-pound superheroine on made-in-America Bob, knowing she'd pin his ass in twenty seconds, but his compassion and curiosity trumped his more pernicious impulses. "Fine," he said, "here in the vestibule it will be."

"I told Bob the truth about us," Crystal began.

"So, I gathered."

"You horse's ass," Bob interjected.

"Hey, come on," Jonas said, losing his temper now, "it was before she knew you. I don't know what you have to complain about, anyway. The minute you showed up she dropped me like a hot potato. You ought to be gloating."

"That's not what this is about," Crystal said.

"Oh?"

"Bob went to see Melanie de Givry today and...well, between what she told him and what I told him when he got home, he knows the whole story."

"The *whole* story?" The taste in his mouth turned bilious.

"I told him we discussed a deal involving millions, but he didn't buy it. So I confessed you were trying to blackmail me into lying at the disposition."

"Lamb, you goddamn scumbag!" Bob roared. "I ought to beat the shit out of you for trying to pull that bullshit, taking advantage of a poor, helpless woman. Using her, you rotten immoral sonovabitch."

Jonas was grateful for Crystal's quick thinking. Better he be accused of threatening to expose her than bribe her. But Bob's chivalrous antics were getting excessive and annoying. "You know, Bob, why don't you give it a rest?"

That was it. Bob's eyes went round as billiard balls.

He'd been looking for an excuse, and Jonas, perhaps unwisely, had given it to him. Shaking off Crystal, he pushed Larry aside and came charging after Jonas who, though he'd never run with the bulls at Pamplona, was now getting a taste of what it must be like. He braced himself.

But Bob only made it halfway to him before May, moving like a tigress after a buffalo, circled Bob and leaped through the air, her scissor-kick catching the lumbering craftsman square on the chin, snapping his head back and dropping him to the floor like a cow in the slaughterhouse.

For a second there was absolute silence. May was crouched on the floor where she'd landed, seemingly ready to spring to life and pounce again. Larry and Jonas were both stunned, Crystal frozen solid as an icicle, ready to come crashing down and shatter. It was her scream that broke the silence.

"Bob!" She rushed to his side, dropping to her knees, her face, framed by her flying red tresses, hung over his. "Bob?" She gently patted his cheeks. *"Bob?"* There was desperation in her last cry.

The behemoth lay motionless, not twitching a muscle, not groaning, perhaps not even breathing. Crystal looked up at Jonas with horror.

"Do something!"

He got down next to her for a closer look at the guy, an ominous feeling going through him, sensing that maybe he was dead. Bob sure wasn't moving. With Crystal starting to cry hysterically, Jonas pressed his finger into the big guy's neck, looking for a pulse, hoping for a pulse. It took a few seconds, but he found one. There was faint movement in his rib cage.

"He's alive," Jonas said. "I'd better get help."

He dialed 911, requesting an ambulance, knowing he'd probably get the police, as well. When he returned he found May looking wary and uncertain, standing next to Larry. They were watching Crystal, whose head was on Bob's chest. She was sobbing now. There was still no sign of life from the big guy.

Jonas figured moving Bob was the last thing they should do and Crystal was inconsolable. After a bit, he decided to try, anyway. He went to her and bent down, putting his hands on her shoulders.

"Help is on the way, sweetheart," he said softly.

Crystal stopped crying long enough to glare at him, her eyes streaked black with mascara. "I hate you," she said. Then she turned her attention back to Bob, pressed her fingers against his slack cheek and began to wail again.

Jonas, sick, stepped back. In the distance he could hear the mournful cry of a siren. What he saw in his mind's eye was a conference room in some law office and an attorney in a three-piece suit addressing Crystal. "Ms. Clear, did you have sexual relations with Mr. Lamb at any time during the course of his marriage to Mrs. de Givry?"

Jonas saw his world crumbling before him. It was over. But one good thing had come out of this. Elise never knew. Maybe that was his reward.

FRIDAY
January 25

Telegraph Hill, San Francisco

Moe was Jonas's baby-sitter that morning, riding in the front seat with the driver. Jonas was alone in back, May Li having disappeared before the arrival of the police the previous evening. He had no idea what happened to her, but he could only assume she'd panicked. Either that or she figured the incident could lead to trouble with the immigration authorities. In any case, she hadn't consulted him before her departure, leaving him in an awkward position.

It had been a chaotic night. Bob had been rushed to the hospital with Crystal at his side. The big guy hadn't regained consciousness. The police had questioned Jonas and they'd tried talking to Larry, though the language barrier posed a problem. It being impossible to get a translator at that hour of the night, they'd postponed the interview, relying for the time being on Jonas's account of events until they were able to talk to Crystal and, if possible, Bob.

The cop who took his statement did acknowledge

that if May was protecting him from being assaulted, it would be akin to self-defense. The decision whether or not to bring charges would be up to the District Attorney's Office. Jonas assumed that Crystal would corroborate his account. She could hardly deny that Bob meant him harm.

Shortly after the police left, Curly showed up to man the fort along with Larry, not that Jonas could see there was anything left to protect. And, since he couldn't sleep without knowing how Bob was, around 1:00 a.m. he and the two Stooges trooped over to the hospital. Bob, they learned, had incurred a rare brain-stem injury. He was in intensive care, paralyzed and semiconscious. But the doctors were hopeful that the paralysis would be temporary and that he would recover full brain function.

Crystal was in a more serene state than when Jonas last saw her, though she was still unhappy with him. He found her in the waiting room with a box of tissues.

"This wouldn't have happened if it wasn't for you and your goddamned Chinese friends," she'd said, clearly not in a rational state of mind.

"Melanie didn't exactly help matters."

"Maybe she's a shit-disturber, but our affair was none of her doing, Jonas. And please, I don't want to hear about your problems. I've got enough of my own."

He certainly wasn't going to argue with her; he was on thin-enough ice as it was. Apparently her account of what had happened between May and Bob was close enough to his that the police weren't putting out an APB on the crouching tigress. But Operation

Black Sheep was in jeopardy, though maybe not quite yet at death's door.

Based on what Crystal had said to Bob, Jonas concluded she hadn't completely betrayed him. At least the word *bribe* hadn't been mentioned. Though Crystal hadn't been in the mood for conversation, Jonas wanted to acknowledge what she'd done.

"Thanks for keeping our arrangement secret," he'd said. "Better I'm a blackmailer. Nice footwork."

"We don't have an arrangement," she'd said darkly.

"Why did you tell Bob I'd tried to blackmail you into lying for me at the deposition?"

"It was all I could think of."

"Well, if Bob's happier hating my blackmailing guts, so be it. Whatever serves your needs is fine with me. I trust, though, you didn't mention that to the cops."

"I'm not stupid, Jonas. But I don't want to talk about this," she'd said. "I'm upset enough as it is and I think you should go."

He had little choice but to back off. And so he'd gone home full of doubt and uncertainty. It had not made for a good night's sleep.

That morning before leaving the house he'd called his attorney, Braxton Weir, to find out how much trouble May was likely in. Weir said that based on Jonas's account of events, she probably didn't have to worry about criminal charges, though the INS might have some concerns. That didn't do much for Jonas's peace of mind.

They arrived at the office. Moe, now the man of

the house, got out and opened the door for Jonas, who was getting so habituated to the lifestyle that he was beginning to wonder if he'd ever be able to do his own dishes again. After climbing out of the limo, he glanced at Moe, a wiry guy with a fringe of bangs across his broad forehead. "What do you think, *compadre?* Will we be safe without mama?"

Moe gave him an uncertain grin. "Okay, Mr. Lamb."

"Enfin!" Gaston said, peering through the glass doors at the street. "I thought he'd never come."

Carly looked, too. "No sign of the woman. That's fortunate. Come on," she said, taking him by the arm and pulling him back to the middle of the lobby. "Get in character, Gaston. Think macho. For the next five minutes you're John Wayne."

"Oh, *mon Dieu,* did you have to say that?"

"Buck up, they're coming."

The door opened.

"You sonovabitch!" she screamed.

"You think I'm paying all that money for shorthand?" Gaston snarled. He grabbed her by the arm, and said, "Come on, we are leaving."

She tried to jerk her arm free, but Gaston kept a firm grip and began pulling her toward the door.

Lamb blocked their way. "Hey, pal," he said. "What's going on here?"

Gaston drew himself up, giving Lamb an indignant look. "It's is none of your affair, *monsieur.* Out of the way."

With the Chinese guy standing shoulder to shoulder with him, Lamb didn't budge. Carly wasn't sure which was more absurd, Gaston's indignation or Jonas Lamb's bluster. But the point was it seemed to be working.

"Is this guy bothering you, miss?"

"He thinks because I signed a contract he owns me," she said, jerking her arm free. "I'm not your slave, Pierre!" she shouted, laying it on as thick as her two leading men.

"You know how much I spent on you?" Gaston fumed, drawing himself up like a villain in some neighborhood melodrama.

Because of the accent, he could get away with it, but were the stakes not so high, Carly might have laughed. "So, take it out of my paycheck. I told you, I quit! Q-U-I-T! Got it?"

"You can't, Carly. I won't allow it."

"Hold on," Lamb said. "You can't manhandle the lady. If she doesn't want to go with you, she doesn't have to. Why don't you hit the road?"

Gaston lifted his brows so high his eyes bulged. "Mind your own business!"

"It *is* my business if a lady is molested. Time for you to go home." Lamb grabbed him by the arm, and the Chinese guy took Gaston's other arm. Together they pulled him to the door and ushered him out.

"This is an outrage! I'll file a complaint with the consulate!"

"You do that," Lamb called after him as he let the door close. He turned to her, taking her in, checking out her legs, obviously liking what he saw.

Carly had split the difference between businesslike and sexy in her attire. She wore a suit, but it was closely tailored and the skirt quite short. Her hair was down, making her more approachable than the cool, no-nonsense look of a chignon.

"You all right?" Lamb asked.

"Yes, thanks for your help. Pierre's basically harmless. Just arrogant. He wouldn't have done anything," she said, sweeping her long hair back off her face, effecting embarrassment.

"I was offended on your behalf."

"Thanks," she said, her cheeks coloring naturally. "Most people wouldn't get involved. I appreciate it."

Carly could see he was searching for a ploy, the difficult first line. "Is there anything I can do?" he asked. "My office is right down the hall. Would you like me to phone the police?"

The man wasn't shy. It was familiar territory, she could see. Resistence, gentle resistence, was called for. "No, I don't need the hassle. But thanks."

As expected, he was disappointed. She offered hope.

"If I could use your phone to call a cab, though…"

"Of course, of course. My name's Jonas Lamb, by the way."

"Carly," she replied. "Carly Van Hooten."

He offered his hand. She gripped it firmly, showing she was unafraid. Compliance, but in the next breath challenge. His eyes told her he was biting.

They walked down the hall, the Chinese guy following. Where was the woman? Carly wondered. What luck! Things couldn't have worked out better.

They reached the entrance to GET, Inc., and Lamb unlocked the door, turning on the lights.

"Care for a cup of coffee?" he asked. "You might as well relax for a few minutes."

Yes, she thought. *He had notions! Yes!* "That's very kind, Mr. Lamb."

He signaled to the Chinese guy, using sign language and words. "Two coffees, please." Then, escorting Carly to the sofa, he said, "It's Jonas, by the way. Pretty girls calling me Mr. Lamb make me feel old. I'm actually decades younger than I look."

It was then Carly Van Hooten knew she had her foot in the door.

She gave him a sweet, shy smile as she dropped onto the sofa, crossing her legs in one graceful motion. Jonas, being unfailingly accurate about first impressions, saw an opportunity. (Not that each and every attractive young lady wasn't an opportunity, but his down phases always left him extra needy.) A quick analysis led him to the conclusion that she was attracted to him. He could feel the vibrations. But the question was, did he avail himself? There was a time when it would have been a slam dunk. And yet, needy or not, he hesitated.

Did he have the time and the energy, considering his plate was already pretty full? She was one hell of a dish, though—petite, honey blond, with the most beautiful green eyes he'd ever seen, a gorgeous girl. Fabulous legs. Girls like this didn't drop in your lap every day. Next week or next month could be too late. He wondered if there was a way to get a foothold then give her a call later, when things weren't quite so hectic.

Jonas dropped into the chair across from her.

"So, where you from, Carly?"

Downtown, San Francisco

She knocked on the door, waited and, after a minute or so, knocked again. Finally it swung open. Gaston, in his robe, his hair wet, stood there, dripping. The way the tie was barely secured, she'd have thought he was expecting Charles or Reece instead of her.

"*Ah, c'est toi.* Sorry, *chérie,*" he said, "I was taking a bath."

"You take more baths than any man I've ever known, Gaston." She walked past him and he closed the door behind her.

"I do my best thinking in the tub. How do you think Archimedes did it?"

Carly glanced around. "I see you didn't spare any expense on *your* room."

"You know perfectly well we picked the Montpelier for you because it's the sort of place a job-seeker fleeing Krause's Appliances in Cleveland would go, whereas the St. Francis is barely suitable for a man with…"

"…your bloodlines?"

"I was going to say with responsibility for a mission of such weight and importance, but now that you mention it, that, too."

"Gaston, you're so predictable." She went and sat on the unmade bed, where a laptop computer winked at her. There was another laptop on the desk, hooked to a wall jack for Internet access. It, too, was on. Of course, the room was hot in accordance with Gaston's preferences.

Crossing her legs at the ankles, Carly leaned back on her hands and stared at him. He folded his arms and stared back.

"So, Bo Peep, am I to conclude from your bitchy tone that things did not go well?"

"Not as well as I expected."

"Then the Chinese girl does have him by the dumb stick."

Carly didn't answer immediately. "I don't think so."

"*Tiens.* What's wrong, then? Surely you didn't fail to spark his interest."

"No, I don't think that's the problem. He had a hormonal reaction. And I don't think it's that I'm not his type, either."

Gaston came and sat next to her on the bed. "Then what could it be?"

"I don't know. I sensed he was fighting himself, that he was torn."

"Perhaps his wife hasn't been dead long enough. God knows Papa waited a whole three months before going off to Biarritz with that artist's model. To be both sad *and* alone was too much for the old fart."

"I thought we decided Lamb married for money," Carly said.

"Those were the indications."

"You know what I sensed? That he was a man fighting temptation, like a husband who loves his wife but has trouble keeping his pants zipped."

"Must be an American phenomenon. Vestiges of Puritanism, undoubtedly."

"Well, I did manage to tempt him, that much I'm sure of." She sighed with frustration. She did not need a failure her first time out in years. She wondered if maybe she hadn't come on a little strong. The Chinese girl had added a note of urgency that had gotten Carly out of her rhythm. Maybe that was the problem.

"So, how did things end?" Gaston asked. "He patted you on the head and sent you on your way?"

"No, not exactly. We talked about my job situation and I gave him my story about running Krause's Appliances even though I was only Marvin's executive assistant. After checking out my boobs and legs for about the third time, Lamb gave me his card and told me to call him this afternoon. He promised to give my job situation some consideration and see if he could come up with some suggestions."

"Hmm," Gaston said, caressing his throat, beads of perspiration forming on his brow. "Could be he wants to find a strategy to get you in the sack, *n'est-ce pas?* On the other hand, it could have been a brush-off." He reflected. "We might have been overly optimistic, thinking he'd welcome you with open arms just because you're capable of inducing an erection."

"Some men fight their desires initially. Breaking down their resistance requires considerable effort. These things aren't as automatic as they may seem."

"At least he left the door open," Gaston said. "I do have news, though."

"Good or bad?"

"Mostly good. I think I may have figured out who the technical genius is behind Mr. Lamb's super ethanol."

"Who?"

"His son. The young man is a microbiologist at the University of California at Davis. He has a different last name. That's what threw me off. Patrick Mayne."

"What's his situation, Gaston? Is he married? Maybe I should be targeting him instead of Lamb. I mean, our ultimate goal is the technical data, isn't it?"

"*Voilà!* I discussed that very thing with Le Genissel. He's already sent people to check out Monsieur Mayne. I have some preliminary data on the gentleman. He's single and attractive. In fact, there's a slight resemblance between him and Antoine."

"Antoine? You're kidding."

"No, have a look. I dug up some pictures of him on the Internet. They're on the computer over there."

She got up and walked across the room to the desk, where she leaned over to take a close look at the screen. Gaston was right, there was something of a resemblance, at least as to general appearance and coloring. The nose was different.

"Switch screens," Gaston said.

She did. The other photos of Patrick Mayne were not as reminiscent of Antoine, but their builds were similar, though it appeared Mayne was bigger than Antoine, who'd only been of average height. "Ironic," she said.

"I thought it might please you."

"I don't know if it does or not."

"Surely it's not a problem."

"No, of course not." She said it easily and it wouldn't be, but it did make her wonder. If she were to seduce Patrick Mayne, would she think of Antoine at the magic moment? When they were still together and she'd had sex with other men, she made a point of not thinking about Antoine because it helped keep her personal and professional lives separate.

"*Bien,* I have other news," Gaston said. "Le Genissel has actually done something useful for a change. He's been focusing on our Chinese friends."

"Don't tell me he's killed the woman."

"No, but he's been watching Lamb. As it turns there was some sort of altercation last evening at his home. Ambulances, police. The Chinese woman fled."

"Well, that saves him the trouble of killing her. He was considering it, you know."

"That particular honor is bestowed on about everyone who crosses his path. The man is a mad dog. But he pays well."

"Whatever. Just so he doesn't step on my toes."

"He's determined to get revenge. He lost a couple of men and blames the Chinese."

"So that's what matters now? Revenge? What about Brebis Noire?"

"*Tiens.* We're talking about Alfred's manhood, *chérie.*" Gaston chuckled. "Well, so much for that. Now that the focus has shifted to Mayne, how do we proceed?"

"I think the best route to the son is through the father. It won't be easy to finesse."

"Surely you don't propose to seduce them both."

"No, not unless that appears to be the only way."

"Carly, if there's a woman alive who can do this, it has to be you."

She turned back to the computer screen and gazed at Patrick Mayne's image, but the voice she heard was Antoine Laurent's. "Hell, if Lamb had a daughter, ten thousand francs says I could bed her in one night." She could hear the laughter of the man buried in that graveyard in the village of Beaumesnil as clearly as if he was standing right beside her. Antoine loved a challenge. But then, so did she.

Carly checked her watch. "It's a little early, but I think I'll call Lamb. Mind if I use your phone?"

"Be my guest."

Carly took Jonas Lamb's card from her jacket pocket and picked up the receiver. She got an outside line and dialed the number. He answered.

"Hi, Jonas. It's Carly Van Hooten. I hope I'm not calling too early."

"No, this is fine. I wish I could tell you I had some hot leads. Like I said this morning, I'm not well connected in the San Francisco business community."

Her heart sank.

"But I have an idea or two I thought we could kick around. Would you care to meet and discuss the matter?"

She felt a spark of hope. "Sure. Anytime."

"Have plans for dinner?"

A big grin stretched across her face. "No." Glancing over at Gaston, she gave him a thumbs-up.

"Why don't I take you out and we can talk. But please, don't get the wrong idea. I wouldn't want to upset you on the heels of what happened with Pierre."

"No problem, Jonas," she replied. "And I wouldn't want you to get the wrong idea by me accepting your invitation."

"*Touché*," he said. "I'll pick you up at your hotel. Shall we say seven?"

"Perfect."

After Carly hung up, she looked at Gaston, who was lying on the bed, staring up at the ceiling, a small smile on his lips. He said, "My, but love is grand."

The Financial District, San Francisco

Melanie de Givry stared at the man across the desk from her. He'd introduced himself as Ramsey Brown, an attorney from Houston, facts corroborated by his business card. He was fiftyish with a square jaw, thick, carefully styled and colored mahogany hair, and a touch of Texas in his speech—the refined variety, rather than corn pone.

"Forgive me if I'm incredulous, Mr. Brown," she said, "but I *know* Jonas Lamb is a flimflam man, and you're asking me to believe he has a technology worth millions?"

"Many millions, ma'am," the man said.

She reflected. "Why are you telling me? That's what I'm having trouble understanding."

"My principals recognize you have a legitimate claim for control of the company. Eventually they'll have to deal with someone, and they'd just as soon it be you...for the reasons you've just cited. Lamb is a loose cannon."

"But you can't be more specific on what this technology is."

"Lamb is keeping the details a closely guarded secret, but reliable sources confirm that what he has is of substantial value."

Melanie shook her head. "And to think, I was going to let him have the stock for a hundred thousand."

"My principals were concerned about that, Ms. de Givry."

She searched for the catch. It was almost too good to be true. The pig in the poke could end up being the goose that laid the golden egg, if Brown was to be believed. How Jonas had done it was beyond her, but assuming he had, he'd done it with her mother's money, so why should the windfall be his? And yet...

"I understand your skepticism," Brown said, "but what possible motive could we have to deceive you? Put yourself in my principals' shoes. Would you want to deal with Jonas Lamb or Melanie and Wilson de Givry?"

Melanie was not easily influenced by flattery, but she couldn't find a hole in the logic.

"Look at it this way," Brown went on, "my people aren't asking anything of you except to pursue what's rightfully yours. My purpose is to alert you so that you don't get taken by Jonas Lamb."

She nodded. "For that, I can only be grateful. Will I hear from you down the road?"

"Someone will be in contact with you, yes, ma'am."

Brown got up to go. Melanie walked him to the reception where they shook hands.

"I apologize for being so abstruse," Brown said, "but my people are in a delicate position. When the time comes it will all be very clear. For the moment, the ball is in your court, Ms. de Givry."

Melanie returned to her office, her blood pulsing. The ball was, indeed, in her court. Best of all, she'd been given another opportunity to put it to Jonas Lamb. That's what pleased her as much as anything. Of course, millions wouldn't be hard to take....

As she sat reflecting, two things became clear. One was that everything was riding on Crystal Clear's willingness to cooperate. The other was that Crystal was in very great danger, because if she were out of the picture, Jonas would walk away with his ill-gotten gains, and he had to know that. Melanie realized it was up to her to make sure that didn't happen. After checking her Rolodex, she dialed the number. The phone rang.

"Yeah?" the woman said.

"Daphne, this is Melanie de Givry. I've got another urgent job for you. *Very* urgent."

Aquatic Park, San Francisco

He sipped Irish coffee and watched the sailboats out beyond the breakwater. Patrick was late and Jonas had the uneasy feeling of a man whose personal and professional lives were on a collision course.

And all because of Carly Van Hooten. Part of him wanted to rush headlong into the game he'd played with considerable success the last few decades—

charm, seduce and conquer. That had been his philosophy and his theme song. But he'd felt the winds of change in his old bones. Perhaps he was a man looking for definition, a composer in search of a coda.

He vacillated because Carly was an exceptional beauty and an interesting, intelligent, complex woman. Actually, something about her reminded him a bit of Tess. They both had class and an inner strength. Carly was more showy, though she remained classy to the core. Tess was more subtle, serious and cerebral, the kind of woman you took home to mother, if you had a mother who could appreciate her.

Larry, who'd accompanied Jonas, stood near the door like a foo dog, grimly determined to keep the master safe. For the sake of his mental health, Jonas had been trying to forget all the women in his life— Tess, the heartbreaker; Crystal, the ball-breaker; and now Carly, the temptress. What a trio. How did a man endure?

He refocused his thoughts on business. The notion of holding all the chips still gave him a rush, but climbing over dead bodies (literally as well as figuratively) wasn't exactly the preferred version of the Horatio Alger story. Success, yes, but at what price? It was a question he'd only begun to ask.

Just then Jonas spotted his son stepping off a cable car. Patrick strode purposefully into the bar and settled on the stool next to him.

"Sorry to be late."

"Not a problem. I have been a little concerned since getting your call."

"Were you followed?"

"Who knows?" Jonas replied. "I've pretty well decided the folks we're dealing with are out of my league. I'm at the stage of concerned resignation."

"I know I've been followed."

"I don't suppose you have any idea by who."

"No, I haven't seen a face. Just a vehicle or somebody on foot, keeping a distance, but always there. On my way here I took precautions to shake them. I think I succeeded. The point, though, is this is getting intense."

Jonas was very close to saying, "Maybe we've bit off more than we can chew. Maybe the smart thing is to find a buyer who'll take your Black Sheep in exchange for a nice fat annuity." Yet he didn't want to be a wuss.

"You called the meeting," Jonas said. "I hope it's good news."

"I wanted to update you and see where things stand with regard to our trip."

"I've got tickets for the Sunday evening flight," Jonas said.

"Super."

"Is your dog-and-pony show ready?" Jonas asked.

"Yep."

That gave him a lift. If they could close a deal with Jimmy, then maybe some of the heat would be off. Things wouldn't reach their final conclusion until the results of the experimental field were in, but it would be good to know they had their ducks in a row. "We've come a long way, son."

"With a few big hurdles to go."

Jonas knew that the final stages of any venture could be the most trying. It was when a man's resolve was tested. It was crunch time.

The bartender came over and Patrick ordered a bottle of mineral water.

"I've been worried somebody's going to rip off or destroy my research. I've taken steps in case their goal is to wipe me out while they're at it."

"Don't you mean wipe *us* out? They'd probably start with me."

Patrick chuckled. "I didn't want to make a point of it."

"I'm getting fatalistic in my old age, so don't give it a thought. What precautions have you taken?"

The bartender brought Patrick his mineral water, then moved away.

The boy waited until he was beyond earshot. "I've given all my documentation to Mom for safekeeping."

"You gave it to *Tess?*"

Patrick poured his water. "With instructions for what to do with it in case something happens to us. I figure it's a kind of insurance." He took a drink.

"Yes, but you've put her in danger, too."

"I didn't force it on her. Anyway, as I see it, this is a short-term arrangement. If we don't make a deal with Jimmy Yee then I'm inclined to give the project to the highest bidder."

"One last shot, in other words."

"Exactly."

Jonas could see Patrick's logic, but he wasn't sure

how he felt about Tess being brought into the deal. He was concerned foremost about her safety, but he also worried about what she thought—about him in particular.

"The other thing is, I gave Mom the package I prepared for Jimmy Yee," Patrick said. "She's going to keep that close at hand so we can grab it before we leave for Hong Kong. And, if I should end up in an alley with my throat slit, she knows to give it to you. I figure somebody's got to put our little Black Sheep to work."

"Tess must have loved hearing that. Was she horrified?"

"More like concerned. About both of us."

"*Both* of us?"

"Yeah. To be honest, I think your stock may have gone up a little when I told her how this all came about."

Jonas was pleased. "I've been thinking a lot about her recently. Regretting the past more than ever, wishing I'd made different choices."

"Trust me, you're better off letting go."

"Yeah. That's what I've been telling myself." It occurred to him then that his Carly Van Hooten escapade had more to do with Tess than it did Carly. He'd been struggling with his feelings for his ex for the better part of thirty years.

Surrender had never been an option. Deep down, through girlfriends and wives, wine and song, one crazy scheme or adventure to the next, there was an undercurrent of regret. And maybe the worse part of it was that Tess had been in denial about him from the time of his malefaction until now. He was more convinced of that than ever.

Jonas finished his Irish coffee. "Don't tell your mom this, but I think she's fighting her feelings for me."

"No, I don't think I will mention that," Patrick said with a grin. He took another sip of water.

"Mark my words, son, she likes me more than she's willing to admit. Tess and I have always had chemistry. Always. And it's still there."

Patrick shook his head with amusement. Jonas peered out the big window at the bay. He'd been thinking about Carly Van Hooten and what to do about her.

"On another subject, what would you think of hiring an executive assistant to keep the office humming…answer the phones, present a public image, that sort of thing?"

"I take it you have a candidate in mind."

"As a matter of fact I do. Lovely girl. I met her this morning."

"Is she Arab or Chinese?"

"She's a Browns fan from Cleveland. Midwesterner, though she hardly fits the stereotype. Classy young lady, actually."

"Jonas, you've got a twinkle in your eye."

"I appreciate a beautiful girl, but that's not what this is about. As a businessman I'm very image conscious."

"Well, that's your department. Do whatever you

think is necessary." Patrick took a long drink of water.

"As a matter of fact, I'm taking her to dinner this evening. If you're free, maybe you could join us. Carly's a crackerjack, son. Bright. Energetic. Hell, if I were twenty years younger…"

Patrick looked at him with surprise. "You'd let a little thing like age stop you?"

"I've been taking a good hard look at my life."

Patrick raised his eyebrow. "I'm beginning to think this talk about Mom is serious."

Jonas nodded. "It is."

"I hope you've got thick skin."

"I do, but that's a topic for another day. How about you joining Carly and me for dinner?"

"I would, but I already told Mom I'd take her to dinner."

Jonas only took a second to seize the opportunity. "That's perfect! Bring her along. She's practically a partner, anyway. And she's got good people sense. We could get her input."

"You're not serious."

"Dead serious. In fact, it's a wonderful idea." Tess being present would help him with his moral quandary. Plus, he'd found that beautiful young girls had a salubrious effect on mature women, particularly mature women who hadn't lost their looks. Jonas took his cell phone out of his jacket pocket and put it on the bar. "Call her now."

Patrick smiled, picked up the phone and dialed his mother's number.

Downtown, San Francisco

It was dark when Jonas pulled up in front of the Montpelier Hotel in the chauffeur-driven limo with Larry riding shotgun. They'd repaired to Marin that afternoon and Jonas was concerned to discover there was still no sign of May Li. The Stooges were on the job, though, seemingly unconcerned. (Who could be sure, really? Jonas's Cantonese wouldn't fill a fortune cookie.)

Patrick hadn't been able to reach Tess when he'd called from the Buena Vista, but phoned Jonas an hour later with the news that he and Tess would, indeed, be joining them for dinner. Jonas took it as an indication that he understood her heart better than her son, though he had to admit it could also mean she didn't trust either of them.

Larry escorted Jonas into the lobby of the hotel. Jonas called Carly on the house phone. "I'm downstairs."

"Give me ten minutes," she replied.

Jonas settled in a leather armchair that had seen better days while Larry positioned himself near the entrance, both waiting under the curious scrutiny of a seedy desk clerk with a gray beard and a superabundance of ear hair. If Jonas had to guess, the guy was probably younger than he. It was a sad fact that one's peers were often the most eloquent indicator of just where a person was in life. The same could be said of spouses.

Several minutes passed before Carly Van Hooten

stepped from the elevator, wearing a stunning little black jersey dress that came to midcalf and black, high-heeled suede boots. Jonas speculated that any love that could make him turn a blind eye to this was love worthy of the gods. His heart had its work cut out.

Carly's only jewelry was a wide gold cuff bracelet and hoop earrings. Over her arm she carried a black cashmere cape. Oddly, Jonas found himself looking at the girl through Patrick's eyes. Would he be as bedazzled as his old man?

"Don't you look lovely," he said, rising from his chair.

Sure he was flirting. A man could be madly in love and still savor a pretty girl. He could also prove himself to be an old fool, which he was determined wouldn't happen.

Carly gave a little laugh, looked up at him with those lovely green eyes, then handed him her cape. He slipped it around her shoulders, then Larry led the way back outside, opening the door of the limo. Carly slipped into the rear seat like Cinderella mounting her coach. Jonas followed her in, figuring he'd better get out his plans for the evening while he still had the clarity of thought to speak coherently.

"Carly, I don't believe I mentioned that my son is a partner in my enterprise, albeit a silent partner. I hope you don't mind, but I invited him and his mother, who remains a very dear friend, to join us this evening."

The girl seemed momentarily stunned, but quickly

recovered. "No, of course not. I'd be honored to meet your family."

A few more beats and Jonas thought he might even have detected delight playing at the corners of her mouth. Maybe the poor thing had been afraid he'd hit on her—not an unreasonable concern—and was relieved they'd have company.

"Tell me about them," she said.

Jonas gave her a quick rundown, avoiding any detail about his marriage to Tess and specifics about Patrick's role in the company. And, of course, he made no mention of GET's business purpose.

Glancing over at her, he saw a gleam in her eye. Her seeming delight with his plans for the evening made him wonder. He recalled one of the few bits of wisdom his mother had passed on to him: "If things seem too good to be true, it may be because they are."

Sausalito, California

Crystal Clear was dead tired when she arrived home in the falling darkness. But at least she felt relieved that Bob had rallied. He'd even had moments of lucidity. They'd talked and the doctor was pleased that he'd been able to move his limbs. Bob still had a long way to go, though. Crystal wouldn't have left the hospital except that the doctor had told her he'd have Security escort her off the premises if she didn't go home and get some rest.

When she pulled up in the parking area, two familiar faces were waiting, the detectives working for

Melanie de Givry—the little blonde with the spiky hair and Chuck Haggerty. Crystal was not pleased to see them.

"What do you want?" she demanded, not waiting for them to volunteer an explanation.

"Ms. de Givry is concerned for your safety, Ms. Clear," the blond woman, Daphne, said.

"Yeah, well I'm concerned for it, too. Did she send you here to tell me that?"

"She sent us here to protect you."

"From what?"

"People who would benefit if you were dead."

"Like who?"

"Jonas Lamb."

Crystal had to laugh. "First you try to catch us in bed together, now you're trying to keep him from what...killing me?"

"Ms. de Givry says that millions of dollars are at stake over your testimony in the deposition next week," Daphne said. "She's tried calling you all day, but couldn't get through. She sent us over to make sure you're all right."

"Tell Ms. de Givry thanks, but I don't need her help. And as far as Jonas is concerned, I can deal with him. Now, I'm beat, so if you don't mind I'm going to bed."

"Would you like for us to make sure your house-boat is secure?"

"No, I wouldn't. Thanks for your concern, though."

Daphne put a hand on her arm. "Please, Ms. Clear, we're really trying to help. Ms. de Givry thinks the FBI may have been behind the warning she got about

Jonas Lamb. They've talked to her about him. And it's not just Lamb you have to worry about. There are others involved who stand to gain from your death."

Crystal was too tired to argue. "All right, come and have a look if it'll make you happy." She wasn't worried about Jonas, but she had to admit trouble did seem to follow him. And she didn't trust his Chinese friends, not after all that had happened.

The two P.I.s accompanied her as they walked along the dock.

"Where's your little girl?" Daphne asked.

"Spending the weekend with her father." As far as Crystal was concerned, it was the one fortunate thing that had happened. It would have been hell trying to deal with a child on top of everything else.

They arrived at *Lamb's Croft,* which was dark. Crystal kept a front room lamp on a timer and it should have been on by now. That gave her pause.

"So, what's supposed to keep the bad guys from coming for me after you folks are gone?" she asked, taking her keys from her purse.

"Ms. de Givry is offering our services for as long as you like," Daphne said. "We'd be happy to stay."

"I don't relish having houseguests," Crystal replied, fumbling with her keys.

Haggerty took the key from her. "Let me help you with that, ma'am."

He opened the door. Crystal went inside.

"I'll put the light on," she said, moving across the dark room.

About the time she banged her knee against the

coffee table and let out a yelp, the firing started—flashes coming from the direction of the stairs with odd hissing sounds. *Thwish. Thwish. Thwish.* She went down amid the pandemonium. There were cries, more shots, running, then silence, punctuated after a time by the faint gasps of the dying.

It took a while for Crystal to pull herself together. When she finally got a light on, she saw Daphne Miles and Chuck Haggerty on the floor in pools of blood.

The Financial District, San Francisco

Jonas had made reservations at Aqua, a trendy, sophisticated restaurant on the edge of the Financial District. The place was favored by the young, hot business set. He'd chosen it as a statement that seemed appropriate when his objective had been to render career advice. (He liked the idea of the young studs ogling Carly and envying him.) But with Patrick and Tess in the picture, his intention was to play the role of gracious host and see what happened.

The place was jumping. Those waiting for a table had spilled out onto the street. With the disappearance of the dot-com millionaires, the San Francisco business scene had slowed down some, but there were still plenty of people under forty in town with money to burn. It was a setting where both Patrick and Carly ought to feel comfortable.

Jonas helped her out of the limo, and the eyes of the men and women alike were on Carly. It was easy enough to see what was going through people's minds. He'd always taken great pleasure in having a beautiful woman on his arm, and the irony was this one had required virtually no effort or sacrifice on his part. But what he was really looking forward to was the look on Tess's and Patrick's faces when they got a look at her.

His son and former wife were already at the table, and when they saw the maître d' escorting them back, Patrick and Tess both looked shocked. Patrick rose to his feet, not quite his usual blasé self as he stared at Carly. Tess seemed surprised, unprepared for Carly's beauty.

Jonas made the introductions. Carly shook hands with both Tess and Patrick, joy and excitement on her pretty smiling face. As the maître d' seated her, Jonas took his chair opposite Patrick and between the two women. He took Tess's hand, giving it a squeeze.

"You look ravishing as always," he said. And she did, her dark hair and dark eyes shining, not flashy in a black suit, pearl-and-diamond stud earrings, gold watch and her engagement ring. Were it not for Walter's ring, she could have been described as thoroughly understated—serious, yet feminine.

Her attention, not surprisingly, was drawn to Carly. "I understand you're new to San Francisco," she said to the girl.

"This is my third day, Mrs. Vartel." The color in her cheeks and furtive glance in Patrick's direction gave her the air of an ingenue, a side of the girl Jonas hadn't seen.

"First trip?"

"To San Francisco, but not California. I spent a few months in L.A. several years ago."

As the women continued exchanging pleasantries, Jonas noted Patrick sizing up Carly. Nice that the kid had a little of the old man in him.

"I'm glad you were able to join us, Tess," Jonas said to his former wife. "You know the business community better than either Patrick or me. Carly's looking for work and I've volunteered to help, if I can."

"Jonas is my knight in shining armor," Carly volunteered. She gave Tess and Patrick a brief account of his minor heroics that morning with Pierre.

"Jonas has an instinct for that sort of thing," Tess observed, giving him a meaningful glance.

The waiter arrived to tell them about the specials and they put aside their getting-acquainted conversation to focus on ordering. Normally Jonas wouldn't take out his glasses to read a menu—not if he was with a young woman—but who was he trying to impress, anyway?

Once they'd ordered, Carly asked Patrick about his role at GET. He explained that it was a sideline since his primary career was teaching. Jonas had been interested to hear how the boy would deal with the issue and was happy to see he'd chosen to be discreet.

With the two younger people immersed in conversation, Jonas turned his attention to Tess. "So, how've you been?"

"Okay. Taking it easy. Spent a little time in Mexico."

"That's what I understand. I'm surprised Walter let you go alone."

"I'm perfectly capable of taking care of myself, Jonas."

"That's not what I meant. I was suggesting that if I were in his shoes, I wouldn't let you out of my sight."

She smiled indulgently. "Walter hardly has anything to worry about."

Jonas thought of their kiss, and maybe Tess read his mind because she looked uncomfortable, then abandoned him for the other conversation. For the next few minutes he listened to Carly charm Patrick and Tess both, admiring the girl's social skills, an impressive performance for a young lady who'd been running an appliance company in Cleveland. Tess, who took Jonas at his word about giving Carly advice, asked a number of questions about her work experience. The girl coolly recounted how she'd taken over the day-to-day operation of Krause's Appliances in Cleveland as the owner lost interest, pressing ahead with his plan to sell the business.

Their conversation was interrupted when the first course was served. The talk subsequently went in a different direction, with much of it between Patrick and Carly. Jonas could see the boy was taken with her, which pleased him—he would have hated to see a very special opportunity lost. Girls like this didn't come along every day.

They were midway through the main course and things were going well, Carly having charmed them all thoroughly, though Jonas sensed in Tess a tiny hint of distrust, perhaps something akin to his own feeling that Carly Van Hooten was...it was hard to put his finger on just what...maybe too perfect. On the other hand, Tess could simply be reacting as the mother of a son—no girl would ever be good enough.

Carly was recounting some of her experiences during her brief childhood modeling career when Larry entered the restaurant, making a commotion up front. Jonas grew concerned when the bodyguard came hurrying back to their table.

"So sorry, Mr. Lamb," he said, bowing deeply, then thrusting the cell phone he was carrying into Jonas's hand.

Knowing the language barrier prevented him from getting an explanation from Larry, Jonas chose to address the caller. "Hello?"

"Mr. Lamb? That you?"

He recognized May Li's voice and more particularly the sense of urgency she always seemed to project. "Yes, May, what's the matter?"

"Very bad thing, Mr. Lamb. Police come to house with translator and ask many questions to Moe about where I am. They think I murder somebody."

"May, Bob's not dead. He's in the hospital."

"No, not man last night. Somebody else. Two private investigators at your boathouse. Lady and man. They dead."

Jonas felt his gut go hard. Private investigators? "Do you know who, May?"

"No, Mr. Lamb. I call to say I didn't do it. They think maybe I do. Maybe since you know me pretty good, they ask you question, too."

That, Jonas realized, was a colossal understatement. If somebody had been killed at *Lamb's Croft,* how could they not think he was a party to it, especially since he owned the houseboat. But apparently Crystal was okay. That was something.

"Where are you, May?" he asked.

"That not important. Mostly I want you to know. Perhaps I can't stay San Francisco, Mr. Lamb. Tang, Shu and Fan can't stay, either. You must hide until Mr. Yee decide what to do. You understand, Mr. Lamb? Important you be careful. Goodbye, Mr. Lamb."

When May Li hung up, Jonas had a feeling he'd never be speaking to her again. He handed the cell phone back to Larry. "Thanks, *compadre.*"

The bodyguard discreetly pressed a slip of paper into Jonas's hand and brought a finger to his lips, indicating silence. Jonas slipped the paper into his pocket. Larry bowed and headed for the door. Jonas's dinner companions, knowing something dire had occurred, looked at him and waited. Carly, who was out of the loop, probably reacted more to the mood of the moment than anything that was said.

"What happened?" Patrick asked.

Jonas told him there had been shootings at his houseboat. "I'm not sure who the victims are. Apparently private investigators." It occurred to him they might be Melanie's people. God knew she had a small army under pay.

"What are you going to do?" Patrick asked.

"First, I'm going to finish my dinner, then I'm going to call Braxton Weir."

Obviously the mood became somber. Tess, in particular, looked ashen.

"You concerned?" he asked her, not caring what she might say in Carly's presence.

"Problems are pretty much routine with you, aren't they, Jonas?"

"Sometimes I'm the victim," he said.

"Not this time. Do the police think you're involved?"

"It wouldn't surprise me."

She was silent.

"You're the lawyer in the family," he said. "Do you have any advice?"

"Make sure you know how to reach Braxton Weir at all times."

Carly Van Hooten looked thoroughly confused. About then Jonas saw a couple of men enter the restaurant. He had a nose for cops, not that his experience with them was all that extensive.

"This may not be the ideal time for job offers, Carly," he said, "but in a couple of days I'll be heading for Hong Kong, assuming I'm not in jail. We need somebody to run the office. Until you find something permanent, would you be willing to be our Girl Friday? We'll make it worth your while."

"Well, I suppose if I can be of help..."

Jonas noted the men up front consulting the maître d', who pointed in their direction. "Tess, I have a feeling I could use Braxton Weir now. Since he's unavailable, I don't suppose you'd be willing to serve as interim counsel."

Tess turned to see what he was looking at. The men made their way to the table.

"Jonas Lamb," one said. He was a big, heavy man—six- three or so, more than two hundred and fifty pounds.

"Yes."

"I'm Detective Ray Tucker, Marin County Sheriff's Department, and this is my partner, Jorge Luz." He flashed a badge. "Could we speak with you, sir?"

The entire corner of the restaurant fell into silence as all attention was on the two cops and Jonas.

"Sure."

"Would you mind stepping outside?" Tucker asked.

"No, not at all. As it turns out, my counsel happens to be present. I'd like her to accompany me."

"Fine."

Jonas gave Tess a beseeching look and she reached for her purse and coat. He got to his feet. "Patrick, should I become indisposed, would you be kind enough to see that Carly gets home okay?"

"Yeah, sure. And I'll take care of the tab."

"Thanks." Then, "Carly, call me in the morning, if you would. And if I'm not available, Patrick can make the employment arrangements."

She had a worried look on her face. "Okay."

Bidding everyone adieu, Jonas, led by the cops, escorted Tess out the front door. There was no longer a crowd out front, but they walked a few steps up the street, where they stopped.

"Is Mr. Lamb under arrest?" Tess asked the detectives.

"No, ma'am," Tucker replied, "we just have a few

questions." He turned to Jonas. "I'll get right to the point. A few hours ago a couple of private investigators were shot and killed at your houseboat. Daphne Miles and Chuck Haggerty. We understand you've had issues with them, as well as your tenant, Ms. Clear, whose fiancé was injured by your bodyguard last evening."

"Is that an accusation or a question, Detective?"

"We're trying to verify the information we've received."

"You got that from Crystal? She okay?"

"Yeah. Can you tell us where you've been this evening, Mr. Lamb?"

"The past hour I've been here."

"And before that?"

"I was at my home in Kentfield until around six-thirty."

"Alone?"

"No, with my security people."

"Where'd you go at six-thirty?"

"I left with Larry—that's his nickname, I believe his real name is Fan—and we picked up the young lady who was at the table inside at the Montpelier Hotel. We came here where we met with the other gentleman, my son, and Ms. Vartel."

"This guy Fan. He Chinese?" Tucker asked.

"Yes."

"The Chinese woman who clobbered Bob MacDonald last night—" he referred to the notepad he'd taken from his pocket "—May Li. You happen to know her whereabouts this evening?"

"No."

"Did she go to the houseboat at your instruction, Mr. Lamb?" Luz asked.

"Jonas," Tess interjected, "I advise you not to answer any questions about your involvement."

"That's all right, Tess. No, Detective Luz, she didn't go there at my instruction. I haven't seen May since last night."

"What about the other security people? Fan was with you, you say. What about the others?"

"I don't know what they did or where they were tonight."

"Where can we find these people?"

"May Li has been staying at my house in Kentfield, guarding me around the clock. The other three are on rotating shifts. They stay elsewhere. I can't tell you exactly where. Possibly in San Rafael. Some sort of furnished apartment, I believe. One of them is most likely at the house now."

"There was a Chinese guy named Tang at the house," Tucker said. "He couldn't speak English, but he called Fan, who gave the phone to the chauffeur and he told us you were here. Where is Fan, by the way?"

"He should be in that black limo up the street."

"He's not. We checked. The chauffeur said he took off shortly after our call."

"Then I can't tell you where he is."

"Mr. Lamb," Luz said, "Ms. Clear says she's a potential witness in a lawsuit you're involved in."

"So?"

"She said her testimony could be damaging to your case, a case in which you stand to lose millions."

"Crystal said that?"

"We asked if she knew of any reason you might want her dead."

"She can't believe I'd have somebody kill her."

"It's not what she believes that matters. It's what happened."

"Well, I didn't tell May or anybody else to kill her. That's the last thing I'd do."

"Jonas," Tess interjected, "I think you've given the officers adequate information and shown cooperation." She turned to the detectives. "Unless you intend to place Mr. Lamb under arrest and bring charges, I'm calling a halt to this right here."

"We're not placing him under arrest, Counselor. At least not now."

"Okay, fine, anything you wish to ask not bearing on his actions?"

"No, ma'am," Tucker said. "Not at present. But there's a good chance we will in the future." He handed them each his business card. "I trust you'll make yourself available, Mr. Lamb."

"If it's okay with my lawyer, it's okay with me." Jonas realized he'd been a bit too flip. "For what it's worth, I had nothing to do with those murders and I seriously doubt May Li or any of the others did, as well."

"Two people trying to protect Ms. Clear are dead, Mr. Lamb."

Jonas felt sick, and not just at the thought of Haggerty and Daphne being killed. It's what Crystal might think that terrified him. "Does Crystal think I'm responsible for what happened?" he asked the detectives.

"She didn't say that. Not in so many words. But she's looking at the same facts we are, Mr. Lamb."

"Hasn't it occurred to you that somebody might want her—and for that matter, you—to think it's me who's behind it?"

"That's enough, Jonas," Tess said, taking him by the arm and pulling him back toward the entrance to the restaurant.

"We'd appreciate it if you stayed in town, Mr. Lamb," Tucker called after him. "And give us a call if you hear from any of your Chinese employees."

Jonas waved over his shoulder, then glanced at Tess. "Somebody's trying to frame me," he said.

"I don't think I want to hear about it, Jonas."

He stopped. "Hey, you're supposed to be on my side. This is me you're talking to, Tess. Remember, the guy you loved?"

"Yeah, the one I also divorced."

"Technically it was an annulment, so in theory the slate is clean and…"

She started to go on and he took her arm, keeping her from leaving. He made her look him in the eye. "You don't think I'm responsible for those murders, do you?"

"If you're asking if I think you're a killer, the answer is no. You're capable of many things, Jonas, but that is not one of them."

"Then why the attitude?"

"I'm getting a flavor of what Patrick and you are involved in and frankly it scares me to death. People being killed in your houseboat, this on top of everything else that's happened. Let's just say I don't find it reassuring."

"I'm not exactly thrilled about it myself."

"And who's this person Crystal?"

Jonas started to answer and Tess cut him off.

"No, on second thought, I don't want to hear. The less I know about your personal life, the better."

"If you're going to be my lawyer, you should hear."

"I'm not your lawyer, Jonas, I did you a favor."

"Crystal's involved in that lawsuit between me and my stepchildren."

"I don't need to hear the details. You've answered the question."

"Tess, I *want* you to know everything."

She sighed, exasperated. He glanced up the street. There was nobody around, the cops long gone.

"The attorney-client privilege applies here, doesn't it? Nobody can make you repeat what I'm about to tell you, right?"

"Jonas, there's no point."

"Look, I screwed up once not coming clean with you, I'm not going to do it again."

"We were married then."

"Well, I still love you, so morally—if not civilly— I'm in the same situation as I was then. You wanted honesty then and you're getting it now. Better late than never."

She rolled her eyes, but he was undeterred. "Crystal Clear was my mistress," he said, not bothering to mince words. "She and I were having an affair during the last eight or nine months of my marriage to Elise."

"Jonas, I really don't want to hear this."

"Well, you *are* going to hear it, so relax and try to keep an open mind." He cleared his throat. "The problem with the affair is that Elise and I had a premarital agreement requiring fidelity, and my inheritance from Elise was conditioned on living up to that agreement. It's in her will. I stand to lose a million bucks and, more important, ninety percent of the stock of GET if it's shown that I was unfaithful. Everything would go to Melanie and her brother, Wilson. As you know, that puts Patrick's and my project in jeopardy."

"Sounds to me like you're screwed." She shook her head. "You really are your own worst enemy, Jonas."

"There's more to the story. When Elise got sick, she gave me dispensation from my vow of fidelity. Her only request was that I be discreet. Neither of us had any idea that anyone would care besides us. But now half the world's got a stake in this thing and people are dying right and left. Can't you see, Tess? I'm technically guilty, but morally innocent."

"*Innocent's* a strong word in connection with anything having to do with you, Mr. Lamb."

"You get the point."

"Did Crystal know about your dispensation from Elise?"

"Yes."

"But now she's stuck in the middle."

"Exactly. Melanie knows what was going on, but she can't prove it. Not without Crystal's testimony. Next week they're deposing Crystal. She knows I don't deserve to get screwed because of a technicality, but she doesn't want to perjure herself, either. I'm sure Melanie's putting the screws to her."

"Your girlfriend is the one I feel sorry for," Tess said.

"But I'm a close second, right?"

Tess shook her head, unable to keep from laughing. Then she grew serious. "You do have a problem."

"Yeah, I came to that conclusion a while ago. But my big worry is what Crystal will do at the deposition. I had her about half convinced to go with the moral truth, rather than the technical truth, but now I'm not so sure. If she blames me for what happened at the houseboat, then I *am* screwed. That's why I think somebody set me up."

"Unless the killer is identified, it will be difficult to impossible to prove."

"Yeah, and meanwhile I've got to keep Operation Black Sheep afloat. Our son's future, among other things, is riding on it."

They headed back to the restaurant, but Jonas stopped her at the door.

"Tess, I've got an idea. Let the kids enjoy each other's company. How about you and I going some place else to brainstorm a solution to my predicament? I'll buy you a drink."

"I don't know about a drink, but I'll let you drop me off at my place. We can talk on the way."

"Or, have a drink there."

"Don't push it, Jonas."

"Or not." He pointed up the street toward the limo. "There's our ride."

"I'd like to say good-night to Patrick first."

Carly was relieved to find the ladies' room unoccupied. She got her cell phone out of her purse and phoned Gaston.

"Ah, *c'est toi!* How was dinner, *chérie?* What did you have? A hamburger or a hot dog? Subs were big in Boston, as I recall."

"Le Genissel, *qu'est-ce qu'il fait?*" What is Le Genissel doing? She spoke in French because of the public setting.

"What do you mean?"

"The police came to arrest Lamb. It had to involve the Gazelle and the Chinese. Who has he killed now?"

"Oh, that."

"Oui, Gaston, ça!"

"He told me he found an economical way to get rid of the Chinese woman."

"Did it occur to him he might be doing in Lamb at the same time?"

"Alfred's not worried about him anymore. He wants us to focus our energies on the professor. And, to be honest, I think he may be right about that."

"So we forget about Lamb?"

"Le Genissel plans to eliminate him. The technology is the key, Carly. As you Americans say, 'We must keep our eye on the ball.'"

"Can't he wait until after I've made some headway with Mayne? My job isn't going to be any easier with the family in turmoil."

"I see your point. How are things going with respect to the lad, by the way? Alfred was eager to know—as am I, of course."

"He's ready to take me to bed."

"My, that was quick. *Je vous en félicite!*"

"Yes, well, I really should get back to him, Gaston. *A bientôt!*" Carly turned to the door, to find Tess standing there. "Oh, Mrs. Vartel, hi."

"Hi, Carly."

"Is everything all right with Mr. Lamb?"

"He has some legal problems to sort out. He and I are going now, so I'm afraid you'll be left in the hands of our son. I hope you don't mind."

"No, not at all. Patrick's a delight."

Tess gave a little smile and nodded. Carly sensed unease. She hadn't had a lot of experience dealing with men's mothers—wives, even mistresses, yes, but never mothers—or had Tess overheard something that troubled her? Carly offered her hand.

"I hope to see you again soon, Mrs. Vartel."

"Yes, I do, too."

Marin County

They had crossed the Golden Gate and were headed for San Rafael. Jonas had talked Tess into accompanying him to see Crystal, which Tess considered insane, though she admitted he had fence-mending to do. "You really think she'll be more amenable to seeing you just because you're in the company of a former wife?" she'd asked.

"Crystal has a lot of respect for the institution of marriage."

"Oh? Apparently your mistresses are as unusual as you, Jonas."

"I said 'respect,' but I didn't necessarily mean in the conventional sense. She's a straight shooter, and your presence will lend an air of dignity and solemnity to the proceedings."

Tess laughed. He'd surprised her yet again. "She could also think that millions of dollars are as important to me and Patrick as they are to you."

"No, Crystal knows what you mean to me."

"You've discussed *me* with your mistress?"

"*Former* mistress."

"Well, I suppose *former* make a difference, considering I'm a *former* wife."

"She knows you're the love of my life, Tess."

"You told her that?"

"Of course. Women confide in their hairdressers, men confide in their mistresses or their secretaries. Everybody needs somebody they can spill their guts to."

"But a woman you're *sleeping* with?"

"Guys tend to think they've got no secrets from the women they screw," he replied.

"Except their intentions."

"Well true, there *is* that."

"Okay, I'll trust your judgment on this," Tess said, "but for the record, I think it's crazy."

After convincing her they should pay Crystal a visit, he'd tried calling the houseboat. He got the cops who were still working the crime scene. When they told him she'd left, Jonas figured it was to be with Bob. He phoned the hospital and the nurse on duty confirmed that Crystal was there. And so they'd set off for Marin.

Tess had something else she wanted to discuss with Jonas and took the opportunity to mention it. "I know you've got a lot on your mind, but I was wondering what you thought of Carly, besides the fact that she's sexy and gorgeous, I mean…assuming you got beyond that."

"Of course I got beyond that," Jonas replied. "She's bright. She's charming. And she's sweet."

"Just as I suspected, you were blinded."

"Am I wrong?"

"No," she replied. "She's all that. And also too good to be true."

"What are you saying?"

"There's something not quite right about her, Jonas."

"Like what?"

"When I went into the ladies' room at the restaurant, Carly was in there talking on a cell phone to somebody *in French!*"

"So? She's traveled. She's very cosmopolitan. And obviously speaks other languages."

"But didn't she say the man you rescued her from was French?"

"Yeah, Pierre."

"Well, doesn't this strike you as odd she'd be talking to him?"

"How do you know it was him? Did she call him Pierre?"

"No, but who else could it be?"

"Tess, there are sixty million Frenchmen."

"In San Francisco?"

"How do you know it was a local call?"

Tess couldn't believe it. All men seemed to have the same fatal flaw—they were convinced that logic and truth were related. "Honestly, Jonas, you were so bedazzled by that face that you can't see the obvious."

"The same face is making you see plot and conspiracy, sweetheart. She's an innocent girl from the Midwest with a sense of adventure. Now, if she'd been Arab or Russian or something, I might have wondered. Anyway, what could her angle be?"

"The same as everybody else. Your Black Sheep."

He stopped to think. "Well, anything's possible, I guess. But she didn't come to me. We had an accidental encounter."

"Outside your office."

"She didn't initiate anything. I did."

"She didn't have to. She knew you were a man."

"The dinner, the job, were completely my idea. She didn't even hint. Believe me, I was there."

Tess could see he was hopeless. "God, for a man who's been married six times and has bedded unknown dozens—or is it hundreds?—of women, you certainly are naive when it comes to how women think and operate."

"Maybe that's what makes me so endearing," he said with a grin.

"Actually, it explains why you have so much trouble."

Jonas reached over and took her hand. "Forgive me for saying this, but you want to know something? I've never been happier than when I'm with you."

"You're like a dog with a bone, you know it?"

She could see him beaming in the dark. The man was a snake. But she let him hold her hand, anyway.

Downtown, San Francisco

The taxi pulled up in front of the Montpelier Hotel and Carly touched Patrick's hand. "Thanks for the ride and the dinner and the conversation," she said sweetly.

"And the job," Patrick said, "don't forget the job."

"Do you think your father was serious? I took it as something said in the heat of emotion. I wouldn't hold him to it."

"No, he'd planned on it. He was talking you up this afternoon, like I said. And you'd be doing us a favor as much as the other way around. In fact, I wouldn't blame you for running for cover after the show we put on, the police coming and all that."

"Important people have enemies. Your parents were both very kind to me. I like them very much."

"And they liked you."

"You think so?"

"I'm sure of it."

"I've been told I may be overconfident, that people can be turned off by it. And it's true, I'm not a fearful person."

"That comes through. And frankly, I like the quality."

"You're a nice person, Patrick."

It wasn't a lie. When she related to people she searched her heart for positive feelings. Her true objectives might not be as represented, but she tried hard to make her gut-level emotions sincere.

The truth was she liked Patrick Mayne. A lot. He did resemble Antoine some, but they weren't at all alike, except they both had a fever, an intensity about them, though the professor's was more subdued, perhaps repressed. She could tell the tiger inside him was itching to get out. That's what she had to play on.

Though what Patrick evoked in her wasn't like what she'd felt for Antoine, it was nearly as poignant—a nostalgic harkening back to her high school years when feelings were raw and primitive, love overwhelming. Patrick Mayne sparked a visceral reaction that she was mature enough to laugh at but still couldn't ignore.

"I guess I should go in," she said, "the meter's running."

"Can I walk you to your door?"

It was the sort of thing a nice boy from the Midwest would have said—an indication of politeness, not uncertainty. "It's not necessary," she said.

Patrick gave the driver a ten, anyway, and they got

out of the cab. Nothing more was said until they were in the elevator when she told him he reminded her of a boy she'd known in high school.

"Is that good or bad?"

"He was good and that was bad."

Patrick didn't ask why. Maybe he sensed what she would have said if she'd been more forthcoming, or maybe he'd had a similar experience. Carly was convinced that even the most moral of men were always on the lookout for meaningful ways to express the secret, dark sides of themselves. Maybe that was what fascinated her most about the type—unpredictability lingering beneath the wholesomeness.

He took the room key from her and opened the door as her high school boyfriend would have done. Once they were in the room Patrick leaned against the door, studying her through narrowed eyes. "Did you have a boyfriend in Cleveland?"

"No," she said, "a girlfriend."

There was a moment of inquiry. "You're a lesbian?"

"Bisexual, technically, I think. But I don't put much stock in labels. I do what feels good and I don't think about it." She waited for his reaction.

"Have there been other women?"

"No."

Patrick reached out and touched her cheek with the back of his fingers. "Does that feel good?"

"Yes."

And so he kissed her.

Patrick Mayne's kiss was less sensuous than Antoine's, but it was sweeter and gentler.

"I'm glad you told me about your girlfriend," he said, their lips still mingled.

"Why?"

"Because now you seem more real to me somehow. Don't ask me why or what that means, exactly, because I don't know."

He kissed her again, and when she dug her fingers into his hair, hair that was thicker than Antoine's, the kiss carried them to the bed, where, after he removed his jacket, they lay side by side, kissing more deeply now as his hand explored her body through the dress. Between kisses he licked her neck and probed her ear with the tip of his tongue. That was sexy. The professor knew how to make love. Any doubts she had had been expunged.

When he discovered she wore no underwear he said, "Do you have any condoms?"

"No."

"I don't, either. I'll go buy some."

"Maybe we should stop here," she said.

"Do you want to stop?"

"No, but there's something to be said for expectation. Presumably there'll be other opportunities."

"I grant you the spontaneity is lost, but there's something to be said for conscious seduction, too. I can get a bottle of champagne and we can start slow, not assuming an outcome."

"Are you sure you're a scientist?"

"It's an interim incarnation."

"I can relate to that. I'm not really a secretary at heart."

"That's evident, Carly." He got up and put on his jacket.

"Take the key," she said.

He got it from the table then went to the door, where he paused. "You're a lot more than a secretary. I just haven't figured out what."

Once he was gone, she rolled to the side of the bed, reached over and picked up the phone and dialed Gaston's hotel. They buzzed his room and he answered on the first ring.

"I'm at my hotel. He went out for condoms."

"Voilà!" Gaston chuckled. "Our professor is a cautious man, but not very well prepared. You, on the other hand, do seem on top of your game."

"Let's not get too excited just yet. Unzipping a guy's fly is the least of it. And this one's no dummy. They're going to Hong Kong in a couple of days, by the way. Is Le Genissel aware of that?"

"Let me ask."

"Is the fucking pervert there?"

"Yes."

"Carly's about to ball Mayne," she heard him say. "Lamb and the professor are going to Hong Kong in a few days. She wants to know if you're aware." She could hear Le Genissel's voice in the background, followed by fumbling, then the Gazelle himself came on the line.

"Are you sure?"

"Yes."

"Can you get the documentation before they go?"

"I seriously doubt it, Alfred. A hundred to one against."

"Then when?"

"A month. Maybe a few weeks, if I'm lucky. He has no incentive to do anything but fuck me, you know."

"It must be sooner. I am under great pressure from my employers."

"A girl can only do what a girl can do."

"Can you get Mayne to stay in the States? Would Lamb go to Hong Kong alone?"

"Alfred, I have no idea what they're thinking or what their intentions are. I've known these people one day. The fact they've offered me a job is a minor miracle. They could just as easily have turned their backs."

"On *you*, Carly?"

"You don't seem to appreciate the difficulty of what I do."

"I know what you can do to a man's mind."

She didn't like the implications of the remark but let it pass.

"We must separate the father and son," Le Genissel said. "See if you can figure out some way to keep Mayne from making the trip."

"Why is that so important?"

"Because, now that we know the professor has what we need, Lamb becomes expendable. Plus, he is...how do you say?...a loose cannon. He may be going to Hong Kong, but I assure you he will not be coming back. Not alive."

San Rafael, California

Crystal was sacked out in the hospital waiting room, asleep on a sofa. Jonas and Tess looked at her from the doorway, Jonas seeing the woman through Tess's eyes.

"She's attractive," Tess said softly. "Why didn't you marry her?"

"I was very fond of Crystal, but she's not my idea of a wife."

"Why?"

"Do I have to say?"

"No, it's none of my business. I shouldn't have asked."

"I briefly considered it," he said, his voice scarcely a whisper, "under the theory she wouldn't testify against me if we were married."

"Jonas, that's disgraceful."

"It was just a passing thought."

"But you thought it."

"Have my comments about us getting together again gone through your mind at all?"

"That's different."

"No, actually it's not. The point is because we imagine something, it doesn't mean we're going to do it. Some ideas are stillborn." He gave her a wink. "Others just premature."

Tess didn't take the bait. Instead, she looked over at the sleeping woman. "I don't think we should wake her. She's probably exhausted."

"What do we do, then? I've got to talk to her."

"I don't know. Let's sit down and wait. Maybe she'll wake up soon."

They sat on the other side of the room. Tess picked up a magazine. Jonas stared at Crystal. It blew his mind that he should be with his favorite wife, watching his favorite mistress sleep. The two represented the best of womanhood, as far as he was concerned. And yet what mattered at the moment wasn't what he felt for them or what they felt for him, it was what they intended—Crystal's intentions with regard to the deposition and Tess's intentions with regard to her engagement. One would determine his place in the world, the other the condition of his heart.

An announcement over the hospital sound system awakened Crystal, and rubbing her eyes, she sat up. Then she saw them.

"Jonas," Crystal said, "what are you doing here?" She didn't sound so much alarmed as surprised.

He got to his feet. Tess did, as well. They went over to Crystal, who was perplexed and sleepy-eyed.

"After what happened at the houseboat tonight, I had to talk to you," he said. "This is Tess, by the way, my second wife."

Crystal looked at her as if she couldn't believe it. "God, Jonas, you're full of surprises, aren't you?"

"It's in his nature," Tess said, extending her hand.

Crystal shook it. Tess and Jonas sat down across from her.

"Didn't the police contact you?" Crystal asked.

"Yes, they made all the usual sounds about being suspicious of me, but that was it. I couldn't help them because I don't know a thing. That's why we've come. I needed to tell you that, Crystal."

She lowered her face into her hands, rubbing her forehead. "I didn't know what to think. I knew you didn't kill those people, but so many crazy things have been happening. I just told the police the truth."

"But not about my offer."

Crystal glanced at Tess.

Jonas said, "I told her all about you and me and my problems with Melanie. Tess is a good person and she's level-headed. I thought she might be able to help me reassure you I couldn't possibly be behind those murders."

"What about your Chinese friends?"

"Their object is to protect me, Crystal. Drawing attention to themselves is the last thing they'd want. More likely somebody's trying to set us up. Somebody like Melanie."

"Look, Jonas, I don't want to be hard-assed about it, but you know what? I don't want to talk about Melanie or the disposition anymore."

"It's *deposition,* sweetheart."

"Whatever," Crystal replied, unfazed. "The point is I feel like a football, I've been kicked around so much. To be honest, I'm not sure what I'm going to do at the *deposition,* but I'll tell you this—anyone who tries to pressure me won't be helping their case, so don't go there. I don't want to hear it."

"I understand. I just didn't want you to think I had anything to do with those detectives being killed."

"Okay, I hear you."

Tess got up, taking him by the hand. "Come, Jonas, the lady has made it clear how she feels and personally I respect her for taking a stand. Let's go." She gave Crystal a wave. "Nice meeting you."

They left the waiting room and were on their way out the main entrance of the hospital when they encountered Melanie de Givry and her brother, Wilson. "Well, look who's here. If it isn't Jonas Lamb and yet another lady friend."

"This is my former wife, Tess Vartel," Jonas said.

"My condolences, Ms. Vartel. So, Jonas, still working on Crystal, are you? What's your latest ploy? Bribes? Pity? Certainly not the truth. That's a foreign concept to you."

"Forgive a pointed question, Melanie," he said, "but do you have a purpose other than to be hurtful?"

"Justice."

"Is that true? Really true, I mean?"

Melanie obviously didn't understand his question.

"If this was really about your parents' estate, you'd be more interested in the money than me. If I'm such an anathema to you, why don't we end our differences here and now? Your complaint has been that I've tried to profit from my marriage to your mother. You resent the fact that she left me a million dollars. If that's what it takes to buy peace, I'll give it to you. But I want my company. That's my settlement offer— you keep the million and I get the stock in Global Energy Technologies."

Melanie smiled. "The news inside obviously wasn't good, was it, Jonas? Thank you ever so, but I'm taking the million *and* the company. If you want to be constructive, why don't you pack your bags and take your snake oil somewhere else." Then to her brother she said, "Come on, Wilson, the stench here is overwhelming."

They walked away.

"My," Tess said, "what charming stepchildren. I hope that's no reflection on your wife."

Jonas shook his head. "That was one of the great mysteries of my sixth marriage, Tess. I never could figure out how such a decent woman could produce such hateful, vengeful children. I think their character was one of Elises's great sorrows, to be honest. She knew they were less than exemplary. Melanie's smart, but she's also a vicious little bitch. And Wilson's a sloth and a leech."

"I feel sorry for Elise."

"Yeah, so did I," Jonas said, looking after his stepchildren. "You know, I hate to think of Crystal alone with them in there. God only knows what Melanie is up to."

"It doesn't matter, because she'll only make things worse for herself. Men have to realize they can't control everything. Women are capable of making up their own minds and Crystal knows what she wants. Respecting that is the best thing you can do."

"See how clever I was to bring you along?" he said. "Genius is all about knowing who to listen to. If I'd had an adviser like you when my second wife was divorcing me, I'd be sitting on top of the world right now."

She slipped her arm in his. "Want some advice about your second wife?"

"Yeah!"

"Respect her wishes."

"That's what you said about Crystal."

"Funny how that works, isn't it?"

Russian Hill, San Francisco

After he'd kissed her for the second time, they sat in the limo outside her building while Tess agonized over his request. Jonas had been direct. "My immediate problem is security," he said. "May Li and her people are history. There are killers on the loose and I'm twisting in the wind. I don't mean to sound like a wimp, but I need a place to stay."

"I know you do."

They both were perfectly aware there were more far-reaching implications than shelter from the storm. This was about them. Did she sleep with him, or didn't she? There was no middle ground. This wasn't about doing a favor for an old friend; this was about the big S and there was no sense pretending otherwise.

"I'll tell you what my problem is, Jonas. I really do love Walter."

"I believe you."

"And it's not that I can't resist you, because I can."

"I believe that, too," he said.

"You want to know why I'm so torn? I had an affair when I was married to Richard."

Jonas turned his head so fast she actually laughed aloud.

"It's true," she said.

"Okay. So how does that figure into what's happening now?"

"You really don't understand women as well as you think you do, cowboy."

"I'll concede the point. But I still don't understand."

"I've spent my whole adult life trying to avoid making mistakes," she said. "And for the most part, I succeeded. Having that fling—it was nothing serious, more like a silly slip than anything else—was a great embarrassment. The good news is Richard never found out. The bad news is I was having sex with another man while Richard was home alone, bleeding to death."

"You can't blame yourself for that."

"Oh, I do. I've felt guilty about it and I'll continue to feel guilty about it, but that's not the point. The point is I thought it was an anomaly," she said. "But I realize now it wasn't. I realize there's another side of me I've spent my life denying. And I've concluded that to marry Walter will be, in effect, a continuation of that denial. Seeing you again, Jonas, has opened my eyes to something very important."

"I could have told you that you still love me, sweetheart. I knew that when you divorced me."

"No, that's not it."

"No?"

"Whether I love you or not isn't the point. I've watched you, Jonas. I've seen you struggle with yourself, face temptation and lose. But the one thing you don't do is deny who you are. My life has been one big pretense. Yours is at least honest—lies and all."

He threw back his head and laughed. "So what's your dilemma, Tess?"

"I'm trying to decide what's best for you, for Patrick, for your business deal and for me. Is this the right time? Are we really ready?"

"Can I offer an opinion?"

"Sure."

"Sometimes you can overanalyze things. The answer is right there in your gut. And you get into trouble when you try to deny what you know to be true."

"If that's your philosophy, it hasn't exactly worked to perfection, has it?"

"I always knew I wanted you, Tess. But I couldn't have you."

"If we sleep together, it's only because I decided I want to. It might end there. Do you understand that?"

"There are no guarantees in life. I learned that a long time ago."

"Okay, then, let's go upstairs."

Tess lay in Jonas's arms, her fingers sunk into the mat of hair on his chest, the feel of him, the rhythm of his body, familiar even after twenty-eight years. It was as though Richard and Walter were passing phases, not to mention Jonas's four subsequent wives. When she thought about it, she couldn't believe she'd actually gone to bed with him. It had taken courage, and caution had always been her MO.

"You know, Jonas," she said, "this couldn't have

happened before now. We had to go through all the things we went through to arrive at this point."

"Much as I hate to admit it, I think you're right. You want to know the main reason you slept with me?"

"Besides the fact that you're irresistible?"

"It gets you out of your engagement to Walter."

She pulled her head back so she could see him. "You know, maybe you are more than just a pretty face."

He laughed and kissed her. She snuggled still closer to him, realizing she hadn't experienced such pleasure since the last time she'd made love with him.

"Since you're so full of wisdom," she said, "explain this. If I love Walter, but that's not a good enough reason to marry him, why is loving you—assuming your premise—enough reason to go to bed with you?"

"You *have* gone to bed with me, Tess, you *haven't* married Walter."

"I still might. I mean, tomorrow morning the world might look very different."

"Then we'll just have to see, won't we?"

She could tell Jonas thought he had her. The funny thing was that maybe he did. Crazier still, she kind of liked feeling she had no choice in the matter, though she'd never admit that in a million years.

"On a completely different subject," he said, "why don't you come to Hong Kong with Patrick and me?"

"Hong Kong?"

"Before tonight I would have thought it was a stupid idea, but it occurs to me the bad guys could assume you're involved whether you are or not.

Anyway, you probably aren't any safer here. Patrick and I have decided Hong Kong is our last shot at the big prize. If we fail, then we go public and sell the Black Sheep to the highest bidder, assuming we have something to sell."

"Is that why you offered Melanie your inheritance for the stock?"

"Yes, I was hoping to go to Hong Kong, knowing the company was mine. Now I won't know until the deposition. If we win, I think we cut the best deal we can and be done with it. What's a few hundred million more or less? I can't think of anybody I'd rather have in our corner than you, Tess."

She only thought for a few seconds. "Okay, I'll go with you."

SATURDAY
January 26

Russian Hill, San Francisco

In Jonas Lamb's experience, there were three kinds of mornings-after—regret, contentment and bliss. The whole object of a man's sex life was premised on avoiding regret whenever possible, shooting for contentment as a matter of course, and accepting the fact that bliss, being both rare and serendipitous, was unlikely. Much to his delight, he'd rediscovered bliss after a hiatus of twenty-eight years. The only bad thing was that contentment would never be the same.

There was no percentage in worrying about the future, however. Enjoy the hell out of the moment you have. That had become Jonas Lamb's philosophy.

He was in bed, listening to the shower running in the bath. Tess wasn't singing, but it took him back to that morning of contentment in Hong Kong with Crystal. It was scarcely more than a month ago, but it might have been a lifetime. Not only was Tess back in his life, but Crystal had assumed a new, thoroughly bizarre role. Fate had cast her as Solomon, the empress of his destiny.

Yet Jonas worried about them all—Patrick and Tess, Crystal, Jimmy and May Li, everybody. But thinking about May Li reminded him of that piece of paper Larry had slipped to him in the restaurant. He'd forgotten about it until now.

He got out of bed and fished the paper out of his jacket pocket. The words "Wu Lo N.S." were written in block letters under three Chinese characters. On the next line, in slightly smaller letters, was "23 Des Voeux Road West." An address, perhaps? What the hell was that supposed to mean? It had to be from May Li. He put the paper in his wallet, figuring he'd deal with it later.

Before he got back in bed, the phone rang. He considered answering it, but opted to consult Tess first. He opened the bathroom door.

"Your phone's ringing, sweetheart," he called as the steam spilled out. "What do you want me to do?"

"Answer it, I guess."

"What if it's Walter?"

"Tell him I'll call him back."

That brought a smile to his lips. That was one thing about women he kind of admired. They could agonize over a decision forever, but once they'd made up their mind, they were like runaway freight trains—there was no looking back. Still in his blissful glow, Jonas almost hoped it was the old boy. But it was Patrick.

"Didn't expect you to be answering the phone," his son said. "Do I offer my congratulations?"

"The important issues remain in your mother's hands. Not to change the subject or anything, but how was *your* evening?"

"As successful as yours, evidently."

Jonas took pleasure in that. They were like sailors comparing notes after the first night in port. There was the additional irony that Carly had started the evening as Jonas's date, but what the hell, this was California.

"So what are you up to?" he asked his son.

"At the moment, Carly and I are on I-80, headed for Davis. I need to pack for Hong Kong and asked her to come along for the ride."

"Good for you, son, she's a hell of a girl."

"Thanks in no small measure to your good taste."

"Are we talking about my choice of second wife, which made your existence possible, or my choice of Girl Friday, which made your pleasure possible?"

"Both, I guess."

"Nice to be so essential."

"Well," Patrick said, "I just wanted to touch base. Say hi to Mom. See you tomorrow at the airport?"

"You bet. And don't be surprised to see your mom there. I asked her to come with us. The way I see it, we're a family and we've got a date with destiny."

"Will you two ever stop surprising me?"

"I hope not. See you tomorrow, son."

He'd just hung up when the bathroom door opened. Tess was in a terry robe.

"Who was it?"

"Patrick."

"He must have been surprised."

"I think he was pleased."

Tess was drying her hair with a hand towel. "So, what did you say?"

He walked over to her and loosened the tie on her robe so he could slip his arms around her naked body. She turned her face up to him and gave him a sultry look. They kissed.

Then Jonas said, "I told him we were trying to get him that little brother or sister he never had."

"Jonas!" she said, whacking him. "You did not."

"It's not a bad idea, though. The bed's not made," he said, tossing his head in that direction. "What do you say we give it another go?"

Davis, California

Carly Van Hooten lay in Patrick Mayne's tub and studied the flames on the tips of her toes, an intense red against the white tile. It reminded her of Anook, who liked giving her pedicures. In a way, Carly enjoyed the indulgence, but also found it boring. That was the advantage of the attentions of men, which were exploitive and therefore dangerous. There was something so satisfying about getting as close as possible to the fire without getting burnt.

She was alone in his house. Patrick had been summoned to the campus by the university police because of a break-in at his laboratory, but not before he'd made love to her for the fifth time in the less than twenty-four hours she'd known him, this last session coming after they'd gotten drunk, alternating slugs from a hundred-and-twenty-dollar bottle of

Mumm. He'd stopped at a liquor store as they'd come to town, saying his good fortune in finding her was cause for celebration.

She'd felt like celebrating herself. She was making good progress toward her goal, and she'd found pleasure in both his company and the sex. The experience proved to her what she'd already suspected—that sex with a man had dimensions unavailable in sex with a woman.

True, Patrick Mayne was the first man she'd had sex with since Antoine, but what took her by surprise was that until now Antoine had scarcely entered her mind. Was it because she was home in America? Or, because Patrick was American? Was she herself more American than she realized?

Maybe the problem was she liked Patrick Mayne. He put her in touch with her needy, womanly side. The conundrum, the source of her confusion and discomfort, lay in the fact that her job was to betray the man.

Carly, her body throbbing pleasantly, realized she'd made a cardinal error—she'd allowed herself to become emotionally involved, creating yet another demon to exorcize. How would she do it, was the question. By killing him? Le Genissel would counsel such a solution. Granted, it was one way to harden your heart. But it was cowardly, and not her style.

Tina Richter and Kristy Ogawa were in the van. K.J., Brad Kozik and Roger Lake were hiding in the shadows of the deserted faculty parking lot. They were all dressed in dark clothing with ski masks handy. K.J. had the gun. Tina felt a little uncomfortable about that. The last week or so K.J. had gotten really belligerent about Patrick Mayne, grousing that if the bastard ever showed up, maybe they ought to shoot him rather than kidnap him.

Tina knew it was the jealous ranting of an immature kid. She and K.J. had had their falling out. Initially they'd argued about the operation, but their problem was that she'd broken off with him and K.J. wanted to take it out on the professor. "Jesus, K.J.," she'd said. "He's not your old man. Get a grip." But that had only infuriated him more.

It was Tina, rather than K.J., who'd come up with the final details of the plan. Brad, who had a deep, authoritative-sounding voice, even if he didn't have K.J.'s balls, had made the call impersonating the campus police. Mayne hadn't sounded pleased. "Shit, not again," he'd said.

"The vandals must have been looking for research materials, Professor," Brad had told him. "Hopefully, they didn't get anything of value. Fifteen or twenty minutes of your time is all we need."

That had been more than half an hour earlier. Mayne should have gotten there by now. Tina worried that he'd called the police back and been told it was a hoax. It was the only part of the plan that had worried her. That, and catching him at home long enough to make the call.

The previous night they'd called Mayne's place until 1:00 a.m. before they'd given up, convinced that he wasn't coming home. "The bastard probably has a girlfriend," K.J. had said, giving her a meaningful, if snide, look.

She wasn't going to let him off easily. "Even fascists have sex," Tina told him. "And for all you know, he might even be good in the sack."

Dressed in sweats, his hair wet from his shower, Patrick Mayne, still in the penumbral glow of sex and champagne, drove onto the campus and headed for the parking lot closest to his office. This wasn't how he'd wanted to spend his time—not considering that this was his last day with Carly before leaving for Hong Kong. But he was suspicious that the break-in wasn't connected to the eco-terrorists. More likely it had to do with Operation Black Sheep.

Not that any of it interested him a lot, given the way he'd passed the last night. Carly Van Hooten, who didn't even have an undergraduate degree, wasn't, by superficial standards, his type. He liked his women brainy *and* attractive, which usually meant an understated academic. Carly was anything but understated. She was also shrewd, confident and just enough off center to be intriguing. Being with her was an adventure, and he liked that. The woman definitely had a dangerous side, too, a pathos and irreverence that he felt at a visceral level. He sensed the largeness of her spirit, the incongruity of her fearlessness and vulnerability.

Carly, he surmised, was a woman who could change a man fundamentally, the type you could leave your wife or girlfriend for, the type who could entice you to join her in a crime spree. She touched a side of him he seldom experienced and knew little about, his unconventional side. That's what made her special.

The wonder of it was that it had happened so quickly. In the blink of an eye she was in his life, and he was having the romantic experience of his life.

He drove into the lot. There were hardly any vehicles around. Parking at the side of the lot nearest his building, Patrick got out of his car and locked the door. He felt the chill air on his wet head and the quiet stillness of the dark campus. He hadn't gone ten steps when the dark figure slipped out from behind a tree, pointing an object at him that, even in the obscurity, Patrick could tell was a gun.

"One peep out of you, Professor Mayne," the assailant croaked, his voice cracking, "and I'll blow you away."

Patrick heard footsteps behind him.

"On your knees, Professor!" the gunman ordered.

Hands forced him down. His wrists were bound behind him. He was blindfolded and gagged. The helplessness he felt only added to the terror. His assailants lifted him to his feet and walked him away. He had to fight to draw enough air into his lungs through his nose. Worse, considering he had a history of asthma, he might even die.

Tina Richter leaned against the side of the van and closed her eyes, trying to concentrate on the sounds of the road as they whizzed down the interstate—anything to blank out the terrible wheezing and snorting sounds made by Patrick Mayne. Earlier he thrashed about so violently that K.J. had kicked him in the legs and told him to cool it or he'd shoot him on the spot.

"I think we should take the tape off his mouth," she'd said.

"No," K.J. had replied. "We don't give him a thing unless he cooperates."

But the wheezing sounded so desperate that Tina couldn't take it anymore. She shone the light on Mayne's face and lifted the blindfold, horrified to see his eyes rolled back in his head, his body trembling.

"He's having a seizure or something," she said. "I'm taking off the tape."

"No!" K.J. commanded.

"Fuck you!" Leaning over, she ripped the tape off the professor's mouth.

He continued to gasp, breathing through his mouth now, though not without difficulty. She wasn't sure he was conscious.

"Maybe it's asthma," Kristy, who was across from her, said.

Mayne's jaw quivered as he continued to fight for air. Tina could tell he was trying to say something. She leaned over his face, noticing despite everything the brilliant blue of his eyes in the beam of light.

"Asthma," he croaked.

"See, asshole!" she yelled at K.J. "I told you. What if he dies on us?" Afraid now, she watched Mayne fighting to get air, expecting him to expire right in front of her. Nobody else moved, but Tina couldn't just sit there and let it happen, so she leaned close to him again and said, "Would you like to sit up?"

After a couple of gasps, he said, "Yes. Please."

Tina lifted his shoulders with difficulty and let him lean his back against her leg. Sitting upright seemed to help. His breathing grew more regular, though he continued to struggle.

"Thank you," he said to her.

She felt terrible shame, even remorse. She glanced up at K.J. and saw him hunched sullenly, his eyes hooded behind the slits in his mask. She wondered at the contempt she felt, concluding K.J. was too full of himself. The little prick with the big cock was king of the heap now and he believed his own bullshit about being a stud. Tina had liked him better when he was just a boy trying to be somebody.

By eleven o'clock Carly was worried. Patrick had been gone for two hours. He was well mannered and he'd struck her as the considerate type. Surely he'd have called if he expected to be detained long. She sensed trouble. Possibly the Chinese.

At twenty after eleven she phoned the campus police, who told her that Professor Mayne hadn't been in that evening and that there hadn't been any reports of vandalism. Using the cell phone Gaston had given her, she called him in San Francisco.

"*Merde,*" he said after she described the situation. "I suppose he could have had car trouble, but if so he probably would have called you. Does he have a cell phone?"

"Yes, we exchanged cell numbers. He was wary about using his house line. Probably because he's afraid it's bugged.

"When we're through, try calling him on his cell."

"Okay," she replied.

"*Merde,*" Gaston muttered again. "Dammit."

"Could it be the Chinese? Surely it's not Le Genissel."

"No, he's not that stupid. He knows you're making great progress."

"Then it's the Chinese. Could they be on to me? Maybe they spirited him to safety."

"*Je ne sais pas.* But that doesn't feel right. Something else is going on. The hell of it is, it's not clear what anybody wants. Have you noticed? First Le Genissel wants Lamb seduced, now he's intent on killing him. The Chinese protect Lamb for reasons that are not clear, and now maybe they've gotten the son."

Carly thought for a moment. "So, what if Mayne doesn't return?"

"Good question. I should probably get my derriere up there. And I'll have to tell Alfred. My guess is he'll get right on this, so expect him to be in touch, probably before me."

"Terrific."

"Just sit tight and hope Mayne shows up. Let me know if you hear anything."

After she hung up, Carly checked the street. There was still no sign of Patrick. She dialed his cell number. It rang half a dozen times before somebody answered, but hung up without saying anything.

Solano County

They were on the deck of the fishing boat, the stars twinkling overhead, the chilly wind that came up from the bay through the Carquinez Straight tossing their hair and making their eyes water. Tina had been leaning against the rail and listening to K.J. and Brad debating what to do, her impatience growing. Finally she decided she had to say something.

"What good is he to us dead? We may not have much sympathy for the bastard, but we've got to take care of him."

"What do you want to do?" K.J. sneered. "Call a doctor?"

"No, smart-ass. For starters we can untie his hands so he can blow his nose and take care of himself. Maybe he needs an inhaler. Somebody could pick one up."

"Sounds to me like you want to play nurse."

"She's got a point," Brad said. "And it won't hurt if one of us is his friend, shows some kindness. Tina's the likely candidate. And she might get more cooperation out of him than the rest of us."

"Okay," K.J. said, "whatever. But if you're going to untie him, somebody's got to be there with the gun."

"Come with me, Brad," Tina said, heading for the companionway. As she started down the stairs she heard him asking K.J. for the gun. She waited below for him.

"What's with all the hostility?" Brad asked when he joined her. "I thought you two were pretty tight."

"Oh, you know how things go. K.J.'s got balls, but

he's still young. It was probably a mistake for me to get involved with him."

"Just don't let it get in the way of what we're doing."

They put on their ski masks and Brad unlocked the door of the hold. Tina turned on the light. Mayne, who was lying on his side on the old mattress they'd put down for him, squinted at them.

"If you won't give us any trouble, Professor Mayne, we'll untie your hands," Tina told him.

"I'd appreciate it."

"You feeling okay?"

"Better, thanks."

"I'm sorry about the asthma. We didn't know."

Mayne looked up at her. "You were the one who took the tape off my mouth, weren't you?"

"Yes."

"I think you saved my life. I thought I was going to die. I couldn't breathe."

"I'm sorry about that. Roll over please, so I can untie your hands."

"I can hardly feel my fingers, they're numb."

"Things will be better now," Tina said as she began loosening his bonds, "provided you cooperate."

"You know," Mayne said, "it might help if you tell me what you want."

Tina glanced at Brad, who stood at the door with the gun. She continued working on the ropes, finally undoing the last knot. To Brad, she said, "Why don't you tell him?"

"We want your cooperation in getting our message across, Professor."

"What message is that?"

"The mutilation of the environment."

Mayne sat upright, leaning against the side of the hold as he rubbed his wrists. As Tina moved over to Brad, she took a good look at the man. Patrick Mayne was even more attractive in person. She felt guilty for putting him through the ordeal, despite her deep hatred for what he represented.

"So it's not about money," the professor said.

"Well, it's not for profit," Brad replied. "Let's put it that way. We wouldn't mind your corporate sponsors contributing to some worthy environmental causes."

Mayne continued to rub his wrists. "I'm not the enemy you think I am."

Tina heard Brad scoff. The professor was a charmer, his blue eyes so sincere. Maybe it was worse than if he were selfish and arrogant and willing to pay any price to get what he wanted. Maybe he wasn't so much a phony as a dupe. "We'll see about that," she said. "So, do you need anything else?"

"Besides my freedom?"

"Yes, besides that. Medicine, maybe?"

Mayne shook his head. "Just don't cut off my air and I'll be all right. But I do have some advice. Don't go public with this."

"What do you mean?"

"Don't announce that I've been kidnapped. In fact, there's only one person who knows I'm missing, and if you act quickly you can stop her from calling the police."

"I don't understand," Brad said. "What's your point?"

"I'm not interested in any publicity myself. I don't want the FBI investigating. I'd like to work out an arrangement with you privately, keeping this between you and me, my family and friends."

"Why?"

"I have my reasons. But you have to let my friend know I'm all right and you've got to tell her not to call the cops."

"If you don't want publicity, why would she call the police or the FBI?" Brad asked.

"Because she doesn't know the whole story."

"Hey, man, this is bullshit."

"Think about it. If I didn't have a damned good reason not to, wouldn't I *want* the authorities trying to find me? Hell, I should be hoping they come swooping down on this place any minute. Trust me. It's the last thing I want."

"That doesn't make sense."

"Let's just say I have problems with the authorities myself. I can't afford the attention."

"Then we've got a problem, man, because publicity is exactly what *we* want."

Patrick Mayne considered that. "Maybe we can have our cake and eat it, too," he said. "If you work with me on this you can get everything you want and more."

"And what, exactly, do you want, Professor?" Tina asked.

"Call my friend. She's at my house. But don't call

on the house line. It's been bugged in the past and it could be bugged now."

"Bugged by who?" Brad asked.

"Maybe the FBI. Maybe somebody else."

"That's it," Brad said, reaching for the door, "this guy's nutso. I'm out of here. Come on."

"Wait a minute," Tina said. "I want to hear what he has to say. Okay, Professor, what do you want us to tell your friend?"

"Tell her I don't want her contacting the police under any circumstances. In fact, let me explain to her why. You've got my cell phone."

"And we're supposed to let you make a call?" Brad said, incredulous.

"Dial the number yourself if you don't trust me."

Brad shook his head. "You know what I say, Professor? Nice try."

Tina wasn't so sure. "Let's go upstairs and talk about it," she said to Brad.

Davis, California

Carly took the teakettle off the stove and poured some boiling water into the mug. Instant coffee. She couldn't remember how long it had been since she'd had any. In searching Patrick Mayne's refrigerator and cupboards she'd gotten a refresher course in Americana. Raisin Bran, Cheerios, Velveeta cheese, Campbell soup, Hershey's chocolate syrup, Skippy peanut butter, glazed doughnuts, Fig Newtons, Heinz ketchup. What an odd way to collide with her past.

As she stirred the instant coffee with a teaspoon,

she had a feeling she wasn't alone. The hair at the back of her neck rose. Spinning, she found him standing across the room. Alfred Le Genissel, dressed in dark clothing, had a faint smile on his lips.

"You look very domestic, Carly. This is the American housewife, perhaps."

"Dammit, Alfred, I hate it when people sneak up on me."

"What did you expect? That I ring the bell? Do not forget the FBI has been watching Mayne."

"How did you get in here?"

"Through the back door. This, you know, is not Fort Knox."

"Couldn't you have rapped on the window or something?"

"I enjoy watching you when you are unaware of my presence."

"Don't do it again," she snapped.

He flushed, pointing a threatening finger at her. "Do not give me orders. I am in charge, and the sooner you accept this, the better."

"You may be paying me, Alfred, but that does not mean you own me. Respect is earned, not bought."

His eyes glazed over, turning cold. "We have more important matters to discuss."

He sat at Patrick Mayne's kitchen table. Carly had known about his twisted desires, what probably amounted to an obsession with her, virtually from the day she'd met him. Antoine, who knew men as well as he knew women, told her never to be alone with the Gazelle if she could help it.

"So, you have bedded your lover and you have already lost him, eh?" Le Genissel said with disdain.

She sipped her coffee, which tasted like dishwater. "I didn't lose him, Alfred. Somebody lured him to the campus and abducted him, most likely."

"Or he could have lied to you."

"To what end?"

Le Genissel pondered the question. "Okay, if it was an abduction, do you have any idea who?"

Carly shook her head. "Could be the Chinese, I guess."

Le Genissel stroked his jaw. "They *have* been a problem, it is true. Perhaps—"

Her cell phone rang, interrupting him. Carly looked at the clock. It was nearing midnight. "Maybe it's Patrick." She pushed the call button.

"Carly Van Hooten?" It was a woman's voice, unfamiliar.

"Yes?"

"Are you alone?"

Carly glanced at Le Genissel, who had gotten up and come toward her. She assumed his intent was to listen in on the conversation. "Who is this?" she asked.

"Answer the question."

"Yes, I'm alone. Is this about Patrick?"

Le Genissel leaned his head down near the phone, turning the receiver partway from her ear so he could hear. She could smell his body odor.

"He wants to speak with you," the woman said.

There was fumbling, then Patrick came on the line. "Carly?"

"Patrick, what happened?"

"Sorry I haven't been able to call before now."

"Where are you?"

"With friends. I can't explain everything, but I need to know something. You haven't called the police, have you?"

"No. I did check with the campus police to see if you were there. I was worried." She felt Le Genissel's breath on her cheek, hating his proximity, even as she tried to put it from her mind.

"Did you tell them I was missing?"

"No. I was concerned, but I didn't say anything to them. What's going on?"

"I want you to get a message to Jonas and my mother. Tell them I'm going to need a million dollars."

"A million?"

"Yes, I have an obligation to my friends. And Carly, this is very important. I don't want anybody contacting the police. Not my parents, not you, nobody. Do you understand?"

"Yes."

"I'll need to be able to communicate from time to time, so would you mind staying there in case I or one of my friends needs to reach you? If anyone asks, tell them you're house-sitting."

"Okay. But Patrick, will you be coming back soon?"

"Yes, I hope so. First, though, I have an obligation to my friends. I'm going to be indisposed for a while."

"What do you mean, indisposed?"

"I can't explain. Just tell Jonas I need the money. It's a top priority. More important than him going to Hong Kong. And don't forget, nobody can contact the police."

Carly heard a voice in the background, a man's. "That's enough."

And the line went dead. She turned off her cell phone and stepped away from Le Genissel. "He's been kidnapped."

The Gazelle, grim-faced, stroked his chin. "Yes."

"It's not the Chinese."

He shook his head.

"Who?" she asked.

"I have no idea."

"What are we going to do?"

Le Genissel's eyes grew cold and hard. "Find him."

"What about Lamb?"

"We will let him go on to Hong Kong."

"Alfred, they were planning on going together."

"That should not be a problem, Carly. Convince Lamb that Mayne has pressing business here and that he wants Lamb to go without him. I am sure you can find a way."

"What about the ransom?"

"Let's let de Malbouzon worry about that. They are asking for a lot of money and that takes time to raise. You can stall them for several days, I am sure."

She did not like the lilt in his voice. She waited. The Gazelle waited, his eyes subtly drifting over her. He wasn't blatant, but she knew what was in his mind. She shifted her weight. He continued staring.

"How many beds are there here?" he finally asked.

"Two."

"How many will we need?"

She held his gaze, though she did swallow hard. "Two, Alfred. We'll need two."

SUNDAY
January 27

Davis, California

Carly couldn't sleep with Alfred Le Genissel in the house. Antoine's warning never to be caught alone with the guy played in her mind. And she knew that the Gazelle was capable of coming through the door at any moment.

Patrick Mayne's bed was redolent with his scent, yet it was of no comfort to her. He was her own intended victim, enjoying a respite while she coped with the predator a step up the food chain from her. There was a time when Carly would see no justice in that, but she saw it now. Maybe in some metaphysical sense she deserved whatever Alfred Le Genissel might do to her. But even if that were so, she could not give him the satisfaction of winning. Not without a fight. And so, having no weapon, she'd spirited a knife from the kitchen to Patrick Mayne's bed.

The Gazelle did not wait until the small hours as she expected. Nor did he silently slip into her bed.

She'd barely turned out the lights when he knocked on her door.

"Yes?"

He opened the door and stepped into the room. He still had on his pants, but no shirt. "I have been thinking," he said. "We need to talk."

Carly, wary, turned on the light. Was it a ploy? "It can't wait until morning?"

"No," he said, approaching the bed.

She tensed, reaching under the pillow for the knife. Le Genissel sat on the bed. His expression was pensive. He did not leer. She was surprised. But she still didn't trust him.

"I have made a decision," he announced. "As I have said, you must convince Lamb to go to Hong Kong without Mayne. While you and de Malbouzon deal with the kidnappers, I will go to Hong Kong and kill Lamb. When I return perhaps you will have figured out where Mayne is. Let's hope so. Do you understand my instructions?"

"Yes."

"I will be leaving very early."

"Okay."

The way he hesitated made her wonder what he expected—that she might invite him into her bed? For the first time he looked at her, though not salaciously.

"So, how was it with the professor?" he asked.

She could see his prurient interest had been aroused.

"Okay. We have rapport. And I think I've established trust. Things were going very well until he was kidnapped."

The Gazelle's expression hardened, his jaw working as he stared across the room. "We never should have let that happen. It is so stupid." Then he looked at her. "You are not to blame, I suppose. But you and de Malbouzon had better find the bloody bastard. You are dealing with amateurs, so you have no excuse for failure."

He left the room.

San Francisco International Airport

Jonas and Tess sat side by side, holding hands, waiting for their flight to be announced. Having slept together two nights running, they were officially lovers. Gratifying though it was, Jonas had to admit it seemed bizarre. "I don't know what this means," Tess had said that morning when they were in the shower together. "Maybe that I'm crazy." Jonas had kissed her and said, "It's a good kind of crazy, Tess. That much I know."

During breakfast they'd gotten Carly Van Hooten's troubling call. Like Tess, Jonas had been uneasy about the news Patrick wouldn't be coming with them, but unlike her he was prepared to put it aside and make the most of their trip.

"I still think it's a mistake to go without Patrick," she said, glancing around the waiting area. There were creases in her smooth brow.

Jonas caressed her cheek. "Carly said that's what he wants, sweetheart."

"If she's to be believed."

"Why would she lie?"

"I don't know, but I would feel better if I'd heard it from Patrick. The bottom line is I don't trust her."

"Do you want to try calling him?" Jonas asked, removing his cell phone from his pocket. "Carly said he expected to be tied up most of the day, but maybe he's free."

"That's another thing. Given the importance of this trip, why would he care what the people at the university think? So what if they consider him irresponsible for leaving town when his office was vandalized again?"

"He's got your responsible gene," Jonas said.

"Well, he's also got your independent streak."

"Which could mean he decided a weekend with Carly would be more fun than Hong Kong with his parents."

"I'm not so sure."

"So what'll it be?" he asked, indicating the phone in his hand. "Do you want to try to reach him or not?"

"I hate to come across as a fretting mom."

"Face it. You *are* a fretting mom. Make the call. If he *is* there, you'll feel better."

Tess took the phone and dialed. Jonas watched her push a wisp of her dark hair back off her face. There was such poetry in every move she made. He'd fallen in love with her elegance, her class, her dignity all over again. More than financial success, winning her heart would be the truest mark of him as a man. With Tess as his wife, he'd never be anything less than a complete and utter success.

"Hello? Carly?" she said into the phone. "It's

Tess…. Hi. We're at the airport and I thought before we board I'd try to reach Patrick. Did he make it home yet…? Oh, that's too bad, I was hoping to have a word with him…. No, nothing's wrong. Except that I'm a little concerned. I'm sure he told you about the arson and the threats that have been made against him."

Jonas could tell from Tess's reaction that Patrick hadn't gone into his difficulties with Carly. When they were at the courting stage, men tended not to complain about such things.

"Yes, well Patrick has been pretty laid-back about it," Tess was saying. "I'm sure he's got the news clippings around there somewhere, if you want to read about it…. It was a band of eco-terrorists called Save the Seed." She turned to Jonas. "He hasn't told her a thing."

"He's got other things on his mind."

Tess went back to her telephone conversation. "Yes, okay. Well, thank you, dear. When Patrick gets home, tell him our thoughts are with him. If we run into any problems in Hong Kong, I'm sure Jonas will give him a call. Please give Patrick our best."

Tess ended the call and sat for a moment staring at the phone.

"What's wrong?"

"Something funny is going on, Jonas. I can tell. It was in her voice, her questions, the way she answered me. I think she was lying."

Tess, sitting by the window, peered out at the ground crew, who, to the man, were bundled up, the gusty wind fluttering their clothing. She ran her conversation with Carly through her mind again, certain the girl had been lying. "Could I use your phone again, please?" she said to Jonas.

He fished it out of his pocket and gave it to her. She dialed information for Davis and asked to be put through to the campus police. She got a dispatcher.

"Is Patrick Mayne in the office?" she asked. "Professor Mayne."

"No, ma'am."

"Has he been there? Or is he with the investigators?"

"What's this regarding?" the woman asked.

"The vandalism of his office."

"You know, you're the second person who's called about vandalism. There hasn't been any the last few days. At least none that's been reported. Mind if I ask who gave you this idea?"

"Never mind," Tess said. "I guess I was misinformed." She hung up and handed the phone back to Jonas. "There wasn't any vandalism. It was all a lie."

"It might have been Patrick's lie, not Carly's."

"I suppose that's possible."

"You know what that probably means, don't you? Your son's in love."

"More like in lust," she said. "Hard as this may be for you to believe, though, I hope you're right."

Solano County

Tina and K.J. got out of the car. The drive down from Davis had been tense. He slammed the car door extra hard.

Tina started up the levee. He followed. "Look," she said, "I know you're pissed because I broke things off, but it's the mission that counts. So I think it would be better if we're not on the same watch anymore."

K.J. grumbled something about the fucking professor. Tina shook her head. It was so much easier before he got full of himself.

They reached the top of the levee. To the west dark clouds were building. The wind blew steadily. Tina led the way down to the boat. They crossed the boarding ladder. Roger came out onto the deck.

"Good," he said, "I'm glad you're here. I hardly got any sleep. Mayne was coughing and wheezing all night."

"This is definitely a problem," Tina said.

"He could be totally faking it, too," K.J. rejoined.

"I'll talk to him," she said. "Has anybody tried calling him on his cell phone?"

"No. And they won't. Brad and I decided to chuck it into the slough."

"Why?"

"Because there's a way to trace down locations of a cell phone when they know the number."

"How are we supposed to communicate with his friend and his family?"

"We'll use our cell phones, a different one each time."

Tina sighed. "Okay, fine. I'm going to go talk to him. I got him an inhaler." She started for the companionway.

"Hold on," K.J. called. "I have to get the gun."

Tina stopped. "You know what? I don't think it's necessary for you to come in with me, K.J."

"What if he tries something?"

"Wait outside the door, and if there's a problem, then you can come in."

He looked at Roger, who took the gun from his waistband and handed it to him. K.J. groused, weighing the weapon in his hand.

Tina went below, stopping outside the hold where Patrick Mayne was imprisoned. She put on her ski mask, removed the inhaler from her purse, waited for K.J. to open the heavy steel door and stepped inside. She found Patrick Mayne leaning against the wall, a blanket wrapped around him. He looked pale.

"Hi," she said.

"My favorite jailer."

She blushed, glad he couldn't see. "I brought an inhaler." She held up the box for him to see.

"That's very thoughtful."

She tossed it to him and sat on the straight chair by the door. "How're you feeling?"

"Better, if you don't count boredom."

"Would you like some books?"

"Sure, but nothing with a kidnapping in it, okay?"

Tina liked his sense of humor. Actually she liked him, which wasn't good. The prisoner was supposed to identify with his captors, not the other way around.

"Have you heard from my friend Carly?" he asked. "Any messages yet from my parents?"

"That's a problem," she replied. "My friends got rid

of your phone. And we haven't decided when or how we'll contact them."

"You obviously don't trust me, but I'm trying to accommodate you as best I can. If you want me to make a propaganda video, fine, I'll do it. All I ask is that you let me work out this deal."

"What deal?"

The professor turned pale. He agonized for several moments, then said, "This kidnapping couldn't have happened at a worse time. My father and I are trying to put together a major business deal. It has nothing to do with food crops, but it is crucial for the environment. And it's terribly time sensitive. I can't explain, but trust me, the importance is much bigger than my freedom."

"No offense, but that's pretty convenient, isn't it?"

Mayne shook his head, sadly. "You're right. There's no reason you should believe me. So, let's focus on what you want. I'll get you the ransom, I'll make your propaganda pieces and I'll go on my way. Hell, the world never has to know there was a kidnapping. You'll have everything you want and you won't even have committed a crime to get it."

"Don't you know how crazy that sounds?"

"Are you telling me that the deal's off, that you want the feds on the case?"

"No, like I say we're considering what to do."

Patrick Mayne slumped, clearly disappointed. Tina was inclined to think he was being straight with them, but she wasn't absolutely sure. "So, why do you do what you do?" she asked. "If you don't mind me asking."

"You mean why am I a scientist?"

"I mean, why do you insist on corrupting nature?"

"I guess for the same reason Salk tried to weaken the polio virus. It seems to me crops that resist pests without the assistance of chemicals that contaminate the water supply and deform wildlife is a good thing. But then, what do I know?"

"It's not that simple, Professor, and you know it."

"Yeah," he said, "you're probably right. I'd just like you to know my intentions aren't bad, even if you don't like my methods." He studied her. "You may not believe this, but I respect your views. And I think I know what you're against, but I'm not sure what you're really for."

Davis, California

Gaston de Malbouzon arrived in Davis midafternoon and was happily at work on the Internet when Carly knocked on his motel room door. The room was five degrees too hot, of course. Gaston was in his bathrobe, a beret set jauntily on his head, his stubby ponytail hanging below it. She'd never seen him wear a beret before.

"Where did that come from?" she asked.

"Americophile though I may be, I'm nevertheless attached to my corrupt, noble roots, if only for purposes of my amusement. Were you followed, Bo Peep?"

"No."

"How'd you get here?"

"Rental car." Carly sat in the chair next to the

dressing table Gaston had converted into a desk and crossed her legs. "We need to talk, Comte."

"About Alfred?"

"The bastard stayed at the house last night."

"Did he do anything unsavory?"

"No, but it's just a matter of time. And I don't need that, Gaston. Life's too short."

"But because of your devotion to me, you'll stay the course, *n'est-ce pas?*"

"I'm not a quitter by nature, but I have to admit I'm tempted. Anyway, I want to know what's going on with Patrick."

Gaston continued navigating the Net. "Are your concerns personal or professional?"

"Professional, of course."

"There's no 'of course' about it."

"What does it matter what I'm thinking as long as I do my job?"

Gaston's attention was on his computer and Carly noticed his growing excitement as he worked. After a couple of minutes he shouted, *"Voilà! Magnifique!"* Then he leaned back in his chair and beamed. "Look at this, Carly."

"What?"

"I just hacked into the Davis Police Department case files. Thought I'd see what their thinking is with regard to your Professor Mayne's detractors."

Carly leaned forward and peered at the screen. "And?"

"I'll have to check this out thoroughly, but I see

we have a lengthy list of potential arson suspects in the Patrick Mayne dossier."

"You know about the eco-terrorists?"

"For a few days now. The professor's disappearance has sharpened my interest in them. My working theory is that they snatched our golden boy. *Golden* being the operative word, *bien entendu*."

"Did Le Genissel tell you about the call I got last night?"

"Yes. Is that the last you've heard from them?"

"Yeah. No more calls."

"I understand you spoke briefly to a woman."

"Right."

"*Bien*. I need to hear all about it. In fact, let's start at the beginning. Tell me everything that's happened since you and the prof connected. You may include or omit as much detail regarding the intimacy as your dignity and conceit will allow or demand. It's up to you."

"Thank you, Gaston. Your consideration is touching."

"As you well know, in the business of crime detection, the smallest detail can be salient. For example, had the boy gasped another lady's name at the magic moment, I should know about it."

Carly recrossed her legs. "The boy didn't."

"Okay, proceed."

Carly brought him up to date, telling him that she and Mayne had had sex five times.

"*Epatant!* And he's in love, is he?"

"He's in fascination. I'm different."

"Then you've found his Achilles' heel." Gaston was delighted. "And so quickly! *Félicitations!*"

"It won't do us any good unless we find him."

"Just so, *chérie*. Am I to assume he's said nothing about the super ethanol?"

"Not a word. Not even a hint. He's smarter than his old man."

"All sons are, Carly. Some of us more obviously so than others."

"What are we going to do about the million bucks? Le Genissel said we'll have to deal with it. When they call, what do I say?"

"For now we'll have to stall them. But ironically, we may end up paying the ransom ourselves. Obviously a million is a drop in the bucket when to our clients it means trillions. The point is we must find our professor by the time Le Genissel gets back from Hong Kong."

"With a couple more notches on his belt."

"It distresses you?"

Carly got up and went to the window, pulling back the drape for a peek outside. It had started to rain. "I don't see that all the killing is necessary."

"The only people Alfred trusts are dead people— preferably dead *and* buried."

She watched the raindrops splashing in the puddles on the asphalt. "So, what's the plan, Gaston?"

"We have to hope the kidnappers will be in touch. They called you on your cell phone, right?"

"Yes."

"Have you tried calling Mayne's cell?"

"Yes, all I get is a recording—'The customer you are trying to reach is unavailable,'" she muttered. "Boy, is that an understatement."

Gaston got up. "Speaking of communications," he said, going to the dresser, "I've gotten special cell phones so we can update each another. It's risky to meet regularly."

He took a phone from the drawer and brought it to her. Carly put it in her purse and was about to check the battery on her other phone when it rang, making her jump.

"Jesus. Scared me to death." She answered. "Hello?"

"The professor wants to know the status of the money." It was a woman's voice, the same one Carly had heard the night before.

"The family is working on raising it," Carly replied. "It's a large sum. It'll take a few days."

"He'd like reassurance you haven't notified the police."

"Tell him we're following his instructions to the letter."

"What's your role in this, Carly?"

She thought quickly, electing to tell the truth as Patrick knew it. "I was hired by the professor's father as an administrative assistant and Patrick and I have become friends."

"What's the big deal Professor Mayne and his father are working on?" the woman asked.

Carly didn't know how to respond, but decided in the end to say what Patrick would expect. "I don't know, actually. I'm new to the situation."

"But there *is* a big deal in the works, right?"

"That's my impression," Carly said. "I think that's what Patrick's father's trip to Hong Kong was about."

"Okay, thanks."

It sounded like she was about to hang up. "Oh, miss," Carly said.

"Yeah?"

"How do I reach you, if I need to talk?"

"You don't. We call you."

The phone went dead. Carly dropped it in her purse.

"What happened?" Gaston asked.

She recounted the conversation.

"Cat and mouse," he sighed. "Well, there's nothing to be done but to press ahead."

She returned to the window to watch the rain. "Are you enjoying this, Gaston?"

"I like the double paycheck." He lifted his beret and scratched his head. "I take it from your question that you are not."

"Not like I'd hoped, to be honest."

"In the modern world everybody's a whore. We, no more than the oil men we work for, or the politicians in Washington who serve their needs. Le Genissel. Lamb and his women. The professor. Whores all, *chérie*. We pray to a different God, that's the only distinction."

Somehow Carly couldn't find the strength to smile, let alone laugh. Some things simply weren't funny to her anymore.

MONDAY
January 28

Hong Kong

Jonas Lamb stood at the railing of Jimmy Yee's yacht, watching the moon rise from behind Victoria Peak. The weather was unseasonably warm, and so Jimmy had suggested an evening cruise around Hong Kong Island and dinner on the yacht before commencing negotiations. Jimmy naturally had to get to know Tess, with whom he'd already become smitten. "My God, old bean," he'd said, taking Jonas aside that afternoon when they'd met for tea at the Peninsula Hotel, "how did you let this one get away?" A damned good question, one that had been his bane for nearly thirty years.

Jimmy loved all women, but Tess he'd recognized as special—more than merely delightful in, say, the manner of a Crystal, who was foremost an amusement. A lawyer and a businesswoman, Tess was a player, which enhanced her standing in Jimmy's eyes because she was about as equal as a woman could get in the Chinese culture.

Jonas had felt like something of a third wheel that afternoon as he and Lily sat listening to Tess and Jimmy going on about the San Francisco real estate market. Lily had looked lovely in a pale lavender *cheongsam* as the four had tea in the marble-and-gold-leaf lobby under the watchful eye of three of Jimmy's bodyguards, but it was Tess who stole the show. Jimmy, puffing on one of his Cubans, had given Jonas nods of approval from time to time as if to say, "You've outdone yourself, old boy."

When Jonas and Tess had retired to their suite for some rest before the cruise, escorted by the security detail that had been with them from the moment their plane landed, Jonas had told Tess she was worth her weight in gold. "I'm having fun," she replied, "even though I know it's dead serious."

There was no disputing the fact that the mood of the visit was very different from his last trip to Hong Kong. First there was the heavy security, more suitable for a head of state than the snake-oil hustler some people thought him to be. Second, there was a sense of urgency that Jimmy seemed to share right along with him and Tess.

Lily had not been included in the evening festivities, which Jonas interpreted as a sign of respect for Tess. And so, it was just the three of them cruising the island, along with the crew and a full complement of bodyguards.

Jonas had been left alone to savor the surprisingly balmy air while Jimmy had taken Tess below so that she could try to reach Patrick on the satellite phone.

(Two attempts from the hotel had been fruitless, the messages left on his machine having produced no return call.) She'd wisely concluded that if she did reach Patrick, he might say a few words to Jimmy, thus shoring up the relationship.

The plan was for Jonas to present the package Patrick had prepared, then in the morning Jimmy would bring in the two experts he'd lined up to evaluate the technical aspects. No firm deal could be made until the results were in on the test crop several months down the line, but Jonas was hoping to pick up some earnest money this go-around, perhaps a few million dollars.

At present the yacht was rounding the western tip of the island and heading south into the East Lamma Channel. The sea was calm, the yacht moving at a leisurely pace. Jimmy appeared, strolling over to where his friend waited.

"We rang up Patrick," the tycoon said, lighting a cigar, "but got no response. Tess is a bit upset. I believe she was eager for me to speak with the young man."

Naturally they hadn't shared their concerns about Patrick, giving Jimmy Yee the party line about Patrick being detained on university business. But Jonas knew Tess's anxiety went much deeper than the business deal. He looked toward the companionway.

"She's freshening up," Jimmy explained, "and will join us shortly." He drew on his cigar, sending a puff of smoke into the East Asian night. "Quite an evening for the end of January, eh?"

"Gorgeous," Jonas said, again eyeing the moon. He

wore a blazer over a polo shirt and khaki pants, a bit more casual than Jimmy, who had on a sport coat and tie.

"I took the liberty of ordering some gin and tonics," Jimmy told him. "I hope that meets with your approval."

"Perfect."

During their conversation at tea Jonas had asked if May Li had made it safely home. Jimmy confirmed that she had and apologized for any overzealousness on May's part. He offered to dispatch a new security team but Jonas had demurred, saying it might be best if he made his own arrangements once they got back.

Jonas hadn't mentioned the slip of paper with the address Larry had given him, though he'd considered doing so until Jimmy admitted May didn't actually work for him. "She's a contract security specialist," he'd explained. "She came highly recommended by a friend." Jonas had wondered what friend, but sensed it might not be politic to ask.

Tess came up from below, making her way toward the men. She wore a navy St. John knit suit and looked stunning with a string of marble-size white South Sea pearls—a gift from Walter, she'd told him as they'd dressed that evening. "I guess I'll have to find some even bigger ones," he'd said. "Let's hope I do well with Jimmy and can afford you."

"Jonas, it's not a competition."

"My dear, that's exactly what it is. Nature's way. Only thing is, instead of fluffing our feathers and preening, we flash our checkbook these days."

And now here she was, the jewel of Jimmy Yee's multimillion dollar luxury yacht, a radiant, confident, classy woman. "Hi," she said, her smile a touch shy.

Jonas slipped an arm around her waist and kissed her temple. He didn't have to tell her how lovely she was. She knew how he felt.

The miniskirt-clad hostess arrived with their drinks. She took a bowl of cashews from the tray she carried and set it on a nearby folding chair, then withdrew.

Jimmy, effusive now, said, "I'd like to propose a toast. To old friends, new friends, new ventures, good fortune and—" he looked back and forth between the two of them "—rekindled romance."

They touched glasses.

"Did Jonas put you up to that, Mr. Yee?" Tess asked after sipping her drink.

"He didn't have to. I'm in his corner in every respect."

"Yes, you men do stick together."

They chatted for several minutes, making small talk, each of them in their way distracted. Tess was undoubtedly worrying about Patrick, Jimmy was probably concerned about the deal, and Jonas had a whole smorgasbord of concerns. The deal, Crystal back home, holding the key to everything in her crazy little head, her deposition looming like a meteor hurling toward earth from outer space, Melanie waiting to pick up the pieces and, of course, there was his relationship with Tess. His former wife was a hesitant lover, a woman who'd given in to pleasure, but was still hedging her bets with regard to the long term.

Jimmy checked his watch. "I'm supposed to call Singapore this evening, and this is probably as good a time as any. Would you excuse me, please?"

"Certainly," Tess said.

After Jimmy was gone, she moved a bit closer to Jonas. He wanted to think she sought the comfort of his proximity, but it was also possible she sought warmth because a cooler breeze had risen. She shivered slightly.

"You cold?" he asked, putting his arm around her.

"A little, but I'm okay."

They stared out at the scattered lights on the dark face of the island and leaned on the railing. He watched her watching the moonlight on the water. Her ring finger was bare; she no longer sported Walter's huge diamond. She'd left it at home.

"Your hand looks much better without that ring," he said, taking it. He kissed her fingers.

She faced him, her eyes shimmering in the moonlight. "Jonas, I know your jokes about us getting together again are half serious, but..." She hesitated.

"They're not *half* serious, Tess, they're *entirely* serious. I do want to marry you."

"All right, entirely serious. All the more reason to be honest with you. I should probably wait until after this deal is resolved and life has returned to some semblance of normalcy, but I just can't. I'm many things, but a hypocrite isn't one...I try to avoid it, in any case."

"What are you saying?"

"I've thought about it a great deal. You and Patrick are *all* I've thought about the last twenty-four hours."

"And?"

"I can't marry you again, Jonas. I'm sorry, but I can't."

"Why?"

"Because, sexual attraction aside, we don't belong together. I'm deeply attracted to you, but that's not what marriages are built on."

"I thought you'd realized we weren't so different, after all. We share the same passions. And I've grown up a little. I'm not the flake I used to be."

"I'm not sure how to explain it, but it would seem like going back. I've made peace not only with you but with myself, and I thank you for that. God knows, it has probably been good for my soul. But marriage is different. You don't need me for redemption, which is what you're after, you know. I want us to be friends, but the future I see has us going down separate roads."

"I don't agree at all," he said glumly.

"I know. But I have to be true to myself. You may hate me for saying this, but I love you dearly, Jonas. I also know we're not meant to be."

"Well," he said, turning to the sea, "I'm not going to argue with you. In time you'll either come to see I'm right, or we'll drift apart." He gave her his patented grin. "Just remember, I saw the truth first."

Tess leaned her head on his shoulder. "I'm sorry. I truly am."

The breeze grew cooler and he rubbed her arm. "I don't know what it is about Hong Kong," he said. "Last time I came here, I brought Crystal and on the flight home she dumped me. Maybe Hong Kong isn't lucky for me."

"Some things just aren't meant to be."

"Well, I haven't given up. My mother used to tell me I'd end up like my old man. She could be right, but you know what, Tess? Being king of the world and having you are both within my grasp. Twenty years from now, when I'm in my rocker, I don't want to wonder what would have happened if I hadn't quit. Point being, you haven't quite heard the last of me. Be forewarned."

She was touched. "I really wish you weren't so cute."

Jonas turned his back to the sea, leaning on the railing with his elbows. He watched the rising wind blow Tess's hair across her face, loving the grace with which she brushed it aside. When she folded her arms, rubbing them, he said, "You're cold. Why don't we go below."

"Maybe we should."

From the corner of his eye Jonas saw a flicker of motion up on the bridge. Jimmy Yee and Captain Lam were engaged in what appeared to be a rather intense conversation as they looked out to sea through a pair of binoculars, which they passed back and forth.

Jonas turned to see what they were looking at. In the darkness he saw a small freighter some distance away, but headed toward them. The ship was without running lights and moving at a rapid clip. Captain Lam gave the boat full power and Jonas could feel it surge in the water.

Tess sensed something was amiss and looked around. "What's happening?"

"That ship is coming right for us," he said, pointing.

With the yacht being smaller and more maneuverable, it seemed like a collision could be easily avoided. There were shouts up on the fly bridge and a crewman came forward with a handheld searchlight. He shined it in the direction of the freighter.

The captain spun the wheel hard to port, throwing Tess against Jonas. He instinctively put his arm around her and checked the freighter again. It, too, swung to the yacht's portside. Two hundred yards was all that separated the two vessels.

With one hand clamped on the railing and the other around Tess's shoulders, Jonas watched the spotlight sweep the hull of the approaching freighter. Suddenly there were flashes on the bow of the freighter and an instant later explosions on the fly bridge. Machine gun fire was tearing the bridge to shreds with glass and splintered wood flying in all directions.

Jonas pulled Tess down onto the deck. The crewman with the searchlight was blown off the bridge. There were cries of agony. The engine stopped. Rounds from the machine gun continued to tear into the hull of the yacht, which started to settle in the water. Jonas lifted his head and saw the freighter less than a hundred yards away, bearing down on them at full speed.

"They're going to ram us," he shouted. "I say we go overboard and swim like hell."

"Okay," she cried, her nails digging into his arm.

He lifted his head and peered around, but with the machine gun firing there was no time for calculation. "Come on," he shouted over the din, "follow me!"

He dashed toward the railing and dove over it, hitting the water flat. Tess splashed into the water a few yards away and came up gulping for air. The dark hull of the little freighter zeroed in on the yacht. It would miss them, but pass by closely enough that they could get sucked into the backwash. Jonas started swimming frantically. Tess followed.

The machine gun fire had stopped, but he could hear the blunt bow of the freighter as it pushed its way through the water. There was an enormous crash seconds later, and an explosion. For the next few seconds bits of burning debris rained down on top of them.

Treading water, Jonas watched the freighter continue on into the night. There were no cries for help, no signs of survivors. Tess was nearby, her pretty face rising and falling with the swells. He checked the dark profile of Hong Kong Island in the distance. It was at least a mile away, probably two. There was a time—forty years ago—when a two-mile swim would have been nothing for him. Now he wasn't so sure.

Already struggling for air, Jonas figured their best hope was that some boat had heard the gunfire, the explosion, or had seen the fire, which was rapidly dwindling and would soon be out. He wondered, too, if the crew of the freighter might have seen them go overboard and would circle back. He looked, but the ship was no longer visible.

"Jonas," Tess said, "look!"

He turned and behind him bobbing in the waves, ten or fifteen yards away, was a white life buoy. "Come on," he said, his spirits lifting as he began to swim.

Tess splashed along beside him. He reached the life buoy ahead of her and, taking her hand, pulled her over. They both clung to it, breathing hard. Jonas looked toward the debris of the yacht, checking once more for other survivors. "Hello?" he called, thinking his voice might be heard if someone else was afloat. He got no response. God, poor Jimmy.

The fire was nearly out now, but the moon was well above the profile of the island. There was enough light for him to see Tess's glistening eyes and the glow of her pearl necklace. He touched her cheek.

"You've got to admit this, Tess," he said. "Life with me is never boring."

Somehow he'd coaxed a smile out of her. "Yeah," she said, "I'll give you that. But we may be down to our last minutes, Jonas. I hate to be negative, but..."

"Do you really love me?" he asked. "You weren't trying to make me feel good."

"No, I do love you. More than I should."

"I mean, love me big time."

"Big time," she said, spitting out a mouthful of water and shaking her head.

Jonas Lamb kissed her temple, wondering if that was God's last ironic gift to a dying man, or a promise of new beginnings. He decided to assume the latter. As his late father used to say, "It's better to be optimistic and mistaken, than pessimistic and right."

Davis, California

The quiet, the feeling of being out of control, were beginning to wear on her. Carly Van Hooten did not like Operation Brebis Noire anymore. Even the money—which was fantastic by any standard—was beginning to seem like a curse. She knew she could slip away, melt into the American hinterland and resurface anywhere she wished. She could put Global Energy Technologies, Inc., Patrick Mayne and Jonas Lamb behind her.

But something held her there. She had to see, first-hand, what happened. There was unfinished business and it wasn't the uncompleted job she'd been hired to do. Carly was being held in place by a compulsion she didn't fully understand. And even though the compulsion had a self-destructive feel to it, she still couldn't let go.

Dawn was breaking as she lay awake in Patrick Mayne's bed, feeling an emptiness akin to the terrible loss after Antoine's disappearance. Her heart seemed to be beating in an empty shell. The world lacked meaning. She wasn't afraid, but she was alone.

The cell phone on the bedstand rang, the phone Gaston had given her. She fumbled in the dark to find the right buttons to answer.

"Yes?"

"I just talked to the Gazelle. Lamb and his former wife are dead."

Carly digested the news, feeling a little sick at heart. "Then we're down to Mayne."

"Yes, *chérie*, but we need to find him. I don't suppose you've heard from the kidnappers."

"No."

"Needless to say, they're key."

"And?"

"I've been studying the notes of the Davis police detectives. They seemed to have done a decent job of winnowing down their list of arson suspects. We, however, have a piece of information they don't."

"Which is?"

"That one of our merry band is a woman. The number of women on the detectives' list is relatively small—a couple of dozen—in comparison with the hundreds of men."

"And?"

"I'm thinking of concentrating on the woman. If your lady calls again, Carly, try to get something out of her that I can use."

"Like what?"

"It'd be nice to know if she's a student, for example. That could cut the names on the list in half. And there's something else. The police have the noms de guerre of a few Save the Seeds out of Berkeley. There's no way to know at this point if they're involved, but if you can use the names to provoke a response, your girl might let something slip. The names are 'Robo' and 'Baby Cakes.'"

Carly turned on the light and jotted the names on a pad. "Okay, Gaston, I'll see what I can do. Any other instructions?"

"Yes, when you hear from the kidnappers, tell

them we've got a million, ready to go. We're prepared to buy Mayne's freedom."

"In case they ask, who is 'we'?"

"You can't say the parents because word could get out through the media that they're dead. Better say you're working with Mayne's corporate sponsors and they're putting up the money."

"Patrick won't know to corroborate that."

"He doesn't have to. Tell them you're a go-between, that the money guys came looking for Mayne and when they found out what happened, they asked you to help."

"Won't Patrick be suspicious?"

"*Tiens*. We can't worry about that now, my love. Once we get him free, we'll deal with his suspicions. First things first."

West Lamma Channel, Hong Kong

They'd been clinging to the life buoy for what seemed like an hour, though it was probably only twenty minutes. At first they'd tried swimming toward Hong Kong Island, both of them behind the buoy, kicking, but the ocean currents were against them and they were actually being swept farther into the open sea. Worse, perhaps, the cold water had begun to sap their strength. Tess shivered so badly that Jonas had to clamp her hands on the preserver because she was having trouble holding on, not an easy task as his own strength was almost depleted.

Funny, but what came to mind was Crystal's tarot

card readings. He thought of Jimmy's quip about them not getting on the same plane.

"We're not going to make it," Tess said through chattering teeth.

"Sure we will, sweetheart. Somebody will come along soon."

They had seen a couple of boats in the distance, the searchlights indicating they were probably rescue craft. They'd shouted at the top of their lungs, hoping to attract attention, but all it accomplished was a further depletion of energy.

"I can't do it, Jonas," she said. "I barely have the strength to breathe."

"Don't give up, Tess. For Patrick's sake, not mine."

That made her cry. She continued to struggle, but her hands kept slipping from the buoy. He knew an eternity of love had to be crammed into their few remaining moments of life. Death had never seemed so ominous or cruel. Or close.

Jonas hated his mortality—the fact that his life meant nothing now. Even his love seemed pointless—a feeble gesture in the face of that formidable dark monster, Death.

"I love you, Tess," he muttered, pressing his cracked lips against her face, his fingers so badly cramped he could no longer grasp anything. Tess kept sinking beneath the surface, each breath she took more hardly won than the last. She was dying.

It was then he saw Death glide toward them in a ghostlike barque. It was silent, serene, promising everlasting peace, the end of the struggle. Tess slipped away. He couldn't hold on to her.

"Ayeeyah!" he heard. *"Ayeeyah!"*

As the water rose above his nose he had one final glimpse of the barque. But then he saw a face hanging over the gunnels. Two faces. A third. All peering down at him. Above them flames glowing brightly in the night.

Something in the deep recesses of consciousness told him a junk was drifting past them, its hull only inches from his face.

Jonas came up gasping. He felt something bump his stomach. Reaching down he touched Tess, his clawed fingers slipping under her necklace. Yanking with his last ounce of strength he somehow brought her to the surface.

The stern of the junk glided past them and Jonas realized the boat was drifting away. Then he saw a couple of crewmen clamber into the small boat tethered to the junk and trailing along in its wake. They were coming after them!

Clinging to Tess for dear life, Jonas prayed as he'd never prayed before. *God, please,* he implored. *All I need is two more minutes. Maybe three.*

Solano County

Tina Richter was drinking coffee in the galley of the fishing boat. Fifteen minutes had passed since the other Seeds, except her and Brad, had taken off. They'd gathered early that morning to decide what to do, and it had been left to her to inform Patrick

Mayne of their decision. She was not looking forward to it.

Everybody was nervous, including K.J., especially after Kristy had reported a visit from the Davis police. The cops had questioned her about the arson, so she'd obviously made it into some sort of list of activists. K.J. had been concerned that Kristy might be under surveillance and so they'd decided she should lie low. Brad reported he'd had a call from Robo, who told him the police were questioning a number of people in Berkeley as well, though none of the Berkeley Seeds had been contacted as yet.

"We've got to stop dicking around," K.J. said. "If nobody's going to report the bastard missing, then we've got to put out the word to the media that we've got him. The whole purpose of this is to get publicity for the cause and so far we've got nothing to show for our trouble. It's totally fucked up."

"What about the ransom?" Roger had asked.

"That's how his family and the corporations get him back. Tina can call his friend and give her the word."

"I want to talk to him first," she said.

K.J. had given her a suspicious look. The guy was really starting to annoy her.

"Whatever," he'd said, dismissing her. "We have to get our announcement to the media ready. I think we should plan on going public tomorrow."

Everyone agreed with K.J.'s plan. Now it was time to give Mayne the word. Tina got an extra mug of coffee for the professor, plus the books she'd brought him, and went out on the deck looking for Brad. "Get the gun. I'm going to talk to him now."

Brad lifted his jacket to show he had the gun in the waistband of his pants. "Want me to go in with you?"

"No, just stay close to the door in case there's trouble."

They went below. Brad unlocked the heavy door and Tina, her ski mask in place, went in, turning on the light. Mayne awoke. He blinked at her.

"What time is it?" He tried to read his watch through bleary eyes.

"Almost ten."

"God, it could be midnight and I wouldn't know the difference."

"Would you like a cup of coffee?"

"Fantastic. Yeah."

"And I brought you some books." She carried the coffee and the books to him.

Mayne sat up, glancing at the book titles before wrapping his blanket around his shoulders and his fingers around the mug. "Sorry about the stench," he said, indicating the chamber pot, "but you guys don't provide the best bathroom facilities."

"Limited budget," she said, retreating to the chair by the door.

"You'll be rich soon enough."

She watched him sip his coffee. "I'm afraid I've got bad news."

There was a look of alarm on the professor's face. "What?"

"We've decided to go public with the kidnapping."

"What about the money?"

"We want that, too. But this is mostly about publicity. We'll want you to make some statements."

Mayne shook his head with dismay. "If you do it my way, you'll have your cake and eat it, too."

"Part of the problem is that we think you're screwing with us. It doesn't make sense that you want to keep this secret."

Patrick Mayne stared at her for a long time. "What if I said my food-crop work—which is where I started, I grant you—is a front for research I'm doing with ethanol?"

"Is that the truth?"

"Yes. The fact of the matter is I'm trying to sell or license the technology and, as you might imagine, being your guest isn't helping much."

"I hate to tell you this," Tina said, "but it doesn't change things. It's all genetic engineering. Ethanol may not be all that important to us, but what *is* important is that you're a visible symbol and we want to make an example of you."

He looked disappointed and she was sorry about that, but what the Seeds were doing was serious, something she believed in deeply. "We're going to make you famous, Professor. Look at it that way."

"Okay, fine, do what you have to do, but let's get this over with. Have you talked to Carly?"

"As a matter of fact, I thought I'd call her as soon as we're done talking." Tina got to her feet. "You got a message for her?"

"Tell her to get me out of here, whatever it takes."

Davis, California

Carly Van Hooten made herself another cup of horrible instant coffee, thinking maybe it wouldn't be so bad with milk. She missed her little coffeemaker back in Paris, just as she missed the life. Awakening in a nostalgic mood, she'd thought about Antoine. For the first time in several days, she hadn't censored her thoughts.

The doorbell rang. Wary, Carly went to see who it was. As she entered the front room she could see a police car out front. She stopped as a wave of fear went through her. The doorbell rang again.

It couldn't be an arrest, she decided. They'd be banging on the door. Steeling herself, she went to the entry and pulled open the door. It was two uniformed officers. There were no guns drawn. Carly breathed more easily.

"Morning, ma'am," the shorter man said. He was Asian. "We're looking for Patrick Mayne."

"I'm sorry, Patrick's not here."

"Any idea when he'll be home?"

Carly hesitated. "He's out of town, actually. Is there something I can help you with?"

"You his wife?"

The question amused her. "No, a close friend."

"Your name?"

"Carly Van Hooten."

The cop made a note. "Double O?"

"Yes. And E-N."

"Do you expect to be talking to Mr. Mayne soon?" the other officer asked.

"Possibly."

"If you could give him a message, please," the Asian cop said. "It's bad news, I'm afraid. There was a boating accident in Hong Kong where Mr. Mayne's parents were visiting. The boat sunk. Their bodies haven't been recovered, but they're presumed dead. There were no survivors."

"Oh, my." Carly was in no mood for acting, but she made the gesture.

The telephone rang. The house line.

"We can see you're busy, ma'am," the cop said. "Please advise Mr. Mayne, will you?"

"Certainly." Carly closed the door and went to answer the phone. "Hello?"

"It's me." A woman's voice…the kidnapper. "How you coming with the money?"

"I've got it," Carly told her. "A million for Patrick, but it's got to be quick. Just tell me when and where."

The caller seemed stunned. "I'll have to get back to you on that."

"Listen, if you want this deal, don't take too long. The situation has gotten very complicated."

"What do you mean?"

Carly figured she might as well be the one to tell them because the word would be getting out soon. "Are you with Patrick?"

"He's nearby. Why?"

"Can I speak with him?"

"No, but I'll relay a message."

"The police were just here. His parents were in a

boating accident in Hong Kong. They're missing and presumed dead."

"Oh, Jesus."

"Yeah, it's terrible. All the more reason to do this thing now. We'll give you the money, but we want Patrick freed immediately."

"Wait a minute, if his parents are dead, who's putting up the money?"

"Corporate sponsors, people who want Patrick free," Carly said.

There was a long silence. Carly could tell she'd struck a chord.

The woman said, "Does this have anything to do with ethanol research?"

Now Carly was the one caught flat-footed. As she searched for the appropriate response, she realized she had to think of Patrick's reaction. "What ethanol research?"

For several moments the woman didn't speak. Then, "Never mind. Just a thought. By the way, you said the police were there. Do they know we've got Patrick?"

"No, I'm respecting his wishes and I hope you are, as well."

"You might as well know, we're going public."

"Why?"

"That's our business."

"No offense," Carly said, "but we're talking about a man's life and lots of money. Is somebody in charge there? I know I'm dealing with a bunch of students, but maybe you should be bringing in a heavy hitter, somebody like Robo or Baby Cakes to handle the negotiation."

There was another silence, seeming confusion, then the line went dead.

Peng Chau, Hong Kong

It was nearly midnight. Jonas, a blanket wrapped around him, sat cross-legged on the straw mat in the corner of the house, the room heated by a portable coal-burning stove. A girl of about ten, who by all rights should have been in bed, watched him from the doorway, serving as a sort of watchdog, though what the concern might be he had no idea. He was at the mercy of these people, having only a vague idea of where he was and no resources. Plus, Tess was in the next room, being examined by the doctor.

At least he spoke some English, unlike their hosts. But Jonas had hardly had a chance to speak with him before he'd gone to tend to Tess. Jonas could hear voices through the thin walls. The doctor, the lady of the house and a younger woman—probably an elder daughter—were doing most of the talking, with occasional grunts and moans that had to be responses from Tess.

It was a miracle they'd been pulled from the water alive. Once Tess was revived, she'd gone into shock, but the men, apparently well schooled in the treatment of exposure victims, had bundled her up and kept her stable until they'd arrived at the island. They'd carried Tess into the nearby house, which apparently belonged to the skipper of the junk. The structure was right on the water, so close that Jonas could hear the waves lapping against the pilings beneath them.

He had been of little help, not thinking clearly. Before they'd helped him get cleaned up and into dry clothes, he'd had the presence of mind to ask the fishermen not to notify the authorities, operating under the theory that they'd be better off if whoever had tried to kill them thought they were dead.

His fondest wish was to get on the first flight home. With Jimmy dead, there was nothing for him in Hong Kong.

Using sign language and a few shared words, he'd managed to make it understood that he wished to speak to May Li by showing the skipper the soggy scrap of paper from his wallet. Jonas knew he was taking a risk, but May had proved her loyalty and, with Jimmy dead, seemed more trustworthy than anyone else he could think of.

Jonas drank more tea and was starting to feel human again when the doctor came out of Tess's room.

"She okay," he announced. "Very bad chill, mind confusion, but she okay. Just need much rest."

"That's wonderful news. Thank you, Doctor."

He bowed slightly. He was a roundish man in his sixties with salt-and-pepper hair. He wore a traditional Chinese suit and a quilted overvest that served almost as a topcoat. He was about as far from what you'd see on *ER* as anything Jonas could imagine.

"I wasn't able to communicate with my hosts very

well, but I tried to explain it would be best if the police weren't notified."

"Yes, they tell me," the doctor replied. "Mr. Lim, the master, already speak to May Li by telephone. She say don't worry, she come soon. You rest, Mr. Lamb."

"Can I see my wife?" The words had come out so naturally that Jonas was almost unaware of the irony.

"Yes, for a few minute. She must sleep. Go now."

Jonas struggled to his feet, his legs as wobbly as a drunken sailor's. He offered his hand to the doctor. "I want to thank you for everything. Do you have a card so I can send you some money?"

"Not necessary. May Li say to tell you she take care everything, including Mr. Lim. No more money necessary."

"Thank you."

Jonas moved to the doorway where the girl waited. She pulled back the curtain for him, and he peered inside a small room faintly lit with candles. Two women were kneeling across from where Tess lay on a mattress. Her eyes were closed, her dark hair swept back from her face.

When he approached Tess's bed, the women got up and, bowing, left the room. As he dropped down on his knees beside her, Tess opened her eyes. She gave him a faint smile. "We didn't die," she murmured.

"No, but we came as close as I hope to get for a while."

She poked her hand out from under the blankets and took his fingers. "Why did this happen? Were they after us?"

"That's my guess. And maybe Jimmy."

"He's dead, isn't he?"

"I think so."

Tess shivered, her eyes glistening. "Do you think they've tried to kill Patrick, too? Could that be why we haven't heard from him?"

"No, Tess, the boy's in love...or in lust, one or the other."

She looked like she wanted to believe him. "A chip off the old block, let's hope."

Jonas leaned over and kissed her. "I saved your life, you know. In China it means you'll have to marry me."

"It does not."

"Honest. Ask the doctor if you don't believe me."

"Well, we may be in China, but we aren't Chinese."

"Haven't you heard the expression, 'When in Rome...'?"

"It's just like you, Jonas Lamb, to take advantage of a woman who's too weak to defend herself."

"I'll take that as a provisional yes," he said, giving her a wink.

"Mr. Lamb. I so happy to see you alive and well." It was May Li at the door. Jonas almost didn't recognize her. She was without makeup and wearing a black Chinese-style quilted jacket and black pants. "I bring a friend," she said, stepping aside so that they could see the older Chinese gentleman behind her. He wore a topcoat and had a fedora in his hand. He had a stately bearing. "This Zhang Jintao," May said. "He very important man. He come to help."

* * *

Chairs were brought and placed on either side of the coal-burning stove. Zhang and Jonas were each brought fresh cups of tea. May went off with the members of the household and Tess was left to sleep.

"I am very sorry for your ordeal, Mr. Lamb," Zhang said after several moments of silence and small smiles. "The events of this night are very tragic."

"Is Jimmy dead?"

"Yes, they believe everyone died. The authorities are unaware that you and Mrs. Vartel survived."

"If this is rude, please forgive me, Mr. Zhang, but who are you, exactly?"

Zhang sipped his tea. "It is a good question. Let us say I am a friend and associate of Yee Jiechi, Jimmy Yee."

"You're employed by Yee Industries?"

"No. I was more an adviser, a consultant you might say. Our ways are different in China, as I believe you know. What is important for your purposes is that Jimmy confided in me. I am aware of your business arrangement concerning the super ethanol, in other words."

"Jimmy told you?"

"I advised him to pursue the opportunity."

"I suppose I should be grateful, but the issue seems to be moot."

"This is not certain, Mr. Lamb."

"Oh?"

"I know this is not the best time to discuss business, considering your ordeal, so with your permission we will defer discussions until you have had time to rest. Let me tell you this now, however. I have financial backers who will gladly step into the shoes of Jimmy Yee to pursue your project. Nothing need change."

"That's certainly good to know," Jonas said, more wary than he let on.

"My intention," Zhang said, "is to put your mind at ease. The details can be discussed later."

"Good," Jonas said. He sipped his tea. "Mr. Zhang, you're obviously well connected. Do you have any idea who was behind the attack on Jimmy's yacht?"

"The authorities believe foreign interests."

"What foreign interests?"

"At this point, it is uncertain."

"Arabs maybe?"

"Quite possibly." Zhang drank from his cup. "Do you yourself have information that may be of use, Mr. Lamb?"

"Over the past few weeks the Chinese and Arabs seemed to be fighting over me."

"With the FBI observing."

Jonas's brows rose. "You know about that?"

"As you noted, Mr. Lamb, I am well connected."

"Can I assume you're willing to help me get Tess home?"

"Indeed."

"As far as I'm concerned, the sooner the better," Jonas said, shivering from the cold. "My concern is knowing who I can rely on. To be perfectly honest, I don't know if I can trust my own government, much less the authorities here."

"I understand. May I suggest that it is possible to leave Hong Kong discreetly, with no fuss and fanfare, and that if such is your wish, it can be arranged."

"Mr. Zhang, you're well on your way to becoming my new best friend."

The man seemed amused by the remark and drank from his cup. "Now I should leave you to rest, Mr. Lamb. I know the accommodations here are humble and we would like to make other arrangements, but we are told Mrs. Vartel should not be moved for the moment. There is more comfortable lodging nearby. In the morning you will be taken there. Meanwhile guards have been posted. You will be safe here."

"You are very generous, Mr. Zhang."

"You are a very important man, Mr. Lamb."

Solano County

Kristy Ogawa's parents were out of town, so the U.C. Davis cell of Save the Seeds met for the second time that day just minutes from the fishing boat in the Ogawa's oak-paneled family room. There were glum faces all around.

"I think we're being set up," Roger said. He'd been wringing his hands nervously since they'd arrived.

Tina, who'd briefed them on her conversation with Carly, checked the faces. Brad seemed solemn, K.J. pissed, Kristy confused. Tina had a feeling Carly had been straight with her, though she couldn't explain how she'd found out about Robo and Baby Cakes.

"If she's involved with the police," Brad said, "coming out with it like that is a strange way to behave."

"She might have been hoping I'd let something slip," Tina replied.

"How did she know we're students?" Kristy asked. "And if she knows about the Berkeley Seeds, how long before the police knock on our door?"

"They already knocked on your door," K.J. intoned. "And thinking we're students is logical. How many possibilities are there? I agree, it was some kind of trick or bluff."

"So, what do we do?" Tina asked.

"I think we continue according to plan," K.J. replied.

"Hey, man," Roger said, clearly distressed, "they're closing in on us. Even if the woman's not working with the police, they can't be far behind. I say we take the money and let Mayne go."

"You know what your problem is, Roger? You don't have any guts. If they had the goods on us, they wouldn't be dropping hints over the phone."

The others looked at Brad, who despite K.J.'s heroics, remained the senior member of the group. He rubbed his chin thoughtfully and said, "We don't have to decide right now. I think we press ahead negotiating the ransom and working on the publicity side."

"And pretend this didn't happen?" Tina said.

"No, I agree we can't waste time. Tina, you deal with the professor and this friend of his. Call her and tell her a million in cash, all hundreds. Let's give her a tentative date for the trade. Tell her Wednesday. We'll provide the details for the exchange later. And if she jerks your chain, hang up. Okay?"

Nobody commented. Tina hadn't said anything about Mayne's claim he was working on a secret ethanol project, figuring it would only confuse things, but she had told them about his parents being killed and Carly saying other people would be putting up the money. Some of them thought it was fishy, others considered it proof that Mayne was serving corporate interests. She'd told the professor the news about his parents because it seemed the only decent thing to do. Of course he hadn't believed her, insisting they wouldn't have left the country knowing he'd been kidnapped. "If it's not true, how would I have known they'd gone to Hong Kong?" she'd asked. "You're sure?" he'd replied. "Carly told you?" She told him yes, that's what Carly had said.

The mood in the group wasn't the best as the meeting broke up. Tina rode back to the fishing boat with Brad. The sky to the south and west was dark. A big winter storm was supposed to hit that afternoon and already a few raindrops were falling.

They'd reached the levee and parked. As they got out of the car, Tina said to Brad, "We have another option. We can issue a big statement, then let Mayne go and forget the ransom. That's the dangerous part, anyway."

"I know," Brad replied. "The thought's occurred to me, but let's hang tight for a while and see what happens."

It was sprinkling more heavily as they went aboard the fishing boat. Once they were below, Tina took off her jacket and put on her ski mask. She went into Patrick Mayne's makeshift cell. "How you doing?"

The professor peered up at her, red-eyed. He looked miserable and it made her feel terrible.

"This is the worst day of my life."

"I'm totally sorry about your parents."

"You don't even know the worst. They were in Hong Kong on my behalf. It should have been me that got killed. My mother in particular is completely innocent."

Tina sat in the chair. "You can't blame yourself for things over which you have no control."

Mayne seemed appreciative. "You're pretty soft-hearted for a terrorist."

"You may not believe this, Professor Mayne, but I'm doing this because I love life. *All* life. That's why I'm against the things you do."

He shook his head, looking sad. "If you only knew."

"What do you mean?"

"I hope I'm wrong, but someday you and your friends might look back on today and realize that by turning me down you'd done more to harm the environment than all the good you could do in a thousand lifetimes. I mean that sincerely."

Tina stared at him, hating it that she believed him. "Can I ask you something, Professor?" she said after several moments. "What's your relationship with Carly?"

"She's a friend."

"Do you trust her?"

He seemed taken aback by the question. "I don't have any reason not to, why?"

"Is there any chance she could be working for the police?"

"Not that I know of. No, I'm sure not. Did she say something to make you think that?"

Tina shrugged. "I was just wondering if she could be deceiving you as well as us."

She left the room and found Brad sitting on a straight chair a few steps from the door, reading a magazine. "That took long enough," he said, glancing up.

"I've got to go home," she said. "Would you mind finishing the watch alone?"

"Aren't you going to call the woman?"

"Yeah, later. I'll let you know what happens."

Davis, California

Their plan was to meet at a pizza parlor on Third Street. They'd talked earlier, and after Carly had told him about her conversation with the kidnapper, her reaction to the mention of Robo and Baby Cakes, Gaston had agreed with Carly's assessment that they were dealing with students. "I think we need to sit down and talk face-to-face," he'd said. "Shall we make it a student hangout?"

Gaston, in his jaunty beret, was seated in a back corner booth, a nearly empty mug of beer before him when she arrived. He was chatting with a waiter who was decidedly gay. The kid looked surprised when Carly took off her wet trench coat and slid into the booth across from Gaston. He promptly drifted away.

"I've forgotten the joys of college life," Gaston said to her, looking after the kid. "I wonder if MIT would grant me readmission."

"You want to go back to school?"

"A change of pace might be nice after years of murder and mayhem. Maybe I could become a professor. After all, I've been tutoring tender young boys in the ways of life for years. It's not like I don't have qualifications."

"Gaston, you'll end up in jail yet. All that remains to be seen is for what."

He reached over and covered her hand, giving it a squeeze. "Let's hope for something worthwhile, eh, *chérie?* Speaking of worthwhile endeavors, I've got a plan to track down our girl. Our friends, Messrs. August and Bardic, *agents de police,* have, through the wonders of technology, provided me with the names, addresses and phone numbers of twenty-seven female students who are arson suspects. After eliminating three foreign students, plus a girl who's in jail, one in the hospital and two who are out of the country, I've got twenty female candidates for us to choose from."

"We can't conduct a surveillance of twenty girls, not in the short time available."

Gaston drained the last of his beer. "Quite right, my love. But you've spoken with the young lady, you know her voice, *n'est-ce pas?* All you have to do is ring up our twenty possibles and chat them up. One is likely to be our girl."

"Very clever, Gaston. So very simple. How did I not think of that?"

"A mark of genius is the ability to think outside the box. Your talents, as Monsieur Mayne can attest, lie elsewhere." Gaston wore a guilty grin. "Which, in your case, is to say *inside* the box."

"Very funny."

Gaston threw back his head and laughed. "I always felt my best professors were the ones with a sense of humor," he said, thoroughly amused. Then, his expression growing sober, he added, "Actually, I think I will ring up MIT and ask about my prospects."

"You do that, Gaston. Meanwhile, how are things going with the ransom?"

"The cash is ready and waiting. I take it you still haven't gotten instructions from the student body."

"Correct."

"Let's hope you do shortly. Our patrons in Texas are eager for good news and Le Genissel is home from the hunt and hungry for results."

"I suppose there isn't much chance he'll lay low and let us handle this."

"When pigs fly."

"That's what I was afraid of. Is he giddy with joy for having killed a bunch of relatively innocent people?"

"Carly," he said, his look stern, "are you losing your edge?"

"No, I'm frustrated and bored."

"*Alors,* gird yourself, my love. I have a hunch things are about to start popping. And don't forget this, we're still collecting a double fee. The first order of business is to find our girl. So get your sweet little ass home and get to work."

TUESDAY
January 29

Peng Chau, Hong Kong

The home, situated on one the island's more prominent hills, was sumptuous. Jonas stood on the terrace, staring at the view and sipping his coffee. It had been served by the houseboy, who was poised to spring into action at the first indication of need. For the moment Jonas was content taking in the view, which featured the skyline of Hong Kong some eight miles in the distance, a jewel sparkling in the mid-morning sun.

The air was crisp but calm and the sun warm. Their hosts had done everything within their power to make them feel safe and comfortable, which added intrigue to the unreality of the situation. The ways of the Orient were, indeed, mysterious.

Jonas had been shaken awake that morning by a young girl. She'd given him a cup of warm tea and let him make his way to the adjoining room, where he'd found Tess in much better condition than the night before. The doctor had arrived shortly thereafter and pronounced Tess fit, though weak. Arrangements were made to move them to "more suitable accommodations."

Soon an entourage arrived including bearers who, under the doctor's supervision, loaded Tess onto a litter. She was carried up the twisting lane to the big modern house at the top of the hill with Jonas walking at her side, the complement of attendants and armed guards in their party making quite a procession, one silently observed by mute villagers standing at their garden gates with reverence on their faces, as though they were being treated to a visit by royalty.

"You must admit," Jonas said to her after she'd remarked on the older people bowing as they passed, "that life with me can be exotic."

"You've become a master of understatement, Jonas."

"Be honest, with Walter nothing like this would have happened in a million years."

"Are you suggesting that's bad?"

"The trip has had its low points, I grant you," he conceded, "but don't you feel really vibrant and alive?"

"Well, I'm not dead, but mostly out of dumb luck."

"And my stalwart valor."

"Yeah," she said, taking his hand, "a little of that, too."

The owner of the house never appeared. But the place was well supplied with servants.

The first thing they'd done was bathe. Tess was delighted to find that their things had been brought from their hotel, which meant her own toiletries and clothes. Jonas also felt more himself in his own pants and shirt.

"This is almost too good to be true," Tess had remarked, as they were being served an English-style breakfast of fried tomatoes, sausages, eggs, toast and marmalade.

"A new twist on the American plan."

Tess still felt weak, so after breakfast she rested, leaving Jonas to explore. He tried to question the staff, but they seemed to lose their English whenever his objective was to elicit meaningful information. He came to the conclusion that no one lived in the house on a permanent basis. It reminded him of the fancy homes corporations provided visiting executives and big-shot customers. He wondered if it might have belonged to Jimmy Yee.

With Tess resting, Jonas took the opportunity to evaluate their situation. One concern was that with officialdom having concluded they were dead, word to that effect would eventually make its way home. There were certain advantages to that (the fact that people were less likely to feel the need to kill you, being chief among them). But there were also disavantages—most prominently putting Patrick through the trauma of thinking he'd lost his parents.

After weighing the pros and cons, Jonas decided it might be worthwhile to give the kid a call, but he soon found that none of the telephones in the house worked. When he inquired of the staff, their language skills promptly deserted them. Jonas decided to defer the matter until someone with authority put in an appearance. Just when that might prove to be he did not know.

"Quite a view," Tess said, coming up behind him. She had on a light gray turtleneck sweater, charcoal wool pants and sunglasses, her hair swept back, making him think of Audrey Hepburn in one of those wonderful old flicks from the fifties and sixties.

"And it's just for you, sweetheart," he said, putting an arm around her. "How do you feel?"

"Much better, thanks. Ready to go home."

"And cut our fun trip short?"

"Somebody already tried that," she replied.

"Yeah, probably somebody who wanted to spare us the ordeal of that deposition. The world abounds with altruism."

"I guess that man hasn't come back yet."

"Mr. Zhang? No, not yet. I wouldn't mind it if he'd put in an appearance, though. This is starting to feel a bit like house arrest. But, considering we owe them a debt of gratitude, it's hard to complain."

"I've been worrying about Patrick," Tess said.

"Yeah, me, too. I even tried calling him, but the phones don't work."

"That's strange."

"Maybe they're afraid we'll shoot ourselves in the foot," he said. "And maybe not without cause. So far I've attracted more bullets than investment dollars."

"It's not your fault, Jonas."

They looked out at the view, their arms around

each other. There was a fair amount of shipping traffic in the channel—a couple of large freighters and a myriad of smaller craft, including ferries, sailboats, motor yachts, junks and fishing boats. One boat in particular was holding steady to a course that would bring it to Peng Chau. When it was a quarter of a mile or so offshore, Jonas pointed it out.

Earlier he had spotted a pair of binoculars on a table inside the house, so he went and got them. The boat was almost ashore at a point near where they'd stayed the night before. He checked out the craft through the glasses.

"What do you suppose P-O-L-I-C-E means in Chinese?" he muttered under his breath.

"Mafia, maybe?"

"You never know."

Jonas handed her the glasses and Tess peered down at the boat, which was in the process of docking.

"There's an older man in a hat and topcoat getting off," she said. "Could it be Mr. Zhang?"

Jonas took the binoculars and focused on the dignified figure making his way across the boarding ladder. He was accompanied by two men in civilian clothes. Uniformed officers remained on the boat. "That's our boy."

"Good. Maybe he has word from Patrick."

Jonas watched Zhang Jintao get into a small automobile that arrived at the dock moments earlier. "No question the guy's got clout." The car promptly made its way up the twisting street they'd ascended that morning. "Let's go inside, sweetheart."

They'd been installed on the comfortable sofa in the front room just long enough for the servants to bring Tess a cup of coffee and refill Jonas's cup when they heard the front door open. Zhang, his hat in hand just as before, appeared moments later.

Jonas got to his feet, waiting for a servant to help him remove his topcoat and take the coat and hat away. They shook hands after perfunctory bows.

"Good morning, Mr. Lamb. Good to see you looking well."

Jonas introduced him to Tess. She leaned forward and shook his hand. "Mr. Zhang."

"You look in fine form, as well, Mrs. Vartel," Zhang said. "Better, I'm told, than your condition last night. I trust the accommodations here are an improvement."

"Very nice," Tess replied. "We are most grateful for the care and hospitality."

"We are most happy to serve you," Zhang said, bowing.

Jonas invited him to sit. "Care for coffee or tea?"

"No, thank you. Coffee is too hard on my delicate stomach and I've had my tea."

"I don't mean to be pushy," Tess said, "but Jonas and I are eager for news, especially of our son, Patrick. I don't suppose you've heard from him."

"No, Mrs. Vartel, I'm sorry to say I haven't any news about your son."

"I'd like to call him and tell him his father and I are fine. I imagine word of the attack on Mr. Yee's boat has gotten back to the States."

"Quite possibly, but because of the obvious danger you face, I'm afraid I must advise caution. Perhaps we can work something out soon, however."

"We noticed you arrived in a police boat," Jonas said. "Are the authorities aware we survived the attack?"

"Certain key officials are, yes, but it's being kept confidential for your safety."

"Any more news on who's responsible?" Jonas asked.

"Some," Zhang replied. "The authorities think they've identified the assailants. The freighter involved is of Russian registry, the craft possibly commandeered. It was found in Macao this morning, the Russian crew dead. Murdered execution-style. As I indicated last night, foreign nationals are believed responsible."

"Russians?"

"No, as we speculated, Arab. Five mercenaries bearing false passports from various Middle Eastern countries have entered Hong Kong over the past couple of days. The police believe that a rather notorious gentleman of Lebanese and French descent was the ringleader."

"You're saying we were attacked by Arab terrorists?" Tess said.

"Not terrorists, soldiers of fortune, though relationships in the Middle East, as you may know, can be complicated and the line gets fuzzy. The police believe the man in charge was Alfred Le Genissel, a well-known figure they call the Gazelle."

Tess shivered and Jonas rubbed her back.

"There are few pictures of Mr. Le Genissel," Zhang said, "but we do have a couple taken recently. They're not very good, unfortunately." He slipped his hand under his coat and drew out two glossy photos from his inside pocket. He handed one across the table. "This was taken two days ago at the airport. It's from a surveillance video." He handed over the second. "And this was taken near San Francisco."

Jonas studied the photo of a man walking down a driveway, the house behind him familiar. "Hey, this looks like my place in Marin. I should say, Elise's place."

"Yes," Zhang said, "my understanding is it was taken after an unauthorized entry."

Both he and Tess studied the photos. From what he could make out, the man did not look familiar, though they could have ridden in the same elevator and Jonas wouldn't have noticed.

"This is the man who tried to kill us," Tess said, shivering again.

"That's what the authorities believe. You may keep those, if you wish."

Jonas handed them to Tess. "For the family album."

She gave him a look of disapproval.

Zhang said, "And now, with your permission, perhaps we can discuss business. I'm sure the subject remains most difficult, but I believe it's safe to say we are both concerned about the future and are under some pressure. My clients, those who, as I indicated last night, wish to step into the shoes of Yee Jiechi, Jimmy Yee.

"Allow me to be direct," Zhang continued. "Your company's discovery is of utmost importance to the world. My clients propose that you be given long-term accommodations here, so your safety can be assured. They propose further to bring your son to Hong Kong to join you. He will be provided the most modern research facilities available to continue his work. This, of course, will be at no cost to you. Once all the parties are satisfied with the results of the discovery, an international enterprise will be formed with your family holding key positions. Profits are to be divided on a scale to be negotiated. This is the offer my clients wish for you to consider."

"Your unnamed clients."

"For the moment, Mr. Lamb. I believe this proposal is substantially in accordance with the deal you hoped to make with Jimmy Yee. May I assume that this meets with your approval, provided profit-sharing percentages can be agreed upon?"

Jonas and Tess glanced at each other. "I think I can speak for the entire family in saying that we are interested in pursuing an agreement," he told Zhang. "Naturally, we'd like to know just who we're dealing with. But, as you say, that will all come out in good time. I'm not sure, though, that it's best for us to stay in Hong Kong. Tess is eager to get home and we both want to see our son and confer with him."

"Our principal concern is security."

"I understand that. It's ours, as well. You've been most generous, but if you wish to do more, we'd prefer you help us get home safely. What we hoped to accomplish on this trip was to get a preliminary commitment from Jimmy, so that we could proceed at full tilt. Since that's no longer possible, I think it's best if we regroup."

"Are you saying you don't wish to do business with my clients?"

"No, to the contrary, our objective would be to sit down with them sometime in the very near future and work out a deal."

Zhang nodded, seeming pleased. "Your desires are understandable, Mr. Lamb. What sort of time frame do you have in mind?"

"Long enough to pull ourselves together. Maybe just a few days."

"That's certainly reasonable," Zhang said, inclining his head deferentially. "And I'm sure we can provide all the assistance you need."

"Thank you."

"When might we leave?" Tess asked.

"If you're feeling up to it," Zhang replied. "The first available flight."

Davis, California

The previous evening, after leaving Gaston with his pizza and beer, Carly had installed herself at Patrick Mayne's kitchen table, where she'd made twelve calls, though she'd only spoken to four of the girls on Gaston's list. No winners. Of the other nine, five were no answers and in three instances she got answering machines. None of the voices on the machines was familiar, but in one case the machine gave more than one name, meaning the recording could have been made by a roommate. The task was more challenging than Carly expected.

When it got too late to continue with her calling, she'd quit for the night.

Once again she'd awakened before dawn. She had breakfast, then got cleaned up and dressed. It was too early to make any calls, so she killed time looking through the books in Patrick's library. His tastes were eclectic, and he clearly liked to read, as did she. Antoine was not a reader, apart from the daily newspaper, which was an addiction of every Frenchman.

When the time came, Carly started by calling those girls she'd been unable to reach the previous night. On her thirteenth call—lucky thirteen—Carly got the answering machine of a girl named Tina Richter. "Hi," the machine said, "Tina's either in the tub or in class and can't speak with you now, but she'd like to hear your message." Then a beep. There was no doubt. Carly'd hit the jackpot. It was the kidnapper.

She decided to inform Gaston.

"I've got our girl," she told him. "Just listened to a voice on the answering machine. It's definitely her."

"Excellent! Bravo! Who's the lucky lady?"

"Her name's Tina Richter."

"Hang on, checking my list. I'm at my computer." After a few moments… "Yes, here she is. A senior from Santa Monica. *Magnifique!*"

"What now, Gaston?"

"We have two choices. Violence or finesse. We either storm the barricades or we use our knowledge to force a deal."

"You mean we pay the ransom?"

"Why not? It's Texas oil money. It's not coming out of our pockets."

The phone on the house line rang just then. "I've got another call."

"Okay," Gaston said, "unless there are urgent developments, we'll speak later."

Carly went and answered the phone.

"It's me," the kidnapper said. "I tried calling last night, but all I got was the answering machine. I thought maybe you went out to dinner."

Carly was struck by the irony of the call coming on the heels of her conversation with Gaston. "I did go out for a while."

"Well, we've connected now. Do you have the money ready? We'll swap Mayne for a million on Wednesday. All hundred-dollar bills."

"Okay, how do we do it?"

"How about if I call you back with the specifics?"

"Okay. How's Patrick?"

"He took his parents' death pretty hard."

"Who wouldn't?"

Tina hesitated, then said, "You and the professor are more than friends, aren't you? You're lovers."

"Did Patrick tell you that?"

"I thought so." And she hung up.

Carly thought for a moment. Was it possible the girl had feelings for Patrick? There'd been a hint of jealousy in her voice. It was risky, but Carly knew she had to talk to Tina in person.

***

The girl's flat was the upper floor of an older house on the east side of town. Carly climbed the steps to the covered porch and rang the bell. Not getting a response, she tried again. An older woman with curlers in her hair opened the door to the lower flat.

"If you're looking for Tina, she left about an hour ago," the woman said.

"You wouldn't know when she's likely to be back, would you?"

The woman shook her head. "Don't know her class schedule. Seems to be different every day. You a friend?"

"Of the family," Carly said.

"Well, if you talk to the parents, they ought to know they've got a wild daughter. Always seems like there's some young man up there. The current one yells a lot."

"Do you know his name?"

"Goes by initials. K something. K.J., I think. Or, is it P? No, think it's J. K.J. They smoke marijuana up there, you know. She's a druggie, Tina is. Wonder the police haven't picked her up. If I was her parents, I'd want to know."

"I appreciate the information."

"Try to mind my own business, but kids nowadays—they throw it in your face."

"Thank you," Carly said, and left. As soon as she got back to her car she phoned Gaston. "You have a boy on your list with the initials K.J.? He's probably a student."

"Let me check. *Attends.*"

R.J. Kaiser   569

Carly waited. A couple of minutes passed, then Gaston came back on the line.

"I've got a Kevin Jensen, a Kenneth Jarrett and two kids with K first names and J middle names. Kyle Jerome Zeigler and Kareem Jamal Williams."

"Any of them young?"

"Let's see, Jarrett's nineteen and Zeigler's twenty. Williams is twenty-two and the others are older. Have you found us another suspect, Carly?"

"I'd say Jarrett and Zeigler are good bets."

"How'd you come up with male suspects?"

"I'm resourceful, Gaston. The switch, by the way, is tentatively set for Wednesday. They want all hundred-dollar bills. Tina will call me with the details."

"Excellent!" Gaston effused. "*Parfait!* Carly, I can smell my own Caribbean island."

"Don't start packing yet. These people are skittish. We still have a few hurdles to get over. I'll be in touch."

Mid Pacific

Tess had been dozing through most of the flight and, when she opened her eyes, saw that Jonas was sleeping, too. He looked so handsome and dear. Serene, not troubled in the least. She'd asked him how it was that he was able to be so calm, and he'd smiled and said, "I'm on a roll, sweetheart. I'm with the woman I love and my destiny is at my fingertips. Not even death could get me."

"Don't get too overconfident, Jonas."

"Oh, I'm not. Dame Fortune has bit me in the ass before when everything seemed to be going great.

We could still get blown out of the water by Crystal at the deposition. But it feels different when I'm with you, Tess. However things turn out, I can't lose. At least, that's the way I see it."

She hadn't admonished him for that because she liked his optimism. His upbeat, fun-loving nature—among other things—was what had attracted her to him in the first place. It was amazing how quickly her feelings for him had evolved—not that she was prepared to make any announcements. Encouragement was the last thing Jonas Lamb needed.

Across the aisle from him, immersed in a book, was Mr. Lu, the security specialist Zhang had arranged to accompany them to the States. The plan was for Lu to stay with them until they'd made other arrangements.

Obviously security was a concern, but what troubled her most was Patrick. She'd wanted to call him from the airport, but there wasn't a chance.

Jonas rolled his head toward her, opening his eyes. "You're awake. Get a good rest?"

"I slept quite a bit," she replied, taking his hand. "Jonas, let's call Patrick."

He checked his watch. "Well, I suppose it won't make a lot of difference whether we call now or when we get home. It's midafternoon in California."

Tess took the phone from the seat back in front of her and placed the call. She got his answering machine and hesitated before deciding to leave a message.

"Patrick, honey, don't faint. It's me. Your father and I are fine, in case you've been told otherwise. They tried to kill us, but we survived, the only ones who made it. We're headed home and eager to see you. I don't know if you're in any danger, too, but please be very careful. I love you. Talk to you soon." She turned to Jonas with glistening eyes and said, "That felt wonderful. Thank you."

As soon as he'd seen the item in the CRES log of message intercepts for China, Ted Myers had hand-carried the log downstairs and waited for the full translation. On his way back upstairs to the Office of Asian Pacific and Latin American Analysis of the Directorate of Intelligence, Myers skimmed the document. It was a report from the station chief of the Guoanbu (MSS), Hong Kong, and it was addressed to the Tenth Bureau (Scientific and Technological Information) of the Ministry of State Security in Beijing, and it was hot.

The station chief was reporting that the "Zen Master" would be meeting with Jonas Lamb of Global Energy Technologies in California to hammer out a preliminary agreement for a joint venture to exploit the super-ethanol technology. Myers knew that the "Zen Master" was Zhang Jintao, a highly respected Hong Kong–based consultant who frequently did liaison work with Western business enterprises on behalf of the PRC. Zhang's involvement was noteworthy in itself. But what really got Myers excited was that Zhang was recommending that GET be paid a good-faith deposit in the range of twenty- to twenty-five million for GET's research data on the genetically modified organisms.

Myers did not return to his office, instead going directly to see his section chief, Ken Kellerman. After he briefed Kellerman and showed him the translation of the intercept, Kellerman instructed him to take the document to the President's Analytical Support Staff, saying he was certain it would be in the morning's national security briefing at the White House.

Davis, California

Exiting the freeway in the driving rain, Alfred Le Genissel spotted the motel where the *comte* was holed up and pulled in. He killed the engine and took a deep breath. He was exhausted. He'd flown from Macao to the Philippines to San Francisco, where he'd gotten a rental car. The entire drive up the interstate had been under a torrential rain. To make matters worse, a couple of accidents had slowed things to a standstill.

Le Genissel went into the office and got a room. He was eager to find out if de Malbouzon had made any progress during his absence and decided to talk to the faggot before getting some much-needed sleep. He rapped on de Malbouzon's door.

The Frenchman, wearing a robe and slippers, appeared, his eyes rounding at the sight of him. "Alfred," he said, "what a delightful surprise."

Le Genissel pushed past him and sat on the corner of de Malbouzon's unmade bed. "Well, what has happened? Have you found Mayne?"

De Malbouzon closed the door. "Almost."

"*Almost?*" he said with derision. "In this business, 'almost' is not good enough."

The *comte* cinched his robe. "You'll get him tomorrow. Is that good enough?"

"You have found him, then?"

"We know who has him. Or, more precisely, we know the identity of two of the kidnappers."

"Then why not liberate him now?"

"We've arranged a ransom exchange. A million dollars and he's ours."

Le Genissel frowned. "Where are you getting the money?"

Gaston smoothed his robe as he crossed his legs. "To be perfectly frank, Alfred, I'd hoped *you'd* put it up."

"*Me?*"

"Well, your sheiks. What's a million to them? So much camel piss." ·

Le Genissel, not liking the *comte*'s attitude, gave him a dark look. "Ransom is a waste of time," he said. "If you know who the kidnappers are, I will get Mayne with much less trouble and far less expense."

"But, Alfred, everything is arranged. This is much cleaner. Don't forget, freeing Mayne is only the first step. Carly has to work her magic on the dear boy."

"We don't have time for that. My clients tell me that governments around the globe are focusing on this, which means our window of opportunity is closing."

"What do you propose to do? Beat the data out of him?"

"If necessary."

De Malbouzon took the water glass of wine from the table next to him and took a slug. "Alfred, with all due respect, this is the phase of the operation where *our* expertise is critical. Please leave the matter in Carly's capable hands. The best thing you could do is get your chaps to write a check and have a satchel filled with hundreds ready for me by tomorrow."

"Who are the kidnappers?"

"Students."

"You have names, addresses?"

Gaston de Malbouzon looked uneasy. "Alfred—"

"Dammit, de Malbouzon, do not argue with me, eh? I am in no mood for your French faggot bullshit. Tell me the names."

The *comte* put down his glass, his expression dour. "All right. You're the boss. We'll do it your way."

"*Merci.*"

"I've got two boys whom we've identified by their initials. We believe it's one of the two, but we aren't sure which. Kenneth Jarrett is one. Kyle Jerome Zeigler is the other. Carly's trying to track down a second kidnapper, a girl."

"Name?"

"We aren't that far with her."

"My brain is numb," Le Genissel said. "Write down those names and addresses."

Gaston went to his blinking computer and, after consulting it, jotted the information on a slip of paper. After Le Genissel snatched it from his hand, the Frenchman cinched the belt of his robe tighter still.

"Is there anything else, *mon capitaine?*"

"A piece of ass and a bottle of wine would be nice. But that's more Carly's department."

"Get some sleep, Alfred."

The Gazelle didn't reply. He walked out of the room. Sleep did beckon, but he was inclined to pay Carly a visit first. If nothing else, it would be interesting to see if she gave him the same story as de Malbouzon.

Carly left the Holiday Cinema on F Street in the pouring rain, having spent the evening far from the madding crowd, though Bathsheba Everdene she was not, even if she felt a bit like her.

Her umbrella doing little more than keeping her head dry, Carly walked up the sidewalk, the wind blowing against her so hard she felt as though at any moment she might be carried away. People were saying it was the worst storm in years.

Over the sound and fury, Carly heard her cell phone ring. She stepped into a storefront entry for protection from the elements and dug out the phone. It was Gaston.

"*Mon Dieu!* Where are you, love? You sound like you're in a wind tunnel."

"I am. And I'm getting soaked. What do you want?"

"Just to give you a heads-up. Our conquering hero, Muhammad, is home from Mecca, but there's still blood in his eye. And he may have a hard-on to boot. Quite literally. Be careful, *chérie,* I fear he's headed your way."

"Thanks for the warning."

"Any further news from our student rebel friends?"

"No, but I haven't been home for a while."

"Just so you know, I told the Gazelle we were springing Mayne tomorrow. He pressed me for details, but all

I gave him was the names of the two boys. I thought that might keep him busy while you deal with the girl."

"But you didn't tell him her name?"

"No, I waffled, said you were working on it."

"Good."

"Carly, Le Genissel really has a bug up his ass. He's against our plan to pay the ransom and his inclination is to resolve this thing cowboy-style. I wouldn't care except, of course, our Texan employers are expecting a somewhat different outcome."

"This comes with being greedy, Gaston. You burned our candle at both ends."

"Perhaps you're right. God may yet turn me into a pillar of salt."

She laughed. "Let's hope not until you've paid the help. When and where do I get the million for the ransom? I expect to talk to Tina this evening and I want to be prepared."

"Come and see me first thing in the morning."

"D'accord."

Alfred Le Genissel was so numb with fatigue that he felt sick to his stomach, yet the compulsion to see her was so strong he couldn't resist. The humiliation he'd suffered in Paris when she'd rebuffed him had been eating at his heart. The incident in the San Francisco restaurant and his last visit to Davis had made him all the more determined to put her in her place.

Carly and the faggot had served their purpose and Mayne was all but in his grasp. Once he had the professor, he would get what he needed from him, his own way. As regards to Carly, what mattered now was that he redeem his honor, bend her to his will.

Le Genissel cruised slowly down the street where Patrick Mayne lived, alert for signs of surveillance. The lights of the house were off, which meant she probably wasn't home. It was too early for her to be in bed, though if she were, the thought of confronting her there appealed to him greatly.

The Gazelle got out the key he'd copied from the one he'd found above the back door. Entering the house, he did not turn on the lights, first checking the bedroom to confirm she wasn't there. No sign of her. But he did see a blinking red light. The answering machine. There was a message. He pushed the button.

"Patrick, honey, don't faint," the woman's voice said. "It's me. Your father and I are fine, in case you've been told otherwise. They tried to kill us, but we survived, the only ones who made it. We're headed home and eager to see you. I don't know if you're in any danger, too, but please be very careful. I love you. Talk to you soon."

Le Genissel was stunned. How was this possible? He slumped onto the bed where he sat with his head in his hands. After a couple of minutes, he pressed the erase button on the answering machine. There was no need to advertise his failure to the world. There was no denying the fact, though. He had himself another problem.

Carly decided to pay her return visit to Tina Richter and get it over with. This time she parked right in front and ran up the steps to the relative protection of the covered porch. Wiping her wet face, she rang the bell.

She'd rung the bell for the third time before a light finally went on in the stairwell inside the glass door. A moment later Tina came down the stairs, though it was hard for Carly to see what she looked like through the sheer curtains.

Peeking out to see who was there, Tina, dark haired and pretty, looking more the college girl than terrorist or kidnapper, opened the door a crack. "Yeah? Can I help you?"

"Tina, I'm Patrick's friend, Carly. We need to talk."

The girl, her eyes as big as goose eggs—it was one of Antoine's expressions—was in shock. "H-how did you find me?" she stammered.

"It wasn't easy. Can I come in?"

Tina seemed uncertain what to say. Her expression indicated she was more inclined to slam the door shut and run upstairs.

"Look," Carly said, "if I was working with the police, you'd already be under arrest."

That seemed to convince her and she opened the door, resignation on her face. Tina, in fluffy slippers, a pair of tight-fitting jeans and a sweater, trudged back upstairs and Carly followed. Once in her flat, Tina plopped in a chair. Carly glanced around the small, eclectic apartment, noticing the distinctive smell of pot. She saw smoke from a pencil-thin reefer curl up from the ashtray on the makeshift coffee table.

"Take off your coat and make yourself at home,"

the girl said. She watched Carly remove her trench coat and lay it over a straight chair. "If I didn't know better I'd say I'm hallucinating."

"You're not hallucinating, Tina."

As Carly sat down, the girl looked her over. "I didn't think you'd be so pretty."

"Thank you, I guess." Carly wore a pink cashmere sweater and gray wool skirt. She crossed her legs.

"Want some weed?" Tina asked, indicating the joint.

"No thanks, I'm working."

"Then I'll finish it, if you don't mind. I need it." After taking a hit, she put the jay back in the ashtray. "So if you're not a cop and you're not working with them, what's your angle?"

"I want Patrick freed, and I'm going to make it really simple. I get Patrick and you get a million bucks. You can be a hero to the rest of the gang. Easy money, Tina."

The girl shook her head. "Maybe it's the Dona Juana, but this isn't making a lot of sense. You've got me, so you could get Patrick for free, probably."

"Yeah, if I involved the police or put a gun to your head. You already know we don't want publicity. And the less messy this is, the better for everybody. So, where is he, Tina?"

"I can't tell you. That's all the leverage I've got."

"Look, don't fuck with me," Carly said, getting annoyed. "I might look soft, but believe me, I could nail your ass to the wall in three seconds flat."

The girl turned white. "He's half an hour or so from here, all right?"

"Is he guarded?"

"Yes, around the clock by two people at a time. We take turns." She took a drag.

"Then we'll have one other person minimum to deal with. When's your next watch?"

"Tomorrow night," Tina said, letting the smoke stream from her nostrils.

"You drive there alone or together?"

"Usually together. Tomorrow I've got K.J. He's the hard-ass of the group. He's just nineteen, but he's got balls."

"I'm sure I can handle him. Arrange to go separately. You and I'll make the trip together."

A sudden gust of wind blew the rain hard against the window, making them both turn with a start.

"What about the money?" Tina asked.

"I'll have it with me. When we get to where we're going, the money stays with you and Patrick goes with me. Clean and simple."

"Almost too good to be true," Tina said, giving a little laugh.

"Not if you play it straight. Be warned, though, I'm not someone you want to fuck with. If you double-cross me, you'll regret it to the day you die."

Tina picked up the toke, studying her through the stream of smoke.

"I'm going to call you in the morning," Carly said, "and we'll talk. Hopefully you'll have your head on straight. But just so you don't get any funny ideas, you might as well know my associates will be watching your apartment all through the night. We really don't want to involve the cops, but if you fuck me over, I'll see that you're put away until you're an old lady with menopause. It's a long time to go without cock."

Carly arrived at Patrick's place soaked from the knees down and the neck up. Eager as she was to get out of the rain, she didn't relish entering the dark house. Not after Gaston's warning.

With the front door closed and locked behind her, she breathed a bit more easily. Even so she checked the back door to make sure it was secure, then checked each room. Satisfied everything was intact, she took her dripping trench coat into the bathroom and hung it over the shower rod. Then she took off her skirt and sweater, laying them across the toilet seat.

Carly looked at her wet hair in the mirror, the corkscrew curls making her think of a remark Antoine once made during a skin-diving vacation in Greece. They'd come out of the water and dropped down on the rocky beach when Antoine reached out and, touching her wet curls, said, "Just like Medusa, you can turn my cock to stone." Antoine had been amazingly literate for a man without a formal education.

Carly peed, dried her hair with the blower and brushed her teeth. Then, wearing nothing but her bra and panties, went to the bedroom for her robe. When she turned on the light, she saw Alfred Le Genissel sitting propped up on the bed. She was so startled she gave a little scream and fell against the door.

"Goddamn it, Alfred, why do you keep doing that?"

"Because I can," he said, looking over her half-naked body. "I am tired of your disdain, by the way. I am still the boss. You owe me respect."

Carly stomped over to the closet, choosing to be fearless rather than frightened, and got her robe. When she'd cinched it good and tight at the waist, she said, "You could still call first like every other civilized human being."

"Where have you been?"

"Taking care of business, believe it or not."

"Be more specific."

"No. You pay for results, not a minute-by-minute accounting of what we do."

"Why do you insist on using that tone with me? A woman must be more gentle. Have you no manners?"

He got up from the bed, took off his jacket and tossed it aside. Carly wasn't sure what he had in mind but, judging from his sardonic smile, her trepidation amused him.

"Tell me about your results," he said. "When can I expect to see Mayne free?"

"I hope by tomorrow night."

"You have a plan, do you?" The Gazelle began unbuttoning his shirt.

"Everything's set, and barring unforeseen developments, he'll be safely with me by this time tomorrow."

He pulled his shirttail from his trousers.

"Why are you taking off your shirt?"

"Because that is what I choose to do," he replied, his voice hard with contempt. "What about Mayne's research? How will you put your hands on that?" He unbuckled his belt.

It was obvious what he intended, the only question was whether she could prevent it. He was between her and the door. Her best chance, she decided, was the knife which was under the pillow on the bed. "Once he's free I can go to work on him," she said. "I'm thinking maybe he and I will go away somewhere, give him a chance to recover and me to restore confidence."

"Be quick about it, eh?" Le Genissel kicked off his shoes and lowered his pants, stepping out of them.

"If you think I'm going to have sex with you, Alfred, you're mistaken. I won't."

"I do not recall asking you what you want."

Carly inched closer to the bed and the knife. "If you assault me, how do you expect me to work with you?" she demanded. It was not easy keeping up a brave front, but she did her best not to show fear.

"You fuck anyone else I pay you to fuck. How do you not see it is no different to fuck me? I do not understand this."

"That is work. This is not."

"So?"

"If we're to work together, Alfred, I can't have sex with you. It's that simple."

"What about Antoine?"

"I loved Antoine."

"Perhaps it is too much to expect you to love me. Instead, you will obey me. Take off the robe."

"No. I won't do it."

He took off his shorts. His dark phallus pointed at her like a rapier. "Take it off!" he roared, having lost patience.

"I'm warning you," she said through her teeth, "don't!"

He moved toward her. Carly, her heart pounding so hard it hurt, couldn't decide whether to lunge for the knife or wait until he'd thrown her on the bed. She was strong and had martial arts skills, but she was no match for Le Genissel and she knew it. Her only hope was to catch him by surprise.

Standing before her now, he slipped his finger under the tie of her robe and pulled on it. The robe opened. He was so close that his distinctive scent reached her nostrils. Despite herself, she began to tremble.

"This gains you nothing," she said coldly.

"That is for me to decide, I believe. Now I want to see your breasts. Do you wish to take off the bra, or should I?"

Carly took off the robe and the bra and stood before him, glaring. Le Genissel's mouth bent at the corners. He touched her breast, running his thumb over her nipple.

"That is much more agreeable," he said. "Very nice." When her nub turned hard, he said, "See, you like it."

"It's only friction. A pig could make it hard."

Alfred Le Genissel's eyes flashed and he slapped her sharply with the back of his hand. "Bitch! Get on the bed!"

Carly climbed on the bed and the Gazelle followed. Kneeling beside her, he pulled off her panties. While he was preoccupied, Carly slipped her hand under the pillow and grasped the handle of the knife. His mind focused on sex and his guard down, she caught him by surprise, swinging her leg and bashing him on the side of the head and knocking him to the floor. She sprang from the bed before he could recover, landing with a knee on his chest and the knife blade against his throat. "I warned you, you sonovabitch!" she screamed.

It took several seconds for the shock to wear off before he smiled. "Very good, Carly. You have shamed me. No one has ever done this to me before."

"You overplayed your hand, Alfred. For two cents I'd slit your throat."

"But that would cost you a million dollars, *n'est-ce pas?* Less two cents, of course. That is very much to lose, and for what? The sake of principle? You would fuck a goat if there was enough money. You think I do not know this?" His grin broadened. "What is it going to be? The satisfaction of spiting me or millions of dollars?"

Carly, hating her uncertainty as much as she hated him, eased the pressure of her knee on his chest just a bit, the blade not pressing quite so hard against his throat. In that split second, Le Genissel snatched the wrist of her knife hand and flung her off him. She landed on her shoulder, but he still had her wrist. On his knees now, he ripped the knife from her fingers and flung it across the room. Then he stood, dragging her to her feet and shoving her facedown onto the bed. With his hand at the back of her neck, crushing her face into the mattress, he lowered his face next to her ear and said, "You distracted me with sex and I distracted you with money. That tells the whole story, *n'est-ce pas?*"

Still pinning her to the bed with one hand, he pushed her legs apart with the other. She felt his hard cock against her backside. Then he thrust hard, entering her. Carly gasped as he tore her flesh. Closing her eyes she made her body relax, going limp, hoping it might deny him pleasure and spare her pain.

Le Genissel was quick. After thirty seconds of thrusting, he came. Carly lay motionless on the bed, refusing to move or cry. He gathered his clothing and went to the door.

"The conundrum of the whore," he said before going out. "You chose money as they all do in the end. It is a very old story."

WEDNESDAY
January 30

Davis, California

Kyle Zeigler and Sala Somani liked to screw in the morning to hip-hop music. They were at the fever-pitch of ecstasy, Sala gyrating like an eggbeater, when suddenly she went flying off of him, screaming. Kyle opened his eyes to see her suspended in the air, one leg kicking freely, the other barely touching the futon where they slept.

A dark man with searing eyes had Sala by her pig-tail. A gun with a big silencer was jammed into her neck. "Where the fuck is Mayne?" he shouted. "What have you done with him?"

Kyle's mouth was open, but no words came out. He stammered incoherently.

"If you do not want me to splatter this cunt's brains over the fucking wall, you had better tell me where he is, and do it now!"

"I...I...I...don't know what you're...t-t-talking about," Kyle stuttered.

"Mayne, goddamn it! Where is he? Where are you keeping him?"

"Honest to God, mister, I...I...have no i-i-idea what you're talking about. Please."

"I shall count to three, you bastard, and if I do not get an answer, she is dead. *One...*" Three seconds passed. *"Two..."*

"I swear to Jesus," Kyle cried, his erection going south, "I...I don't know anybody named Mayne. If I did, I'd tell you. Please, for the love of Christ..." He began to sob.

The man barred his teeth.

"Last chance..."

"No, no," Kyle implored. "God, I don't even know what this is about. You must have the wrong person. It's a mistake. Please...please..."

"Shit!" the man shouted, issuing oaths in some foreign language. As Kyle watched, he let go of Sala, who crashed down on him.

Kyle peered over her shoulder at the red-faced man whom he was certain was going to shoot them both. But he didn't. Instead, he strode angrily toward the door, muttering under his breath.

Russian Hill, San Francisco

Mr. Lu, whom Jonas had nicknamed "Groucho" because of his prominent eyebrows, arrived while they were having breakfast.

"Did you get the gun?" Jonas asked.

Lu opened his coat and took the nine millimeter

automatic from his belt, handing it to him. "Do you know how to operate it, Mr. Lamb?"

"When I was in the army I carried an M-16, but I fired a .45 several times."

"This is different. Let me show you."

With Tess standing at the kitchen door watching, Lu gave Jonas a rundown on the weapon, how to unlock the safety, change cartridges and so forth.

"Okay," Jonas said, "thanks."

"You are certain you don't want me to stay with you?" Lu asked.

"Yes, Tess and I discussed it. I just wanted something I could use if somebody breaks down the door. This should do the trick."

Lu shook his head. "Well, it is your life, Mr. Lamb."

Jonas considered the irony of that. It was perhaps the biggest day of his life in some respects and here he was in fear of losing it. Lu had called last night to say that they had information Alfred Le Genissel may have come to San Francisco, though, of course, he had no way of knowing they were still alive. Even so, his proximity was unnerving.

"Thank you for your help, Mr. Lu," Jonas said. "And extend my thanks to Mr. Zhang. If you talk to him, tell him I'll be in touch soon."

"I would be most pleased to convey your message."

Lu bowed and left. Jonas locked the door and put on the security chain. Tess came over to him as he weighed the gun in his hand. She put her head on his shoulder.

"What has our life become, Jonas?"

"Trouble. In the short run, at least. But, being an optimist, the long-term prospects strike me as better."

"I saw the way you were looking at the gun. What were you thinking?"

"About turning in my M-16 before shipping out of Vietnam. I told myself I'd never hold a weapon in my hand again, if I could help it. Now, thirty-five years later, here I am, ready to shoot somebody."

"You didn't ask for this trouble."

"You don't think so? Greed has its own reward, you know."

"Do you consider yourself greedy?"

"I don't know, Tess, but I wonder. I've always played the game hard, though my goal was never to hurt anyone. Maybe it's rationalization, but I've always tried for outcomes where everybody's a winner."

"Is that your intention with Melanie, too?"

Jonas grinned, shaking his head. "Now, there's a woman who could try the patience of a saint."

"I think she's out for blood."

"Yeah, mine," he said, looking at his watch. "You know, it's almost time, sweetheart. We've got a date with destiny."

"Yes, we've got to get ready. But can I ask a favor first?"

"Sure."

"Will you call Patrick? He won't return my calls. Maybe he'll talk to you."

"It's awfully early."

"Maybe you can catch him before he goes out. I'd

just feel better knowing that Le Genissel isn't on his trail, too."

"Okay, if it'll put your mind at ease." Jonas went to the phone and dialed Patrick's number.

A woman answered.

"Carly?"

"Yes?"

"It's Jonas."

She didn't speak, but he pictured the shock on her pretty face.

"Carly?"

"My God, I thought you were dead. The police said you'd died in an accident."

"It wasn't an accident, but we did survive. But I thought you and Patrick knew. Tess called yesterday and left a message on the answering machine. Didn't you get it?"

"Uh, no, we didn't. But Patrick did say the machine hasn't been working right."

"Then I'm the bearer of good tidings, I guess. Can I speak with him?"

Another hesitation. "He's not here, Jonas. But he'll be back this evening. Shall I have him call you?"

"Yeah, but first you might want to tell him we're alive and well."

She laughed. "Good idea."

"So you decided to stay in Davis rather than run the office?"

"Yeah, Patrick said he needed me more here."

"I bet he did," Jonas said, chuckling.

"No, seriously. He's had problems."

"You mean the vandalism at the lab?"

"Yes."

Jonas didn't know whether to challenge her or not. Tess would ask him about it, so he decided to get the skinny. "You know, Carly, we called the university and they said there hadn't been any vandalism. What's going on?"

"Uh, well, that's what Patrick told me. I assumed it was true."

"I see. Well, Tess is eager to speak with him, so please have him call." He hung up and looked at Tess.

"He's still unavailable?" she said.

He nodded, thinking.

Tess said, "Something funny is going on. I think we should drive up there, Jonas."

"Well, let's resolve things with Crystal and Melanie first, then we find out what's up with Patrick. Don't forget, he's got a stake in the deposition, too."

Davis, California

Carly stood outside Gaston's motel room, waiting impatiently for his overnight guest to dress and leave. Finally the kid came out, giving her a bashful grin before slinking off down the hall. She went inside.

The *comte* showed more annoyance than embarrassment. "It would have been nice if you'd called."

She didn't bother replying to his comment. "I don't suppose you have a gun, do you?"

"A gun? I thought you came for the money."

"I'd like both."

"Why a gun, *chérie*? Is there something I should

know?" He studied her. Carly's cheeks colored. Gaston understood. "It's Le Genissel, isn't it? *Le salaud,*" he said with disgust. "The bastard."

"I don't want to hear anything about him writing the checks. *Understand?*"

Gaston put his arms around her. "I'd shoot him myself. Are you all right?"

"I don't want to talk about it, Gaston. But I'll tell you this, the man's crazy and he's going to fuck up this operation. Lamb is alive, by the way. Le Genissel didn't get him, after all. I've decided not to wait until tonight to get Patrick. I'm going to pick up Tina after I leave here. I want it a done deal before Le Genissel figures out what's happening."

"What about the other kidnappers?"

"I'll have Tina call in advance and tell them that she's on her way and that they should leave. She'll do whatever I tell her. Just get me the money."

He went to the closet. "You ever seen a million in cash?"

"No."

"I hadn't, either. What surprised me most was how heavy it is. They brought it in this little suitcase with wheels."

He rolled it out. Carly opened the case and checked a couple of the packs of bills, rifling through them. Then she zipped it closed.

Taking the handle, she said, "Well, I'm off. Wish me luck." She went to the door where she paused. "Gaston, if Alfred should contact you, will you give him a message, please?"

He looked uncertain. "Sure."

"Tell him he knows his whores."

The Financial District, San Francisco

They entered the coffee shop on Kearny Street at 9:00 a.m. Crystal was sitting in a rear corner booth, wearing a canary-yellow knit suit and a sullen expression. She was alone, a mug of coffee in front of her.

"I hope you know what you're doing," Jonas said out of the corner of his mouth.

"Trust me," Tess replied, "I do."

They'd had a hell of a time tracking her down. After that last traumatic scene at the hospital, Crystal had gone into hiding. They'd finally gotten word to her through her attorney, requesting a face-to-face meeting before the deposition. Tess had spoken to her. It had taken fifteen minutes of cajoling and solemn promises there'd be no arm-twisting.

As they approached the booth, Crystal scarcely made eye contact with him—not a good sign. She did reward Tess with a small smile, however (the sisterhood of Jonas Lamb's women?)—not a bad sign. Naturally Tess said the right thing, which, after all, was to be expected, considering she was a woman.

"How's Bob?"

"Doing much better, thanks. They moved him out of intensive care. Yesterday, he got out of bed for the first time. He's grumpy, which the doctor says is the surest sign he's getting better." She laughed, clearly elated.

"Wonderful!" Tess said. "I'm so happy for you. The last few days must have been hell."

"God, were they ever. I really thought I'd lost him." Crystal beamed. "But I haven't." She held up her hand. A diamond twinkled on her ring finger. "The first full sentence he said to me was 'Will you marry me?' Can you believe it? The stinker already had the ring. He sent me over to his place to get it." She rolled her eyes. "It was in his underwear drawer."

Jonas signaled the waitress for two coffees as Tess took Crystal's hand for a closer look at her ring. "Crystal, it's beautiful! You must be so thrilled."

"I am. I couldn't believe it." She studied the ring herself. "I think I'm going to exchange it for an emerald cut, though. I really prefer emerald cut. Or princess cut. And maybe a little bigger. I mean, he *can* afford it, right?"

"How exciting! I'm so pleased for you!"

The women beamed at each other like a couple of giddy schoolgirls.

Jonas, who'd taken it all in, had a sudden insight that explained everything (or at least the huge gaps in his understanding of the female mind). When it came to their emotional lives, women were perfectly content with each other. Men were superfluous except to the extent they made women feel *wanted*. That was a man's function in a woman's life—that and maybe to impregnate her and to bring home some bacon. But another woman's compassion, support and understanding were the essential nutrients of life. Everything else was gravy.

The other side of the coin he'd understood for ages. A woman's purpose in a man's life (apart from sex and food) was to make him feel *needed*. A woman lived to be wanted and a man lived to be needed. It was the yin and yang of human psychology. It also explained why men concentrated on *doing* things while women concentrated on *feeling* things. *Jesus,* he thought, *I'm ready to go off to the mountain.*

Then they both looked at him.

He ventured a sheepish grin and said, "Gee, Crystal, I'm happy for you. Congratulations!"

She accepted that, but didn't trust it. Why should she? Men, Jonas included, were wanters, not feelers, and at last report he wanted to be king of the world. Thankfully, Tess stepped into the breach.

"It's very considerate of you to meet with us, Crystal," she said. "I know this is a very difficult day for you."

The waitress arrived with their coffees. After confirming they didn't want anything else, she warmed Crystal's cup and left.

"I hate to see Jonas get screwed," Crystal said, "but I don't see that I have any choice, especially after what happened to Bob. I mean, it's things like that that teach you what really matters in life, right?"

Jonas felt his gut sink right to the floor.

"I know what you mean," Tess said, "but let me confirm something. The only thing keeping you from helping Jonas is the perjury problem, right?"

"Yes. And the thought of helping Melanie makes me sick." Crystal looked at him. "Sorry, Jonas, but we weren't in bed doing origami all those months. And you *were* married at the time, like it or not."

"Nobody disputes that," Tess said. "But let me put on my lawyer hat for a moment. You can confirm this with your own lawyer, but the fact is, although it's a crime to lie under oath, it's not a crime to lie *about* what your testimony is going to be."

"What do you mean?"

"You can say anything you want to Melanie about your relationship with Jonas. You can tell her that you never had a sexual relationship with him and you can tell her that's what your testimony is going to be."

"But what's the point?"

Tess gave Jonas a sly look, almost a wink. This had been her idea and he had to admit it was ingenious. Tess was worth her weight in gold.

"If Melanie believes you, she'll think her goose is cooked. You see, Crystal, we're not asking you to lie under oath, we're asking you to lie to Melanie."

"What good will that do?"

"It gives Jonas a chance to negotiate a settlement. If Melanie believes he's in the dark about what you'll say under oath, then she'll figure he's more likely to settle. And if she thinks your testimony will hurt her case, then she'll want to settle, too. Obviously, though, we have to work out a deal before the deposition, because once you tell the truth under oath, it's over and Melanie gets everything."

"That's pretty sneaky," Crystal said.

"But it's not illegal for you to deceive Melanie, only the court."

"If your plan fails, I still tell the truth in the deposition and I'm safe, right?"

"Exactly."

Crystal ventured a tiny smile. "I kinda like this. Never will a lie feel so good as putting it to that little bitch." She reached over and gave his hand a squeeze. "And it'll make up for some of the crap you've been through, too. Right, Uncle Jonas?"

Tess gave him a look. "*Uncle* Jonas?"

Davis, California

Carly sat on Tina Richter's front steps, hoping she hadn't been double-crossed. The girl wasn't home. Carly had knocked on the door of the old lady downstairs who told her she hadn't heard Tina go out that morning, but that on Mondays and Wednesdays she usually left early for class.

The problem was Le Genissel was working leads, trying to get to Patrick, too. If the bastard got to him before she did, it could get messy, especially for Patrick.

The funny thing was Carly was no longer sure what was motivating her. More than once she'd thought of the million dollars in cash sitting in the trunk of her car. She didn't want to screw Gaston, but if she just up and took off, she'd have little trouble disappearing forever.

But something, maybe Le Genissel, was making her hang in there. She wanted to kill the son of a bitch, but she also wanted to beat him at his own game. Maybe beat him even more.

After half an hour, just when she was sure Tina had skipped out on her, the girl showed up, dragging herself up the street, her shoulders rounded. She was surprised to see Carly.

"What are you doing here?"

"There's been a little change of plan. We're going now."

"Why?"

"I've got my reasons, the main one being to get to Patrick before somebody else does."

San Francisco

Melanie de Givry was at her wit's end. She paced back and forth in the conference room, muttering under her breath. That son of a bitch, Jonas Lamb, had gotten to Crystal Clear, somehow, some way. Melanie also knew she was dead in the water, a fortune lost in the blink of an eye.

Worse, she may have overplayed her hand when she'd told Crystal, "Whatever he's offering you, I'll double it." That had infuriated her. Melanie's profuse apologies had barely been enough to calm her. At least Crystal had the decency to warn her what her testimony would be. What if she hadn't? What if Crystal had simply raised her right hand and said her relationship with Jonas was purely platonic?

Melanie checked her watch. In two hours the deposition would begin. In three hours she'd be a billion dollars poorer unless she found a way to save herself.

Melanie began to perspire. Her life, her future, depended on finding a way to turn the tables on Jonas Lamb. Then it occurred to her. It didn't have to be all or nothing. What was wrong with half a billion? It galled her to think of sharing anything with the bastard, but it was certainly preferable to seeing him walk away with everything.

It would mean arranging a settlement conference before the deposition. That gave her precious little time. She'd call his attorney now.

There was a knock just then and a secretary stuck her head in the door. "Excuse me, Ms. de Givry, but you have an extremely urgent call from a Mr. Ramsey Brown in Houston. Do you wish to take it?"

Lord, Melanie thought, *what now?* "Yes, I'll speak to him."

"You can use the phone there, if you like," she said, pointing to the side table at the other end of the room. "I'll transfer the call."

She went away and Melanie went to the phone and sat in the adjacent chair, her heart pounding, her temples throbbing, her destiny hanging in the balance. What if Jonas refused to deal? And what did Brown want? God, it had to be good news, because after Crystal's bombshell, she couldn't take another blow.

The phone next to her rang. She picked up the receiver. "This is Melanie de Givry."

"Brown calling from Houston, Ms. de Givry. There's been a new development further to our discussions, so I'd like to inquire about the status of your lawsuit with Jonas Lamb. Have you worked out your differences? I need to know where things stand."

"I was about to call him to arrange a settlement conference, as a matter of fact."

"Is there some difficulty?"

"Well, as you might expect, Mr. Brown, we're facing the prospect of a long, drawn-out litigation and it's probably in both our interests to have a nice clean settlement so that the company can do business unimpeded."

"That's certainly desirable from the standpoint of my clients. I hope, though, that whoever ends up in control will be amenable to working with us."

"I intend to see to it. What's the development you alluded to?"

"I've been informed by my clients that Mr. Lamb plans to meet with a foreign investor in a couple of days to negotiate rights to the technology. I've been further advised that the investor will be offering an advanced payment in the order of twenty- to twenty-five million dollars to secure rights. My clients will tender an offer of thirty million dollars to Global Energy Technologies for the exclusive right to negotiate for a period of one year, provided GET agrees immediately. We'd hoped to make the deal with you, Ms. de Givry, but the important point is that we preempt the competition. I'll be leaving for San Francisco this evening with a cashier's check for thirty million. I would like to meet with either you, Mr. Lamb or both of you as appropriate to finalize the agreement. Can I count on you to make the necessary arrangements?"

"Yes, of course. I think, though, that tomorrow afternoon would be the soonest we could meet with you."

"That would be fine. Please advise me. I'll be staying at the Four Seasons."

"Okay, I'll be in touch."

Melanie hung up, wondering what in the hell she was going to do. The first thing was to get the deposition delayed, because once Crystal gave her testimony, it was all over. Then she'd sit down with Jonas and work something out. It would be one of the more unpleasant experiences of her life, but essential. Fortifying herself with a deep breath, Melanie dialed Braxton Weir's number.

Davis, California

The fact that Kenneth Jarrett lived in a dormitory did not help matters. Le Genissel sat in his car, watching the building. He had confirmed that the kid was there, but he couldn't go barging in and drag the little bastard out. And so he waited, hoping the kid would go out to buy himself an ice cream or something.

The Gazelle knew he didn't have much time. The police would be looking for him before long, if they weren't already. He had to find Mayne, put a gun to his head, get the technology, finish him off and go. And, since Lamb and his wife had survived the attack on the yacht, he'd have to track them down, too. But the first priority was to find Patrick Mayne.

At last he spotted the boy coming out the front door. But the kid wasn't alone. He was with a middle-aged man. And it didn't look like a happy situation. Both of them had scowls on their faces and were exchanging words. They went to a car up the street, the man all but shoving Jarrett inside.

Le Genissel started the engine and followed them. Incredibly, they drove to the same motel where Gaston de Malbouzon was staying. A coincidence? Maybe. The town wasn't big. But the pair didn't go near the *comte*. Instead they went into a room on the ground floor near the back. After parking, the Gazelle went to the door of the room and listened. Inside he could hear the two arguing.

"I don't give a goddamn what you want, Kenny," the man shouted. "I took off from work, drove all the way up here so you'll damn well know I mean business. I'm pulling the plug. If you want to go to college, you can get yourself a scholarship or go to work and save the money. You're not getting a free ride off me any longer. Not if you're going to screw around instead of hitting the books."

"That's totally unfair," the kid protested. "You don't want me to have a life. You want me to be like you."

"Is that so bad?"

Le Genissel tried the door and found it unlocked. Checking to make sure nobody was around, he took his gun from under his coat and stepped inside. The man and the boy both turned, shocked by the intrusion.

"What do you think you're—" the man said, stopping when he saw the gun in Le Genissel's hand.

"You Kenneth Jarrett?" he asked the boy.

"Y-yes," the kid stammered, disbelieving of what he was seeing.

"Who is he?" Le Genissel asked, indicating the man.

"My father."

"What do you want?" the elder Jarrett demanded.

Le Genissel ignored him. "Where's Mayne?" he asked the boy.

The kid stood frozen, mute.

"I said, where is Mayne?"

"What is going on?" the father demanded.

The Gazelle aimed at the man and fired. Jarrett fell backward to the floor. The kid looked at his father, then at Le Genissel, incredulous.

"Jesus!"

Alfred Le Genissel went over and grabbed the stunned boy by the arm and shoved the muzzle of the gun up under his chin. "Are you going to tell me where Mayne is or do I blow your head off?"

Motionless on the floor, the elder Jarrett made terrible gurgling sounds as he took his last breaths. Kenneth Jarrett looked down at him out of the corner of his eye.

"Yeah," he croaked. "I'll tell you."

Solano County

Carly, who was driving, gazed at the level, barren land. Ahead a conical-shaped mountain rose above the distant hills. "What's that?"

"Mount Diablo," Tina replied.

"Is that where he is?"

"No, we're keeping him in an abandoned fishing boat tied up on a slough in the Delta."

"You're sure your friends aren't going to be there?"

"I told them to go, like you said."

"Will they listen to you?"

"Yes. It was my plan. Most of them defer to me."

"This kidnapping was a gutsy thing to do, Tina. Not very smart, but gutsy."

Tina told her where to turn.

"What happens after you've got the professor and we've got the money? We all pretend like nothing ever happened?"

"Something like that."

They came to the levee. There were no other vehicles around.

Tina said, "The boat's on the other side."

"Okay, here's the drill. You and I are going to go get Patrick. When we get back to the car, I take the case with the money out of the trunk and leave it with you. Then Patrick and I will take off. Your friends can come and get you."

They got out of the car and climbed up the levee. From the top Carly saw the rusty old fishing boat. Unless Tina had duped her, Patrick was there, waiting to be rescued. She felt an odd surge of optimism, expectation, even joy. Operation Brebis Noire might yet turn out to be a success. Everything depended on whether Patrick would accept the fact that certain money interests had trusted her to secure his release. She had her story prepared, but it was Patrick Mayne's emotions, rather than his logic, that would determine the outcome—of that she was fairly confident.

Carly had Tina walk ahead of her as they crossed

the boarding ladder onto the deck of the boat. Everything was quiet. Carly knew she was taking a chance walking into the kidnappers' den, but they couldn't be sure what resources she had at her disposal.

They heard a sound coming from below and Carly took Tina's arm, stopping her. Carly listened. It sounded like banging. Then she heard a muffled voice.

"What's that?"

"It might be the professor."

They descended the steps, going down the companionway. The banging got louder. Once they were below, moving along the gangway, Carly could make out the words.

"Water," Patrick called through the door, his words muffled, "I need some water. Is anybody there?"

"Open the door, Tina," Carly said.

The girl threw the heavy bolt and pulled the door open. Patrick, unshaven and rumpled, wearing the same sweat outfit he'd had on the night he was abducted, stood there, his eyes rounding with incredulity at the sight of her.

"Carly!" It was both a laugh and a shout.

Then he glanced at Tina, confusion settling over him.

"How'd you like to go home?" Carly asked. "I've paid the ransom. You're free!"

"My God!" he exclaimed, elated, grabbing his head with his hands in disbelief. He didn't run from his cell as she might have thought, a bit wary, instead, looking Tina over as though trying to understand. "You're the friendly one, aren't you?" he said.

The girl lowered her head. "Yes, Professor Mayne, and I'm sorry you suffered."

"You look better without that mask."

She blushed, looking terribly embarrassed.

"Tina's going to take the ransom and quietly fade into the sunset," Carly explained. "If you'll agree, I take you home and all is forgotten."

"I don't have to make any propaganda videos? No statements? They didn't go public, after all?"

"No, Patrick," Carly said, "we're back to where we were before this happened."

"Thank God. I want a glass of ice water and a hot shower, in that order."

He looked like a boy on the last day of school and Carly couldn't help a big grin, matching his. Patrick stepped through the door, took her by the shoulders and gave her a big kiss on the cheek.

"I smell foul, I know, and I apologize," he said. "But I'm happy to be out of here!" He gave a shout of joy and headed toward the companionway, a spring in his step.

Before they got to the stairs, a boy came stumbling down, followed by Alfred Le Genissel, a gun in his hand. He shoved the boy against the wall and, eyeing them, said, "Well, what have we here? A welcoming party?"

Carly groaned, absolutely sick at the sight of him. She'd come so close...*shit!*

"So, Carly," the Gazelle said, "beat me to the punch, did you? And all this time I thought you were nothing but a pretty face."

She couldn't believe what he'd just said. The idiot had blown everything. Patrick looked at her. She was furious. "Alfred, you dumb shit!" she said through her teeth. "I had everything in hand."

"What's going on?" Patrick said. "Who is this guy?"

"This guy is in charge," Le Genissel said. "Now, shut up and move over there against the wall with the kid. You, too," he said to Tina.

Patrick's expression was beseeching now, the joy that had been on his face only moments ago, dead. She felt sick at heart.

"Hmm," Le Genissel said, stroking his chin. "The party has grown too large. Carly, you and the professor go back in the cell for a moment." Then to the kids he said, "You two stay right where you are. Face the wall."

Tina and the boy, looking terrified, turned to the wall. Carly heard a splattering sound and saw a puddle of pee at the boy's feet. He began to sob. Carly knew what was coming and he probably did, too.

"Carly," Tina said, "you told me—"

"Shut up!" Le Genissel shouted. Then to Carly, "I told you to take him in the cell."

"Alfred, this isn't necessary. Nobody else is coming here until midnight. Lock them up. Anyway, what are they going to do? Tell the police somebody stole their kidnap victim?"

"I killed the kid's father."

"We'll be long gone. Lock them up, Alfred."

He scoffed. "You are too soft-hearted for your own

good, Carly. No, we are doing this my way. Get in the cell."

Carly put her hand on the Gazelle's arm. "As a favor to me?"

He leered. "Why should I do a favor for you?"

"Then why not shoot me, too, if you don't care?" She ran her hand down his belly and lightly over the front of his trousers.

Le Genissel gave a half laugh. "You are incredible."

"Please, Alfred. You spoke of the future. Am I to understand you didn't mean it? Was what you got last night what you *really* wanted?"

He began to perspire, shaking his head with disbelief. When she rested her hand on his bulge, he drew a long breath through his nose. "If I do what you ask," he muttered, "you will owe me. And I do not mean like last night."

"Fine."

He looked hard into her eyes, questioning whether or not he could trust her, wanting, as all men did, to do just that. Carly gave him her sweetest smile. The Gazelle thought for several moments, lives hanging in the balance. He shook his head. "There's no reason for me to believe you. Not after last night."

"I hated you last night, true," she replied, "but now you have something I want and I'll do what I have to do to get it."

"You want their lives? How can that be so important?"

"Maybe what's important to me is winning. It's really quite simple, Alfred. I want *you* to submit to *me*."

"I don't understand you," he said.

"We both know what I am."

He took another moment, then said, "Okay, lock them in the cell."

Davis, California

"I've discovered the true secret of the species' survival," he said. "When a woman has the chance to spend the evening with the man she loves, a man on the brink of becoming a billionaire, and she chooses instead to drive a hundred miles to check on her baby, you know it's a species that will never die out."

"Very funny," Tess said. "Come on, I'm tired of waiting. Let's go inside."

They'd been parked in front of Patrick's house for fifteen minutes, having gotten no response when they rang the bell.

"In Patrick's shoes, I'm not so sure I'd appreciate Mom and Dad snooping around my pad while I was away. For all you know they're in bed."

"If Patrick didn't want me in his house, he wouldn't have given me a key," Tess replied.

"Forgive me, sweetheart, but that's the rationalization of a nosy mom."

"I know something strange is going on. Like I told you from the very beginning, I don't trust Carly. I know she's been untruthful. As a minimum I'm going inside and see if there are signs of..."

"Of what? Foul play? I can guarantee you they've been sleeping together."

Tess rolled her eyes. "Is sex all you ever think about, Jonas Lamb?"

"Pretty much."

"I guess that's the other reason the species will never die out. Well, call me what you will, I'm going to have a quick look. Do you want to come or stay here?"

"I'll take the moral high ground and stay."

Tess gave him a look and got out of her BMW and made her way to Patrick's door. Jonas watched her take her keys from her purse and go inside. Then he sighed. What a day.

He'd hoped to get Melanie and the deposition behind him, but everything had been moved back a day and continued to hang over his head. The fact that Melanie wanted to settle was encouraging, given her unwavering hostility, but on what terms? Had his ruse with Crystal worked? It seemed to have gotten Melanie to the negotiating table and that was something. It could also be that she was preparing a trap of her own. One thing he was confident of, though— he wouldn't have gotten this far if Tess hadn't come up with her brilliant negotiating strategy.

Just then Jonas noticed a car slow and come to a stop a few doors up, parking on the same side of the street as the house. He couldn't see the occupants clearly because of the reflection of the sun on the windshield, but he thought he'd gotten a glimpse of blond hair on the driver's side. When the door opened, sure enough, Carly Van Hooten stepped out. The door on the passenger's side opened next and Patrick climbed out.

Jonas chuckled. Tess was about to get a hell of a

surprise. But then he got a surprise of his own. A third person got out of the back seat. A man. He looked down the street the other way. Then, when he peered back in Jonas's direction, Jonas recognized him. It was the man in the photo Mr. Zhang had showed them—Alfred Le Genissel!

Jonas felt his heart constrict. His blood seemed to stop flowing. Judging by the way Le Genissel held his hand under his coat, he had a gun on them. Carly went to the trunk and removed a suitcase, which she dragged to the sidewalk. She extended the handle, then the three of them trooped to Patrick's front door, Carly pulling the case. Patrick hefted it up the steps for her and opened the door, oblivious to the fact that his mother was inside.

Jonas watched in horror. Le Genissel, he reminded himself, had tried to kill them once, why not again? But what should he do about it? Remembering the automatic Mr. Lu had given him was in the glove compartment, he took it out, examined it and removed the safety. He tried to decide whether he was better off taking matters into his own hands or calling the police. By the time they arrived Tess could be dead and maybe Patrick and Carly, too. There was no telling what Le Genissel had in mind.

Right or wrong, Jonas knew he had to act. Getting out of the car, he ran to Patrick's front steps, then slowly climbed them, dreading the sound of gunshots as he crept to the door. He knew his best chance was to catch Le Genissel by surprise. He carefully turned the knob. To his great relief, it was unlocked.

Opening the door a crack, he heard voices. Patrick's stood out.

"She has nothing to do with this," he said angrily. "Leave her alone. My God, I thought she was dead, I come home and find her alive and now you want to kill her? What kind of a maniac are you?"

"One who wants your technology, Professor. If your mother is so important to you, tell me where the research materials are and I will let her live."

"Let her go and I'll tell you," Patrick replied.

"Are you deaf, Mayne?" Le Genissel roared.

Jonas heard a loud thump and Tess's scream. Somebody had been struck. He couldn't wait another second. He charged into the house and found Tess and Patrick in front of the leather sofa on the far side of the room. She was helping him to his feet. Le Genissel stood in front of them, his back to Jonas, the gun in his hand. Carly was off to the side.

"Drop the gun, you sonovabitch!" Jonas shouted. "Drop it now, or I'll shoot your sorry ass!"

Alfred Le Genissel glanced over his shoulder. "Well, it is Papa Lamb."

"Drop it, I said!"

"If I drop my gun, Mr. Lamb, I lose my leverage. You may shoot me and you may kill me, but not before I have gotten off a shot." He extended the gun in the direction of Tess and Patrick. "Which one do you wish to die, Mr. Lamb? The choice is yours."

"I *will* shoot you!" Jonas cried.

"And I will shoot one of them. Will it be the wife?" he asked, shifting his aim a few degrees so that the gun was pointed at her. "Or will it be the son?" He moved the muzzle back the other way so that it was aimed at Patrick's chest. "Which of them do you wish to die?"

Jonas struggled to think. Should he fire or was Le Genissel right? The bastard could probably get off at least one shot. His insides in a knot, he glanced at Carly, who offered no help, standing motionless by the suitcase.

"Mr. Lamb," Le Genissel said, "you have not made a decision." He swung the gun back to Tess. "Her?" Then the gun went back to Patrick. "Or him?"

"Jonas," Tess said calmly, "the next time he points the gun at me, shoot him!"

"No!" Patrick cried. "Shoot him when it's pointed at me!"

Le Genissel kept shifting the gun back and forth. Jonas was dizzy with indecision. If he shot the son of a bitch in the head, maybe he wouldn't fire. But he was too far away to be sure of his shot. He began inching closer, directly behind Le Genissel, scarcely able to draw a breath, his finger tightening on the trigger, memories of Vietnam flooding his brain.

"Lamb!"

A few steps more.

"Lamb!"

Jonas was two feet away and from the corner of his eye watched the man's gun hand swinging back and forth between his wife and son, more quickly now. If he could time his shot just right, Le Genissel might miss them both.

While his eye was on Le Genissel's gun, the man they called the Gazelle ducked and spun quickly. At the same instant Jonas squeezed the trigger. The automatic fired, but the shot missed. Le Genissel's gun hit Jonas's, knocking it from his hand and sending it skidding across the floor.

In the split second that followed, Le Genissel slammed the butt of his weapon against Jonas's shoulder, knocking him down on the coffee table. "You choose yourself, Lamb?" Then, inexplicably, he laughed. "You are a fool. Now you cannot save either of them."

"Alfred!"

It was Carly. Le Genissel glanced over his shoulder at her. She had Jonas's automatic in her hand and was pointing it at him.

"Carly, what are you doing?"

"Drop the gun and turn around," she said. "You're not killing anybody. Even if you do get off a shot, it won't matter to me who you shoot, so your little trick won't work this time. Drop it now and turn around or you're dead."

He dropped the gun and turned to face her. He shook his head, grinning pathetically. "What are you thinking? You know what is at stake."

"The conundrum of the whore," she said, glancing down at the suitcase. "Do I choose the money or my loyalty to you, Alfred? Which will it be?"

"No, Carly," he said, seeming to get her point. "Don't be foolish. Think about the future, not last night. You asked me not to kill those kidnappers and

I didn't. For you, Carly, for you. Think about all the jobs we will do."

"What was it that famous sage, Alfred Ahmed Le Genissel, once said? I believe it was, 'In the end, they always choose the money.'"

He extended his arms beseechingly. "Carly... please."

She pointed the gun at his heart and fired. Le Genissel went flying backward over a chair, ending up in a motionless heap.

Tess helped Jonas get to his feet. The two of them and Patrick all stared at Carly.

"I'm very sorry about this," she said. "He would have killed you all, eventually—not that I didn't get a certain amount of satisfaction shooting him." She looked at Patrick. "It wasn't supposed to work out like this, the violence, I mean. I'm sorry. And to be honest, I regret taking this job because I like you, Patrick. It made deceiving you a very difficult thing to do."

"You really were working with that guy?"

"My job was to charm your secrets out of you, not take them by force. The only reason this killing happened is because Le Genissel is a psychopath. Or was," she said, looking at the motionless corpse. "The world's better off without him."

"But why did you do it?" Patrick asked.

"The short answer is for the money. The point is you still have your GMOs to do with as you like. But I have a small problem," she said. "I'd like to leave and I'd like some time before the police start looking for me. The thing is, you have a corpse on your living room floor. You have an obligation to call the police, I know. How can I assure myself of a three- or four-hour head start is the question? I hate to tie you up for form's sake, but I'll leave the decision up to you."

"Carly," Patrick said, "we owe you. You not only saved our lives, you saved those kids at the boat. If you need four hours, you've got it."

"Thank you." She tossed Jonas's gun on a chair.

"But I wish you'd stay and see this through," Patrick said. "We'll vouch for you. What you did was like self-defense." He turned to his mother. "What do you call it?"

"Justifiable homicide."

Carly shook her head. "You don't know me."

"Maybe not entirely. But I've seen your heart."

"There's a million dollars in this suitcase," she said. "It's what I want. Alfred knew that, but at the critical moment he forgot. And he paid the price."

Patrick went over to her and placed his hands on her shoulders. "This is not you, I know it isn't."

She seemed touched. "You've got a world to save, Professor. Go save it." She kissed him on the cheek. Then, taking the case, she pulled it to the door and went out.

Patrick faced his parents, looking bewildered.

Jonas understood completely. He understood as well as if it had been him. He held Tess's hand. He felt her shiver.

"Let's go in the kitchen," she said. "I can't stand to be here with that man, even dead."

The three went into the kitchen and sat at the

table. No one spoke for several moments. Jonas glanced up at the clock on the wall. Tess did, as well.

"I guess we won't be calling the police for a while," she said. "We'll need an explanation for the delay and whatever story we tell, it had better be the same one."

"How about the truth?" Jonas said. "I know that's a novel concept coming from me, but the girl saved our lives and we felt such an obligation that we just didn't have it in our hearts to deny her her wish. They may not be pleased, but neither was Alfred Le Genissel exactly Mother Teresa. Nobody will cry crocodile tears."

"I can live with that," Patrick said.

He and Jonas turned to Tess.

"Don't look at me," she said, "I'm just a lawyer. What do I know about justice?"

Patrick was still bewildered. "I wish Carly had stayed," he said, "but this is the next best thing, I guess."

"You really cared for her, didn't you, honey?" Tess said.

"Yes, Mom, I did."

"Your father and I had different opinions of her. I'm not sure which of us was right. Maybe we both were in our way."

Jonas reached out and took their hands, looking at his wife and son. "I'm especially grateful to Carly for bailing me out," he said. "I damned near blew it in there. If either of you had been hurt, I don't know what I would have done. But I just couldn't shoot the guy," he said, "not while he had that gun pointed at the two of you. He gave me an impossible dilemma."

"If he'd shot Patrick I would have been furious with you," Tess said, giving him a smile, "but I know you were in an awful situation." She pressed his hand to her cheek. "Anyway, if it wasn't for you, I'd be in the bottom of the South China Sea. Remember? You can't be Superman every day."

"Well, I'm definitely not cut out to be a trigger man, that's for sure," Jonas said. "I think I'd better stick to white-collar crime."

"What's this I hear?" Patrick said. "The old man performed a heroic deed? Saved the fair damsel?"

"It's a long story," Jonas said, "best saved for another occasion."

"Okay, but I have something to say that can't be saved for another occasion," Patrick said.

"What?"

"I've done one hell of a lot of thinking the past few days and I realize I've made a huge mistake."

"What mistake is that, Patrick?" Tess asked.

He got up and went to the cupboard and got a glass and filled it with water at the sink. He guzzled it down and filled the glass again, bringing it back to the table. Looking at each of them in turn, he said, "I've been using you. You, especially, Jonas."

"What are you talking about?"

He took a deep breath and said, "The bottom line is I'm not sure my GMOs, the Black Sheep, will work."

Jonas leaned forward, not sure he'd heard what he thought he heard. "What?"

"I don't know whether we can produce super

ethanol or not. In fact, it's been looking like a long shot for a while now."

"Patrick, what are you talking about?" Jonas said. "Last summer there was a seventy-five-percent probability of success. Since then all the tests and experiments have proven out, everything's been coming up roses. Are you saying that's not true?"

"Yeah. Basically it was a lie."

"Patrick," Tess said, incredulous, "why?"

"My intentions were good. When Jonas and I first talked, I figured he'd do a more credible job if he was convinced he had a winner. From the beginning I thought we'd end up selling out to some energy company, but I also knew they'd be hard-nosed about the research and test results. I figured our best chance was to get several of them competing, climbing over one another to throw money at us. I hadn't abandoned hope of making the GMOs perform as expected, but I knew that it would take time and money to work out the kinks. Then, when Jonas suggested we bring in outside capital, I thought it would give us the leverage we needed.

"I know you had big plans," Patrick continued, "but I also knew they were unrealistic. When you got back from this last trip to Hong Kong, whether you'd gotten a check from Jimmy Yee or not, I was going to suggest we go to the oil companies and try to make our deal. But then I got kidnapped and you and Mom were killed. Or so I thought. I can't tell you what hell I've been living through, thinking I'd sent you to your deaths over a project I wasn't even sure would work. Then when you walked in the door today, I thought you'd been spared just so I could watch you die all over again." Patrick lowered his head, tears filling his eyes. "I've been hating myself the past couple days."

Tess rubbed his hand. "Well, we're all okay, honey, and it's over now."

"Thanks to Carly."

Jonas continued to digest what he'd heard, feeling like he'd been kicked in the stomach. "So the Black Sheep don't work."

"It's not that they don't work. They do. The problem is that in all the lab experiments they stopped replicating after several generations, in effect losing their potency. Something's preventing the organisms from passing on their altered genetic structure. I tried dozens of variations but couldn't overcome the problem. It's a long shot, but there may be a chance that the process will work better in field crops grown under natural conditions."

"Then our Black Sheep aren't quite dead yet."

"Yeah, but the point is I've caused all this death and suffering for what might turn out to be a total bust."

"I went into this deal with my eyes open and a profit motive in my heart," Jonas said. "I wasn't trying to cure cancer." He struggled to get it all in perspective. "To think, all we've accomplished is to get a lot of people excited over nothing. How ironic is that?"

"So, what do you do now?" Tess asked.

"Well, if I understand correctly, there's still an outside chance our Black Sheep will come through. And even if they don't, there must be some value to the technology. Am I right about that, Patrick?"

"Oh, I can keep trying and I still might succeed, but as I said it will take time and money. And there's always the chance another researcher will find a solution building on the groundwork I've laid. My research is not worthless by any means. But it's not worth anywhere near what we thought."

"There you are, Tess," Jonas said. "We're selling potential now rather than a sure thing. So what if we're looking at a hundred thousand instead of a billion?"

She shook her head, amused. "What are you going to do tomorrow with Melanie?"

"She's still holding the stock and my inheritance from Elise hostage. I'd like to salvage something, if I can. Crystal's ploy either worked, or it didn't. I guess we'll find out."

THURSDAY
January 31

San Francisco

It was eleven in the morning, the first day of—as they say—the rest of his life. Jonas waited for Melanie de Givry in the conference room of her attorney's offices on the thirty-second floor of the Bank of America Building. Across from him was a sweeping panorama of the East Bay. It reminded him of that day he'd visited Jimmy Yee at his office in Hong Kong—how he'd thought of Jimmy as the master of the universe. God knew, he'd aspired to that himself. But everything had changed now. Jimmy was dead, in a sense a victim of Jonas's dream.

Patrick's news about the Black Sheep had turned things upside down, sobering him. Jonas was in a survival mode now, though of course Melanie thought they were there to duke it out *mano a mano* for a billion bucks. What a fantastic, if tragic-sad, ride they'd been on.

The door opened and Melanie walked in. She did

not say hello. She did not sit at the table. Instead she went to the huge window. For a minute she stared out at the view as though the lumbering old oil tanker headed across the bay to Richmond was actually worthy of note. Then she turned to him, folding her arms across her chest and crossing her ankles as she leaned against the sill, a miniature George Patton in drag.

"Look, Jonas," she said, "I'm going to save us both a lot of time and trouble. I know about the technology and the fact that GET, Inc., is worth a fortune. I know about your foreign investor and his plan to tie up the technology for twenty-five million, so let's don't bother posturing over principle or sentiment or any other bullshit. I say we get all our cards on the table and get on with it."

He had to admire her chutzpah, even if he didn't like her. But how did she know about Zhang Jintao? And where did she get the figure twenty-five million? Zhang hadn't mentioned a specific figure to him. Was it a ploy, or did Melanie have better sources than he? "Fine with me," he replied.

"You know that regardless of what happens at the deposition we're going to be in court for ten years, if we don't settle this."

"Yeah, I know."

"You cheated on my mother," Melanie said. "I know that for a fact. And, though she provided the operating capital, it was your son who developed the technology. Much as I hate to admit it, you've got some equities, even if you don't have much of a case."

"Like you say, the lawyers will probably debate that for ten years."

"Then I take it we're agreed that a settlement would be in both our interests."

Her tone was matter-of-fact, but Jonas sensed ardor, perhaps even desperation under her cool veneer. What did Melanie know that he didn't? Or was it simply that she didn't know the facts? "I'm willing to listen to anything you have to say."

"I may as well tell you that I, too, have been approached by a potential buyer," she said, "somebody interested in the technology. My buyer is aware of your buyer's intentions and he's frankly said he'll pay to preempt him. If you and I can agree on what to do with GET, we can have a cashier's check for thirty million dollars in our hands in a matter of a day or two."

Jonas's heart went bump, but he maintained a placid expression and stroked his chin. "Or we can wait until next week to see if my guy will up the ante. Nothing helps a negotiation like good old-fashioned competition, you know."

Melanie seemed uncomfortable with the suggestion. She didn't say anything, but Jonas knew what she was thinking—next week was a problem because Crystal's deposition was *this afternoon*. It was then that he realized Melanie was in a dilemma. How did she press for a quick settlement without tipping her hand? Jonas leaned back in his chair, grimly sober.

"I take it you'd like to divide the stock," he said. "What do you have in mind?"

She stared at him for maybe a minute, then said, "We're going to end up at fifty-fifty, so why don't we just do it and be done with it?"

"You want half my company."

"Ninety percent of which is presently owned by my mother's estate."

"Which Elise willed to me."

"As we both know, it'll be ten years before that's finally determined."

Again he stroked his chin. "And what about the thirty million? That's a nonrefundable deposit, right? Cash on the barrelhead."

"Right."

"And you propose...?"

"How about we split the cash fifty-fifty, too?"

Jonas gave her a weak smile and slowly got to his feet. "Let's let the lawyers go at it for a couple of rounds, shall we, Melanie? Then if we're both in the mood, we can talk about settlement again. That way we get to see if my guy is a little more generous than your guy."

"You really want to piss half away on lawyers?"

He swallowed his smile. "Odd that you see the folly in that."

"My guy's offer is good for today only," Melanie said. "We either do this, or lose it."

He thought for a minute, noting her eagerness, convinced that she was indeed caught between the rock and the hard place. "How could we possibly run the company with equal shares?" he asked rhetorically. "We'd never agree on anything."

"Then we do have a problem, don't we?"

Jonas didn't sit again, but he didn't walk out, either. "There are two variables as I see it. Control and cash," he said. "What it comes down to is the value of one percent of the company. Am I right?"

"I suppose like most men you're big on running things," she said.

"I guess I tend to hog the remote control, but nobody's ever offered to pay me to give it up. My preference would be to defer a decision until next week. If we put me in charge, that's what I'll elect to do."

Melanie fell into a brooding silence. Jonas stayed right where he stood, maintaining eye contact. Jimmy Yee once told him that he who speaks first in these situations loses.

One minute passed, then two. Melanie knew the game, but she was also the one under pressure. She thought she knew what Crystal was going to say under oath and she didn't know about Patrick's confession about the GMOs, his sickly Black Sheep. But most telling of all, she was driven by greed and hatred. For whatever reason, Melanie wanted the remote control. Jonas could see it in her eyes.

"Okay, here's my offer," she finally said. "I get fifty-one percent of the company and final say. You get the thirty million."

"Plus my inheritance from Elise."

"You want me to give you the money *and* eat crow."

"Yes."

Again she stared at him, motionless, unblinking. Jonas stared back. He knew what she was thinking.

Until yesterday she'd been convinced it would all be hers. She would gain a fortune, but just as important, she would deny him all but the ten percent of GET he already had in his pocket. Now suddenly he had her giving away the store.

"You already have a hundred thousand of it," she said.

"You're right. It's nine hundred thousand due me."

Melanie drew a long, slow breath. "Okay, but that's it," she said. "GET is my baby."

"I don't know what you were promised, Melanie, but any purchase of GET's technology is going to be conditional."

"I'm aware of that. And I also know the people I'm dealing with. Including you. You're taking the bird in hand because you're a small-time operator, Jonas. But that's okay, we each get what we want."

"And deserve?"

She smiled for the first time. "You said it, not me." She looked at her watch. "Well, I'll call Crystal's lawyer and tell him the lawsuit has been settled and the deposition canceled. I suppose you'd like your lawyer to sit down with my lawyer to draft an agreement. We'll have to sign everything before you get your check."

"Fine."

Melanie walked around the table on her way to the door, then paused when she came to where he stood. Jonas offered her his hand. She looked at it and shook her head. "No, your signature will do, thank you." She walked out of the room.

Jonas did not close his eyes, but he saw his mother's shining face before him, and he heard her say, "I didn't think it was in you."

Yeah, Mom, it was!

That made him feel good—better than the thirty million, better than knowing he and Patrick and Tess could be set for life, better even than beating Melanie at her own game. His whole life he'd needed to hear his mother concede his worth. And now he had.

Out in the bay he could see a freighter inching its way somewhere, maybe home. He wasn't going to be king of the world, and even the thirty million could get swallowed up in litigation. But that was okay. Tess was meeting him for lunch. His biggest and most important challenge still lay ahead.

EPILOGUE

It took a while for the police and the FBI to sort out the story behind the activities and death of Alfred Ahmed Le Genissel. Jonas, Patrick and Tess were able to provide the motive for his actions, but his employers were never identified, though it was suspected they were Middle Eastern.

Carly Van Hooten disappeared without a trace. The authorities were unable to establish a connection between her and Le Genissel, though it was determined that prior to coming to California she'd spent several days in Cleveland, where she'd obtained a fictitious employment history by bribing an area businessman with money and sexual favors. Her true identity remained unknown despite efforts made through Interpol and various foreign governments. "Carly Van Hooten," it seemed, was a nom de guerre.

After being released from the fishing boat by his friends, Kenny Jarrett fled to his parents' home in Bakersfield where he was arrested by police for suspicion of the murder of his father. He broke down under questioning and admitted to the kidnapping of Patrick Mayne and the firebombing of the university building, implicating his friends in the process. It was determined that Le Genissel was responsible for Cal Jarrett's murder and the assault on Kyle Zeigler and his girlfriend.

Tina Richter, Brad Kozik, Roger Lake and Kristy Ogawa were all arrested and, like Jarrett, charged with conspiracy, kidnapping and arson. "The Davis Seeds," as they became known in the press, pled guilty. Patrick Mayne appeared at their sentencing and asked the court to show leniency toward the defendants, Tina Richter in particular. Their sentences ranged from three to seven years in the state penitentiary. Tina wrote long rambling letters to Patrick during her incarceration. He occasionally responded.

Comte Gaston de Malbouzon's involvement in the affair, like that of his employers in the oil industry, was never discovered. He returned to France initially, but was granted admission to MIT to complete work on his bachelor's degree in computer science. He subsequently went on to do graduate work and teach in both the U.S. and France. The *comte* supplemented his income and amused himself with occasional forays into the dark side of the social fabric. He was seen on two or three occasions in the company of a petite, very attractive blond woman.

In June Crystal Clear married Bob MacDonald. Jonas and Tess attended the wedding. Jonas gave Crystal his houseboat as a "wedding present," signing the card, "With appreciation, Uncle Jonas." Crystal planned to keep the houseboat as a rental, renaming it, *On a Clear Day.* Jonas had his dance with the bride and they wished each other happiness.

The results of Patrick's experimental field crop were not as bad as he expected, though not good enough to justify production on a commercial scale. Additional developmental work was required. Melanie de Givry, desperate for a return on her investment, negotiated a sale of the rights to the technology to a consortium of oil companies under a profit-sharing arrangement with enough up-front cash to cover GET's expenses. The industry promptly buried the project. Melanie filed suit against the consortium in federal court, alleging bad faith. Legal observers believe the case could be tied up in court for years.

In Washington there was a heated debate over the administration's energy policy initiatives to reduce the U.S. dependency on foreign oil. After receiving tips from unnamed sources, an investigative reporter with the *Washington Post* uncovered an alleged conspiracy between top administration officials and key executives in the U.S. oil industry intended to stifle the research and development of alternative fuel sources and additives.

The vice president, acting as point man for the administration, denied improper involvement with the private sector and defended administration policy to encourage private—as opposed to government-sponsored—initiatives in the area of energy development. He blamed the opposition for "inflaming irrational passions in the name of misguided environmental concerns that serve no purpose but to weaken the American economy, thus rendering it vulnerable to foreign competition and ultimately endangering national security."

Congressional investigations were initiated and hearings held. One oil industry researcher testified under oath before the Senate Committee on Energy and Natural Resources that, because of lax security, suspected undercover intelligence operatives from the People's Republic of China may have stolen data on a secret "super-ethanol" project operating under the umbrella of the consortium of U.S. oil companies.

Executives of the companies, testifying before the committee, denied the accusation, stating that the project was essentially defunct, that it had been experimental, that even if data had been purloined, it had no viable commercial value and therefore national security was in no way jeopardized. One executive suggested that the accusations may have been fabricated and embellished at the instigation of a disgruntled California entrepreneur who'd brought a lawsuit against the consortium in a desperate bid to extort money from the companies at the expense of the American consumer.

After turning all his data over to GET, Patrick Mayne resigned from his teaching post at the university and, in partnership with his parents, formed a biological research firm to develop and fund biotechnology projects intended to protect and enhance the global environment. He regularly received inquiries from various foreign interests about super-ethanol technology, but he always referred them to GET, as per the agreement with Melanie de Givry.

Patrick dated occasionally but never got over Carly Van Hooten, going so far as to hire private investigators to track her down, but without success. Tess was upset with her son's inability to move on, but Jonas sympathized, having spent years regretting missed opportunities at love. Who was to say where foolish romanticism ended and fated love began?

Jonas bought a house in Pacific Heights in San Francisco and a nice, but not ostentatious, sailboat. During the first year, Tess spent a lot of time at his home, but never quite moved in. Between the family's biotechnology firm and her charitable endeavors, Tess stayed very busy. In December Jonas took her to Paris where, on Christmas Eve, in a suite at the Ritz after a bottle of champagne, he proposed marriage. Tess rejected the proffered moniker, "Lucky Seven," but nevertheless agreed to marry him. They tentatively planned a Valentine's Day wedding.

It was such a lovely winter night that Tess insisted they go for a walk. As they strolled arm in arm across the Place Vendôme, the snow falling from the night sky, Jonas saw a limousine pull up in front of the hotel. A beautiful young blond woman decked out in fur and jewels emerged on the arm of a distinguished gray-haired gentleman. They were too far away for him to be certain of the woman's identity, but Jonas was pretty sure he knew who she was.

Patrick, who had been attending a scientific conference in London, was scheduled to join them in Paris on Christmas Day. Jonas didn't mention seeing the blond girl in the limo to Tess (even soon-to-be-happily-married men needed their secrets), but he was sorely tempted to tell his son about the sighting. Jonas Lamb was above all else a romantic, and romance in the heart of a romantic never dies.

"Twisted villains, dangerous secrets…irresistible."
—*Booklist*

New York Times **Bestselling Author**

STELLA
CAMERON

Just weeks after inheriting Rosebank, a once-magnificent Louisiana plantation, David Patin was killed in a mysterious fire, leaving his daughter, Vivian, almost bankrupt. With few options remaining, Vivian decides to restore the family fortunes by turning Rosebank into a resort hotel.

Vivan's dream becomes a nightmare when she finds the family's lawyer dead on the sprawling grounds of the estate. Suddenly Vivian begins to wonder if her father's death was really an accident…and if the entire Patin family is marked for murder.

Rosebank is not in Sheriff Spike Devol's jurisdiction, but Vivian, fed up with the corrupt local police, asks him for unofficial help. The instant attraction between them leaves Spike reluctant to get involved—until another shocking murder occurs and it seems that Vivian will be the next victim.

kiss them goodbye

"Cameron returns to the wonderfully atmospheric Louisiana setting…for her latest sexy-gritty, compellingly readable tale of romantic suspense."—*Booklist*

Available the first week of October 2004,
wherever paperbacks are sold!

If you enjoyed what you just read,
then we've got an offer you can't resist!

Take 2 bestselling novels FREE!
Plus get a FREE surprise gift!

R.J. KAISER

| 66713 | SQUEEZE PLAY | ___ $6.50 U.S. ___ $7.99 CAN. |
| 66614 | GLAMOUR PUSS | ___ $6.50 U.S. ___ $7.99 CAN. |

(limited quantities available)

TOTAL AMOUNT $_____
POSTAGE & HANDLING $_____
($1.00 for one book; 50¢ for each additional)
APPLICABLE TAXES* $_____
<u>TOTAL PAYABLE</u> $_____
(check or money order—please do not send cash)

To order, complete this form and send it, along with a check or money order for the total above, payable to MIRA Books, to: **In the U.S.:** 3010 Walden Avenue, P.O. Box 9077, Buffalo, NY 14269-9077; **In Canada:** P.O. Box 636, Fort Erie, Ontario L2A 5X3.

Name:_____
Address:_____ City:_____
State/Prov.:_____ Zip/Postal Code:_____
Account Number (if applicable):_____
075 CSAS

*New York residents remit applicable sales taxes.
Canadian residents remit applicable GST and provincial taxes.

MIRA®

www.MIRABooks.com   MRJK1004BL